FUCHSIA

Lady Carolyn Byrd

First Published: 2019

ISBN- 978-0-9817864-6-9

Dedication

Fuchsia is dedicated to every woman who has ever been faced with abuse (verbal, emotional, sexual or physical). The silent pain of your truth is real. The emotional pain of your truth is undeniable. The residue of the trauma can't have the final say on your life.

Rise my sister, find your light, get your voice back, regain you! Shake loose the opinions of others and Re-define You. Every part of you is like a petal on a flower, discover all the beauty, and all the hidden treasures of you!

This piece is to the re-defined and rediscovered you!

Contents

FOREWORD

How HONORED AND blessed am I to have been asked to write this Foreword for the inspirational novel Fuchsia. I am not only elated to have been chosen because Carolyn Byrd has served as an instrumental force of spiritual guidance in my life but also because I, like Fuchsia, whom I bonded with immediately, am on the spiritual journey of maturation and transition. I am Teela Brown (Teela B), Actress, Author, Model, Fashion Stylist and Influential Speaker.

I met Lady Byrd through a mutual friend in 2015. Even before I knew anything about her, I was referred to her healing esthetic products. I reached out to her and that ordained transaction served as the initial encounter leading me to the many experiences of how inspiring, nurturing and incredibly gifted in the field of healing she is. My first impression of Carolyn (what I knew her as, at the time) was that she was very beautiful, youthful and honest. But there was a very subtle and lingering presence of Kingdom about her. I soon learned that her hands, heart and mind were created to offer tranquil experiences of love, wellness, and victory to those she encounters.

I can remember a time when I was in mental distress transitioning from my despair to my triumph. As I began intentionally walking towards my destiny and cementing milestones in my career as an entertainer, the broken and shattered pieces of my mirror that were never cleaned up or "dealt with" from my childhood, began to pierce my steps. I was confused, sad, depressed and afraid. Dysfunction was all I had known and I had never been at that vantage point in my life. Without fore warning from me of my pain, Byrd invited me to her spa to perform a lash extension service. Needing the boost of confidence, I obliged. When I arrived, not only did Lady Byrd provide me solace by enhancing my physical appearance, but most rewardingly, she began to plant the seed that would help heal my soul by ministering to me. She poured into me from her overflowing cup of life experience, prophetic anointing, transparency, and genuineness. On that day, combining her talents and spiritual gifts in the way only she can, Lady Byrd exemplified the greatest act of wellness I have ever experienced. When I left her, I felt at peace with the next phase of my promised life. I had never been so excited to move on with my life!! With her unconditional willingness to uplift and the powerful use of her gift of healing, I have been able to progress towards a more whole and authentic image of myself through my mirror.

Under her mentorship, I have been able to heal in areas of struggle that stem from my childhood filled with emotional neglect and identity crisis. She has served as a friend, mentor and sometimes the glue that has held together the pieces of my shattered self-image. When expertise advice was needed to heal my marriage, Lady Byrd was there. When moments of doubt of my deliverance and success plagued my mind, Lady Byrd was there.

As Byrd has nurtured me on my journey of increase, through this inspirational novel, Byrd has extended that same nurturing to the reader.

Much like Fuchsia, growing up, one could find themselves exploring and adventuring through life to find the core and foundation of who they are. Though your stories may be a bit different, you are able to recall familiar emotions and experiences as you journey through Fuchsia's being. These realizations serve as markers for your own life and will be able to compare the then, now and future of your own journey. Someone once said, "Sometimes you have to remember where you've come from, appreciate where you are, and look forward to where you are going". This novel will effortlessly cemented that necessity in your mind. As you travel further with Fuchsia, you begin to realize that though your journeys may be different, you and Fuchsia alike both come from self-doubt and despair and are going to the same place of healing and triumph.

Though this novel is written with an inspirational undertone, you will find yourself amused and captivated as you follow Fuchsia and her comrades through their adventures. Lady Byrd has creatively used her spiritual gift of healing to create a character serving as a self-reflective mirror that is searching, honest, and relatable. She has written the novel in a way in which there is a clear inspiring and entertaining message of survival to overcoming. Byrd has also offered an effective way of portraying the relationships Fuchsia has formed with the other whimsical characters in the novel. This can and will provide deeper insight into bonds you have formed in your own life. There is no doubt that the reader will experience healing in their areas of struggle as they journey, fall and rise with the wonderfully and craft fully, animated character Fuchsia.

I owe a great deal of my affluence to Lady Byrd. Her obedience to sharing her gift of healing for my uplifting and others is endearing. In this novel's formation, it is satisfying to know that it serves as an essential reference for inspiration. Because of Byrd and with the help of Fuchsia, my journey of maturation and transition has been redirected and recharged. I have arrived at my first stops of victory as a spotlighted runway and print model as well as a budding stage and film actress. After reading creation, I know that there are immeasurably more opportunities awaiting my arrival. Won't you allow yourselves to book a trip with Fuchsia to your next level of triumph; as you mend together the broken pieces of your reflection?

It will be a viable, yet amusing adventure to remember!

Much Love,

Teela B

Wife, Entertainer

Baltimore, 2019

CHAPTER ONE

Hey, Mac pull up, the old lady trying to pull out her driveway."

"Tell her to hold up! Damn! She can wait a minute, can't she?" The trashman angrily shouted back at his colleague.

"The rumbling of the trash cans, the shouting of the men scurrying down the road once again awakens me," sighs Fuchsia. "I thought I closed those blinds before I went to bed," she muttered as Lady, her white teacup poodle with pink bows and tiny bells jingling, stretches her yawning little body moving from the foot of the bed to plant her morning kiss.

"Alright, okay, that's enough," smiling as Fuchsia rubs her little head.

"Well Lady, do you know what today is?" she whispered in Lady's ear. "Today is the big day; a day I never believed would happen to me. Who would ever think that I would be getting married, an ole' fly girl? Hard to catch- let alone keep; one who knew no hope, who saw no future, came from brokenness. I was the girl known as the badass, trash-talking brat whose momma couldn't handle her, the runaway; you name it, they called it. It's not that some of them weren't true, but the problem was no one took the time to get to know me. Nonetheless, I'm glad you never once judged me, Lady," smiling as she rolled to the floor slipping into her favorite pink flops.

With a long stretch, glancing at the mirror, "Wow, time has changed some things, huh?" she thought as she, one by one, removed the pins that held her hair in position while asleep, and section by section, her hair bounced past her shoulders and rested as though they were perfectly placed.

I'm looking more like momma these days. Smiling slightly at her reflection in the handcrafted mirror resting on the beautiful mahogany dresser, "Momma I wish you could have shared this part of my life to know the woman I am today and see your little Fuchsia take the steps of faith and *get hitched* as grandma would say," she muttered.

As Fuchsia made her way to the bathroom, Lady began to whine.

"Okay, okay let me brush my teeth and wash my face, then I'll feed you, girl".

All the way down the stairs in the hallway, she and Lady would do their morning chase – roll the pink ball. Between the jingling of the bell and her bows, it was like morning music as Lady fetches and bring back the ball only to go and fetch again, laughing as if it was the first time they ever did it.

"Lady you are the simplest of all my friends, you are easiest to please!"

The chiming of her phone began to pierce the quietness of the house.

"Good morning! You still around right? I don't need to send out the search party, do I?" sang the voice on the other end of the line.

"Hey Sasha, I knew you would be the first to call! Yes, I'm still here, and no, I'm not planning my escape! I told you I'm not the runaway bride!

"I told you three that I'm all in, plus I ain't crazy; only in the movies can a sister get away with that. Girl, you know Marvin would hunt me down! That man is in love with me!"

Cracking up with an outcry, "Don't start this morning, give me a break this day *pleassse!*"

"Do you need me to do anything for you today?" asked Sasha.

"No, actually. I made sure I'd done everything, maybe too much of everything, so that I could take my time, reflect and be beautiful on this *daaay,*" Fuchsia sang in A flat tone.

"Girl, didn't I tell you about trying to sing? Well, I'll let you slide with that one cause it's your day, see you soon." They laughed and hung up.

"I know this phone will keep ringing; maybe I should turn it off, what you think Lady?" Grinning as if she expected an answer from her fluffy four-legged friend.

While Fuchsia awaited the whistling of the teapot, she opened the French door that leads outside for Lady and reached for her favorite tea mug, old and worn looking, but one thing that grandma Lydia gave her that she cherishes to this day. The day she gave Fuchsia the mug, it was too big for her little hands, but grandma Lydia said "It's the perfect gift Fuchsia; you'll grow to match its size." Fuchsia's little five-year-old hands could barely hold the mug, but her eyes were fascinated with the colors and details engraved in it. The perfect color "Fuchsia," with gold trim and lettering reading, **_wonderful are your ways oh Lord_**. At five she did not understand as she does now twenty-five years later.

Grandma was special to all who met her. "Grandma Lydia was no joke!" Fuchsia giggled as she remembered her Grandma who was strong for such a petite woman. She had so much wisdom, and her laugh would make you crack your side. She sounded like a screeching train making a sudden stop, and made everyone feel at home. Grandma baked the best biscuits and brown sugar cookies. *Boy! I wish I had a biscuit today*, smiling to herself. *Grandma would be proud of me, her little Fuchsia. She often would* say, *'Girl one day everything will change, you just wait and see.'* Grandma was a praying woman, and, of course, Fuchsia gave her much to pray about.

"Thanks, grandma," Fuchsia whispered while looking up towards the ceiling. "I really miss you, but I know you are still with me, always in my heart," she said as she placed kibbles in Lady's Stainless-Steel bowl.

Fuchsia made her way to her oversized taupe rocking recliner that sits in her Morning Room, with her favorite loose tea 'Sunrise' she orders regularly from her favorite tea shop. Curling her feet under her, she sips her tea, watching the birds fly around the garden.

Phone chimes, again, began to fill the room.

"Sasha! What now?"

"Girl, pull your thong together! I just wanted to tell you I'll be there at one o'clock, and the others by one-thirty. You know I got to be the first to shower my girl with love! See you then." Sasha said, hurriedly.

"Man! Sasha's a mess," she said as she opened the French door to let Lady back in the house. She sighed with a smile on her face, gazing down at the small yet still visible scar just below her left knee.

CHAPTER TWO

I t was a cold winter morning; the sun was sparkling through the mini blinds as tiny hands tried to reach over the radiator to peak outside.

"Fuchsia! You better not knock over that vase again!"

"Ok momma, I won't," Fuchsia said, mumbling under her breath. "Don't knock over my vase," she reiterated sarcastically.

"What you say? Don't make me come in there," Momma shouted back as she came along with arm extended to take a swing.

"Nothing!" Fuchsia said, avoiding the hand.

"Momma, what we doing today?" Fuchsia said with excitement.

Fuchsia loved Saturdays. She, Mitch, her older brother, and Momma would spend the day out together. The bus, 'The Number Five,' would take them from their home through the city to downtown every Saturday afternoon. There, they window-shopped and, sometimes, stopped at the Five and Dime store to pick up a few things as they made their way through the Saturday crowds.

Momma had every Saturday speech, that is when she catches the two kids just as they would reach out to touch the nick nacks on the stands. "Look, don't touch. I only came to get a few personal items we need, don't have much money," but she always walked out the stores with bags full of stuff.

Leaving the Five and Dime store, they would walk towards Lexington Market, looking in all the store windows along the way.

The closer they approached Lexington Market, the familiar smell of roasted peanuts filled the air causing their mouth to water. If they acted good, momma would buy a bag for them to share and eat on the bus ride back home. Momma could spend hours here going from stand to stand, looking at everybody's fruits and vegetables and comparing everybody's meat. Mitch and Fuchsia, however, would laugh and play together. Every now and then, one grocer would hand them a piece of something from their stand.

"Hey Mitch, you going with me and momma today," Fuchsia said as she busted through his bedroom door.

"No shut my door for I hurt you! Get out, now Fuchsia!" Mitch shouted, throwing his football at her.

"Momma, Mitch throwing balls at me. Help! Momma, help!" Fuchsia screamed, escaping Mitch's bedroom.

"Punk!" she cursed.

"Don't come back or I'm gonna hurt you."

Mitch used to enjoy Saturdays along with Fuchsia, but now, Mitch rather hung out with his friends. He's changed since he turned eleven. He said she was too young to hang around him; up until three months ago, it had always been Mitch and Fuchsia, laughing and playing together. Even though they were four years apart, Mitch always took her by the hand and said, "Come on squirt. Somebody got to look out for you; you know it's dangerous out here." Mitch knew if he didn't, momma would be on him for sure.

"Momma," Fuchsia called as she slid down the stair rail.

"Girl, what I tell you about sliding down those stair rails? You gonna bust your behind open. Get off the rail!"

"You always say that but I haven't yet," she laughed, sliding off the rail and landing on her feet in the hallway.

"Fuchsia, stop talking back. You talk too much," her momma said while cleaning the stove. "Get over here and help me finish this kitchen so we can get dressed and go."

"Why don't Mitch have to clean?" Fuchsia said, stomping her feet as she entered the kitchen.

Momma looks up and gives Fuchsia a look that meant *that's enough or else*.

At the bus stop, momma looked at Fuchsia and said, "Fuchs," a pet name for her, "This Christmas time may be a little tighter than before, so I need you to only write down two things you really want. No more than that. Do you hear me?"

"Yes momma, but why only two? I saw a pair of boots I really want in the shoe store."

"Well, you can get one other thing with the boots if they don't cost much, and what shoe store? When did you go to a shoe store?" momma said with a disturbed expression.

"The one on the main road. You know the kid's shoe store on the corner, I saw it the last time we caught the bus. We were at the bus stop; remember I tried to show you, but you walked on."

"Fuchs, I don't know, I'll see."

"You always say that, 'I'll see.' When you gonna see momma?"

"Come on girl, here comes the bus," grabbing her by the arm as the bus pulled up.

Fuchsia loved sitting by the window of the bus; she daydreams watching people and buildings. She looked up at her momma and thought to herself; *I wonder what momma looked like when she was little*. Momma wore her hair up always in (what she called) a French bun, always neatly pinned with a little flower on the side. She would say, "I carry a little piece of you with me every day Fuchs, cause you remind me of hope." Whatever that meant, she sighed. Momma was quiet most of the time, but when she was in a good mood, she would laugh really hard, like she had some kind of animal trying to get out.

"Angie," grandma Lydia would call momma when she caught momma staring off in space, "You need to trust the Lord, that's all."

Boy! Momma would get mad at grandma, and roll her big brown eyes then stare out to space. Momma and grandma didn't always get along, and no one could tell why. Momma's skin was so smooth; it looked like soft crème butter. She always wore a dress everywhere we go, and she wasn't much taller than Mitch. She'd never leave home without her lipstick, telling me 'a girl should always look nice,' so I always had to have my hair brushed and have my faced washed even if I was sitting on the porch. Momma sure is pretty; all those men are always looking at her, especially her legs, making the other mothers on the block roll their eyes whenever she passed by.

This particular Saturday, they stopped at the corner store; a teenage girl from the block was going in as they came out. She called Fuchsia a half breed, as she came walking behind momma. All the walk home, Fuchsia was confused trying to figure out the half of what she could have been. She looked a little like momma and little like Mitch, *so what is my other half?* she thought as she tried unwrapping the Watermelon Now & Later candy.

As they approached the corner of their block, she noticed Grandma Lydia sitting on the porch chair patiently waiting for them to return home. Running up the street to greet grandma Lydia, almost tripping momma, she didn't notice the wooden stick sticking out the marked freshly-poured cement. By the time she noticed, it was too late. She fell, scratching her knee pretty bad against the stick. Falling over, slightly missing landing in the cement, she let out so loud a moan that caused grandma running to meet them.

"Fuchs, what I keep telling you about running? I told you one day, you gonna fall and hurt yourself! Now, look what you done! Come on, let's get you to the house," momma said as she reached down to help her up.

Grandma Lydia reached them just as Fuchsia was standing on one foot with the bleeding leg up in the air. "Oh Fuchsia, let grandma take a look. Ok, give me your hand; when we get in the house, I will fix it."

With tears streaming down her cheeks, she nodded and placed her tiny hand in grandma Lydia's hand. When they reached the house, grandma Lydia helped her up the stairs to the bathroom, putting the toilet seat down so Fuchsia could sit on it. She cleaned the cut and was just about to bandage it when Fuchsia stopped her and said, "Wait. Before you cover it, I want to see if I can see the other half, maybe it's inside cause I don't see it on my face or body." She said as she examined the bloody leg.

"What on earth are you talking about, little girl?" Grandma Lydia said with a concerned expression. "what other half?

"You know, the half of my breed."

"Where you get such nonsense, child?" Now, grandma Lydia was beginning to get upset. "Where you get that half breed mess from?"

"When we was coming out the corner store just now, that teenage girl with those big eyes called me a half breed. So, I'm trying to see if I can see it in my skin with the open scratch. Do you see it? Can you show it to me?"

Struck by Fuchsia's innocence, Grandma touched her face gently, lifted her tiny chin up to look her in the eye and began gently speaking, "Fuchs, Baby, people are cruel and cruel people say some dumb hurtful things sometimes."

"Ouch! That hurts," she screamed, interrupting Grandma Lydia, as she withdrew her leg from grandma's hand.

"Now, Fuchs, behave and stop acting like a baby. Let me put this bandage on; this might leave a little scar, but you will be fine."

Folding her arms, she poked her lips out at grandma, "Well, you hurting me like those people you talking about."

"Hush Fuchs, that's not the hurt I'm talking about. You hurting because I'm trying to fix you up; the hurt I'm talking about is one of meanness. And that mean spirit is because they don't know any better, they get that dumbness from their parents and the parents before them."

"Grandma Lydia! You told me never to call people dumb. How come you say it then?"

Putting the first-aid kit away in the medicine cabinet, she picks Fuchsia up and sits her on the edge of the sink. "Sweetie, I'm not calling them dumb per se. Fuchs, I'm saying their actions are dumb. What's important for you to know is, baby, you ain't no half; you a whole person. God made you as he made you just like he made them."

Grandma was taken aback. "Fuchs, why you frowning like that?"

"Because..."

"Because what?"

"Because I don't understand. I'm confused! You telling me that God made them dumb? One day you tell me God don't make no mistakes; he made us all beautiful, and we all wonderfully made. Now, you tell me he made people dumb?" She said, trying to wiggle off the sink.

Catching her by the arm, "No Fuchs, baby, I'm sorry you confused. People's actions can confuse us all but try to understand what I'm saying.

"We have no control of how we got here; we control what we do with our lives after we get here. Fuchs, you have a rich soul full of all the other rich souls before you, never forget that."

Rubbing her hands across Fuchsia's forehead, then down to every part of her little face, "We just like that rainbow in the clouds; it's colorful. Every color has its own brightness that when put together makes the most beautiful thing your eyes ever seen.

"Fuchsia, you are like that rainbow full of color, some white, some light brown and some dark brown all wrapped up in one beautiful package. It doesn't make you better or worse than anyone else; it just makes you a blended human being – one full of all the wonders of each color of the rainbow."

"Oh, I love rainbows. Grandma, don't you?"

"Of course, I do. It's one of God's creations. So, every time you see a rainbow, remember what I'm telling you today. You are like that beautiful rainbow in the sky. You are made with a little of this and a little of that, making a whole Fuchsia. And Fuchsia, never let anyone define you because of the color of your skin. Never let anyone try to block you because you are not dark enough or cage you because you're not light enough."

"Cage me?" Fuchsia's eyes widened with fear. "Grandma, I'm not an animal! Only animals live in cages like in the zoo." Tears began to flow down her cheeks. "I don't want to be put in no cage! You making me scared."

Grandma swept Fuchsia up in her arms, holding her close to her breast, "Shhh, baby shhh. No, no one is gonna cage you. You just be you, and one day, if people would only try, they will love you because of your inner beauty and if they look close enough they will see you are no different from them.

"Remember, love does not separate, it joins together all who would try and open their hearts to receive it. So, don't go searching for no half nothing; you just be the whole part of all the halves and stand out because you were chosen to show what true love looks like when we all come together as one. Let your light of love shine through. Fuchsia, be the light of love; help bring people together, and I promise you that you are not alone. There are so many more of us rainbows in the world if only people could see past the individual colors and see all the colors as one." She kissed Fuchsia on the forehead as a seal to her words.

"Grandma, are you a rainbow too?" She asked curiously

"Yes, I am."

"what about Mitch and momma them too?"

"Yes baby, they are too because your momma came from me and you guys from her," she explained as she put her down on the floor. "We just a family of mixed colors."

"Grandma Lydia, how come Momma never talked much of her childhood? Just said 'that was then, and this is now,' whatever that means."

Taking her by the hand and walking out of the bathroom then down the stairs, "Well Fuchs, it's hard for some people to talk about life. They just try to forget."

The next Saturday, momma and Fuchsia did their usual house cleaning, got dressed and headed for the bus downtown. Walking along the pavement to the bus, Fuchsia reminded her mother of the boots she wanted, and momma replied, "We will see Fuchs, we will see."

They stepped onto the bus, put the bus fare in the bus meter, and made their way to the only two seats left side by side. Fuchsia looked down at the leg she scratched up last week and said to her momma, "See momma, it's gonna be ok. Right momma?"

"Yes Fuchs, it's gonna be ok," patting her on the knee.

Smiling Fuchsia looking out the window noticed a girl her age waiting for the bus to come to a complete stop, "Momma, look she got on my boots!" Fuchsia said as she nudged her momma. She knew not to shout in public.

"What boots, Fuchs?"

"The ones I told you I want. Look, she got them on," she said as she slumped back in the seat and rolled her eyes.

"Fuchs, they hers. Her momma brought them for her, they not yours."

"I saw them first, now, I don't want them no more," Fuchsia said with tears in her eyes.

"Oh Fuchs, stop being a baby. Now, sit upright."

The little girl with her momma sat right in front of Fuchsia and her momma, but Fuchsia stared out the window the rest of the bus ride.

"Fuchsia, get up. It's seven o'clock; time to get ready for school," momma said as she opened Fuchsia's bedroom door. "Fuchs, come on, get up. I'm about to fix your breakfast, now get up!"

Angie opens the blinds and, in, pops the sun shining right in Fuchsia's eyes.

"I'm sleepy, do I have to go to school today?"

"Get up now."

She hurriedly freshened up, dressed and ran down the stairs. Remembering not to ride the stair rail, she jumped the last three steps and ran into the kitchen, shouting, "Momma, can I please have the last of the cereal?"

"No, I came down first. I want it," shouted Mitch as he shoved her from the counter.

"Mitch! Have you lost your mind? What I tell you about shoving her like that? You don't get to put your hands on your sister, do you hear me?" Momma said as she turned from the sink and caught him shoving Fuchsia.

"Now, let her have the cereal, you're the big brother plus I have some waffles for you. You know she loves that cereal."

"Momma!"

"Mitch, please. Don't, not today."

"Ok!" he reluctantly responded as he pushed down the button on the toaster to heat his waffles.

"Alright, you two get to moving before you are late." She opened the door and handed them their lunch. "Love you," kissing them both on the forehead as she does every morning. She closed the door behind them to get ready for work.

"Man, I don't know why I have to walk you to school. Can't you walk yourself or find a friend or dog, something – just not me?" Mitch said as he snatched Fuchsia arm to cross the street.

"I'm gonna tell momma!"

"So? And she'll find you in the trash if you do. Watch me, I'll put you right in it like our worn-out shoes," he laughed.

"I ain't no shoe! Why you always so mean to me now? I ain't done nothing to you!"

"Oh, go on, I'm just playing. You know you my best girl," he said as he shoved her gently. "Come on, hurry up. I got to go; I'm running late."

"Not her again!" Fuchsia said, rolling her eyes. "What she doing at my school?"

"Who you talking about, little one?" Mitch said, gazing around.

"The girl with my boots from the bus," she said as she again rolled her eyes at the girl.

"Come on girl, get in the building; I got to go. You too little to have all that attitude. Chill Fuchsia, chill," Mitch laughed as he pushed her into the school doors.

"Fuchsia," said Mrs. Brooks. "This is our new student; her name is Sasha, and she will be sitting next to you. Will you be her helper?"

"Alright," Fuchsia said politely as she looked down at Sasha's feet to see those boots.

"Hi, I'm Sasha," she said sweetly.

"I heard," replied Fuchsia under her breath.

"Fuchsia, she will sit with you in the lunch room as well," said Mrs. Brooks

"How old are you?" Sasha asked Fuchsia while pulling her sandwich out of her snow-white lunch box.

"I'm seven going on eight, why?" she replied harshly.

"I just turned eight Saturday, my mom brought me these new boots; I was just asking," she said shyly

"So, I used to want them, but now I don't!" Fuchsia snapped, as she got up to throw her brown paper lunch bag in the big grey trash can across the room.

As she returned to the table where they were seated, Fuchsia hadn't noticed that someone spilled their milk, she slid and fell under the chair where Sasha sat. With tears streaming down her little eyes in embarrassment, she hurried to her feet only to slide again. The children began to laugh all except Sasha who reached out her hand to help her up.

"Oh, are you ok?" Sasha said, wiping Fuchsia's face with her hand. "Look, your leg bleeding."

Fuchsia cried as she saw the blood running down her white tights; the scab had come off the wound where she fell a few days ago. Sasha ran to tell the cafeteria aide. That day was the beginning of their friendship.

The next day in class, Fuchsia was happy to save the seat next to her for Sasha.

"Hi Sasha, I saved your seat for you," she said while sliding the chair out from the table for Sasha to sit.

"Ouch! Fuchsia, I'm gonna tell the teacher you hit my leg with that chair," said Jimmy whose seat was next to Fuchsia.

"What boy? Why you screaming like an old chessicat? You better shut up for I hit you in your lip again!"

"So, that was a mistake? You lied. Fuchsia, you lied!"

"See, there you go again, you tattle-tail! I'm sorry, ok Jimmy, I'm sorry!" She snapped back, rolled her eyes and helped Sasha with her bag.

"Some people just full of drama!" Fuchsia whispered to Sasha.

"Miss Fuchsia, I can wait until you finish talking to your friends. Then, I can teach the rest of the class, ok?" The teacher said, standing over-top Fuchsia and Sasha.

"If you like," Fuchsia muttered, then turned and placed her feet under her desk.

Motioning at Jimmy with her finger, "I'm gonna get you, just wait and see!"

The rest of the morning, Jimmy kept away from eye contact with Fuchsia.

"Ok girls and boys, get your lunches out and line up by two's so we can quietly walk to the cafeteria," the teacher instructed the class.

"What you bring for lunch today?" Sasha asked Fuchsia.

"Food! What you think? What you bring?" she clinched her brown paper bag in her hands already knowing that it contained the same daily food.

The lunch bell rang as the children all lined up and began walking to the lunch room. Two by two as the teacher instructed them, there was laughter and talking as they all made their way down the hall.

Sasha and Fuchsia walked side by side each holding their lunch in their hands. Finally, Sasha speaks up.

"Fuchsia, why you so mean to me?"

Fuchsia walked on silently. They reached their class-assigned lunch table, placed their lunch on the table and set next to each other. Suddenly, Fuchsia blurted out in Sasha's ear, "I ain't mean, I just speak my mind!"

Startled by Fuchsia's response, she calmly said, "But why does your mind have to speak to me like that? I thought you wanted to be my friend, Fuchsia?" She dropped her head and began opening her lunch box.

Fuchsia, realizing she had hurt Sasha's feelings, reached out her hand with her lunch bag in it. "Here, you can see what's in my lunch, but I can tell you quicker: peanut butter and grape jelly sandwich, an apple, and a Twinkie. It's the same lunch I had yesterday and all the other yesterdays."

They both burst into laughter as Sasha pulled the food out of her lunch box.

"Well, today you can share mine! My mommy sends me all kinds of snacks. She said it's because I can't make my mind up about what I want to eat, so, she packs everything and what I don't eat I take it back home. So, here Fuchsia, you can share mine," she said with much excitement.

"See, I have cookies, crackers, chips, an apple, and orange plus a turkey and cheese sandwich! Here I'll trade you today for your peanut butter and jelly, that's my favorite!" She said as her eyes light up.

"Thanks, Sasha, thanks! This Turkey and cheese sandwich is so good!" Fuchsia said between bites. "Does your mommy make this kind of lunch every day?"

"Yes, every day! But from now on, I will ask mommy to pack extra for my new friend!" She said as she hugged Fuchsia around her shoulders.

"Why you hugging me?" She said while trying to break loose

"Because I'm happy you my friend."

"Well, you can be happy, but you don't have to be all mushy with the hugs!" She bites into a chip.

"Why no hugs Fuchsia? I only hug cause I like you and so happy you are my friend. I hug my mommy all the time cause I love her. Don't you hug your mommy?"

"Well, I ain't your mommy, and no I don't," she said with sadness in her eyes.

After school, Mitch was waiting at the usual location, sitting under the tree beside the school building throwing the ball against the tree and catching it.

Fuchsia runs towards Mitch as soon as she spots him, running past the huddle of kids laughing and playing in front of the school. Suddenly, there was a loud whistle screeching through the air.

"Young lady, please, stop running!" yelled a teacher.

Fuchsia stopped in her tracks and briskly walked to Mitch.

"Ha ha ha, she caught you!"

"Shut up and come on, let's go!"

"Hold up, why you rushing? What's the hurry?"

"Nothing! Just want to get on home, that's all!"

She walked and watched the cars ride up the street. She saw Sasha and her mom walking towards a small yellow Volkswagen wagon car. They were talking and laughing with each other; her mommy's arm was around Sasha's shoulders as they walked along to get in the car. She watched as Sasha's mom kissed her lips and buckled her in her seatbelt.

"Momma! Fuchsia screamed as she burst through the front door of the house. "Momma, where are you?"

"Fuchs! What's wrong?" Angie said as she came running down the stairs with the feather duster in her hands. "What happened?"

Stopping in her tracks at the bottom of the staircase, she threw her bag on the floor next to the radiator. "Nothing happened, Momma."

"Then why you come in here screaming like that scaring me to death?"

"How I scare you? All I did was called you?"

"Fuchs, you screamed my name in a panic! So, what is the big fuss about?"

Waving the feather duster at Fuchsia's head, "Pick up those books off the floor, and start dusting the living room and these rails on the banister since you have all that energy!" She said as she turned to go back up the stairs.

"What dust? Momma, it looks like that's what you were already doing. So, why do I have to dust? I been in school all day, I'm tired, plus I want a snack."

"Fuchs, do as I say!"

"Momma! I just wanted to ask you for a hug, that's why I called you." Fuchsia dropped her head, picked up her books and laid them on the white wooden kitchen chair.

"Oh Fuchs, stop being a baby! And where is your brother! I told him to come straight home today?"

"He's stopped on the corner with his friends, told me to go in the house, and he will be in soon," she said, wiping the one tear from her eye as she picked up the lemon-perfumed dusting spray and the dusting cloth.

"That boy, always doing what he wants to."

"Mitch do what he wants, and I get in trouble. All I wanted was a hug," Fuchsia mumbled, sniffling, trying to hold back her tears as she remembered the look on Sasha's face as her mom kissed her.

Fuchsia stood in the living room staring at the wood coffee table; removing the colorful flower centerpiece and placing it on the floor beside the table, she sprayed the table with the dusting spray and began wiping the table making sure to rub in the spray and not leave streaks. She then replaced the centerpiece and began unbending the silver sprayed pedals – they perfectly matched the silver vases on the side tables next to the sofa. Momma loves silver accents in the house; she said it just compliments the house and is not too cheesy, whatever that means. She did the same to the two side tables and the lamps set on them, the fluffy pillows on the grey sofa and matching chair. When she was done, she went into the small dining room to dust the dark wood dining table and chairs, and buffet that matched.

Finally, just about an hour after she was all done, she placed all the dusting supplies in the kitchen cabinet under the sink. Fuchsia moved her step stool over to the sink so she could wash her hands, then dried them on the tea towel hanging from the hook over the sink.

"Fuchs! What are you doing? You too quiet down there!" Momma hollered from the upstairs bathroom.

"Nothing Momma, I just finished washing my hands. I was gonna get me a snack, I'm finished dusting the living room tables, and I did the lamps too."

"Did you do the dining room?"

"Yes, already done. I knew you would tell me to do that too, so, I did it already."

"Well, come get this dust mop and dust those floors."

"Oh momma, can't Mitch do them when he comes in like he used to dust them? I want to eat my snack!"

"Who you think you talking too? Do as I say, Fuchs! Now get up here and get this dust mop, before I come down there!"

"Fuss, fuss, fuss. That's all you do – fuss, fuss, fuss," she mumbled as she climbed the stairs.

"Bong, bong, bong," Fuchsia could hear momma alarm clock sounding down the hall. Sitting up, she began unwinding herself out from under her pink sheets and blanket that tangled her through the night. She reached for the pink and purple quilt that grandma Lydia gave her and fluffed them in the air. Jumping up out of her bed, her feet hit the cool wood floors. She opened the light pink cotton curtains that covered the windows in her room. From her bedroom window, she could see the decorated pumpkins on the porches across the street as she peered through the remaining yellow and orange leaves left on the tall tree that normally blocked her view. The blowing wind was slightly moving the branches to the left and right just enough to see Mr. Brown walking to his green Ford, and Mrs. Green walking her black poodle.

"Fuchsia, time to get up!" Momma sang from her bedroom door.

"I am up momma," wiping the moisture from her eye.

"Well, get in the bathroom, and hurry this morning. Don't be long getting dressed either. I got to leave early this morning, and I need you to be dressed before I leave!"

"Okay, okay. Hey momma, did you remember to get me a bag of Halloween candy for class and a bag for the trick or treaters?" She said as she ran into Angie's room.

"Fuchs! Didn't I tell you to get in that bathroom? And NO, I did not get candy! I ain't thinking about no Halloween! I don't have any extra money for no candy, plus you don't need no more candy! Now get in that bathroom now for you make me late for work!"

Fuchsia headed back towards the bathroom from momma's bedroom door, kicking her feet against the footboard of the hallway. Across the bathroom, she heard the sound of music coming from Mitch's bedroom; she tapped on his bedroom door, then slightly opened it.

Mitch room was blue colored. The walls full of posters of his favorite basketball players and favorite bands. The dark blue cotton curtains blocked out the daylight while the light bulb on the ceiling fan just gave enough light to see all the tennis shoes all around the floor. His clothes-hamper beside the closet door was overflowing with clothes. The oversized bean bag chair was full of albums and his bed full of washed clothes. Mitch didn't hear the tapping on the door, nor did he hear the door open.

Sliding quietly into his room, she walked over to the foot of his bed.

"Hey Mitch, you up?" She said softly while shaking his foot.

"What the!"

"You better not curse!" she jumped back as he threw his pillow at her.

"What I tell you about coming into my room? Get out! Plus, it's not half past 7 yet! Get out for I hurt you!"

"I just wanted to ask you a question, that's all."

"Well, ask me after I get up! Now go! And don't come back or else!"

Picking up the pillow he threw at her, she hurled it back and ran out his room slamming the door behind.

"Fuchsia, what are you doing? Don't make me come in there and use my brush on your behind first thing in the morning! You hear me girl! You got five minutes or else I'm coming!"

Running into the bathroom, she slammed the door behind and sat on the toilet with her arms folded and lips pouted.

She rushed to brush her teeth and wash her face; she quickly fixed her hair into a single ponytail. Hurrying to her room, she grabbed some jeans and a blue sweatshirt; reached in her drawer, got her socks and put her blue and white tennis on.

Sliding down the banister, she jumps off right as momma was coming out of the kitchen.

Angie caught her right as she landed on her feet. "Didn't I tell you not to slide down that rail?" she said as she grabbed her by the arm and squeezed.

"Girl, you just asking for a spanking this morning! What's wrong with you? Fuchs, why you got to be so hardheaded?" She said as she released her grip off Fuchsia's arm.

"Ouch, that hurts. You pinched me with your nails."

"I'm gonna do more than pinch you in a minute. Now, get in that kitchen and eat that cereal. I got to go before I miss my bus. I will see you after work today; I should be home by six O'clock."

Angie walked over to the bottom of the stairs and looking up the stairs said, "Hey Mitch, I'm leaving. You and Fuchs be careful gonna school today, you know how those fools act on Halloween. And don't be late, please. I don't feel like getting no calls today from that school cause you late again. Mitch, you hear me?"

Opening his bedroom door, "Yeah momma, I hear you. See you later."

After eating, Fuchsia ran back upstairs into her momma's bedroom closing the door behind. She walked over to Momma's dresser with the mirror on it and began opening momma's makeup bags.

Pulling out all the colors of eyeshadows that momma don't use and the red lipsticks of different shades, she painted her eyelids green and blue, applied red blush and red lipstick. Searching through momma's jewelry box, she found the biggest clip-on earrings and put them on her ears. Going through the drawers until she found a colorful orange, green, and pink scarf, she folded it into a triangle, wrapped it around her head and tied it at the back of her head. She grabbed another scarf, a bright yellow and white scarf; she wrapped it around her neck, then ran out of momma's room.

"Hey! What in the world? Fuchs, you done gone crazy and momma gonna get you! What you doing girl?" Mitch laughed as he caught her coming out of momma's room.

"It's Halloween! I'm a gypsy stupid!"

"Yeah, you gonna be a dead gypsy when momma see you! You look like some type clown," shoving Fuchsia as he laughed.

"She ain't gonna catch me cause she won't be home till 6 O'clock and I be all cleaned up by then, and you better not say nothing or else I will tell momma I found cigarettes in your room!"

"You little snitch! I told you to stay out my room! Come on. We got to go. You walking to school like that?"

"Yup! It's Halloween and momma wouldn't buy me a costume, so, I made my own. Plus, it looks better than the one you wearing," she said as she ran down the stairs with her books to the front door.

"What costume? Ain't nobody wearing no costume! I don't do those kids things no more!" he said locking the door behind him.

"I'm talking about the one you was born with! Ha ha ha," she jumped off the last three steps unto the sidewalk.

"Ha ha ha, very funny. But the girls like it," he said as he ran his fingers over his new growing mustache.

In class, everyone had on their costumes and brought their candy for the class to share except Fuchsia. She told the teacher she left hers on the dining room table by mistake. There was enough candy to go around for everyone because Sasha's mom brought extra and even brought Fuchsia favorite Reese cups.

After school, while walking out the school doors, Sasha ran over to Fuchsia.

"Hey, want to come over to my house for trick or treats? We can hand out candy at my house when the people come."

Pausing for a moment, Fuchsia knew momma wouldn't allow her to go over to anyone's house and she hadn't met Sasha's mom.

"Nah, I have to hand out candy from my house because my momma brought a bunch of good candy and if she came home from work and it's still there, she gonna be mad! But thanks, plus you not gonna trick or treat yourself? Me and Mitch is going later." Fuchsia said as she turned to go meet Mitch by the tree.

"Okay, see you Monday."

"Oh, you never know. I might be one of the treaters who knock at your door; my mom is taking me out later!" Sasha said as she ran to her mom who was waiting at her car.

Fuchsia's heart sank as Sasha's voice kept ringing in her ears, 'I might be a treater at your door.'

"What's wrong with you?" Mitch said as she walked up to the tree.

"Nothing!"

Through the walk home, she silently thought about fixing the lie she told Sasha; what if Sasha knocked on her door and she didn't have candy, what was she gonna do? The whole walk home, she kept seeing candy wrappings of all the eaten candy and began picking up the wrappers from chocolate ones that wasn't messy or torn.

"What are you doing Fuchs! You the trash man now?" Mitch said as he shoved her.

"I'm minding my business like you should! Plus, I gotta make a Halloween poster for class on Monday! So, shut up and stop pushing me."

Mitch's friends caught up with him as he walked Fuchsia home, joking and tussling along the way. Fuchsia walked ahead of Mitch and his friends, picking up candy wrappers on the way. As they approached their block, Mitch pulled away from his friends and caught up with Fuchsia.

"Hey, you okay? You been quiet the whole walk home."

"I'm okay, you been playing with your friends."

"Yeah but you been strangely quiet though. What's going on in that head of yours? Cause I know you conjuring up something, I know that look of yours."

"I'm just thinking, that's all! Oh, go on with your friends anyway! I can walk the rest of the way home, I know you ready to go on with them, so go!" Snapping at Mitch, then turning to walk home.

"Why you so smart? I was just trying to talk to you! Go on with your mouthy self! I'll watch you from here, so hurry up, run, so I can go!"

Running towards the house she turns back and shouted, "Dummy! You and your friends just dumb!"

"Little lady, that was not a nice thing to say to your brother," a voice seemed to echo through the trees. It was like Grandma Lydia was in the trees.

Fuchsia looks up towards the sound of the voice and spotted the next-door neighbor looking out her upstairs window, barely seeing her through the screened window.

"Oh, hi Miss Netti," she mumbled as she opened the screen door to put her key in the lock. Hurrying into the house, she slammed the door, dropped her book bag on the floor besides the stairs, ran into the kitchen and turned on the small TV that sits on the kitchen cart. Opening the white cabinet doors over the sink, she grabbed a small glass mixing bowl, then pulling out the drawer besides the stove she grabbed a large spoon. Looking through the cupboards, she moved the flour, sugar, salt and pulled out the chocolate momma used for baking. Taking a glimpse of her favorite after school cartoon, *The Flintstones*, she waited for the phone to ring. Like clock work, same time every school day - ring, ring, ring.

"Hi momma," she said as she picked up the phone.

"Hey Fuchs, how are you, school, where is your brother?"

"I'm okay, school was the same. He's with his friends."

"That boy, whew! Did you remember to lock the door when you came in?"

"Yes, I did."

"Okay, I will see you after work."

"Hey momma, can I make me a snack? I won't make a mess or turn on the stove."

"Fuchs, don't make no mess!"

"Okay, I won't." She hung the phone back on the wall besides the kitchen cart.

Walking into the dining room with the spoon in one hand and the bowl in the other, she walks over to momma's freshly potted plants and began scooping out some potting soil, some from both the pots. Making sure that she pats down the remaining soil around the plants. Tossing the potting soil around in the glass bowl, she sang the theme song of the show. She walks over to the small countertop between the stove and sink to continue mixing the soil, picking out the tiny rocks and throwing them into the trash can besides the back door. Singing out loud as she scoops out some chocolate and mixes it with the potting soil and adds a few drops of water to make it blend.

"It's not creamy enough, hmm let me see." She takes out the creamy margarine from the refrigerator.

"Two scoops should do it."

Dropping the scoops into the potting soil and chocolate, she mixes until it looks slightly stiff but creamy. Looking over at the clock on the yellow kitchen wall that read four thirty, she got her book bag, pulled out all the used candy wrappers, placed them on the kitchen counter and smoothed them out. She scooped out a small spoonful from the bowl and began filling the wrappers, rewrapping them each again.

"Done! My chocolate trick surprise!" Giggling, she carefully placed each one in a large plastic bowl and placed the bowl beside the front door on the radiator cover.

"Now, I have trick or treat candy too!" she waited excitedly at the window beside the front door for her first guest to knock on the door.

"Ding Dong," the doorbell chimed.

Opening the door with a huge grin on her face as she recognized her first trick or treater, little Oscar, the kid next door dressed like a ghost.

"Trick or Treat!" He shouted as the door swung open.

"Here, you can only have one, I don't have many left," she sang out as she placed one in his jack-o-lantern bag.

"Thank you Fuchsia," he said as he ran back to his big brother.

Bursting into laughter as she closed the door behind him, "I got tricks not treat at this house!"

Peaking out the window for the next guest, she glances again at the kitchen clock that read five fifteen.

"Come on, hurry up people!"

Suddenly the back door burst open, scrambling with the large bowl of tricks, she hid it under her coat she left on the floor by the stairs.

"Fuchs, what you doing?" Shouted Mitch as he stood in the kitchen staring at her.

"Nothing! Why you scare me like that and why you here?"

"I live here, remember! And what you hiding in there?" He said as he walked towards her.

"I ain't hiding nothing!" She screamed back as she tried to keep the bowl hidden under her coat.

"Ding Dong, Ding Dong, Ding Dong," the door bell keep ringing.

"Well, ain't you gonna answer the door?" he said with a smug look.

"No, cause momma didn't buy no candy!"

Walking to the door swinging it open, a girl dressed in a princess costume shouted loudly, "Trick or Treat! Is Fuchsia home?"

"You know Fuchsia? How could such a cute little princess know my sister the mud ball?" Laughing as he opened the screen door to let her in.

Hiding behind the door Fuchsia whispered, "shut up and tell her I'm not here!"

"Come on in, what's your name cutie?" Mitch said as he shoved Fuchsia from behind the door.

"I'm Sasha. Hi Fuchsia, I told you I would come to your house for trick or treat, my mom drove me. She's in the car waiting.

"Hi," with her head hanging down. "Yeah, I see."

Snatching the hidden bowl from under from under Fuchsia coat, "Here, offer your friend some of your candy, Fuchs," Mitch said as he pushed her forward.

"Stop Mitch, I'm gonna tell momma! You play too much!" Tears started streaming down her face.

"Here, offer her the same candy you gave my friend's brother."

Looking confused at Fuchsia and Mitch, "What's wrong Fuchsia?"

"Nothing, you don't want my candy, because I think the store my momma brought it from sold her stale candy. I'm sorry but I have to finish my chores before my momma gets home. See you Monday," she said as she tried to get the door opened.

"Nope, not that easy Fuchs! Here Sasha, why don't you open a wrapper yourself and see if it's stale or not?" Mitch said as he handed her a wrapper from the bowl Fuchsia had made.

"Okay," Sasha said as she began opening the wrapper. "What kind of candy is this? It don't look like regular chocolate candy."

"Go on, tell your friend what you been doing."

"This smells like dirt!" Sasha said. "Oh no, they sold your momma dirt!"

Mitch interrupted, "No, they didn't sell my momma anything! Fuchsia made this up herself to trick people into eating dirt."

"Well, you always said we have to eat a little dirt before we die!" Fuchsia said trying to make Sasha laugh.

"Fuchs, you giving people dirt to eat! mixed with chocolate! You lucky my friend's mother didn't see this!" Looking back at Sasha, "Sorry we don't have no candy here," he grabbed the bowl from Fuchsia and took it to the kitchen.

Sasha put her arms around Fuchsia, "Ha ha ha, you the funniest person I know! You got tricks not treats! Ha ha ha," she kept laughing.

Giggling back, "That was kinda funny, wasn't it? You should have seen that little boy's face light up when I gave him that candy! I wanted to laugh in his face!"

Both the girls stood by the door giggling softly so Mitch wouldn't hear.

"I better go for my mom come to the door, see you Monday."

Six O'clock on the dot, Fuchsia hears the key in the door and runs from the kitchen, "Hi momma!" She said as she grabbed the bags in momma's hand.

The look on momma's face said it all, "Don't hi momma me! Girl, you lost your mind, did you?"

"What you talking about momma, what I do?"

"What you do? Are you really asking me this Fuchs? I saw Mitch at the bus stop and the little boy. You could have made that child sick! Why would you do such a thing Fuchs? Where is that bowl of junk?" Momma said as she walked into the kitchen.

Angie was so angry at Fuchsia that she dropped her purse on the floor and everything went rolling around the kitchen. "Look what you made me do! Where is that bowl?"

Fuchsia reached in the kitchen trash can where she threw it in, and handed momma a piece of the wrapped soil chocolate.

"Momma, I'm sorry."

Angie opened up the wrapper and stared at it, "I just don't understand why you would do this? Did you think this was funny? What if someone's child had eaten this? Talk to me girl!"

"I asked you for candy and you said no Momma."

"So, you think because I said no means you would hurt other people's kids?"

"I wan't trying to hurt nobody, I was just tricking them, plus ya'll say a little dirt don't hurt nobody."

"Fuchsia, this ain't no little dirt! Ok, here then, you eat a piece of your little dirt and see how it feels to be given dirt as a trick!" She handed the chocolate soil mixture to Fuchsia.

"Momma! You gonna make me bite this? No momma, please, don't."

"You didn't seem to mind giving it to someone else's kid, so go on, take a bite right now, and you better swallow it!"

Tears streaming down her cheeks, she closed her eyes, took a small bite and began to chew.

"Now spit it out in the trash and go brush your teeth! No TV for the rest of the weekend! And No, you can't go outside either! And the next time I tell you no, you better accept it as NO!"

Running frantically upstairs to the bathroom with tear filled eyes, she threw her face in the sink and began rinsing her mouth out. A smile came over her face as she looked at the dirt between her teeth wishing Sasha could see this.

Monday morning, Fuchsia couldn't wait to share with Sasha her Halloween adventure at school. Getting dressed before time, she rushed down to eat breakfast before momma made it to the kitchen.

As soon as Fuchsia arrived in class, Sasha immediately turns to Fuchsia, "I had a blast with you on Halloween! What's our next adventure Fuchsia?" She said as she burst into laughter.

At the lunch table, Fuchsia and Sasha laughed during the entire lunch break, whispering and plotting their next adventures.

CHAPTER THREE

Wedding day

I always knew Sasha would become a nurse or something like that," Fuchsia said as she jumped to answer the doorbell. "May I help you?"

"Yes, I have a special delivery for a Fuchsia Green," said the voice on the other side of the door.

"That's me, hold on second," Fuchsia said as she tightened her long satin white robe with fuchsia and pink ribbons. "Oh wow, who are these from?"

"Don't know, I just deliver." The delivery man handed her the most beautiful bouquet of flowers she'd ever seen. She closed the door, raced to the coffee table and quickly opened the envelope. Her heart raced and tears streamed down her cheeks. She stood in awe as she read the card attached to the most beautiful vase of Fuchsias. "Wonderful are your ways oh Lord. Always with you, Grandma Lydia." With trembling hands, she removed the wrappings.

"How? What? I don't understand," she wept in the memory of grandma Lydia.

"Grandma, I wish you could be here, I miss you so." Fuchsia cried seated on the sofa. *Who would send these to me?* She thought.

Suddenly a soft knock at the patio door startled her. *Who could be at the patio door?* She thought as she wiped her tears and walked to the den.

"ooohh!" she screamed as she opened the white French patio doors.

"I knew I'd surprise you, you didn't think I'd miss my baby sister's day, did you?" Mitch exclaimed.

She jumped into his arms, buried her face in his chest and wept like she was eleven years old again. Mitch held her small framed body and kissed her forehead.

"Grandma would be so proud of you Fuchs, and I wanted a part of her to be with you today. I know you'd need a hug, so I made sure I'd be around when the delivery man came," he said to her while wiping her eyes with his thumb.

"When? I don't understand." Still sobbing and shaking, she closed the patio doors.

"I came in this morning; the flight landed at a quarter till 6. You know it's hard to hide anything from you but this one thing I knew: you would have the most beautiful fuchsias' garden around your house. So, I hurried from the airport and cut some out of your garden then bribed the florist to put them in a vase and deliver them to you. Yep! I paid for that, but my best girl is getting married today, and nothing was more important to me."

"But you said they wouldn't give you the leave because you just got stationed there?"

Dropping his duffle bag on the floor beside the patio door.

"Yes, but I talked to my sergeant. Told him I needed to be here, and he granted me forty-eight hours. So here I am, I knew I had to be here," he said as he wiped her tears. "Besides, who else is going keep the runner from running!" he laughed

"Oh Mitch, this time you don't have to worry! I really love Marvin!" she asserted. "Are you alone, where's everyone else?"

"Patrice? The doctor wouldn't let her travel the distance. She's eight months now, so, she and the little ones stayed behind. She understood I needed to be here with you."

"I'm glad you're here Mitch, you just added to my joy, you hungry?" She walked towards the kitchen.

"Who's cooking? Not you, I know!" he laughed as he gazed around the large kitchen with all white cabinets and silver handles.

"Oh, cut it, your baby girl has come a long way, you said it yourself, grandma Lydia would be so proud, and besides, I gave the staff off today."

"Did you just say, staff? Wow! Ok but let me make breakfast for you, it's your day. You do own pots and pans up in here in this gourmet kitchen, right?" Said Mitch jokingly, he walked over to the stainless-steel stove that perfectly matched the stainless-steel refrigerator.

"Funny."

"For real, your place is beautiful," he marveled at his baby sister's growth, "Just like you," he added, running his hands across the light grey granite countertops with white swirls. The large white Island that sat in the middle of the kitchen with six tall high back swerve stools also had the same pattern.

"I missed you so," she said warmly.

"Me too. Ok, enough of the mushy talk. What do you wanna eat, still like fried bologna and American cheese?"

"Come on, that's still your gourmet dish!" she burst out laughing.

"Nah, when I saw you, it brought back memories of me making you my famous fried bologna and cheese sandwich!" He boasted.

"Ok, but don't tell nobody I still love 'em, hot and cheesy! Umh, the best!" she said laughing as she bent down to pull out a medium nonstick copper pan from the large sliding drawer full of neatly stacked pans. She placed it on the smooth electric stove top.

"What you mean you don't eat them now, you all grown up?" Rolling up his sleeves he walked over to the small stainless-steel sink that was in the center of the large Island.

"Well let's say that I have slightly elevated to a hot mozzarella cheese with beefy tomatoes and a hint of mint! Uhm, uhm good!" She said as she opened the stainless-steel double door refrigerator.

"I always knew baby girl would go bourgeois!" he said shaking his head as he finished drying his hands.

"Whatever," she smiled. "If grandma was still alive, she'll say 'stop that talk, Mitch! she ain't nobody bourgeois, she's my little Fuchsia, she just a little fussy that's all, now leave her be!" she said shaking her forefinger with her hands on her hips as her grandma did.

Handing him the packages of assorted sliced cheeses, a ripe beefy tomato, some fresh mint leaves and stick of butter.

"Yea, Yea, Fuchsia could do no wrong in grandma's eyes, ears, or mind," he laughed. "I'm glad you didn't go stock raven mad until after she died, or you would have killed her!"

Mitch turned on the stove, cut a piece of butter, threw it in the pan and began making their grilled cheese sandwiches.

Sliding into one of the high back stools at the counter with sadness in her voice "I know, glad she wasn't around, but sad she's not here." Then with sudden energy in her voice, she blurted

"Besides, you sure don't have room to talk! If you were not so busy doing you, you would have seen me before I lost me! Anyway, that part of my life is over; the books are closed, a new book is opened in my life. She's gone, dead and buried with no resurrection!" Jumping up walking over to the cabinets above the counter beside the refrigerator. She reached in and grabbed two juice glasses.

"Somebody was looking out for you, even though I wasn't. Funny isn't it? How life can start one way, take a turn that leads nowhere, a turn that should have killed you but then out of nowhere a new road springs forth. Glad we both found new roads."

He sliced the ripe beefy tomato as the cheese melted on the hot grilled bread in the pan, placed the tomato gently onto the hot cheese then closed up the sandwich.

Fuchsia looked away and stared at the flowers and said, "It was more than looking out for me, somebody prayed for me, and I'm glad about it." She sighed as she began pouring the fresh orange mango juice in both glasses.

Mitch cut both their sandwiches right down the middle as momma used to, placed them on the white glass plate Fuchsia handed him and gave her a plate. "How's your bougie bologna and cheese sandwich, my dear?" Mitch asked braggingly.

"Boy! I just took a bite, but it's Oh this is sooo good, big brother," she smiled as she caught the cheese leaking out the bread.

"Tell me about this Marvin that I'm about to release you to," he said in his deep masculine protective voice.

"Mitch only God, that's all I can say, only God. He is the perfect one for me, he understands me, he calms me, he cares for me, he just knows me better than anyone else in this world."

"Wait, wait, wait, not better than me," Mitch said in a jealous tone, dropping his sandwich on the plate.

"Big brother this time I have to say yes, better than you, but you are a close second, besides you went off and married Patrice without my consent, didn't you? It was you who said she's your angel sent from above, rib taken from your cage, blah blah blah."

"You got me, on that. You looking at a brother who missed his only sister grow up, wasn't there to protect her, wipe her tears and fight her battles. He now knows that there is another man taking a place that was left vacant for so long. There were so many nights that I cried myself to sleep knowing that I let you down," he said with tears in his eyes.

"No Mitch, please don't. I'm fine now; I'm a survivor."

Sipping from his glass of juice, he slid his hand across the Island and held hers.

"No. I promised that if I ever got to hold you in my arms again, I would tell you how sorry I am to have let you down, it's one of the reasons I never wrote you in lock up before you left. Baby girl, when I saw your eyes in the courtroom, they were the only eyes I could see for ten years. Man, you talking about pain, I knew I messed up I knew that was it for me. It was so hard for me to let go and fall in love with Patrice because I let down all the women in my life and I couldn't bear hurting another, but she was so patient and persistent, so I finally gave in. When I found out you no know longer lived in the neighborhood and no one has seen you for years, I was crushed I'm so glad I had Patrice because I shut myself in my room for days I wouldn't eat and couldn't sleep. That's when I began to pray, I remembered grandma's prayers, so I started to talk to God. Patrice is a good woman you'll love her when you meet."

"I know she is, she has to be to catch such a wonderful guy," She said as she gently wiped away a tear from his cheek.

"Baby girl please forgive me for leaving you alone. You know I tried reaching any and everybody asking where's my baby girl, and no one knew. Some said that they heard you were different places, and some said they heard you were dead. My world crumbled Fuchs, it crumbled, but it made me determined to be the best husband and father to my family. Man, I used to look at my little girl who is so much like you and I would cry so hard to myself when I laid her down to rest, I was broken. The day I got your message on Facebook, I screamed and did something I never thought I would do. I shouted thank you Lord for answering my prayer. You are real! Patrice came running in. She thought something had happened to one of the kids, she was shaking, crying and trying to calm me down. When I calmed down, she just held me and said, 'thank God, thank God.' You see that's why nothing was gonna keep me from you this day. I swore I'd never let you down again." Mitch stood up and reached for her; he wrapped his arms around his baby sister once again. Kissed her forehead as she laid her head on his chest.

A sense of family and peace came upon her as she buried her face in her brother's chest.

"Mitch, I'm so glad to have you here to hold me today, I have never felt so loved by you as I do this moment."

"I know." they held each other wept with joy.

"Ok do you want your baby girl to have puffy eyes on her great day?" She said upliftingly as she broke away.

"No. Of course not but can I tell you if you did, you'd still be the most beautiful girl in the room."

"Awww!" Smiling, she picked up her plate and headed to the dishwasher

"Hey, you gonna finish that incredible sandwich or am I gonna be forced to eat it for you?"

Bursting into loud laughter that filled the kitchen, Mitch picked up his sandwich "Not this time you little Pacman! You still can eat huh?"

Giggling "only if it's good!"

"Tell me, how big is this wedding anyhow?

"About three hundred."

"What! Who is it you said you were marrying?" he said laughing.

"Mitch, cut it out."

"How large is the wedding party?"

"Four girls, four guys, nothing big, and now my big brother."

"I guess I won't know anyone huh?" he asked.

"Uhm, you remember Sasha?"

"You two still kicking it?"

"We found each other again, and she's still Sasha."

"Wow, what's she doing now, she married, kids?"

"She's a nurse, lives in South Carolina, no husband, no kids, no animals, just Sasha."

"What, is she still fine?"

"Yes, she's still Sasha, I just told you!" she said, smiling and shaking her head.

"Girl, when you brought her home, I was like a hot rooster in a chicken coup, man when momma said, 'boy you better leave that girl alone, she's too young' I could have jumped off the roof! She had a body like she was twelve!" he laughed in reminiscence.

"You a mess! Can I tell you a secret? She thought you was cute too."

"For real? Man, momma was blocking," he laughed.

"Let's see who else is at the wedding. There are Candi, Melondy, and Tommie."

"Tommie! You got a dude as the bride's maid?" Placing his empty plate and glass into the dishwasher.

"What? fool!" She said as she spun around in the high back stool to face him.

"Tommie is a girl, short for Tomeika! Now, she used to fight like a dude, but she always had my back, she was like my big sister or brother," she laughed.

"When I would get caught in a jam, Tommie had my back. She could knock a dude straight out! Guys would say leave little momma alone cause she got a killer, big sister. She would throw down in a dress and pumps, now that's a real roller! One night some guys tried to pin me down, and I had to run, they didn't know I knew how to run, boy I broke through a neighborhood, and someone recognized me as Tommie's sister, got on the phone, called Tommie and said your little sister just flew down the bridge and a pack of dudes is after her, within five minutes Tommie was under the bridge the dudes cornered me and was trying to handle me, thought they was gonna pass me around like an old bone. I cut one as I swung my blade and it got rough, that dude hit me so hard in my back, I fell as I tried to run. I hit my head as I was trying to get free. Suddenly, I heard a scream.

"She picked one dude up, threw him down and stomped him. Another tried to grab her long hair, man! she turned around and kicked him in the nuts and wore him out. By the time the others saw who she was, they started moving back. One said 'Tommie, didn't know she was with you.' She said 'she's not. She's a part of me, that's my sister and you better not even look her way again!'"

"You sure she's not a guy? He laughed flopping on the stool beside her."

"Yea, I'm sure she survived Juvie, and the streets most of her life, her dad used to beat her like a man from the age of five, so she knew how to hold her own but if you saw, her you would not be able to tell the life she once lived. I'm grateful to her. She was my protection then. When I got off the streets, Tommie followed me. She's married with a three-year-old son, Tavone."

"Wow, baby girl life must have been hard, huh?"

"Let's just say it's been," she mumbled as she stood up and began clearing the kitchen table.

"Well, it's ten o'clock, let's see, what would I be doing if you weren't here, hum. I guess I would be sitting in my big chair reflecting over my life and rejoicing about my future. Who would have known that a girl like me would have a turn like this? Sometimes I still find it hard to believe that this is my life, every now and then I pinch myself to make sure I'm awake," she said smiling as pushed the stool neatly under the Island top and the plates in the dishwasher.

"Don't get me wrong, I grateful for my new life, and I appreciate the old one. The things I been through has made me a better woman today; I can get up in the mornings and not feel the pain of the night before. No, it's even better than that, I can get up in the mornings." Sighing, she turned and looked Mitch in the face and says, "Well, now that you are here, you can sit with me and reflect."

"Whenever I'm about to go up another notch or change directions, I always reflect over the last season making sure I learned the lessons and left nothing undone. Want to join me? It may seem painful, but it really keeps me balanced and not full of myself. I know it's only something greater than me that kept me: God!"

"Sure, I would love to reflect with you, I want to really know what I've missed in your life," Mitch said as he stood up and pushed his stool under the counter. He poured another glass of freshly squeezed orange juice.

Mitch reaches down to pet Lady saying, "she's a good pup huh?"

"Yea, she's a good ole girl, had her since she was six weeks, she's two four now, been she and I until Marvin came along, now we three peas in a pod! When Marvin comes over, she is so excited like he visiting her! She whines when he leaves and all. I tell her, look, Lady, he can't stay yet, the time not right, in due time he will, then we go on up to bed. She's our little girl."

"Come, let's go into my lounging room, do you want to take your juice? It's okay. You the first man I allowed to enter that room, so you know you special!"

"You kidding me, baby girl as fine as you are, nobody? What about Marvin?

"Not even Marvin," she smiled.

Fuchsia and Mitch walked up the staircase made of hardwood, at the very top in the center was a beautiful Swarovski crystal chandelier which could be seen from the huge oval window over the double side door. The staircase turned slightly to the left which led to an open loft with a crème jacquard chaise wide enough for two. Right on the center wall was an enormous picture set in a wood grain frame with crème & gold trim and right in the center was a fuchsia garden, the room smelled of fresh flowers with a slight hint of spice. To the right of the chaise in the center of the room was the most beautiful glass French doors with brass knobs one could only see out and not in. Fuchsia open the double French doors that lead to the most beautiful bedroom Mitch ever saw, custom drapes that flowed from the ceiling to the floor, a bedroom suite fit for a Queen. The entire suite was crème with inlays of gold, all hand-crafted. The headboard was a handcrafted garden with the bed set so high that a step stool was attached to the side of the bed. The carpet was plush crème with an inset embossed center with fuchsia flower, surrounded by gold and crème stems. Mitch knew this had to be a custom design for his baby girl. They walked through the bedroom to a very serene intimate room off her bedroom, that had a cozy love seat, two lampstands, small personal refrigerator, center sofa table with photo albums.

"Wow, this is different from the rest but really nice," Mitch said

"I need to have a room that keeps me grounded where I can just sit, relax, meditate, reflect and pray with no interruptions. This is my spot. As I said, you the first man up in here," she said as she picked up an album labeled stage one. "These are pictures of my beginnings; you know you in here too."

"What, from where, where you get pictures of me? Mitch asked curiously.

"When I left momma's house, I took all the pictures I could crumble in my little duffle bag: you, grandma, momma and me. I didn't want to forget nobody" she sighs.

Mitch reached for the blue spiral album labeled stage one, as he opens to page one, a smile unfolds on his face, "Wow I remember this day this was the day momma brought you home wrapped in a pink blanket, you were so tiny and wrinkled! Your hair was so silky with little locks of waves that rested just above your eyebrows; I used to run my hands through your waves. Momma said 'Mitch this is your little sister, her name is Fuchsia. Ain't she precious? Now I have a big man and baby girl'. Boy! could you scream, that first night I was so scared something was wrong with you, I said Momma will she ever stop crying!" Mitch laughed while flipping the pages.

Fuchsia laughed as she reached for a covered dish and pulled out a jar breaker and curls her feet under her as she leans on her brother's leg, "Oh I love this picture!" she burst out with loud laughter.

"Oh my, now that's the picture of all pictures!" Mitch said as he tried to take the picture out of the album.

"Oh no you don't!" Fuchsia scrambles to get the picture, "come on Mitch, don't, you can't take it! It's the only one, pleaaaasssssssse, I'll get you a copy, for real Mitch, don't, please!"

Mitch jumps uplifting the picture above his head with loud laughter like the days when they were young, and he would tease Fuchsia and play keep away. He darts away from her twisting and turning as she jumped and danced singing "pretty please Mitch, with ice cream on top, pretty please!"

They jumped and played liked little kids laughing and giggling until Fuchsia rolled up like a ball shouting "Stop, stop, my stomach, don't make me laugh no more Mitch," tears from laughter rolled down her cheeks as they used to when she was younger. What a great feeling, she smiled to herself. It'd been so long that anyone made her laugh like that.

Finally, Mitch sat down on the chair beside her and said, "Baby girl, big man sure missed you." He kissed her again on her forehead.

"Not more than I missed you," she giggled as she places a yellow jawbreaker in her mouth. sucks on her jaw breaker.

"I can't believe you still eat those." He reached inside the jar and pulled out a blue one.

"Every now and then I crave for that little piece of me. That's why I don't let no one up here, so I can keep that part of me to myself."

"Your secret is safe with me, only if you give me one." He said as he gently pushed her forehead. "Now about this picture, will you make sure I get a copy of this one?"

"You bet I will. Don't momma look so sweet? I love this picture too, my favorite of all of us." She murmured as they stared like little kids at the picture with momma and the two of them. She remembered that day as if it were yesterday. Momma wore a long white silk dress to her ankles with buttons from the collar to the hem. The sleeves were long and flowed at the wrist with little white pedals as buttons. Momma's hair was perfect that day because aunt crystal did it for her, it was the only time she wore it out, boy was it long, it flowed down her shoulders like a peaceful river. Her beautiful eyes shined as she added simple makeup she would say, "To add definition and color." Her lips were perfectly colored with a little hint of reddish brown and a touch of gloss, "Remember Fuchs, always look your best," she would say as I watched her in the mirror.

"This was a special day for momma, she turned twenty-one and wanted a family picture." She said.

"She dressed us in cream for that picture, even though you fussed about wearing those clothes, you never liked wearing church clothes. Momma would promise you a new baseball glove if you'd just do this for her this one time. 'After all, it's my day, Mitch, it's my day.' The photographer placed the most beautiful white cloth on the floor and told momma to sit on it. She rolled her legs behind her on a slant as the photographer straightened out her dress, making it wide all-around momma, then he said to me 'come princess, what's your name?' I said 'Fuchs.' He said 'Fuchs,' momma interrupted and said, 'it's Fuchsia, Fuchsia is her name.'

"He said 'well, Fuchsia, how old are you?'

" 'I'm four, four years old and my brother, he seven and momma twenty-one today.' I said with a smile. The photographer said 'that's nice' as he looked at momma funny. 'Come Fuchsia' he said, 'let me see that beautiful dress, you look like a princess.' I said, 'I'm not princess, my grandma said I'm her Fuchsia.' 'Oh,' he said 'well, you pretty as a princess to me.'

"My dress was made of white eyelets and lace with the biggest round collar. I loved that dress; momma always made sure my socks was white with lace and white patent leather shoes, she said always makes a little girl nice. The photographer had Mitch sit in front of momma with his legs facing the same direction as momma's, leaning slightly on momma's knees then he said, 'Come, little princess, oh I mean Fuchsia, and sit here in front of big brother.' He made my legs face momma, then slightly bent my knees back to show off my shoes.

"When he said 'cheese,' momma smiled sweetly and looked wide-eyed at the camera and suddenly you leaned over slightly to take a look at my face, said after the picture you wanted to make sure I was smiling, and the photographer took the picture, the picture was so precious momma said, 'so precious that I'll take that one.' "

Mitch continues with laughter as he turned the pages with smiles of memory all over his face. He said, "Seems like such a long time ago, but yet like yesterday" as he sees pictures of himself, Fuchsia and Momma. "I wonder how the old gang is today, been so long since I heard or seen any of them.

"Before I got released, I made up my mind that the streets was no longer gonna be my thing, I had to cut all ties if I was gonna make it. That was the worst eighteen months of my life. Locked away from the people who really loved me, and I really loved them. None of those guys came to see me once, the same ones who told me, 'we will always be there for each other.'

"Boy! when the chips were down, I found myself all alone. I realized that the ones who really mattered was the ones I turned my back on. I became so bitter and angry with myself that it took years before I could forgive myself for letting you guys down. Especially you, Fuchs, especially you," Mitch said as he squeezed his baby girl's hand gently.

"Mitch, what happened to make you turn like that? Those friends of yours were the worst, especially Bobby. I hated him the most! Ooooh, he used to irk my nerves! Whenever I went to look for you, cause momma wanted you to come home; he would catch me in the alley and say to me, 'what's up squirt, you know if you weren't Mitch's sister I'd take you up under this bush and give you something big n' hot'. My face would burn in anger, and I would turn to run and tell him: if my brother found out, he'd cut your throat with your dirty self!" He would throw bottles at me shouting 'don't let me catch you out at night alone in these alleys, cause you sure would find out, and Big Man would watch me give it to his baby girl.' Man, he made my skin crawl with his rotten teeth. Who in their right mind would want him to touch her, yuck!" They both burst out laughing remembering Bobby.

Suddenly Mitch stopped laughing and said, "I can't believe that old head was trying to hit on my baby girl, he must really been mad! People used to tell me before I started running with him, 'that's a nasty one, you better always watch your back' but he would tell me 'Big man, I would never cross you because I know you would come back while I was sleep and cut my throat.' And I would have tried earlier if I had known He was messing with you."

"What you mean! You would have tried earlier, Mitch what you do? Or maybe I shouldn't know! She said sternly "Tell me you didn't kill him, did you, Mitch."

"No, I didn't, someone else did, after I attempted. We got into an argument over money, and he said one thing wrong. He said, 'boy I blow your momma house up if you messed with me!' I jumped off the rooftop pulled out my blade and was about to stab him and five o' rolled up on us. We all broke and ran, the next week someone found him shot dead, so someone beat me to it."

"Wow, I didn't know that!"

"I was gonna do him in before he even thinking of blowing up our house!" He said angrily.

"Hey, can I ask you a question that has been forever on my mind?"

"Sure, what's up?"

"Mitch, what happened? What caused you to not want to hang out with me any longer, to start hanging out with those hood rats? Why Mitch, just please tell me what happened? Fuchsia said with a concerned look, as she sipped from her cup tucking her legs under her as Lady came to cuddle beside her.

"Oh, baby girl, baby girl, that's a jaw-dropping question, I'll try and answer, but what if I tell you that I really don't understand myself? I don't know what was drawing me to the streets. You, momma and I were fine. So, it's hard to explain; it was like power had come over me. I became intrigued with Teddy, Johnny, and Ray. Seemed like they had it going, they could stay out longer. Their momma didn't mind the things that momma wouldn't allow. They would wear all the latest clothes and tennis; I thought they were the coolest. It wasn't until I was in Juvie that I found out that Ms. Rosa was not their real mother, that their momma died of an overdose. She was their aunt, like a foster mom to them. She was collecting the money and didn't care what they did as long as it wasn't in her house. The money she was getting for keeping them, she used to drink and gamble, so the boys took to the streets hustling to feed and clothe themselves. They were products of unfortunate happenings. You know, they never talked about their home or family, and they were always angry. It's like they hated momma for no reason, I thought, until I found out it was because their momma had died, OD and they were bitter. "

When momma would walk past the corner gonna or from the bus stop, she would stop and say 'big man, make sure you eat, sitting here on this corner all day wasting time ain't no future in life, promise me you'd take care of yourself today' I would be so embarrassed cause she would then try to kiss me, and I'd brush her off. Baby girl, I wanted so bad to kiss momma's cheek and say, "momma, I'm ok. It's alright. I got this, just you be careful" but Teddy, Johnny or Ray, one of them would start the remarks like 'ain't no momma love like that, she fake; she want to make you a wuss, man.'

" 'Real dudes know the truth and can see past it, she know we don't fall for that lie, all momma's lie, even yours, punk! If she keep coming pass trying to make you look weak, we gonna bust her lying lips and send you on home with her. You little punk.'

"Fuchs, I didn't want nobody thinking I was no punk, so I had to prove myself to them. See they used to sit around the playground at school and pick on the other guys. I just use to watch and say I don't want them to pick on me, so I started befriending them little by little. I tried to act like I was as hard as them. Johnny being the oldest of the three would run up on the back of me and pop me on the back of my head and say 'the boy with the punk hair looking like a little golden child, you ain't nobody special. Just cause your hair all curly wavy like don't make you no better, you still a little punk' he would say as he'd flick my hair. Fuchs, you know dudes like me had it just as hard as the little light skinned girls. My insides would just curdle at the sight of him, so I figured I better join them then have them humiliate me any longer."

"Mitch, why did you say nothing to momma? You know momma would have protected you; you know she wouldn't play with someone touching us!" Fuchsia said with an instant attitude.

"Yeah, Fuchs, but I didn't want momma to fight my battles, I was eleven, not seven anymore. At the time I thought it was my only choice, I didn't see another way out that would be less harmful to me or you two."

"Sorry Mitch, I wasn't in your shoes, I was not thinking, you were never a fighter before that. That's why I couldn't understand the change. They were nothing like you Mitch, nothing." She said, her voice lowered in sadness.

"I know baby girl, I know but boy, did I grow to fight soon after, I had to, if not I would have to fight them."

"I know! I was so surprised that time I walked to the corner store and saw you fighting like that! Boy! my eyes opened up so wide with bewilderment. I shook in fear, was that boy gonna hurt my big man, tears started running down my cheeks when that boy hit you so hard in the face. I thought *oh Mitch gonna die. I gotta go and get momma.* As I was turning to run home, I heard a scream of pain. When I looked back, I saw that board in your hands and blood on his head. I didn't know whether to cry, laugh or jump for joy, so I did all three!" She said laughing.

This lady came running off her porch with a broom screaming, 'Get off my boy!' She saw me jumping and laughing, stopped and said 'What's wrong with you, are you some kind of crazy child? Go home you little fool,' she shouted." Fuchsia said, still laughing.

"I never told momma, didn't want her to whip me cause of the lady, so I ran off to the store still smiling saying to myself Mitch sure beat him bad, bet he won't mess with my brother again."

"Baby girl, I didn't know you were there, why you never said anything?"

"Cause I didn't want you to tell momma, I was not supposed to be on that corner!" she said still laughing.

"I guess you right; momma was no joke!"

"This is what I don't understand, why momma let you hang out with them boys?"

"Well she didn't at first, she used to see me, and I would duck and run. Then when I finally come in at night, she would drop me like hot cakes. She would come out of nowhere and bang me upside my head, saying 'Big man I'm not playing with you, I'll hurt you, keep trying me.' Then she would murmur 'You gonna worry me to death.' He said choking back tears.

"Baby girl I never meant to hurt her like I did, trust me, I just got caught up. Then one night momma waited up for me and this time she didn't come out swinging, she just sat in the chair by the front door and when I closed it, she sat there, turned on the light switch and said, 'Mitchell Samuel Green, I give up, you want to be

62

a man, then be a man, you wash your own clothes, clean your own room, cook your own food, cause I'm not taking care of anyone who believe he's a man who won't respect me or my house. So, Mitch, you on your own, do what you want cause I can't do no more! I have no more strength, no more tears, I'm tired, tired Mitch. I love you, but my love can only reach so far, the rest is up to you. Now when you ready to be a family again, I'll be right here waiting. One day you'll see those punks don't care about you. You just wait and see, they just want you to mess your life up like theirs.' Momma said with tears rolling down her face as she hurried up the stairs to her bedroom and that was the last time momma said anything else about it."

"Mitch, No!" Fuchsia snapped. "I remember that night; it was the night I heard momma praying, asking for help and strength. When I entered the doorway of her room, I saw her trembling and rocking in her chair, she was crying so hard she didn't see me and all she kept saying is I'm tired, I'm tired, please give me strength. When I looked closer, she was holding your picture close to her chest saying, 'Please help; please keep him safe.'

"Momma didn't look up, so I went down to the kitchen to find dinner, and when I went to the stove and looked in the oven where momma would sometimes keep the food warm if she cooked early that day, I only saw one plate that night, and the food was on my favorite plate, so, I knew it was mine. My heart dropped as I ate because I knew something was terribly wrong. That night, I ate alone and went to bathe afterward. I looked into momma's room, and she was still in chair rocking but this time no tears, she said in a soft broken voice 'Fuchs, did you eat and bathe?' I nodded, and she said, 'Go on to bed now.'"

"Yeah, that had to be the night, cause it was the first time there was no dinner in the oven for me," said Mitch as he bent over the table to get the next album with stage two written on it.

"Wow, that's how the scar healed, like a jagged edge?" Fuchsia said, she noticed the scar on Mitch's lower back when he bent over.

"Yup," he said, reaching back to touch the scar. "It's a reminder of my change, sometimes I just touch it and whisper thanks. If that day never happened, I don't know where I would have ended up, certainly not where I am today."

"Why do you say that?"

"Because that day, I was supposed to do something that would have gotten me charged as an adult and my future would have been different."

"I don't understand, what do you mean you were supposed to do something?" she asks curiously.

"Fuchs, by that time I was doing crazy things: robbing, stealing, selling, beating dudes down, guys in the neighborhood were scared when I showed up cause I was known on the streets as the dirty fighter but that day was gonna be different because I was supposed to kill somebody that night."

"What? Who? Why?"

"Oh, baby girl, I had changed a lot. That's why I didn't want you around. I didn't want you to know the big man I become. The more I did, the more I did, if you know what I mean."

"Still, why would you be gonna kill someone when you were only fifteen, Mitch you were still a child."

"Listen, baby girl, by then I was no longer a child, I had changed, that's why I couldn't come home much anymore, cause I had to always watch my back and I couldn't watch mine and yours too!"

"But..." she said hesitantly.

"Come on Fuchs, I know it was jacked up, I know. I can't even justify my actions then. I was about to change one situation, but another man interrupted my premeditation and changed the course of my life. I would've still been doing time baby girl, and it would all be for nothing, nothing. Turf wars, young dudes don't know what they are doing, it's all a game of the mind. I got caught up, first because I wasn't strong enough to handle the mental anguish, instead of communicating with momma, I allowed the mind game to damage my family relationship and where did it get me? In a dark alley behind a dumpster barely breathing, couldn't see, blood running out my mouth, missing teeth, broken ribs, and a four-inch-deep wound that just missed my lungs.

"Baby girl, to this day I don't know who or what hit me! All I know is that day was my time to prove I was not a punk and that I had no fear of taking a life. Baby girl you know I was no punk, and I knew it, but the mind games of proving yourself is deep.

"I know this now, but I didn't know that then, so I fell for the trap. Life has a way of grabbing you by your kahuna's and redirecting your path. I thought I was a man until that day. I thought I was untouchable. I thought people was scared enough to not touch me, little did I know it was all a part of the game. I remember crossing over the tracks, and when I woke up, I was in a hospital bed with momma crying saying, 'Oh big man, what you done got yourself into?' Then you come bursting into the door frantically screaming and crying, at that moment I wished I was dead!" Mitch said and then turned to stare out the large framed window behind them.

Fuchsia gently interrupts him, "That was second of the five worst days of my life! Momma and I was in the house alone, Kevin was out with his drunk friends. I just got out of the tub about to get ready for bed, and I came down the stairs to get something to drink, all I had on was bed shorts and tank-top. Then a sudden loud bang on the door shook the atmosphere; it startled me. I still remember the empty cold feeling that came upon me. That old skinny girl you use to run with came falling and crying through the door when momma opened it; momma screamed 'What's wrong! What happened?' That girl said she didn't know; she wanted to know if I knew! Momma yelled 'Know what? Fuchs been in house all day, she ain't been feeling well today. So, what you talking about young lady, what?'

"Then she had this look like she was a deer caught in headlights, 'I walked up to her and said you better start talking now before I snatch that hair you brought.' She started crying, saying 'I thought you knew, they found Mitch behind a dumpster near the tracks early around six.' Momma screamed and burst into tears saying 'My baby, where is he. Tell me where he is.' She said the hospital off Liberty. Boy, before I knew it, momma had on jeans, and you know momma never wore jeans in public! Momma said 'Come, Fuchs.'

I ran out the door shaking in my bed shorts, my hair was wet, and my flops were in my hands. We headed up the street and momma hailed a hack as we was jumping in the car, that ole' skinny girl tried to jump in with us, boy momma looked at her and said 'Where you think you going?' That girl stopped in her tracks again looking like a deer," Fuchsia laughed.

"Momma said 'You should have come to get me early, not five hours later, find your own way. Then I said 'No, don't show up at all, and I better not find out you had anything to do with it, better not be so.' When we got to the hospital, it was so crazy in there, people all over the place, momma broke through the people shouting, 'Where's my son, where's my son?' I never seen momma look so distraught before. Momma was moving so fast that she left me, and I was looking for her, all I could do is follow her voice, I could hear it in the distance saying, 'Where's my son?' Then I didn't hear her anymore; I was looking in all the emergency rooms in the direction the nurse sent me. Then I heard a whimper 'Oh Mitch,' my heart stopped when I turned and looked through the curtains, your face..." she stumbled in speech as though a lump was forming in her throat.

"I know somebody really wanted to destroy my pretty boy image," he said smiling, holding back tears as he listened to his sister describe that day.

"Yeah, but it didn't work! I thought you were done in for sure but tell me this. How did the police put those robberies on you? I never understood that."

"Easy, they had been trying to catch me for a while, see I never stayed in one spot long, so it was easy to finally catch up with me that time," he shrugged. "You know the old saying every dog has his day and it was my day, but for real, that beating saved my life," Mitch said with a sign.

CHAPTER FOUR

Wedding day

I know Fuchsia is up; it's 11:00 am, she better answer this phone!" Tommie says to Candi as they climb out of Tommie's white Jeep to go to their favorite Bagel shop.

The phone began chiming again; the phone rang, breaking through that one moment of silence she and Mitch were having. "I knew it was too good to be enjoyed, too quiet.

"Hellooo," Fuchsia sang, "Yes, may I help you?"

"No, you may not! I called you to help you! I was just saying to Candi, 'I know Fuchsia is up, it's 11:00 am, she better answers this phone.'"

"What you mean I? You mean we called?" interrupted Candi screaming into the phone Tommie had up to her ear as they darted across the busy street.

"Where are you two?" Fuchsia questioned as she could hear the car horns blowing.

"We just getting out this big chunky Jeep of Tommie's, on our way into the bagel shop." Candi chuckled.

"Hey, watch it, don't you see these fine ladies trying to cross the street!" Candi shouted in her rough voice at the driver of the black BMW who swung to the left just missing them.

"I know she's not acting out today!" Fuchsia laughed "She promised me she would be on her best behavior today, even if it choked her!"

"Well, you better get a grip!" Tommie said laughing "You know, you asked the wrong one to behave today."

"What! You little make pretend snoothies!" Candi shouted into the phone.

"Snooty? You trippin'! Hey Tommie, she shaking that booty of hers, ain't she?" Fuchsia blurts.

Tommie laughs, "You know she is, twitching that thing around." She twitched in the shop. "You know I'm good, I'm not gonna spoil your day Fuchsia, but his, I just might think about," Candi said in a sultry tone looking at the tall guy besides the counter.

"Girl, she's a trip! Same ole' trip just a different location," Tommie said while pulling her arm. "Let's go, 'fore you get somebody in trouble, you promised Fuchsia, no drama today."

"Why you French poodles' always feel as though I'm trouble?" Candi said in a high-pitched voice as she raised her nose in the air, standing at attention.

"Now, that's more like it," Tommie whispered to Candi still laughing.

"You girls are wired up this morning, did you sleep well?" Fuchsia joked.

Mitch was looking at the joy on his baby sister's eyes as she communicated with her friends. It was as if she was four again playing with her Barbie dolls, she was animated then and still today the same. While she was on the phone, he got up "Which way to the bathroom?"

Fuchsia motions with the head to her master bath. When he opened the door, he was stunned at the elegance of her bathroom, he looked back at his baby sister and said, "In here?"

with a questioned look. Fuchsia shook her head and smiled not dropping the conversation.

The bathroom was all marbled from the floor up to the mirrored ceiling which housed a beautiful multi-tiered chandelier. The sun was beaming through the two beveled windows which joined the two corner walls. The windows had to be eight feet tall and surround the beautiful pearl porcelain claw foot tub whose claws were brass, resembling the paws of a lion. Mumbling to himself, "Whew! Just whew, he thought to himself who is this Fuchsia what does she do?

As Mitch walked out of the bathroom, a sweet fragrance was lightly resting in the atmosphere as if someone blew a kiss, a kiss of perfume while he walked by. Fuchsia's phone call ended at the same time he reached her.

"Baby girl, now that's some bathroom! I didn't know if I was to use it or take a photo of it! And what in heaven's name is that scent I smell? It was as if it blew out the sky as I walked by!"

She smiled, "Wouldn't you like to know? It does gently blow as it senses motion. Thanks, you know I love nice bathrooms."

Changing the subject, "those girls are crazy, they were just checking in on me to see if I needed anything. I told them my big brother is here with me. They can't wait to meet you, and they promised me they would be on their best behavior," she shrugged.

"What kind of girls are they that you got to make them promise to behave?" he was curious.

"Nah, that's just how we go, they are actually the only two from that life that I keep dear and near. We go way back, been through too much and seen plenty to lose contact. Besides, all three of us turned our lives around, so we have a past and present in common. We shared the bad times now we share the good times." She adjusted her body and tucked her feet under her as they continued sitting on the fluffy beige loveseat.

"Which one did you meet first, or did you meet both together from the same neighborhood?" He asked with a curious look. "Hey, any water in this fridge?" reaching to open the stainless steel 3.5-cubit refrigerator in the corner of the room.

"Hey, now look who's asking all the questions! Yes, there's water, and organic juices as well, help yourself." Nodding her head while raising her perfectly arched eyebrows. "Ok, one question at a time, let's see, I met Candi first."

She began to think to herself on the day she first met Candi. The expression on her face saddened. She loves Candi but to recall their meeting is having to unlock the secret parts of her life that she never talks about. Fuchsia drifted off into another space in her mind as she began to share the most painful times of her life with her brother who should have been there, who should know the sister that he walked out on and left to deal with and cope with so many things, after all, she was so young, too young to have experienced so much pain.

Taking a swallow from the bottled water. "Baby girl, you ok? You don't have to talk about it, let's change the subject, what do you need me..." before he could finish Fuchsia interrupted him.

"No, It's not ok. Maybe this is my day to really let you know what happened so that I can really say I forgive you," she said in a sharp tone with hot tears flowing down her cheeks.

A sense of hurt began to overtake him. "Whoa, hold up, what are you saying? Really, forgive me? Fuchs, Baby girl," he started to choke as he was trembling by the thought that his baby sister still held a pain that deep.

"Please, Big man," she said softly. "The door is open; I must continue through," she said as reached for the box of Kleenex and began wiping her eyes.

They both knew it was more than talking about her friends; it was the pain of abandonment that was stilled locked in her subconscious. Remembering the pain and anger, she felt when he left her and momma all alone.

Fuchsia tightened her legs under her reclined chair, laid her head to the side and just stared off. She started talking softly as if she was telling her story for the first time in her life. Her thoughts drifted off into another world, a world that no one was able to gain access, she had actually built up walls that had invisible locks all around. She knew this day would come; she prepared herself for this visit years ago. Fuchsia could feel the tears getting hotter, one side of her wanted to shut down and close the door but the other side knew this was that day and it had to happen. She blinked her eyes hard to stop the tears and allow access to her painful world. As she took a deep breath as she remembered the day grandma Lydia died.

***

(19 years ago)

Waking up that morning, Fuchsia knew that day was different. She felt something different about that day. "Momma?" Fuchsia said as she climbed up in her bed; she loved the feel of momma's soft bedspread.

"Yes Fuchs, what is it baby?" momma said as she rolled over and lifted the covers so that Fuchsia could cuddle up with her. It was an unusually cold morning for September.

"Tomorrow is my big day; I'll be eleven. I'm almost a teenager. What we going to do for my birthday?" she said with a big grin.

"Well first, we have to get through today. Fuchs, don't you remember it's grandma birthday today?"

"No, I didn't' forget, I just want to know what we doing tomorrow. I know we going to see grandma today like we do every Sunday," Fuchsia said and kissed her mother's soft face.

"Well let's get going. Get your bath and do your hair real pretty for grandma today turns eighty." Momma was grandma Lydia's only girl and youngest child. Grandma had Angie late; she would say, "Real late, she's my miracle baby."

"Ok momma, what should I put on today for grandma?"

"Put on your pretty yellow dress, the one with the white buttons down the front. Grandma likes that one on you, she said it makes you look like sunshine on a cloudy day."

"Ok, but do I have to put on those white fluffy socks! I'll be eleven tomorrow and you said when I turn eleven I can wear pantyhose. Can I, please momma?"

Angie smiled, realizing her baby girl is growing up. "Yes, now get going, we want to beat grandma home before she returns from church."

Fuchsia ran to her room to get her yellow dress and the brand-new pantyhose that momma brought on sale a couple of months ago. She just had to have them when she saw them. *No more baby socks,* she thought to herself. Fuchsia ran into the small bathroom she used to share with Mitch before he stopped coming home. She loved bubble baths and "smellies" – the sweet perfumes she would take out of momma's bathroom.

Fuchsia ran her bath water, slid under the bubbles and began to sing 'amazing grace,' one of grandma Lydia's favorite songs. "I was lost but now I found," she sang. *I don't know when grandma got lost but I'm so glad she got found cause I sure would miss grandma*, Fuchsia thought to herself, singing and smiling.

"Little princess, will you hurry up! We going to miss our bus! Snap, snap, let's go!" Momma sang.

"I'm getting out now, rush, rush, rush."

"What you saying in there?"

"I'm rushing, here I come."

Fuchsia hurriedly pulled her panties up. She looked at herself in the mirror as she pulls her lace undershirt on. *One day I have boobs like other girls and be able to put on a bra too*, she thought to herself as she tried to push up the flat skin where she, one day, hoped for them! She reached for her new pantyhose, took them out of the pack – they looked so nicely creased she held them up to her waist, looking in the mirror.

"Fuchs!" Momma burst through the door, startling her.

She scrambly dropped her panty hose, saying, "You scared me! Momma!"

"If you don't stop prancing in the mirror and hurry up, I'm going to..."

"I know, I know, knock me out."

"Little girl, not today, not today."

Fuchsia sat on her bed and wore her pantyhose which fitted her just right. Then she grabbed her yellow dress, slid it on and hurried to button all the white buttons. She pulled the brush off her dresser and brushed her hair into one ponytail; then reached into her closet for her black shoes, slid them on and ran down the carpeted hallway to momma's room.

74

"I'm ready, here I am."

"Fuchs, take those shoes off, they don't match. Get those white shoes and put them on!"

"Yes," she said as she drops her head and rushes back to her room. "What's wrong with these shoes?" she mumbled. Fuchsia loved those black shoes, they made her feel a little bigger.

Taking her time walking back up the carpeted hallway, she stopped to look at all the family pictures on the hallway wall as if she never saw them before. There were baby pictures of herself and Mitch, momma and her brothers and one picture of Grandma Lydia in the middle.

"Little girl, if you don't hurry down these stairs now!" Momma shouted from the bottom of the staircase.

"Coming momma! Geese!"

"Girl, didn't I tell you don't take that tone with me!"

"Yes," she mumbled, carefully walking down the stairs so as not to slip.

A sudden strong wind began to blow as Fuchsia and momma began walked to the bus stop. The wind was warm but chilly.

"Whew! Momma, that was a big wind, with heat in it. Did you feel it? Momma, did you?"

"Yeah Fuchs, I did," Angie said in a sad voice. "Come on bus, hurry."

"Momma, the bus heard you. Here it comes," she said excitedly.

Momma was very quiet, staring out the window just looking through the whole bus-ride. The trees all looked so beautiful this day as if they were all smiling; the yellows, oranges, and red leaves waving as the sun peeked through them. Momma reached up to push the button for the bus to stop.

"Come Fuchs, this our stop."

They got off the bus and hurried down the street. "Momma, grandma is not home yet, is she? It's too early for her to be home from church," she said, looking down at momma's wristwatch.

Momma didn't say a word. They briskly walked silently across the street and then up the block. The block was empty this Sunday, no kids running and playing, teenagers on the stoops with loud boom box on the latest jams. Whenever grandma Lydia is home and she's not cooking, you could find her sitting in her recliner next to the big window looking outside at all the happenings on the block.

As always, Fuchsia would count the number of stoops to grandma's building, "One, two, three, four, five, six and grandma's place," she said as she skipped along.

"Momma can I ring the bell this time?" She loved hearing the chimes as the tunes seem to bounce off the walls in the small apartment.

"Yes, go on," momma said as she reached for the key to the outer door to grandma's building. If Grandma wasn't in the window, momma would ring the bell first to let her know they were coming up.

Fuchsia raced the stairs to the third level where grandma stayed, the only apartment on the top. Momma came up behind as Fuchsia waited for her to reach the floor. *Today momma seems sad,* Fuchsia thought to herself. Momma put the key in the door, took a deep breath and, with Fuchsia, walked in on her heels. As they approached the living room where grandma always sat if she was not sitting in her bedroom window, she noticed the lamps were still on. *Grandma never turned lights on in the day, she would say God's sunlight is enough for the day*. Momma switched off the lamps when suddenly, the doorbell rang.

"May I help you?" she shouted softly, looking out the window.

"Anna's Bakery."

"Oh, Fuchsia I forgot I had the bakery to deliver grandma's favorite cake. Please, go down and get it for me. Here, give the guy this tip."

"Ok momma," she said with such a joy. She ran down the three flights of stairs, slung the door open, handed the young man two dollars and took the cake box. "Smells good," she said to the young man as she closed the outer door. "This my favorite too! Triple layered coconut cake with lemon in the middle," she whispered as she walked carefully up the three flights of stairs.

While Fuchsia was getting the cake, Angie walked into the kitchen to turn on the teapot to make a cup of tea. She noticed the dishes from last night were still in the sink, *which is unusual for momma,* she thought as she turned to go to her mother's bedroom. The door was cracked open slightly and an unusual smell was peering through the opening. Angie's heart started pumping rapidly as she pushed open the door slowly. Momma's chair was turned slightly to the side as it would be when she is getting in or out of it. Angie could see the silver and white waves of curls resting on the arm of the chair as she moved forward. Tears rushing out of her eyes, she came closer to touch the chair; words melted out of her mouth in a tremor, "ma...ma," she said as her knees became weak and started to give out on her.

"Ma... Momma," she muttered again. Angie was at the foot of the chair where her mother's legs were dangled to the floor as if she barely made it to her chair. The blue princess phone was still on her lap as if she was about to make a call. Angie kneeling in partial fetal position at her mother's feet, with her hands holding her mother's hand, began to weep uncontrollably, "Momma, Momma, no, not yet. I'm not ready to let go yet, momma I need you, don't leave me yet."

Fuchsia finally made it back to the third floor, the door was still opened, she ran to show momma the cake. "Momma, can we open it up to smell until grandma... Momma! Momma! What's wrong with my grandma?"

Fuchsia dropped the cake and ran to momma who didn't see or hear Fuchsia. She leaped over Angie into the lap of her grandma Lydia and wrapped her little arms around her frail neck. Fuchsia was immediately introduced to her grandma's cold lifeless body before Angie could look up to hold her back. Fuchsia's scream was so loud that the neighbors in the building heard it and began to call the police. Angie tried to pry her daughter's little fingers apart "Come Fuchs, come. I know baby, come to momma."

"Look at me grandma Lydia, it's me Fuchs. Look, I'm wearing your favorite color," she screamed. "Grandma, I came for your birthday, I'm here. It's me, baby girl..." Tears streamed down her face as she unlocked her arms from grandma Lydia's neck, and gently reaches to touch her face. She touched her cheeks, her eyes, her mouth. "No grandma, you can't go, not now. It's too soon! Who's going to watch over us? Grandma, who's going to pray with me, grandma? Grandma, please wake up, grand..." Fuchsia buried her head in her grandmother's hard cold chest, holding on to her favorite house dress. Angie tried again to lift Fuchsia up, but she wouldn't let go; she held so tight to grandma Lydia until all Angie could do is wrap her arms around them both.

When the police arrived, the neighbors motioned them up the stairs. They came through the unlocked door that Fuchsia left open. As they entered the room, a call went out for a paramedic; the officer found the three of them balled up in a chair. "Ma'am, are you ok?" the officer said. "Are you hurt?"

Angie looked up with big bright-now-turn-red eyes, "My mother has passed away." She broke down again.

"My condolence, paramedics are on the way. Can you stand? Is this your little girl?"

"Yes, I can stand and yes this is Fuchs. She loves her grandma, I can't get her to let go."

"Fuchs," the officer said. "What a beautiful name, can we see your grandma?"

The officer tried to lift up the frail Fuchsia who suddenly collapsed in his arms.

"Fuchs! No Fuchs!" Momma screamed.

The officer motioned to his partner now standing in the doorway, "Check on the paramedics. I need an ETA now, tell them to hurry!"

The Paramedics ran into the room; one ran to check grandma and the other put oxygen on Fuchsia's little face.

"What's wrong with my baby!" Angie screamed at the paramedics

"Ma'am, she's going to be ok, please let us help her."

"Pulse good, blood pressure little low. Shock, she went into shock. Ma'am are you her mother? When the body can't cope, it can go into shock. We are going to take her to the hospital. Is there anyone you can call?"

"Yes, my mother, but she won't answer because she's gone."

The ride in the ambulance seemed so long. Filled with fear and pain, Angie sat quietly holding Fuchsia's hand until they arrived at the hospital.

"Fuchs," Angie said as Fuchsia eyes were beginning to open. "Don't talk, momma's here, everything going to be fine. You just got a little overwhelmed, but you are ok. Thank God, I couldn't have something happen to you too. Do you want some water or juice?"

"Yes momma, I'm so thirsty. Whose room is this? Why we here? I want to go to see grandma Lydia, is she back yet?"

Angie reaches out to hold Fuchsia's hand, it was the first time that she ever lost anyone and someone so close. To comfort and explain death to her daughter while grieving for her mother, words were scarce in her mind. *This is what my mother would handle, she always had the correct words, she was full of wisdom.* Whispering, "Lord what do I say to my child? Give me now the words to say," she prayed.

"Fuchs, listen to me," she said very softly and calm. "Grandma Lydia was getting older, she may not have act like it or looked like it, but she was. Your grandma loved you so Fuchs, she loved all of us so much. She enjoyed life and enjoyed her family and most of all she loved God so and He loved her. He loved her so much that He wanted her to come and live with Him in His Heavenly Home. Grandma is living in a better home, no more aches and pain like she used to have in her legs, no more colds and earaches, no more worry about anything. Her new home is full of peace and joy.

"Fuchs, remember when grandma Lydia would say 'I'll always be around even when you don't see me, as long as you keep me in here,' Momma said laying her hand over her heart, 'then I'm always around.' Honey we may not see grandma face to face, but she is always with us. She's in the words she used to share with us, she's in the pictures we have taken, she's in the dolls she gave you, in the stories she would tell you, in every laugh you share with her, every song she sung to you, she's still there.

"Fuchs, they are called memories, and can't nobody take them away from you. It's okay to cry, tears are good. Grandma would say, "They cleanse your soul and wash away all the debris from the pain. But one day, the pain will leave, and we will be left with memories and tears don't wash them away, they make it clearer so we can see them in our minds." The tears ran slowly down her face as she had talked to Fuchs, she cried hard, "Fuchs, you will one day see grandma again, for she will be waiting for you in heaven. I promise you, grandma Lydia, you will see her again."

"Momma, will you see her again too? She asked her momma tenderly.

"Grandma always said that I would, and I believe her... I'm going to do my best Fuchs, I'm going to do my best."

There was a soft knock on the door, it opened, and a short man with dark hair and glasses came in. "Well, good morning. How is my little patient this day? You gave your momma quite a scare. Let's see, can I touch your little hand?

"Yes," she said looking at him crossly. "Who are you? Momma, how I scare you? I'm sorry, momma."

"It's fine Fuchs, this is doctor Schmitz. He just want to check on you so we can go home that's all, right doctor?"

"Yes, as I said yesterday, we only wanted to keep her overnight for observation. Has she been talking at all?"

"Yes sir, and I talked to her about grandma Lydia."

Doctor Schmitz eyes peered over his glasses on his nose and he said, "Is that right, Fuchsia?"

"Yes."

"Well, do you have any questions that I may help with?"

"Are you going to see my grandma again in heaven?"

"Well, I..."

Angie suddenly came to his rescue, "Fuchs, he didn't know grandma, he never met her."

"Oh ok, I'm hungry. Can we go now? Momma will you make me some blueberry pancakes for my birthday breakfast," she said with surprisingly perky voice.

Angie's eyes widened. With all that happened, she forgot it was Fuchsia's birthday. "Sure, you got it! Anything else?"

"I wonder if big man remembered and coming over for breakfast with me."

Angie's heart dropped. *Oh, I forgot to send someone to tell Mitch*, she thought as she scrambled to get her shoes on.

Doctor Schmitz looked up from Fuchsia's chart, signed release papers and handed them to Angie. "Young lady, you have to take it easy for a few days, not too much excitement for you, ok?" he said to Fuchsia, then he turned again to Angie and motioned her to the room door.

"I know this is a hard time for you and your family, allow her to grieve and talk about what has happened, it will help her to heal. But also find things to do that makes her happy to ease the tension in her mind. She's a smart little girl but she is just that – a little girl. If you have any problems or she seems to become overwhelmed, please take her to her pediatrician. Sometimes, patients can relapse in emotional distress. Can I share the same with you, grieving is normal and necessary but you too must do things to occupy your mind and bring joy to yourself. If you need someone to talk to for yourself or your daughter, we do have grief counselors we can recommend."

"Thanks Doctor, we will be fine. Thanks again for everything," she said as she extended her hand to shake his.

"Alright, if you change your mind we are here. Oh, and by the way Fuchsia, Yea I plan on meeting your grandma one day," he said as he smiled and walked out the room.

"Well, little miss eleven years old, let's get you dressed, head on home, and celebrate your big day."

Angie's three older brothers had all been notified and are on their way home to help Angie make the arrangements for grandma Lydia. They had all moved to Georgia, that's where grandma Lydia was born. She moved from there when she was eighteen years old and never went back, but all her sons returned to her home State before Angie was born. She gave birth to Angie and didn't want to leave, she said she loved her church and her pastor and God didn't tell her to leave.

Momma and Fuchsia called a cab from the hospital and went home. When they got home, momma told Fuchsia to take a warm bath and put on something nice; she was going to the corner store to get a few things for breakfast.

"Be right back, remember to not open the door for nobody. I have my keys, you sure you will be ok, Fuchs?" she said as she peeked in the bathroom.

"Yes momma, grandma's here with me; I feel her, I'm ok."

Momma stopped in her tracks and open the door again and looked at her daughter with a worried look, "Oh Fuchs, maybe I shouldn't go."

"No, momma, you told me that she's in the songs that grandma would sing, so I'm about to sing for grandma."

With a sound of relief, "Oh okay, go on and sing, be right back."

Angie just wasn't going to the corner store, she was on a mission to find big man. *How dare he missed his sister's birthday and not be with us for his grandmother's death*, she thought to herself. Angie raced up the street looking down all the alleys on the way, she knew where he usually hung out but was checking all the spots on the way. "That boy, sometimes, I want to just knock him out cold until he comes back to where he belongs," she said to herself. "I got to go looking for him, while his sister needs my attention, and I just lost my own mother, ooh!" fussing in low voice as she walked along.

"What's up beautiful, what you doing round here?"

Angie turned back to see the man behind the voice. *What? This old man who can barely stand on his own two feet asking me what I'm doing around here when he looks like he needs a doctor.*

"Excuse me sir, this ain't the day," she said as she wrapped herself tightly in her sweater. Finally, she reached the block where her son normally hung out. "On one of these porches filled with young people, I know he's some..." she said to herself.

"Big man, it looks like your momma done lost her way!" A shout came from across the street.

Suddenly from another porch came running towards her a boy in a hooded dark sweat jacket zipped up the front and dark jeans. Angie couldn't see his face until he reached her.

"Momma, didn't I tell you not to come over these streets, what you want? It's not safe," big man said as he came closer. When he looked in her eyes, he knew something was wrong. "Where's Fuchs? Momma, where's Fuchs?"

"She's home now, she's bathing. You know today her birthday, don't you?"

"Oh man, I forgot the date. Wait a minute, home now, what you mean?"

"I just brought her home from the hospital..."

"What? What happened? Is she ok?" he said as he took his mother's arm and turned to start walking her home.

"Big man, where you think you going?" shouted a voice from the porch.

"Leave it, I need to go with my momma!" He shouted with such a violent force.

"Momma, what happened?"

"She went into shock," Angie said with tears running down her cheeks, she turned and looked at her only son. "Yesterday, your grandmother passed away on her birthday. When Fuchs saw her, she collapsed on her and wouldn't let go of her. The paramedics came and when they lifted her off. she just fell out like a lifeless body; they said it was too much for her. Big man, you know she loved grandma Lydia, I don't know what..." Angie broke down, crying on the next corner.

When she pulled herself together, she turned to look at her son. He was sitting on the steps of the house on the corner. He had his face in his hands weeping. She ran to him, "Oh, big man I know, come let's go home. I promised Fuchs I wouldn't be long, she don't know I came to look for you," she said as she helped him up. It's been so long since she saw big man broken like this. "Come, we can't leave her long, the doctor wants us to watch her."

"Momma, I'm so... sorry," with the tears flowing. "I haven't seen grandma Lydia for two years and I promised her I was coming by to see her. Momma, I let her down, momma I'm so sorry. Not grandma, she was our strength."

They hurried home picking up eggs on the way. Angie and big man didn't say another word on the way home. When she put the key in the door and opened it, they could hear Fuchsia talking as though someone was in the house with her. They both ran up the stairs, then stopped in their tracks at the top of the stairs. Fuchsia had finished her bath and was kneeling in the corner of her bedroom dressed in her bathrobe.

"Lord, I know you would not leave momma and me alone with no one to pray for us. Grandma said you would never leave us, never alone. Would you please stay with us even though grandma is with you? One more thing, my brother, Mitch, can you send him home to be with me on my birthday, and to be here to hold momma and my hand at grandma's funeral like I saw on the movie on TV? Somebody was always there to hold somebody's hand..."

As the words were coming out of her mouth, a hand reached down and grabbed hers; startled Fuchsia jumped and opened her eyes, and when she saw Mitch, she jumped in his arms and wrapped her feet around his waist and cried in his arms. "Grandma said He answers prayers, so, I decided to try it," she said holding on to her big brother. "She's gone Mitch, she's gone." They both cried in the corner where they found her praying.

Mitch stayed around for the funeral as Fuchsia prayed for, he held her and momma's hand and never left their side the whole time. Two days after the funeral, big man was back to the streets as usual.

CHAPTER FIVE

Christmas was grandma Lydia's favorite time of the year; she would come over the house, decorate and cook all day, making cakes and pies. "Momma I really miss Grandma Lydia, don't you?" Fuchsia sadly said as she walked into her momma's bedroom, climbing unto Angie's bed. "Momma, can I help you in the kitchen this year?"

"Sure, Fuchsia," momma sang as she twirled around her bedroom.

"You sure look happy today, momma."

"I am, Fuchs. I must say I am."

Angie took one more peek in the dresser mirror; she adjusted her bra to prevent exposure and did one final turn. She picked up her favorite bottle of perfume, sprayed her neck; she added some to her wrist and rubbed her wrist together. *Wonderful,* she thought.

"Momma, why you keep smiling at yourself?" Fuchsia asked. She can't remember the last time she saw momma so happy.

"Well Fuchsia, I have to tell you something...Well, I need to have a mature conversation with you. Come sit here with me for a moment. Fuchs, you're almost a teenager, Mitch too. Soon, you will be all grown up; you will move out, get married and have your own family. When Ray, your father left me, you were only seven days old.

"One day, he went to work and never returned. We were not married then because I believed he really did love me. He would say, 'When two people love each other, they don't need no piece of paper to prove it.' I believed him, so when he walked away from us, I had nothing; no money, no job, nothing but two beautiful children in a one-room apartment that I could not afford. I had to move back home with grandma Lydia, and she would remind me that she told me so, that "Ray is up to no good, protect yourself, Angie." Well, honey, I found out that he went back home to his wife and five children that I never knew about. They had a house out in the suburbs with three bedrooms, a yard, and a front porch, all the things I always dreamed of for our family. I was miserable for years because I believed the lies he told me, every time he said he had to go visit his sick grandmother and wouldn't come home for days at a time. When he would come, he would bring me gifts, flowers and fancy perfumes; then he would take big man shopping to buy him whatever he wanted. Momma said every time he came over before we got our own place, 'I smell a rat.' I would say, momma, please don't embarrass me.

"Fuchs, I know I never talked about Ray, but he is your father. I don't know where he is or if he still lives here or dead. I have no pictures to show you because I burned them all when I found out. Ray was thirty years older than me, and he took great care of me until that last day when he never came home. He may have been as old as momma, but he always made sure I was happy. People would tease me and say he's just my sugar daddy, not a husband; I guess they were right.

"Well Fuchs, I made up my mind that I was going to raise my two children by myself and I never wanted to date again, that's why you never saw me with a man. Honey, things are changing now. As I said, you going to grow up and I will be left all by myself, and to tell the truth, I don't want to grow old alone. Fuchs, I met a nice man. His name is Kevin, and he wants to marry me, Fuchs, really marry me. Kevin's a nice man, he's not older nor married with children like Ray, but he is respectful. That means you will be his only daughter; it will be you and me and Kevin. Fuchs, he's going to marry me and move us across the tracks! He has a big house;

you'll have your own room and bath like now, but you will have a back yard, porch and your own dog! Honey, we going to be a family."

"But we already a family momma, you, me and big man," she snapped.

"Now Fuchs, don't you want to see me happy and not lonely? I don't want to be sad no more. I need somebody to hold and love me, just me!" she shouted at Fuchsia.

Fuchsia, seeing the look in momma's eyes, "Yes momma, I will be happy for you." She stood up from the bed and began walking out momma's bedroom.

"Great! I knew you would understand. I invited him to Christmas Eve Dinner and maybe Christmas too!" she said excitedly.

"Great," Fuchsia mumbled under her breath. She left straight for her bedroom. "Just when I thought finally things are getting better between us, here comes Kevin. Who is this dude, what he want?"

Fuchsia went to lay upon her bed with tears in her eyes. *Who wants to move across the tracks? I like these sides of the tracks,* she thought to herself.

"Grandma, what would you say if you were here? I would have to move from my only friend, Sasha. Who I'm going to have fun with over the tracks? Who cares Kevin got a house? I like the one we in now. I don't need a yard or porch, I ain't no puppy," she said as she cried herself to sleep.

"Fuchs," momma called as she opened her bedroom door. "You napping? Get up and straighten out your hair. Wash your face and put on your best behavior, Kevin downstairs waiting to meet you."

Fuchsia sat up on her bed wide eyes unaware that she fell asleep. "Man! I thought it was a dream," she said as she touched the dried tear crust around her eyes. "Ok, here I come."

"Little girl, didn't I tell you about sliding down those stair rails, where're your manners?" Momma shouted as she jumped up off the sofa and ran to help Fuchsia off the stairs. "And why didn't you put on that nice red skirt with the pleats in the front?"

"Cause we in the house and I like this skirt." She loved denim clothes; skirts, jeans, shorts. she loved them all but momma hated them. She would say, "Little ladies should wear little lady clothes, denim is workers clothes." She didn't like it when Fuchsia put them on to go outside. "They are in-house clothes," she would say.

"Well besides momma, we in the house!"

"Kevin, I apologize. This is my daughter Fuchsia, she's a little hand full, but she's a good girl, don't give me any trouble."

"Well Angie, she's more beautiful than you said, her pictures don't tell it all!" Kevin said as he stood up to greet Fuchsia. He walked over and reached out his hand to shake hers. When she reached back, he held her hand tight and kissed it.

"Yuk! Why you do that?" She said as she snatched her hand back.

"Fuchs!" momma shouted. "Say you sorry, go on say it."

"I'm sorry, Mr." she said with an attitude.

"Fuchs! Behave now."

"What I do? I don't like my hands kissed."

"See Kevin, that's why we need to move from this neighborhood. She picking up too many bad habits, especially since my mother passed. I lost one to these streets; I can't afford to lose another."

"Fuchs, why don't you come and sit next to me while your mother sets the table?"

"Nah, I'll go and help her."

"Fuchs, sit with Kevin and get to know him."

He gives me the creeps, she thought to herself. *With those wet puppy lips, yuk*! She shrugged at the thought and wiped her hands on the back of her skirt.

"You're big for your age, aren't you?"

"No, I'm just the right size. You don't know many eleven years old, do you?"

Kevin stared at this little feisty girl; he looked at her almond-shaped eyes with beautiful full hair like her mother. Her lips were perfect little hearts with the most stunning black mole beside them. "That's a beauty mark," he said as he noticed all the details of her face. Her nose was as keenly shaped just the right size for her little round face. He observed her neck and noticed another beauty mark – yet another distinctive mole on her neck. He stared down her small but slightly developing curves as her skirt with zippered side pockets seemingly outlined her tiny frame.

"Why you looking at me like that? You know you should just take a picture, I promise you it will last longer!" she said as she jumped up and went in the kitchen with momma. "What's wrong with him? Is he crazy or something, just keep staring like he stupid?"

"Fuchsia please be nice, please!" momma snapped.

Two months later, momma married Kevin, and life as she knew began to change. Momma got a new job which required she worked three nights a week. Momma would say, "I'm so glad I have Kevin here to be home with you Fuchs. If he wasn't here, I wouldn't be able to take this new job and make more money because there would be no one at home with you." She said this so many times as she got dressed to resume her job. *But why don't I feel so good about it,* Fuchsia would ponder each time momma would say it.

Mitch met Kevin once and said he wasn't feeling him as well. "Keep your eyes open baby girl, you know where to find me if you need me," Mitch said as he left the house. That was the last time Fuchsia saw Mitch until she saw him in the hospital.

Kevin moved Angie and Fuchs across the tracks as he said. It was a quiet neighborhood; lots of trees and few people came outside even at night. The houses were different; they weren't connected like the house they used to live in. Fuchsia stood in amazement as she could walk around the whole house from outside. They had three bedrooms still, but this time, the bedrooms were so much bigger, and now, they had a "basement, not a cellar," momma would say. "Our last house, it was unfinished downstairs, this house is a finished room downstairs where we can sit and enjoy."

After Mitch got stabbed and sent to Juvienile, Kevin started acting creepier.

"What do you mean creepy?" Sasha said, laughing over the phone. "You make him sound like a bug."

"I can't explain it; it makes my skin crawl."

"You sure you not reading something wrong girl because you know how you are. Fuchsia, you don't trust nobody but big man!" she snapped at Fuchsia

"Forget it; you sound like momma. I'll talk to you later," she said as she hung up the phone in the kitchen. Tears bottled up in her eyes as she looked around the kitchen feeling trapped. *Who will believe me?* she thought. *Everybody thinks I'm just overreacting because of Mitch and grandma Lydia being gone so close to each other.* "I'm not overreacting, he makes me nervous," she said to herself as she slammed the dishes in the sink.

"What's wrong sweet pea?" the voice whispered from behind her.

"It's Fuchsia, and when did you get back?" she said as she picked up her glass and headed towards stairs to her bedroom.

"Wait, why you leaving?" Kevin said looking at her with that simple grin he always had.

"I'm going to my room. Where's my mother, I thought she was off tonight?"

"She was, but I gave her money and told her she needed time for herself. She's gone shopping; she'll be home later," he said with a smirk.

"She left me here alone here with you," she muttered.

"what's that?"

"What?"

"What you saying?"

"Nothing," she said as she stepped on the first step to go to her bedroom.

"We can hang out together."

"No, we can't. I want to go to my room."

"You mean the room I let you stay in, right?" he said with an attitude.

"No, the one my momma put me in."

"I'm the one who put your momma in this house, so you in the room I let you use. And if you don't watch your mouth, you won't have that, and you know your momma loves this house. Do you understand what I'm saying little girl, do you? Are we clear?" He said and snatched her arm as she tried walking up the stairs.

"Get off me!" she cried out and pulled away, dropping her glass.

"Pick it up! And no glass better be left on my floor!"

Fuchsia ran to the broom closet beside the kitchen and got the broom, dustpan and paper towels. She shook with fear as tears ran down her face. Kevin stood over her with the belt he pulled out of his pants as she cleaned up the mess, sobbing and trembling.

"You don't have much to say now, do you?" he mumbled.

"No," she said in so much fear.

"No what?"

"No, Kevin."

"No Sir, Mr. Kevin."

"No sir, Mr. Kevin," she repeated with quivering lips.

"That's better, remember this is my house, and I let you stay here, and you do what I say. Everything I say you do or else... Do you hear me?"

"Yes sir, Mr. Kevin."

"Oh, and one more thing, your mother don't need to know about this. This would hurt her, and she don't need no more pain after your grandmother's death, and your knuckleheaded brother's ordeals. Do you understand that?"

"Yes sir, Mr. Kevin," Fuchsia said as she went up the stairs to her bedroom.

She shut her door and climbed in her bed fully dressed, crying like she never cried before. "Momma never hit me before," she cried until she drifted off to sleep.

"Good morning, Fuchs, you sure went to bed early. You must have had a hard day at school yesterday. I came in your room and you were buried under those covers fully dressed. I tried waking you, but Kevin said you must be tired because you been in there all evening," momma said as she was at the stove cooking her famous Saturday flapjacks.

"Morning momma," she said as she sat in the chair next to the kitchen window looking out into the back yard.

"You feeling ok?" she said as she walked towards her with the wooden spoon in her hand.

"My head hurts."

"Did you take something?"

"No, I don't feel good today."

Momma felt her forehead, "No fever, Fuchs. Does your stomach ache again, like cramping?"

"Yes momma, this morning I got the spot you told me about," she said without looking at her mother.

"Oh Fuchs, why didn't you tell me? My baby is growing up. Well, you are twelve now, it's time. No longer a baby but going into womanhood. Did you get the personals I put up this day for you?"

"Yes ma'am, I did. I did all you told me to do this morning when I woke up. I rinsed my panties and hung them in my bathroom."

"Do you want some hot tea with your slap jacks?"

"No, I'm not hungry," she said as tears filled her eyes. She remembered what Kevin had said the night before.

"No flapjacks for you? Fuchs, that's your favorite breakfast."

"I have no appetite today."

Suddenly, Kevin walked in the Kitchen from the basement as though he was somewhere listening. He walked up to Angie and kissed her from behind. "Oh, did I interrupt girl talk?" he said with a smirk, looking at Fuchs.

"No," she said as she jumped up to return upstairs

"Oh, excuse me. I didn't mean to interrupt you two."

"Fuchs," momma said, "be nice. Just because your flowers are blooming doesn't mean you can be snappy."

"I'm sorry, Mr. Kevin," she said with her puffy eyes filled with tears.

"You know how we go baby girl," he said as he pulled a chair and sat.

Fuchsia cringed at the thought of him calling her baby girl and continued up the stairs.

"Fuchs, I'll be up in a few to check on you. Ok?" momma said.

Fuchsia stayed in her room the entire day until sunset, but Momma didn't show up. Kevin kept her busy all day. That day was the beginning of many. Momma never recognized that she was losing Fuchsia day by day. Whatever Kevin said stuck, even if it meant closing Fuchsia out. Days became a whole year; she became more withdrawn as she was being prowled by Kevin. She never again said anything to Sasha about it. Sasha felt as though Mr. Kevin was the greatest because he would show her the side he showed momma. Fuchsia felt lonelier day by day, missing grandma Lydia and Mitch with no one to talk with. She would go to school, return home and back to her room.

CHAPTER SIX

B ong! Bong!! Bong!!!" the alarm sounded. Momma opened up Fuchsia's door just as she was turning off the alarm.

"Fuchs remember I'm working a double today, make sure you come straight home from school. No hanging out at that library, no need in worrying Kevin today, remember it's his birthday. So, be polite and tell him a happy birthday, will you?" she said and shut the bedroom door.

Fuchsia pulled the covers over her head, "Oh! They make me sick! Kevin this, Kevin that!" she exclaimed.

Lifting the bed covers off her body, she slid her tiny feet into the pink and white slippers beside her bed. She reached for her pink terry cloth bathrobe, twisted the belt around her waist. Yawning and stretching, she opened the door to the bathroom and could hear momma closing the front door, heading to work. She paused at the doorway, and her mind went back to the morning memories of her and momma before Kevin. Now, momma just leaves, no "See you later," nor goodbyes but closed doors. How she sighed and proceeded to her routine in preparation for school.

"Ring, Ring." Fuchsia ran to answer the phone knowing it was Sasha.

"Hey, almost ready, will be leaving soon. I meet you at the bus stop," she said to Sasha.

Sasha transferred to the same school after her family moved on the same side of the tracks during the summer. Fuchsia was so excited to have her best friend close again; they lived just around the corner from each other now.

"Where you think you going without fixing me something to eat on my birthday?" shouted Kevin from his bedroom.

"I'm late. I gotta go," she said as she grabbed her books and ran out the door.

"Come on, run. Here comes the bus! Come on for you miss it!" shouted Sasha from the bus stop half a block away. "Wait a minute, here comes someone else," Sasha instructed the bus driver.

"She better hurry. I got a schedule to keep," the bus driver said, seeing Fuchsia through the side mirror.

"Whew! Thanks for waiting."

"That Kevin make me sick!" He ought to just roll up under a rock somewhere and just die!" she said to Sasha as she took her seat still panting.

"Dang! Y'all fighting again!" Sasha said, laughing. "It's like the wild wild west up your camp!"

"It's his camp, let him tell it. I'm just a leaf on the tree, nothing more."

"Have you heard from Mitch at all?"

"No, not since we saw him in court. Momma don't talk much about him at all; we haven't gone to see him cause Kevin says don't make it easy for him. He says he needs to learn his lessons, and we don't need no trouble at our house, and momma listens to him. I don't know; it's like she's in a daze sometimes. She don't see anything he does wrong, so I just stay up in my room when I go home. Some nights, I don't eat dinner at all because I don't want to go around him when momma's not home," she said as she adjusted her books in her book bag.

"Smack! No wonder you eat like a hog at school," Sasha said, giggling. Sasha always laughed a lot, she always had a sense of humor, seeing the best in all situations.

"Oh, shut up. Come on, get off this bus."

"But seriously," her tone changed. "Really listen to me, if you never see me for a while, know that I love you and always will." She said as she stood up from her seat.

"Girl, what you mean if I don't see you for a while?" Sasha got concerned.

The door opened as the bus stopped in front of the school. As the kids alighted the bus, the shoving separated the friends for a moment. Sasha struggled through the group of students to catch back up with her friend.

"What do you mean, Fuchsia?"

"Just that, I've been thinking. Sasha, it's hard. Every day, it's something new. It's getting too much. I can't sleep at night unless momma's home. He walks back and forth past my bedroom door, and sometimes he tries the knob. Sasha, I'm scared. I have bad dreams; it's hard to concentrate and to make it so bad, he threatens me about momma. And if I get close to saying something, he shows up out of nowhere like he got eyes and ears everywhere. I and momma can't go anywhere alone, because he always got to go with us. He tries everything to keep us from being alone together. I can't do it anymore."

"For real, you want to leave? For real?" Sudden sadness came over Sasha as they entered the school building.

"No, I don't, but I don't know what else to do."

"Real talk, Sasha. You the best, thanks for being my friend." She held Sasha's hand as they both went to their homeroom classes.

The day seemed unusually long in school, but lunchtime finally rolled in. Fuchsia and Sasha had different lunch periods, so, instead of the usual hanging with her classmates, Fuchsia went to the library and sat in the corner all alone. All morning in class, she couldn't focus; she just daydreamed. Daydreaming became a way of escape for her, especially at home. Grandma Lydia always told her, "Never lose your dreams because your dreams are all you have. One day Fuchsia, your dreams will become a reality if you believe."

For days, daydreaming has been the only thing that seemed to keep her mind; she never realized how much she did listen to grandma Lydia until she passed away. Her words came to her every day. Most days, it was hearing grandma Lydia's voice in her mind that kept her going. "Oh, how I miss you, grandma," she whispered, gazing at a distance.

Fuchsia's mind drifted off into a picture of a future she'd been creating for herself. Picturing herself at the age of eighteen and living on her own with her own apartment and having a car. *One day*, she thought. *One day*. Fuchsia learned to create her own place, and she loved this place where she was in control of what or what didn't happen.

A sharp voice suddenly interrupted her thoughts, "Excuse me, young lady, you are about to be late for your next class," the librarian bent down looking at her watch. "Let's get going."

After school, Sasha had track practice. So, Fuchsia left immediately to go home.

The bus ride home was crowded and loud; the usual boy's horse-playing and a few older kids from the high school were on the bus. The driver would squeeze the kids on the bus, shouting, "Move to the back." Fuchsia made her way to the middle, she didn't like the front and certainly not the back of the bus. As

Fuchsia reached for the pole to catch her balance, a hand groped her buttocks. She jumped in embarrassment, almost falling over the lady who sat quietly on the bus.

"Watch it! Next time, you might draw back a nub!" she said as she looked at the guys standing around her.

"What's up little momma, you don't like?" a voice shouted from behind.

The bus broke out in laughter as the boys and a few girls thought it amusing.

"No, I don't like and I ain't your momma!" With a loud voice, she snapped back hard and strong, but on the inside, she could feel her heart racing as if it was trying to escape her chest.

"Nah, you sure ain't but I know I can make you call me daddy!" said the same voice which was hiding behind the bodies of other boys.

Suddenly, another voice came from way in the back, "Alright man, that's enough! Leave the girl alone, plus she's a baby, and you know what that means," a deep voice seemed to echo from way back of the bus.

"Yeah, she's still a virgin!" the voice shouted back.

Laughter filled the bus; boys slapping high fives, some buckling over the seats with others.

Feeling so violated, she wished she could disappear at that moment. A small, fragile hand reached up and touched hers; the hand felt so safe. Fuchsia barely saw through the tears she was holding back. She gazed to see whose hand was squeezing hers, and it was the hand of the little white-haired lady. She looked at Fuchsia with so much love and sympathy, then motioned her not to say another word. She reminded Fuchsia so much of grandma

Lydia. Fuchsia suddenly felt so much peace; the lady held her hand without a word until Fuchsia rang the bell for her stop. She looked at the white-haired lady and softly said "Thank You" as she stepped off the bus.

Dropping her books on the nightstand in her bedroom, she kicked off her shoes, reached for her slippers, and suddenly, fear gripped her as a hand grabbed her arm, holding her tightly and pulling her into his large body.

"Stop! What you doing, get off me!" she said scrambling to break loose. "What's wrong with you? Get off me! Let me go! I'm going to tell my momma!"

She fell on her side to the floor as she was trying to break away from his grip, her heart beat fast. *Why?* she thought.

Raising her voice, "Kevin, I said get off me!" She could smell the alcohol as he snatched her small body up from the floor and pressed his lips on her face aiming for her lips. Feeling the prickly hairs of his moustache on her face, she screamed "Yuck, you stink! Let me go!" Screaming louder, "I'm not playing with you, this ain't funny. You are hurting me!"

She broke free and hit the floor again. She scrambly got up; just as she caught her balance, he picked her up and threw her on the bed. She bounced hard and hit her head on the bedpost knocking her dizzy with the throbbing pain.

"What you doing, why you doing this?"

"Please Kevin, I won't tell momma. Please, you hurt me. I didn't do anything to you." Tears rolled down her face into her ears and hair as she tried to wiggle free of his grip.

Suddenly, he smacked her in the face. "Shut up! I told you I'm the head man in charge, and it's my birthday, so, I get what I want." He tried again to press his lips on her tear-filled face.

"I'm not your present!" she said, kicking him in the stomach as he tried to jump on her.

He fell on top of her, one hand holding his stomach and the other grabbing her long hair. He pulled her hair so hard that Fuchsia felt the tension in her scalp. He smacked her again in her mouth until blood started to emerge.

"You don't think you going to walk around here and not pay your dues," he said as he pushed his lips unto her bleeding lips.

"No stop! Please, I'll find a job," she said breaking down in frantic tears. "I promise I'll go today..." she wiggled to get his foul-tasting breath off her lips.

"Not today, you won't." He gripped her tiny breast squeezing tightly; pain erupted in her tiny, fragile breast.

"Oh, ouch! You hurting me, I want my momma," she cried out, trying to break free from his horrifying grip, feeling the blood of her now swollen lips run down her chin.

"I said shut up! Come on, let's go wash your face, you got blood everywhere!" he said as he got up and snatched her by the arm up off the bed. He pushed her out into the room he shares with her momma. "Get going. Come on, wash that face." He pushed her into momma's bathroom right into the sink and threw a used washcloth at her in the face.

She turned the cold water on, with little strength, and began washing her face. Trembling, she turned to look at Kevin who was standing there in the doorway of the bathroom with no shirt on and a crazy look in his eyes.

"I promise if you let me go, I won't tell momma," she said. Falling to her knees on the bathroom floor beside the sink, she begged.

Anger rose up in him hearing her beg, he picked her up and toss her to the bed he shared with her momma. "Your mother loves me; she won't believe you anyway. I'm the best thing she ever had, so beg all you want. In fact, I want to hear you beg more. Come on, call my name."

"Please, Kevin don't," she began to plead for her life as Kevin tried to climb her.

"No, not like that!" he said as he wrapped his big hands around her throat. "Say it like you mean it!"

This time, Fuchsia wouldn't say a thing. She just cried and stared up in the ceiling. Hating her life, her mother for not being there, Mitch for getting locked up, grandma Lydia for dying, she began holding her breath in hopes of dying so that it would be over.

Kevin released his grip of her neck and stuck fingers in her mouth to pry them open, she fought, locking her jars tightly. He reached for her waist, snatched and tore her top down the front, exposing her white bra. Kevin flipped her lifeless body over onto her stomach, attempting to pull her pants down as he rolled her. With his body pressed hard against her, she had no more fight in her. She laid there, shaking and whimpering as he pried at her zipper. His hands almost on her private area, she wiggled again to get loose, barely unconscious, "Please Kevin, please."

"Now that's it, Fuchs, that's it. I'm not going to hurt you; I promise you going to enjoy it. I'm getting you ready for womanhood."

"Please, please, I won't tell momma."

"Tell momma what?" Angie threw her bags at the bed, "You don't have to tell me, I see what you doing."

"Angie! Baby, how long you been home?" Kevin stumbled as he tried to get up from the bed.

"Long enough, get up you two!" She ran towards her bed and swung her arms widely towards Fuchsia.

"Girl, get out of my bed! How dare you in my bed, Fuchs, for real! In my bed! I heard you telling my man 'Please, I won't tell momma!' I knew you were up to something, that's why you wouldn't come out when I'm around. You no better than a tramp on the street! This what I would expect from one of those gutter rats in the neighborhood but not my own blood! Get out my room!" She screamed as she pulled Fuchsia up from her bed.

"Momma, no! Momma, I ain't..." with swollen lips and teary eyes, she could barely get the words out.

"Shut up, I can see. Kevin's a good man, why would he want a child when he got a woman right here? You trouble just like your brother," she shouted and slapped Fuchsia across her right cheek.

Fuchsia fell to the floor, stunned, looking up at her momma's face through the tears in her eyes.

"Go on, get out!" She shoved her daughter out of her room, slamming her bedroom door behind her frail body.

"Baby, I told you that girl is trouble. I was lying here in bed waiting for you, for my birthday loving from my one and only," he said as he reached to pull Angie into his arms.

"I was awakened to her laying in our bed; baby, I tried to put her out, but she kept prancing around. I asked her what's wrong with her, don't she know I love her momma? She said she was my birthday present. Angie, she's just a kid, where she learned to trick a man like that? I thought you said she was a virgin? Angie, she no virgin, not acting as she did in here. Baby she was trying to trap me, I was so weak from drinking today I couldn't fight her back. She knew I was drunk and took advantage of me."

Looking in her eyes, "Baby, I'm so glad you came home in time, you saved me. Baby, she trying to get me locked up and away from you. She kept saying she won't tell momma, but I know it was a trick. Thanks for saving me, baby. Come here; you saved your man, your house, everything. You baby, you saved us," he said as he kissed her and took her to bed.

Trembling and barely able to stand, Fuchsia stared at herself and bruises in the mirror. "What did I do to deserve this," she cried and picked up the new razor she just purchased for her shaver. "Momma, I didn't do it, it was Kevin." She slid to the floor and leaned on the bathroom door. "Who would miss me?" She took the blade, trembling, she began to put pressure on her left wrist.

She threw the razor into the trash at the instant when she heard grandma Lydia's voice whisper "Fuchsia, never give up on yourself." She cried until she choked, gasping for air. She crawled over to the toilet, dropped her head into it and began to vomit until it seemed as if the lining of her stomach was collapsing. She had blood red eyes staring back at her as she looked into the mirror, face flushed, hair wringing wet from perspiration, and barely standing up, she ran water in the tub to bathe.

As usual, she'd dry off in front of the mirror, but this time the reflection was not one she was familiar with – bruised neck, scratched arms and hurting waist from tussling to break free, a swollen lip, and the outline of momma's fingerprint on her cheek. One single tear rolled down her cheek, "Why God did you leave me? Grandma said you would never leave me, but today I'm all alone," she mumbled as tears again rolled down her face.

Reaching for her big fuchsia colored duffle bag given to her by her grandmother, she began fumbling through her dresser draws taking out things of importance. She took ten sets of panties and bras, socks, five pairs of jeans, three sweaters, five shirts, all her favorites. Placing them all neatly and tightly in the duffle bag, she walked into her bathroom, picked up her toothbrush and toothpaste, a bar of soap, deodorant, comb, brush and packed a side pocket tight with the toiletries. Fuchsia went again to her closet in the far-right corner, in a box of sanitary pads, she removed the rolled sock where she hid money that Mitch gave her over the years, money she never told momma about. Mitch called it emergency money. He would tell her to keep it hidden in case there was an emergency and he was not around; she would always have. Quietly going back and forth from her bedroom to her bathroom across the hall, she doubled check to make certain that she packed everything she needed.

Tip-toeing, she went to the linen closet near momma and Kevin's room to get one towel and two washcloths. Fully dressed in her jeans and jacket, she eased down the stairs, carrying her duffle bag waiting until she was near the door to put on her tennis shoes. Just as she was about to open the door, she remembered her scrapbook of pictures she was working on the week before. She tipped to the kitchen to grab it from the counter. She looked around one last time to make sure she had not forgotten anything. When she sighted the mug that grandma Lydia gave her at the age of five, she picked it up along with the scrapbook and stuffed them into the duffle bag. Her heart raced, and tears flowed down her cheeks as she opened the front door hoping so much for momma to come down to rescue her from the situation; she waited five minutes with the door opened hoping she would just get up and notice her daughter's absence but to no avail. Fuchsia finally stepped out onto the porch, placed her key under the rug mat and closed the door.

She pulled her hood over her head and walked two blocks where she flagged down a city cab, she saw turning the corner. Tossing her duffle bag on the back seat beside her as she closed the cab door, "Thanks, Greyhound bus station please," she instructed the driver.

"Traveling alone, huh?" the driver asked her as he drove off.

"Nope, meeting my big brother. He's already there. I'm late, can you please hurry?"

"Get you there as soon as I can."

"How much more for fast? My brother's going to be angry, and you don't know my brother."

"No extra charge. I'll step on it, little momma."

"Thanks," she replied, staring out the window.

"Can I help you, young lady?" shouted the man at the ticket window.

"Yes. Georgia, please," she said. She looked at the people sitting all around with the stench of urine and liquor all in the air.

"Where in Georgia you going?" he shouted angrily.

Her heart started to race; she trembled with fear. She never thought about that, all she ever knew was the city she was leaving, and the place grandma Lydia was from. Looking above the man's head, she saw a poster that said Atlanta, Georgia. She blurted, "Atlanta."

"Well, you better hurry. The bus pulls off in ten minutes, so you better run," he said, handing her the one-way ticket.

She barely made it, running and dragging her duffle bag, as the driver was just about to close the bus door. She mustered up the strength to lift her bag up and tossed it in the opening of the bus.

"Come on little lady; I got a schedule to keep, get on the bus."

As she climbed on the bus, she looked around at the few passengers on this midnight ride to Georgia. While she scaled through for the right seat, "Alright little lady, please take a seat anywhere you like so we can get going," shouted the driver.

Fuchsia chose a seat by the window next to an older woman who looked at her and nodded, there she felt safe. Staring out the window as the bus pulled from the station, *the city looked different at night*, she thought. She passed all the places she once traveled with momma and Mitch when they were younger. A warm tear glided down her cheek as she pulled her hood down over her face and leaned her head against the window, peering at the city she once called home.

"What's your name sweetie?"

"Fuchsia. Fuchsia, that's my name," she said without looking up.

CHAPTER SEVEN

Hey Fuchsia, wake up; we are in Atlanta," the older woman said. "You must have been tired; you fell right to sleep and slept all the way here. Are you hungry? I saved a sandwich for you; would you want a turkey and cheese?"

Startled, she first was about the Greyhound bus ride. "Yes, please," she said as her belly panged of hunger.

"Baby, while you were asleep, I prayed for you," the older woman began as she handed Fuchsia a sandwich.

"I don't know what you are leaving, but I asked the good Lord to put a shield around you for where you are going. I prayed for your peace and that He would always send you someone to watch over you, that you would always have a place to lay your head, that you would never be hungry. Baby, the path called life is rough sometimes, and the journey we travel may seem hard, but if we keep our heart clean and our hands in God's hands, He will guide and keep us. I prayed that your momma wouldn't grieve to death, that she will one day understand the truth and that you two will connect again with forgiveness in your hearts.

"Baby, we all make mistakes. It's part of life, but our mistakes should never dictate who we are. I know you are running and the last few years have been hard for you; one day you will have to stop running and face your pain. Baby, just don't give up; don't give up on you, you have a great future ahead. You may be questioning now but, by and by, you will understand. Where ever you are going today is not your final destination but just a pause on your way to destiny." She gently reached out to touch Fuchsia's hand and squeezed softly.

It was as if she knew what Fuchsia had just been through.

Without looking up from her sandwich, she kept nodding her head as the bus pulled up to the station. The older lady who didn't give her name lifted Fuchsia's head and said, "The man who did this will forever regret last night; it will haunt him every day, don't you worry. Baby, lift up your head and never walk with it down; always look up, there you will find Him, the Lord," pointing to the sky.

As they stood up to get off the bus, Fuchsia turned and wrapped her arms around the woman and held her tight. "Thanks for watching over me, I know my grandma Lydia sent you to me," she said as she alighted the bus and disappeared into the crowd.

Everything looked different, the people, the streets, and stores. She began walking not knowing where to go or who to trust or what to do, but she knew she couldn't stay at the bus station. Thoughts ran through her mind of home. *What is momma thinking now that she's gone? How will Mitch know that she left home? Will she ever go home again and see momma? Oh! Sasha, I'm going to miss her,* she suddenly felt alone. Feelings of despair, loneliness began to overtake her until her feet started feeling like lead; she saw a green wooden bench and decided to sit for a moment to get her bearings together. It looked like the people were moving fast on their way to places, homes, workplaces; it then overwhelmed her that she had no place to go.

"What did I do?" she said looking at her big duffle bag filled with her life, "What did I do?"

The sun was beginning to set; the people were becoming fewer and fear began to creep upon her. Looking at her watch, she hadn't noticed that she had been sitting there so long watching people move along the busy street.

"Lil bits, what's up? I've seen you sitting here for hours, hope you know this ain't no bus-stop any longer?" A sharp voice cut through and interrupted her thoughts.

Startled Fuchsia looked up to see the biggest boobs she ever saw on a girl, with the smallest waist and wide hips. Her eyes traveled up to the face of this body, short wavy hair, piercings in her nose, tongue and earrings up to her earlobes; under all those piercings was an attractive young face.

"Okay, now that you studied me, you want to answer my question Lil bits? Why you been sitting here all this time?" the voice questioned again with a little more tension.

"My name is Fuchsia, and I'm new here," She shyly responded.

"That's better. My name is Candi, and I lived here all my life," her voice softened up a bit.

"Oh, is this a nice place to live?"

"Depend on who you ask, who you with?"

"You, I guess... you the only person I know here."

"Me! Lil bits," she laughed, then sighed as she saw a familiar look in Fuchsia's eyes.

"Have you eaten anything lately?" Her voice became softer with a tone of care.

"Not since the old lady on the bus woke me up and gave me a sandwich," Fuchsia said and tried to conceal her face with her hood.

Acting as if she hasn't noticed the bruises on Fuchsia's face, "Come on, let's go over to the diner and get you something to eat. How old are you anyway?"

"I'm thirteen," she said as they walked across the street avoiding the traffic.

"You from up north, ain't you?"

"Yes," she said and stepped into the diner.

"Somebody looking for you?"

"Honesty, I don't know; don't know if I'm even missed," dropping her head as the words rolled out.

"Hey Jack, just the two," she shouted to the waiter.

"What's up gorgeous? Pick any table, be right there," he shouted from the back of the diner.

"Come, let's sit over here next to the window. You know it's dangerous for you to be walking these streets especially you being green and all."

"Green? What you mean green?"

"See, that's what I mean. You don't know anything. You are a prime target for one, the man; two, one who thinks he's the man; three, one who don't want any man." Her voice became stern again as though she was correcting Fuchsia.

"Huh? I understand 'the man' cause my brother used to run from 'the man' but who are the rest of the men?" Confused, she sank into the chair.

Laughing, "Oh Lil bits, I got a lot of teaching to do. No worries, I got you."

"You a school teacher? You look so young," sitting back up in the chair; she became relaxed seeing Candi laughing.

"What? Oh boy, you really don't know anything, do you? So, how you end up on the streets?" Raising one eyebrow, she took a sip of water the waitress placed on the table.

"Two cheeseburgers and cheesy fries, please Ann? Candi said to the waitress who was now standing in her soiled apron to take their order.

She turned to Fuchsia saying, "You like cheeseburgers, right? And cheesy fries?"

"Never had cheesy fries before and yes I love cheeseburgers," she hid her bruised face from the waitress. She picked up her glass of water and took a sip.

"You going to love their cheesy fries, best in the area, plus it's good ole comfort food; it's that kinda day."

"Back to the conversation. I'm a B student at my old school; I'm not slow," Fuchsia said.

Lowering her head in shame, she continued. "My momma's husband tried to do things to me that I didn't want; momma came home and caught us on her bed, and she blamed me." Tears welled up in her already puffy eyes.

Candi placed her hand on Fuchsia's chin and lifted her head, "Hey, hey, know this: it's never a kid's fault when a grown ass man has sex with them! Or even touch them! So, you have nothing to be ashamed of! I know that it has been tough for you." The look in Candi's eyes bespoke sympathy and anger.

"But I didn't let him do anything. I fought back. He choked me; see my bruise on my neck and my lips," she said, pulling her hood back off her face.

"Yea I see, they look fresh, like they are new," Candi adjusted the hoody back in place to not draw attention to them as the waitress brought their food to the table, placing a plate each in front of them.

"Last night; it happened last night," she said as she bit into her cheeseburger. "I was so scared; what hurt me most was momma didn't believe me, and she smacked me in my face right in front of him! I knew right then that he would try it again because he won momma over to his side."

"Wow! It hurts the most when you feel betrayed especially by your mother, who was supposed to look out for you and protect you. So, what you going to do now?" Candi said with concern.

"Well, I don't know. I never thought past running. I guess that was a stupid move, wasn't it? Fuchsia was overcome with shame, even as she noticed, through the big glass window of the diner, the sunset.

"Hey, Hey, we will figure something out for you okay?"

"You were right; these cheesy fries are so good!" Fuchsia said, stuffing the last fries in her mouth.

"Where do you live?" Fuchsia said softly.

"Not far up the way, I have my own apartment."

"Really? Where your parents? How old are you?" She was astonished.

"My parents were killed in an accident when I was ten. So, I lived in a group or foster homes being passed around until I was almost thirteen, about your age. I'm now eighteen, almost nineteen.

"I know how you feel. Every home I went into, the men act like I was sent there for them. So, I left the system, became a runaway, as they put it and took to the streets until I was old enough to get my own apartment in my name. You remind me of myself except

I knew the streets and how to take care of myself, my older brothers taught me that."

"You have brothers too, how many? I have one, Mitch, but he left us for his friends a long time ago."

"Yeah, I had two. One dead now and the other locked up. They, like me, was passed around the system. Nobody wanted three kids, so, we was split up, and every so often, one would break free and run away to come looking for me. I would sneak out of whatever house I was in and hang with my brothers until we get caught and got sent to another house. They stopped trying to send my older brother back to a house because he was seventeen. He got killed trying to stop a man from raping my other brother, Troy, who was fifteen at the time.

He, James was his name, found out where Troy was staying. One night, he went looking for Troy so he could break out again. We had a secret code that wherever they sent us, we would leave a tiny white ribbon hanging out the window of the bedroom we slept in so James could find us. So that night, James climbed up to the second floor of the house to tap on the window with the white ribbon, but when he peeked in the window, he saw the big fat man on top of Troy's naked body. Troy had a cloth stuffed in his mouth. The man was so into raping my brother that he didn't hear James open the unlocked window. James hit him from behind and knocked him off my brother; they then whipped his fat ass! All the commotion woke up the house, the man's wife got her gun and shot James dead on the spot. She shot Troy in the back; he's in a wheelchair today because of it." Candi paused and drank from the glass of water left on the table.

"Did they lock up the fat man for raping your brother?"

"No, that fat man was a judge and had connections. Troy had a court-appointed attorney who was new, the wife testified that my brothers planned to kill her husband and that he never did such a heinous act, that he's an upstanding citizen in the community and my brothers were Juvieniles delinquents with no parents; the jury sided on the fat man's side, and Troy got fifteen years. So, I knew there was going to be no hope for me. When I got the chance, I ran."

"You slept on the street outdoors?" Fuchsia asked curiously

"No, but if I had to, I could have. I slept in different places wherever with whomever I could. Look, you can stay with me for a week until you find out what you going to do, but I don't want no stuff. I don't bring guys to my house. Nobody who knows me from the street knows where I live and I want to keep it like that, you hear me?

Smiling and nodding her head, "Oh thank you, Candi! I see why they call you Candi cause you so sweet."

Picking up the last of her cheeseburger, "This sure is a good cheeseburger too, is all the food good here?"

"Yes, you can pretty much find whatever type of food you want. Do you have a favorite kind?"

"I don't know much about different kinds. Only what momma would make when she was home."

"You momma a good cook?"

"Yes, she is, but grandma Lydia was the best. She's dead now."

"I'm sorry to hear that. You only have one brother, any sisters?"

"Yes, one brother, big man; he's in Juvenile. He should be out sometime before the year ends, I guess. He used to be my best friend until he took to the street with the guys in the old neighborhood."

"How old is he?"

"Seventeen now."

"Just the two of you?"

"Yes, just us and momma 'til Kevin came."

"Who's Kevin?"

"Momma's new husband. She married him after grandma Lydia past."

"Oh, I see."

"Is he the one who did this to you?"

"Yeah, I can't stand him! He's been trouble since he came. Momma don't see through his stuff; she believes everything he says. If he said the cow jumped over the moon, she gets giddy like she's lost in his words."

"You tried to tell her about him?"

"Too many times. Then, he started keeping us apart so I couldn't say anything."

"Wow, your momma fell for him hard," she said, shaking her head.

"If grandma Lydia was still alive, it would have never been. Grandma could see through anything, and she wasn't afraid to tell what she saw."

"You was close to your grandma."

"I was. Boy! she could fix anything. She would just start praying, and everything would turn around. Kevin would not have made it this far. It was like grandma had radars, momma wouldn't mess with her. She knew grandma would be on it."

"I never knew my grandmother; she died before I was born. My parents were the only children. So, when my parents were killed, there was no one to take care of me and my brothers. None of their friends wanted responsibility. Who wanted the responsibility of three kids! My daddy used to say that my mother was sweet as candy, so when they finally got a girl, he said that I was his little candy. I wish that the three of us could have stayed together, but since that never happened, and losing them was devastating for me, I became a loner," she said, shrugging her shoulders.

"I'll be your sister; I always wanted a sister."

"Huh?" Candi's face was a board of a puzzle game.

"Can we become sisters, since we both alone? You need someone to love, and I need someone to love and protect me. Ain't that what sisters do?" Fuchsia said innocently.

Stunned Candi sat there for about two minutes staring at Fuchsia thinking *Is this some type of joke or prank someone just pulled on her*. Then, she saw the tears and pain in Fuchsia's eyes. She remembered being ten feeling lost when her parents were gone; sitting in the funeral seemingly alone, feeling abandoned, not understanding why such a little girl with the weight of despair on her tiny shoulders. She vowed to herself growing up that "I would never let a little girl feel that pain and pressure if she could help it."

"Sure, we can be sisters, Fuchsia. Yeah, we can be."

"Oh, thank you, thank you." She looked up towards the ceiling and said, "Thank you."

"Why you do that?" Candi asked with a puzzling stare.

"Because I know that grandma Lydia is watching over me. Then, there was this older lady on the Greyhound who said she prayed for me while I was asleep. She said she prayed that I would be safe and have a place to lay my head."

"Oh, Oh, I see. Come, let's get going; it's getting late, and I know you probably want to bathe." Candi looked at the check that the waitress laid on the table and pulled out cash from her pocket.

"I got a few dollars; I can pay for mine," Fuchsia said while reaching in her pocket.

"No, that's all right. I got it."

"Thanks," she said softly.

They began walking towards the corner. The walk was short only a few blocks. The two didn't say a word as they walked together. They finally came to a building with four front steps and a red door. Candi put her key in the door and opened it. It opened to a hallway with two doors, one on the right and Candi's door on the left. She opened hers which had steps that led to the second floor. A sweet smell filled the tiny space; it was a small one-bedroom apartment, with a kitchen and living room which had a sofa.

"Here, this can be your bed out here. I'll give you space in my closet and in my dresser drawer. It's small but it's home, and it's peaceful," Candi said, motioning Fuchsia towards the living room space.

"Oh, I like it," she said, smiling, putting her duffle bag on the sofa.

"Great, we can make it work. It may be a little tight, but we can do it."

"I promise to be neat and clean. Momma taught me how to clean house; I promise I won't be a bother. I'll cook too if you want."

Laughing, "You, cook what?" Candi turned the light on in the kitchen.

"I can, really. I'll do my part."

"Ok, if you say so. Sometimes, we will eat out, ok? I like to eat out a lot. You eat pizza and Chinese?

"Never had Chinese, had pizza sometimes. But I'll eat whatever you say. I'm not going to be a bother."

"Never had Chinese! Oh, I got a lot to teach you." Both of them giggled.

"Ok, if you say so."

"If someone asks you who you are to me..."

"You my sister," Fuchsia interrupted.

"You got it, lil sis! Now when I'm not home, don't open the door for no one. Nobody comes to my house, so nobody should come here looking for me. Got it?"

"Yep, I got it! I just won't answer the door!"

"That's it! Now I leave during the night a lot, but I promise I'll be back by morning. Will you be okay by yourself? If there is an emergency, Ms. June lives downstairs; that other door, that's her place. I'll tell her my little sister is staying with me, she's sweet and mind her own business as I do. So, do you think you will be ok?

"Yes, I stayed home before. Can I watch TV?" she asked while standing in the bedroom doorway.

"Of course, there's only one right now, but I'll get one for you in the living room."

Candi entered her small neat bedroom in the back of the apartment next to the bathroom. She kept everything in place, clean and smelling so good. Fuchsia sat on the sofa which she found out turned into a bed and began unpacking her duffle bag. As she pulled out her mug that grandma Lydia gave her, the pain of past memories began to choke her in the throat. Thirteen years old and no momma, grandma, or Mitch. For the first time in her young life, she felt lost; tears began to roll uncontrollably. *What has happened? What has she done? Will she ever see Mitch again? Is Momma crying too at this very moment? What if she dies, who would know? Would someone come to find her?* Fuchsia rolled up on the sofa bed and cried herself silently to sleep.

"Momma!" Fuchsia screamed out of her sleep. She jumped up frantically, grabbing the covers and wrapping herself unaware.

"Momma!" she screamed again; the room was dark, she scrambled to the floor trying to find the light switch when a door swung open and feet were coming her way. Trembling, she searched to see the hand reaching out to touch her.

"Hey little one, are you okay?" Candi said as she turned the lights on. "It's ok; it's me. Did you have a bad dream?"

"Candi, I'm sorry; I forgot where I was. I was dreaming about Kevin, he was chasing me, and just as he caught me, I started screaming for momma. I saw her face, she turned her head and walked away and he..." she sobbed laying her head on Candi's shoulder.

"It's ok; you are safe. You are here with me now, and I promise you that nobody will ever hurt you; I will make sure of that," as she held Fuchsia by the hand. "I didn't go to work last night. I would, but when I came through after bathing, I heard you whimpering in your sleep. So, I grabbed a blanket and covered you and decided I'll take off a few days to get you settled.

"I remembered what it was like the first time I had to stay in a new place, I felt so alone and scared too. I'm going to purchase some night lights first thing in the morning so that you can always see at night if you wake up, okay?" she said as she tucked Fuchsia back in the sofa bed.

"Good night, go back to sleep; remember you are safe now."

"Candi?"

"Yes?"

"Thanks."

"No problem. I've been there, so I understand. Night-night," she said as she walked back to her bedroom, this time, leaving the bathroom light on and her bedroom door open.

The next few days, Fuchsia and Candi hung out. Candi took her to all the stores, showed her around, introduced her to the people she needed to know especially Ms. June from downstairs. She used to be a school teacher in a private school for many years. She told Candi, "That child needs to be in school, don't let her waste her mind doing nothing." Candi told her that she couldn't because Fuchsia had no records to put her in school. Ms. June looked at them both knowing in her heart that there was some truth being left out but also knowing that if Candi brought her here, there must be a good reason. So, she agreed to teach Fuchsia during the day so that she would not be uneducated.

CHAPTER EIGHT

Time seemed to just swiftly move on. The days became easier and nights were so much at peace. Candi worked at night and Fuchsia homeschooled with Ms. June during the morning hours, Monday through Friday from eight until half-past eleven. Ms. June would say, "Three straight hours of pure teaching was all you need a day." "That is fine with me," Fuchsia would reply.

Candi would come home between six and half-past six every morning; she would walk in, lay her keys on the table, walk right to Fuchsia as she slept and rubbed her head, saying, "I'm home baby girl, I'm here." Then, she would take a shower and go to bed. She would sleep until about one o'clock, then get up and spend the day with Fuchsia. They would talk about everything, go shopping or take long walks together.

Candi would often say to her, "I finally feel like my life is important and I matter since you came along. Before you came, I just existed; you gave me purpose and meaning. One day, I'm going to open a shelter for girls like us who have nowhere to go and need a safe place to call home. Baby girl, you helped me realize that there is such a need. I'm saving money now, for the first time I feel all the money I make has a purpose. One day, I won't have to do what I do, but until then I just grin and bear it. However, I can guarantee you this baby girl; you won't have to do my kind of work and I better not find out no time that you did! I do this that you don't have to." This she said, at least, once a week to her.

Fuchsia would never ask what she did because Candi told her the first night, "Never ask about my work, just know I have to do this, but I won't be doing it too much longer."

Then, she came home one morning with Princess, a puppy boxer. "You know Ms. June downstairs, but I figured you need company upstairs with you. One of my best clients gave her to me; I thought she would make a good addition to our newly formed family and plus, she'll keep you company at night."

One day, while Princess rolled in the grass, she sat on the bench and watched the leaves sway on the tree, she perceived a sweet smell. Fuchsia thought to herself, *uhm, that smells likes Momma favorite perfume.* She jumped and looked around as if she expected to see her, but no momma.

Princess ran and jumped on her lap as though she knew that Fuchsia needed a friend, a tear broke through her piercing stare and rolled down her face. It had been weeks since she thought of momma, she finally was able to sleep throughout the entire night without jumping up in tears. This time, her tears were different; she was no longer angry at momma or scared that Mr. Kevin was coming to find her and take her back. No. This felt different; she had peace inside for the first time since Grandma Lydia had died. The wind blew gently across her face of tears as if they were wiping them as quickly as they fell.

Fuchsia began wondering how momma was doing, *Was she eating, still working, living in the same house? Does Sasha come by to see her or even call her? Is Mr. Kevin still around? How is Mitch? Is he home yet from Juvienile detention?* This was the first time in months she was able to think without fear overtaking her. Getting up from the bench with princess' leash in hand, they walked towards home; she felt the urgency to write letters, one to momma and the other to Sasha. Then, a thought interrupted her; *They would know where I am! Oh no, that can't happen! No, I won't let it happen!*

Ms. June was coming out the door to their apartment house just as Fuchsia was going in. "Whoa little lady, what's wrong, why your face broke up like that?"

"I'm sorry Ms. June. I was just thinking about writing my momma a letter to see how she was doing, but then I thought someone would come to Atlanta to find me, and I don't want to go back! Ms. June, I feel finally free, and I don't want to go back! But I want momma to know that I'm fine and not to worry any more, her Fuchs is fine!" she cried out.

Ms. Jane hugged Fuchsia. "Baby girl, where's your sister?"

"She should be up by now, I think. Ms. June, I'm not trying to cause no problems here at home," she said nervously.

"I know you're not. Come on, let's talk to Candi." They headed upstairs to Candi's apartment.

"Candi!" Ms. June called as they reached the top of the stairs.

"I know. I heard," Candi whispered as she sat at the kitchen table taking a sip of coffee. "Baby Girl, if you send one from anywhere in Georgia, it will be postmarked from Georgia, and they will know you live somewhere in Georgia."

"I got it!" Ms. June shouted "I got it! You remember I told you I'm going to Oregon next week to visit my sister who moved there ten years ago, and it will be my first time there? Well, when I get there, I can drop Fuchsia's letter in any mailbox from there; just don't put a return address on the envelope."

"Ms. June, I told you that you are a genius!" Fuchsia said as she jumped up and kissed Ms. June's fat cheeks.

"Well, that's settled. Write your letter, seal it and give it to Ms. June," Candi sighed as she got up from the table and hugged Fuchsia. "Didn't I tell you a solution is always one step from you if you just believe and have no fear. Now, go on, write your letter and give it to her and then we going down Peach Tree, I need to get a few things from the store, okay?"

"Yes! Thanks, Candi, you the best sister in the whole world!" she said as she reached out and squeezed Candi around her small waist.

Sitting on the sofa with princess curled up beside her, Fuchsia began to write her letter. She had crumbled several pieces of paper trying to say the right words but barely got through momma's letter because of the emotional tears. "Finally, I'm done," she said to Princess whose ears popped up as though she understood. "Now, I have to write to Sasha."

"Dear Sasha, please don't be mad cause you haven't heard from me since I left, but I'm fine now, finally free. How is school, hope you doing great? You know you will always be my best friend. I can't tell you where I am but know I'm well. My hair started growing back in the back; I guess because I'm not twirling it up out of fear anymore. I think I'm getting taller finally cause my jeans are getting too short. I haven't made any new friends, but I got a sister who looks out for me; you know I always wanted a sister, and she's pretty too. It's just me and her and our little dog who lives with us. Sasha, I miss you so much, but I know I can't come back no more. I hope one day, we see each other again. Can you do me a favor? Can you go and check on my momma, please and don't go when Mr. Kevin is home? I don't know what he would do to you, and I can't bear to think he could hurt you too. Please kiss momma for me, tell her I really do love her and miss her so much.

I'm sending you a picture of me and my dog; her name's Princess, but I cut out the background so nobody could find me. Now, don't laugh at my little legs in the pictures, I'm finally not ashamed of my thighs. My sister says ain't nothing wrong with my legs; she really looks out for me like grandma Lydia sent her to me. She's a little older; you would love her. I promise you that I would keep in touch with you. Love you, Sasha, you will always be my best friend no matter how far we live apart."

Fuchsia

Licking the envelope, a tear ran down her cheek as she remembered the friend she left behind.

She prepared for bed early and smiled at herself in the long length mirror as Candi swooped by into the small kitchen to grab a half of sandwich she laid on the table earlier.

"Shoot! I'm going to be late!" She took a big bite while trying to slip her sweater dress over her head. "How do I look, does this dress make my butt look big?" she said, wiggling her butt for Fuchsia to see.

"Look big? Nah, it is big!" Fuchsia laughed hysterically.

"What, you don't know? My butt is my greatest asset!" She turned giggling and walked over to place her glass in the sink. She stopped to see her reflection in the small mirror over the sink, "And I ain't bad looking either!" she snickered.

"Huh? What you mean by that?" Fuchsia said still laughing as she watched Candi shake her big butt.

"That's alright. One day, you will understand," she said, putting on her earring and hopping on one foot to get her long black boots on.

Fuchsia sat on Candi's bed watching her as she put on her finishing touch. Candi was very pretty and much taller than Fuchsia. Her hair waved a brown color with gold streaks; she has a small diamond earring in her nose and three going up both earlobes and another tiny one in her tongue. Her waist was so tiny with wide hips as her clothes perfectly rested in all the right places.

"Candi?" said Fuchsia.

"Yes?"

"Can I ask you something?"

"Yeah, what's up?"

"Why you have so many holes in your body? I mean it don't look bad or nothing, I just want to know."

As the question flowed out of Fuchsia's mouth, Candi had finally wiggled both her boots on. She stood up looking in the curious eyes of Fuchsia, her smile faded, and sadness overtook her eyes.

"My mom loved jewelry, diamonds to be exact. Whenever I would miss her so, I would add another one to me because it made me feel close to her. I didn't want to forget her face, so I pierced my nose and put her reminder there, and I kept going 'til I felt I was full of her memories. People do all kinds of things to remember people; mine was adding diamonds to my body. Because it reminds me of the jewel she was," she said as a tear ran down her cheek.

"Oh Candi, I'm so sorry." Fuchsia jumped up to hand her a tissue from the dresser.

"No need to be, I'm better now, plus you gave me the purpose to move forward." She wiped the tear away and did a final check on her makeup. "Ok now, I'm really running late! Gotta go, love you baby girl! See you in the morning," she said as she scurried out the door.

CHAPTER NINE

Whew! *I can't believe it's been a year since I left home,* Fuchsia thought to herself as she was waiting on the bus' arrival. "What's taking the bus so long?" she mumbled out loud as she leaned on the pole, holding an application for a job she was trying to get at the soda Coco Cola Plant.

"What is a stupid worker's permit? Just permit me to work for you, that's all," she mumbled again. "Everything so difficult!" *Candi told me I might have problems because of my age and people gonna want to know my social security number, and if I give it, they will track me. I just thought I would try*, she thought as she kicked the paper laying on the sidewalk beside her foot.

"What's up sweet thang?" a voice came from behind.

She looked back and saw a guy with freckled face smiling with teeth full of gold. She looked around to see who the dude was talking to.

"I'm talking to you, Shorty. No need to look around, just look in a mirror. What's your name."

"It sure ain't Shorty," she snapped at him and looked away, up the street for the bus.

"Who you talking to like that? Do you know who I am? I bet I'll slap..." his voice became louder and angry.

"Slap what! You better sidestep now for I bust you up! And you know who I am and that I would!" shouted this short fiery young lady.

Stunned Fuchsia backed up to the pole, heart racing, knees knocking, and hands trembling. *Who are these people and why all this commotion? I'm just trying to get the next bus up town,* she thought.

"Aw Tommie, what's this got to do with you! I ain't got no beef with you; chill, babe chill. I'm just poking fun with the little honey," the freckled face guy said.

"Yeah, right! If I didn't put my patty in the bun, you woulda tried to wrap the sandwich! Go on man, you know I know what you little punks up to! Can't you see the girl ain't like those scanks you mess with! Go on up the block for I bust your lip, again!" The short lady shouted as she approached Fuchsia.

"Come on man, let's roll. Shorty trippin'," the freckled face guy said to the other guys who walked up behind him.

"Oh, hold up. Oh, snap; that little slant eyed babe you ran up against last year, ain't it?" bursting out in a loud laughter, shouted the fat guy amongst them as he ran down the street pulling up his pants which fell from his waist.

"Young blood, it's ok. They won't mess with you again, I promise you that!" She stood in front of Fuchsia, smiling. The sun was glaring in her eyes as it was preparing to set, reflecting such a warm hazel color. Upon her almond color face with a small pugged nose, her long hair was gently swaying in the warm breeze. Brushing the hair out of her face with one hand as the other reached into the pocket of her short denim skirt which revealed her muscular short legs, she extended her hand to Fuchsia, "Hey, I'm Tommie, and who are you?"

"Fuchsia, but everyone calls me Fuchs. Thanks for helping me out. Where did you come from? I mean I didn't see you."

Laughing, "I was walking behind you since you came out the building. When I saw them crossing the street, I knew they was up to no good. So, I dropped back a little to see if they would mess with you; they trouble in these parts." Tommie said.

"Did you really bust him in the mouth before?"

"Did I? I was new to the area too like you and they tried the same move on me, but there was one problem. When they tried to drag me down the side street, they was expecting me to be like the ones running for their lives. Girl, my father when he was alive ran a boxing gym; he trained men welter weights and I was his only daughter and the only girl he ever trained. He said it was just for fun because he would never let me box; then, I had five older brothers who either boxed, who took some sort of self-defense. Three are fifth degree black belts who teach in their own gym. The other two are kick boxers, so you know my life was not a timid one! And just in case someone gets the upper hand, I always carry two switch blades and know how to use them with precision and will use them. Oh, let me stop. I don't mean to make you afraid, I'm really quiet. I just don't like bullies or trouble. Enough about me, what you doing in these parts?"

In a soft gentle voice, Fuchsia responded, "I was looking for a job. My sister said I don't need one, but I want to help out."

"What? You nuts! If your sister tells you that you don't need a job, why go against the grain? Wish I had it that good at your age, man I had to work, me and my brothers. After my dad got killed, mom was about to lose everything, so we pitched in to help, there went any hopes of college. Trust me, savor the moments you have now!" she said as she bent over to fix the strap on her denim sandals.

Fuchsia caught a glimpse of the flames tattooed on Tommie's back peaking from beneath the back of her halter top.

"Wow, flames. That's interesting, I never saw that one before."

"Yeah, my dad had flames tattooed on his fist. They used to call him fist of blaze. I loved my dad; people say I got his hot temper so they would call me baby blaze. My flames are of my dad, and if you look close, here take a look, you will see the white Lily in the middle, that's my soft side because of my mom," she said as she turned so Fuchsia could see.

"Your dad wanted another boy?"

"I knew that was coming next," Tommie interrupted. "No, it's short for Tomika. Don't worry, I get that all the time," she said, smiling, pointing to the bus coming towards them.

They boarded the bus together laughing and talking loudly like she and Sasha used to do. Tommie told her how her dad was killed in the gym late one night when he was locking up, how it crushed her mom. The family believed the hit was meant for one of the guys who locked up at night but had to attend a funeral that night, so her dad closed in his stead. That devasted their family and her mom never recovered from his death. She lived in a nursing home after her nervous breakdown. This happened when they lived in the Bronx. At the age of eighteen, Tommie moved to Atlanta; it would be a year next month. Tommie lived alone in a one-bedroom apartment building, five blocks east of Candi and Fuchsia, and worked as a barber.

"Was it hard for you to find a job when you moved here?" Fuchsia asked curiously.

"Well, yes and no," shrugging.

"Did you know anyone here when you moved?"

"You sure ask a lot of questions, you sure you're not a reporter?" she joked while handing her a business card. "Here's my number, keep in touch and maybe we can hangout sometimes."

"Oh, I would like that; don't have many friends here, just my sister Candi."

"It's getting dark. How far you stay from bus stop?"

"It stops on corner. I don't have far to walk, why?"

"Just checking because you don't appear to be one to hang in the streets late."

"I'm not, I mean I don't? So, what you saying; I look like a baby?" she said with a slight attitude.

"Chill little momma. I ain't putting you down, I'm just saying you look different in a good way. You don't appear to be a hood rat, but then you might be an undercover one!" she burst out in laughter.

Fuchsia looked at her in amazement, she never met anyone like Tommie before. "No, I don't think so," thinking to herself whatever a hood rat is, it doesn't sound clean.

"You little tough, but you still green?"

"Now here you go with the green jokes."

"What? What you mean?" laughing again. It was the first time Tommie laughed so much since she moved there.

"I like you, it feels good being able to be myself without having to justify myself. People look at me in all kinds of ways, asking questions about the flames of fire on my back, why my eyes so slanted with a pug nose. 'I don't know fool!' I would say under my breath. You know people would have the nerve to say I'm the devil with flames on my back! Crazy! All they had to do is ask me like you did and I would tell them, people judge without any knowledge. I know people who are real devils and they wear their cross faithfully. I'm no saint, but I'm no devil either."

"Yeah, people are cruel. My grandma Lydia would say 'Read the book first before you judge its contents.' "

"Your grandma is wise. I'd like to meet her; does she live here too?

"Nah, she's gone on to heaven. She used to tell me, 'When I leave here Fuchs, I'll be waiting for you to come. So, make sure you get your reservation, for heaven's a place with reservations only, and you must meet the one with the ticket Fuchsia.' She would say, 'You got to get to know him here so he can call you there.' Boy! Grandma Lydia had some sayings! She never thought I was listening, but I was. I miss her so."

"Wow! She sounds wonderful and funny."

Smiling, "She was. Here's my stop. Thanks again Tommie, I will call you."

"See you later, lil momma and you're welcome," waving to Fuchsia as she got up to alight from the bus.

Fuchsia looked back and smiled as she stepped off the last step. "Whew, it's got a little chilly out," she rushed down the block. Thinking to herself, *I know Candi going to drill me, but she don't understand.*

"Lil bits, where you been?" angrily shouted Candi down the stairs.

"I been out looking for a job; I told you I wanted my own job!" She snapped. This was the first time she ever snapped at Candi, it made her own eyes open wide.

"Who you shouting at? You must have lost your everlasting mind! I've been worried about you and you going to come back with this type of attitude! For real, I ain't the one, not today, not today miss thang!"

Coming back to her senses, "I'm sorry, didn't mean to make you worry, and shouldn't have snapped. I just thought I would try to get a job and just what you said would happen, it did," she said as she flopped on the chair in the kitchen.

"I tell you from experience and what little I do know. Some things you just got to trust me on."

"No disrespect but trust you like you trust me and you won't even tell me what kinda work you do?"

Stunned at Fuchsia's remark, she put the pot of rice down on the stove and said, "What difference does it make what I do? We eat, have roof over our heads, cloths on our back, and you can watch cable all day every day. So, I ask, is it really important?"

"No, but I want to know," she said with a curious tone.

Staring off at Fuchsia with a puzzled look, "I help keep older men from becoming lonely."

"That's a job?" Fuchsia exclaimed with a puzzled face. "Who pays for that? I talk to old people all the time, maybe I should become your assistant!" she said with laughter.

"Absolutely not!" Candi snapped with such sternness in her voice.

This was the first time Fuchsia saw Candi at that level of anger, it scared her.

"Wow, what did I say wrong? We was only talking about old people. It ain't like I said that I was selling drugs." She got up from the table to get her plate of food.

"Little girl, it's more than just sitting on the porch having a conversation. Most times, it's doing things with them that makes your skin crawl! It's more than laughing at their dry jokes as they

136

try to put those old wrinkled lips with the smell of old spice on your lips!"

"Yuck! Double yuck! Fuchsia screeched.

"Little girl, I'm beyond yuck, but it pays the bills!"

"Do they... Do you... you know have sex with them?" This time, Fuchsia wasn't laughing as she put her fork down, turned her whole body around to look at Candi.

"It's part of my job, Fuchs. It's part of my job," she said as she slid into her kitchen chair.

The rest of the evening was very quiet neither of them talked to each other the rest of the night.

CHAPTER TEN

(Wedding day)

O h wow! Baby girl, so..." Mitch said as he sat up in the chair with the appearance of shock on his face. "You telling me she was a prostitute? Please tell me you didn't get turned out!"

"Turned out into what?" Fuchsia became defensive, then jumped into attack mode, stood up with her hands on her hips, and raised her voice. "Everyone on the streets are not there because they choose to, some of us had too! And better than that, big brother, every girl out on the street ain't giving up the goods. There are some who are great companions for some poor old dude who sometimes want company! People always want to judge especially in areas where they know the least! Some of them have values too, but because of lack of skills or confidence to pursue anything else, they do what they gotta do! Man!..."

"Whoa! Hold up Baby Girl!" Mitch interrupted. "Why you all twisted up like this? You can lower your tone. You may be grown and about to get married and all but I'm still your big brother! This is me Mitch! I'm not judging you or your friends. I just got tossed a ball I wasn't ready to catch. Come on Fuchs, come on!" he said as he turned and struck the wall, then slid to the floor and broke down in tears.

"Mitch, Mitch, I'm so sorry." Lowering her voice in compassion, she cried, "Mitch, Big Man, look at me please. Please, it's not what you think." She buried her face in his back, "Please don't, not today. I need you to listen to me. Mitchell! I'm a virgin!" she shouted as she pushed him as hard as she could until his head hit the wall.

"What, what are you saying? You weren't on the streets?" wiping his eyes as he turned to face his sister.

"Yes, I was on the streets, and yes, I'm still pure."

"How could that be Fuchs? You think I'm stupid or something?" he threw his hands in the air while still on the floor.

"Thanks for believing me," she dropped her head in disappointment.

"That's because I've never met a prostitute who claimed they were untouched. Excuse me for not understanding! And then, not just any ole street walker but I just found out that my sister was a hooker!"

"Ouch! Girl, are you crazy!" holding his face as she struck a hard blow to his right cheek.

Standing up over top of her brother, she pointed her finger at his face and with anger in her voice she shouted, "First of all, I'm a grown woman! And not you or anyone gonna walk up in my house and call me a hooker! You don't know me, nor do you know anything about my life! Where were you when Kevin tried to rape me? Where were you when the boys in the neighborhood tried to gang rape me? Huh? Where were you when I didn't have food? Huh? Where were you when I was homeless, had to wash in the sink of a store, hiding from cops? Where were you? Where were you Mitch? Oh yeah, in the street!

"It wasn't your hands that picked me up; it wasn't your arms that held me at thirteen when I was lonely! It wasn't you who taught me how to survive the streets! No, it was my homegirls. Yeah, those you call hookers! You don't know them, they happened to be my family! When my brother and mother turned their backs, it was them who took care of me! They fed me, cloth me, and taught me. They made sure I was educated and protected! You didn't, big brother, you didn't!"

She screamed from the top of her voice all in one breath standing over him.

Mitch saw so much fire in his sister's eye. It was like she transformed before him. Her whole face changed, the redness in her eyes were not because of tears; it was like he could see the fumes of flames piercing through them.

A gentleness came upon him, his voice softened, "Look, let's just calm down. This is not the day for all this; besides, you are right, I'm wrong, I apologize for being so insensitive." Mitch said as he reached up from the floor to get his sister's hand. "Hey, Hey, I'm sorry. You are right, please forgive me."

Fuchsia helped him up, "No, you are not the only one who is insensitive, I'm in error as well. I guess I'm so defensive because I never liked what I was doing."

Hugging her brother tight around his waist, she laid her head on his chest, "Mitch, please believe me. It's important to me that you do. I never could get with an old man trying to slide his old fuzzy tongue down my throat, but I had to help in my share of living. You know Grandma Lydia instilled in us 'Everyone must give their share in the house; no work, no eat."

She took a step back and held her head, "Man, all her words still swim through my mind! I hear her all the time, that's the reason I'm still a virgin. She drilled me hard about a pure clean garden. 'Never let no man plant his seed in your garden unless he went through the proper channels to take possession of the entire land,' she said mimicking her grandmother's voice.

Laughing, "What! That woman was something else!" Mitch responded.

"Yeah, she was. So much so, I could never drop my draws! Man, I was so afraid that she would show up!" she said bursting out in loud laughter. "For real Mitch, I couldn't do it. So, Tommie taught me how to work a man and never give up the goods. I soon learned that old men just want companionship most of the time, so, I learned to cater for them. I'm real good at cards, checkers, and yes, bingo!" smiling, she winked her sweet gleamed eye at him. "I'm a game player!"

"Really? Wow, Baby Girl, look who really turned out to be street wise."

"I had awesome teachers. I love those girls, and they wouldn't let anyone, anything hurt me. If one of them got a whiff of danger, I was on locked down, and they would take my place. At first, Candi didn't know because she wasn't having it, but I kept showing up on the streets in the areas that Tommie hung out frequently. Someone would tell Tommie they saw me, and she would throw a fit. Green, that's what she would called me."

"Green?"

"Yeah, green." She twisted her lips and crossed her eyes. "She called me green because she said that I didn't know anything and that my momma named me a color anyway!"

They both burst out in laughter as the phone rang.

"Hello," she sang in her top note voice.

"What you doing? You chickened out yet? You need me to create a diversion so you can escape?" said Tommie on the other end of the line in her usual one breath sentence.

"Talking to my brother, and no, and no to your crazy gestures."

"You know all you got to do is say the word, and you out of there. Wait! Your brother? Okay. Hey, on a real note, we are stopping to get something to eat; what you want as your last supper?"

"Shut up and give me the phone." exclaimed Candi in the background. The sounds of a push raddled the phone.

"Ok, you two," Fuchsia said in her motherly voice.

"Tell her who ranks in this platoon!" Candi said.

"But I'm the sexiest and I must say, the cutest," Tommie shouted in the background.

"Oh no, not today. Can we put that away?" Fuchsia interrupted. What you heifers want, what time you coming?"

"Oh yes, that's why we called. We on our way, what you want to eat? You want homegirl cuisine or miss prissy chow?" Candi asked jokingly.

"What! You know we better get her healthy vittles! It's her wedding night! It will be just a mess to get gas tonight!" shouted Tommie in the background.

"Yeah, I guess you right," responded Candi.

"Just bring me some Sushi. You know which ones I eat. Just make certain it's fresh please, comrades, and a Vitamin water. Thanks, see you in a few," sighed Fuchsia as she ended the call.

"Hey Baby Girl, why the sigh?" With concern on his face, Mitch turned, drawn to his sister's side as she walked out the room stepping into her huge walk-in closet.

Shrugging her shoulders like she always did as a child when she was nervous, "Nothing," she whispered.

"Hey now, your comrades may know you well, but I knew you first and better. I might not have been there when you needed me most, but I'm he who was there when momma water broke the day you came into this world. I'm he who helped momma change your soiled diapers, he who wiped your runny nose, and rocked you to sleep when you were afraid. Yeah, I was the first guys' arm you would crawl up into because you weren't feeling well, and momma wasn't home. Fuchs, I'm still he. Please, let me be. It's still safe with me, please trust me again.

"Baby Girl, I'm not the enemy. Please let me in, don't lock me out. I promise I'll never leave you again unless you want me to," Mitch extended his arms towards his sister.

"It's just... I... We... Well, Marvin has never seen me naked. What if he doesn't like what he sees? What if I can't please him?" she said, shrugging her shoulders.

"No Baby Girl, don't think like that. He loves you and besides, you are perfect! Look in the mirror, you are perfect. Look at those beautiful brown eyes. Your hair is still long and ravishing like mommas."

He began to twirl her around by his hand, "And sweetheart, your body! Good thing you getting married cause you make a brother have to stay strapped to fight off all those men for you! Trust me, any healthy man would be looking at you! If you weren't my sister, I'd be looking like all the other healthy guys! You have bumps in all the right places. Woman would die to have your body."

Mitch released her hand and lifted up her chin, "So, we good and settled on the body issue. Fuchsia, I know this is where you miss momma and grandma Lydia, but they are not here, and I'm honored to be here with you on this momentous occasion." He playfully took a bow.

"See, Baby Girl, this is special as it should be with any woman or man in that aspect. I'm proud of you as I know Grandma Lydia is. To keep your garden sacred, un-tampered with, un-touched is so powerful. It's nothing to be ashamed of; it's something to be empowered by. Not many people can truthfully make that same claim. Yes, there are some who have vowed to be celibate, but how pleasantly pure the garden that has never been touched."

With sensitivity in his voice, he whispered in her ear, "When your husband visits the garden, he enters a dimension where no man has ever gone before. You know that was the way it was intended from the beginning. You, my baby sister, is like a fresh field where the fruit is ripe, not one is bruised. No vines or thorns to crowd one out, no over grown weeds, or signs of decay."

Pausing while holding her in his arms, he again lifts her head and looks into her eyes.

"So, Baby Girl, you are the best field any man can acquire. And without knowing Marvin, I'm sure he will gently unlock the door of your garden with the tenderest turning of the key. Just relax and let the sweet pure love that flows from your garden welcome him home."

Fuchsia's eyes lit up, "Oh Mitch, I never heard it sound so romantic and sweet, thanks. Man, I didn't know you was that deep nor sensitive."

"Yeah, but let's keep it our little secret."

"Married life agrees with you!" she pushed his shoulder.

"I love being married, really we both do. I take my vows seriously, and I honor my wife. If it wasn't for the new baby, she would be here too by my side."

"I promise you for Christmas, I'll come to visit you, okay? I can't wait to meet the woman who captured you.

"Hey, thanks for the father daughter talk. Now, I need the momma daughter opinion on my negligee!" She said as she breezed from the closet.

"I would ask my girls but due to their history in the bedroom, they would put me in jungle meets girl attire!" she sneered.

"Now, wait a minute. That may not be too bad, but don't kill the man before you can enjoy him!" Bursting with laughter for a few seconds, then turning back to look into the face of his baby sister, "Baby girl, it still puzzles me how women, no matter how fine they are, never see themselves as good enough. What happened to my strong confident little sister?"

She shrugged. "Life man, life."

"I understand life because we all have traveled through the journey of life, but there was a time you would prance in the mirror smiling at what you saw. I can tell you now, it used to pluck my nerves then! But now, I see that part is missing from your persona. Tell me, what shattered that girl to develop into a woman who is not aware of her worth? I'm not trying to bring you down, I'm just a concerned big brother who doesn't want to see his sister unaware of her value."

Looking stunned and embarrassed, but yet grateful, Fuchsia responded with *searching* in her voice. "I never really gave it a thought until now. I guess when we lived; just you, me and momma, home was different, it was safe. I felt pretty and perfect because there was no one in my life to make me feel anything different."

She stood still for a moment, then walked towards the window.

"And if they did, I would challenge them until they saw otherwise. Life was so sweet and loving. It was the best until change happened. When momma brought Kevin home, it all went to pieces; I was so afraid and confused. It caused me to withdraw from momma and my friends. Sasha was the only one I would talk to and, sometimes, she thought I was just making things up. I couldn't sleep at night because of fear, I would not dress up anymore because of fear."

She walked back to the sitting area and sat on the Loveseat. "He made me so afraid that I began to think something was wrong with me. Was it my fault that he would mess with me like that? Fear can mess a person up. I had no one to validate that I was okay, that there was nothing wrong with me and that he was the sick one. Momma was so wrapped up in him she couldn't see the forest through the trees."

Twiddling her fingers, "It's ok to love someone but it's not okay to love them more than they love themselves and allow that love to incapacitate you until you have no life left. I became the center of his disease, the temptation of his darkness. His words was cruel, his actions was even worst. I was too young to encounter such dysfunction. And the worst part is I was entering adolescence where my body was already changing and I could not comprehend the changes, so, I believed it was all my fault because my breast started growing and I could not stop them; then my pants started filling out with natural curves, I became ashamed of my body."

Her voice became soften, "Oh, how I missed grandma Lydia. I could ask her anything and she would tell me everything. But momma missed all that was happening with me because her focus was on a man who didn't even notice her for looking at me!"

She slightly tilted her head to the left as she looked up at her brother who was now leaning on the wall in front of her. "Mitch, you know what's so funny? The reason why I'm who I am today is because of Ms. Dorethea. Ms. Dee, I would call her. I tell you the truth, it was as if grandma Lydia sent her from heaven to help me!"

"Really, how's that?" Mitch said as he reached into his duffle bag for his cell. "Oh, we been talking so much. I never checked my phone, and the wifey has texted me twice, plus, you never showed me the room I'm to use while I'm here." He quickly answered the texts.

"Oops! You are so right, what a bad hostess I am. I was so caught up, I totally forget this your first time here!

"Now, Ms. Dee would have pulled me up on that so fast! She'd say, 'Honey, a good hostess always makes sure the needs of their guest are met before the guest asked for it!' " mimicking Ms. Dee's voice.

"Excuse me fine Sir, please follow me!" Chuckling as she headed to her master suite.

Looking up from his phone at Fuchsia, "This Ms. Dee. seems like you really took a liking to her, will I meet her today? I would love to thank her for taking such care of you in me and momma's absence."

"I just flunked Hostess 101!" Laughing, as she walked her big brother around the half-circled wall. The half-circled wall looked over unto the great room which was adorned with an elegant oak railing the width and was enough for three persons to walk side by side. As the half circle walkway laid with the plushest carpet came to end, the most exquisite flooring met them. The hallway was long with several closed doors with knobs adorned in different colored crystals.

Mitch was in amazement, thinking to himself, *Who is this woman? I have never seen such elegance in my life.*

He silently began counting the doors as they walked by. "One, two, three, four, five, and they stopped in front of door six with a beautiful blue tone knob.

Fuchsia turned the knob, opened the door and said, "This is your room. It's the most masculine of them all and..."

"Fuchs, what! Oh, my heavens! How? What? Baby girl, you got me amazingly confused," Mitch stood in awe as he entered the room. It was as if he stepped back in time but this time, it was upgraded for a king.

"I always dreamed I would see you again; so, when I redesigned this house, I designed this room with you in mind. 'I had to have a room for Big Man,' I would say, and no one has ever stepped foot across this thresh floor but me."

Standing in the middle of the room, she continued, "On your birthday, I would come here and pray asking God to let me see you again. On my birthday, I would come in to talk to you. On the anniversary of grandma Lydia's death, I would come in here and curl up on this your bed, remembering the day you held me in your arms when she died. I decorated, by memory, the things I knew you once loved, like baseball, but I upgraded for a man."

Mitch couldn't believe what he was seeing or hearing; a lump seemed to be stuck in his throat. He went over to a wall which was decorated with custom three glass mantles trimmed in wood and inside each one was autographed baseball paraphernalia. Right square in the middle was a 16 by 20 picture of him in his little league baseball outfit resting in the most beautiful custom wood trimmed picture frame.

"Oh snap, I forgot about this picture. How old was I, and where did you get this?" Mitch gleamed as he reached out to touch the picture.

"The night I left momma's, I took with me my favorite things and pictures; this was one of my favorites of you. I used to love to watch you play baseball, hitting those home runs out the field. So, I had it retouched, enlarged and framed; it was one of our best summers."

"Baby girl, you off the chain. Man, my wife would love this! You did the room in my favorite shade of blue," he said with a big smile.

"Oh, how I remember. You used to say not too dark and not too light, but boy blue! Momma used to be upset with that; she would say, 'How I know what shade that is boy blue?'

Walking over to the bed, she touched the comforter, "I used to smile saying I know it when I see it. You don't know how many fabric swatches I had the designer bringing me for this room. I knew you didn't like fluffy comforters, 'Cause I ain't no girl,' you used to say. You weren't a big fan of curtains. You used to say momma spend too much time looking at them. So, I had them make these custom window shades that let in just the right amount of light as the sun rises and just enough of privacy in the evenings if you forget to close them. I took a step further in imagining what you would like as a man and ordered this desk and chair with the fixings, I hope it suits you."

"Suit me? Girl, if I didn't have a wife and kids, you wouldn't be able to get rid of me!" He spanned the high back plush navy-blue leather chair and flopped down in it as it reclined.

Smiling, this is the day she always dreamed of; the day her big brother would be sitting in his chair talking to her in this very room. "Look, what I couldn't figure out was what type of man you would be. Jacuzzi or shower? So, I did this room with both, and besides, when you and Patrice come to visit together, she would be comfortable as well."

"It don't matter to me one bit. I'm still the guy who just want to jump in and get out. No frills, just a bathe type of man. Remember I'm a military man. Now, my wife, she would go nuts in this bathroom."

"Still just a plain old simple guy, Mitch."

"Baby girl, only one thing. Now, know I'm not being picky because this is off the chain in amazement! But you know how I would love watching sports on TV when I was a kid, so, where the TV?" Standing in the center of the room with a confused grin on his face.

"You dropped your luggage on it! No worry, it won't do any harm. Oh, where did I put that remote?" Walking over to the oak wall unit which housed a king bed, she opened one of the smoke glass doors which concealed the book shelves and pulled out a compact remote. Turning towards Mitch, "Here it is." Then, she aimed it at the foot of the bed to the oak chest. At the foot of the bed, she pushed a button and a narrow top panel opened, a flat screened TV raised from the chest and rested on top of the chest facing the bed.

"What!" Mitch jumped and grabbed his head.

"This is simply awesome, baby girl. Man! Wait until Patrice hears this. No, I better wait until I'm home before she thinks I'm not returning home," he said as he stood up and walked over to sit on the bed. "You really didn't spare no expense, did you. Now, tell me about this Ms. Dee. She must be something else; I'm ready to plant a big kiss on her when I see her."

A moment of sadness came over her face. "Well, unfortunately, you can't. She passed away just about a year and eighteen months ago. It was fifth worst day of my life because again I was left alone, so I thought".

"She reminded me so much of grandma Lydia. Her wisdom, elegance and charm. She was something all the way to her grave; it was at her funeral Marvin and I reconnected."

"I'm sorry to hear that. I wished I could have met her as well. Was she sickly or anything?"

"No, she was the healthiest woman I knew. Very strong and strong willed. No one messed with Ms. Dee. She died a peaceful death like she said she wanted and would, almost like grandma Lydia died in her sleep except she was much older. Ms. Dee was ninety-six and looked like she was seventy-five. Ms. Dee would walk the dogs in the neighborhood every morning with her fifty-pound companion. She would say, 'Every morning, I would get up when the sun came up, pray. Put on one of my walking suits, juice my fruit and vegetables with protein drink up, get my tennis shoes and say let's go, Champ.' "

Champ was her dog 'He was a little this and a little, that' she would say. She named him Champ because she said he represents all the people who overcome their issues with their identity and become champions in their own rite. Man, she could say some things that make you think. She and champ would walk about an hour; she come in drink water, sit down and read her bible. She would never talk on the phone until after she said she and God spoke first. She would say, 'Fuchsia, that way, I'm spared from the wrong conversations.' If someone knocked on her door or phoned first thing in the morning before she finished her daily rituals, she would say you must have a word for me from the Lord; if not, go back and talk to Him, then call or visit me later and either hang up or close the door!"

Bursting into laughter as she shook her head, "Man! Persons who didn't know her would be stunned but those who knew, they knew better," Fuchsia said, unzipping Mitch's garment bag to hang up his suit. "Nice suit, but you know I ordered your tuxedo just in case you could make it."

"Thanks, that I know but this is my *just in case* back-up suit," he laughed. "Fuchs, how did you meet this wonderfully inspiring woman? She really does seem like grandma Lydia."

Fuchsia closed the closet door, walked over to sit in the chair, and folded her arms.

"Well, one day, I met this older gentleman and I say gentleman loosely. He was very polite, and he was loaded, you know, wealthy. Now, remember I never slept with any of my clients; it was just to escort them to events, just eye candy, that's all. This old dude saw me at a play with another client and he smiled and tipped his hat as my client and I sat in the balcony of the theatre to watch the play.

"I was used to the stares; I got stares all the time. Old ladies used to roll their eyes; one lady tried to trip me one night at a gala event. As the evening progressed, I noticed that this old gentleman kept staring at me. Now mind you, I always wore a long classy gowns and dresses, I would go to the second-hand stores and get them when they were marked way down to my budget which was next to nothing. The play was just about over, and I excused myself to visit the ladies room. When I was returning, standing at the balcony entrance way was that same old gentleman with this sweet smile on his face; he asked me my name. He said it's an unusual name, but he liked it. He handed me his card and said, 'Call me tomorrow,' and opened the curtain for me to return to my seat.

"So, the next morning, I called him. His name was Fred, short for Frederick. He asked me if I would have lunch with him; I said yes. See, to me it was a job. Well, I got dressed in a soft form fitting dress but not revealing, that was my personal dress code. I caught a cab as usual to meet him and exited the cab about one half a block away; never wanted anyone to trace back the cab number to find out where they picked me up. A standard policy we always did to cover ourselves. I walk into the restaurant and said I was there to meet someone whose name I gave. The mamaitre'd tradee looked at me, smiled and led me to a private section in the restaurant. When I stepped through the doorway, there was a pianist playing, and he was sitting at a table for two with a waiter standing beside him with a huge bouquet of all types of pink flowers.

"He said 'I knew your name was a color or flower in the pink family, so, I ordered all kinds of pink flowers. I hope you like them.' *Wow*, I thought, *who is this man?* He ordered lobster, and did all the ordering, asking me nothing except if I drink. I said only occasionally, not much on drinking. While at dinner, he asked me if I would accompany him to two upcoming functions; one at an opera house and the second was in another state. So, of course, I questioned what state. *There are several that directly connects to Georgia which one was he referring to?* He said Florida; it's just for a weekend for business conference retreat. He would take care of everything and take me shopping to make sure I had the attire for the gala banquet. That while he was at the daytime meetings, I could hang out at the pool or spa. I thought it was a wonderful plan, this would be a mini vacation; I never had one. Then I thought, *Man, I don't know this old dude, how do I know he's on the up and up?* It was as if he read my mind; he said, 'I know you don't know me, but I can give you references; ask the staff here, they can tell you I'm an upstanding citizen in the community.' So, you might say I was gullible. I escorted him to his first function and was treated like royalty. Never in my life have I ever experienced all that.

"He treated me with grace. He wouldn't let me lift a finger the whole night; I was blown away. So, the next day, after the event, we made a date to go shopping for weekend wears. He literally brought me everything down to my panties, saying it was his honor to do so for such a beautiful creature. I should have known better. Well, that night, after shopping, we ate dinner at the same restaurant. That's when I found out he owned it. He asked me if I wanted him to drive me home. I said no, I'll catch a cab as usual. So, he said, 'You catch a cab every time we are together, don't you trust me yet?' I said yes, but my life is private. So, he told me, 'I have been trying to track you down to surprise you, but all the cab drivers say you get out at a busy intersection and not usually the same area. I asked him why he had been trying to track me down. He smiled and said, 'Yeah, but it didn't work; you a sharp girl.' I smiled and reassured him it's not about him. It's a code of ethics my roommates and I live by, just trust me on that. So, that evening, I went home, and Tommie is at the house sitting at the table with Candi, eating. This was strange because it's around ten in the evening and they both work nights.

"I said, 'Hey, what's going on?' They both said simultaneously, 'You.'

" 'Me?' I said, dropping my shopping bags. Then it began.

"Candi snapped at me, 'That's right there. That's what's up.

" 'What you talking about?' "

"Tommie jumped between us and threw her arms up. 'Okay ladies, let's not get too emotional and say things we can't take back.'

"Candi pushed Tommie out the way, screaming, 'Fuchs! Since when we get personal with any one client!'

"So, feeling myself, I ranted, 'Who said I'm personal? I'm grown now or can't you see? I'm a twenty-year-old woman! Oh, you talking about these bags; what's wrong, you jealous that the old dude want treat me right and I ain't got to give up my stuff to get it?'

"Before I could finish my sentence, Candi stepped back with open hand and slapped me, knocking me to the floor. She said, 'Don't you ever talk to me like that again, you selfish wench!'

"Tommie reached down to pick me up; she was horrified by what was going on. She screamed at Candi, 'Whoa, wait a minute! That was uncalled for Candi. I think you took it a little too far and that's not what we discussed!'

"I was livid! I snatched away from Tommie and started going in on her, 'Get off me! What you mean that's not what we discussed? You in on this too? Screw you both!'

"Well, of course you know Tommie, gangster and all. She started in on me too. 'Now listen hear, Fuchs! I'm not Candi; I won't use an open hand but my fist and my four-inch boots!"

Candi started screaming, 'She just hard headed! Ever since you met that man last week, you been acting like you got a tampon shoved up your behind. You don't know him nor what he is about or want from you, and you better not have given him none either. I better not find out you opened your legs!' pointing her fingers in my face.

" 'Or what! I have not been acting like I got something stuck up in me. Again, you sound jealous!'

"Tommie got in my face and was like, 'Shut up and listen now, you pissing me off! She's not jealous. We trying to warn you that we don't trust the smell of this; we been doing this way longer than you. So, don't go round twisting this thing because someone is going to get hurt and it certainly won't be me! Do you hear me now or must I go further! Fuchs, don't push me, please, don't. You know you my girl, but I will hurt you if you disrespect me, do you understand what I'm saying?'

"I tried to walk away still thinking I'm grown. 'Let me go! I know what I'm doing; this man means me no harm! He has actually been a gentleman every time we been together!' I was now crying but tried to sound like an adult.

" 'Fuchsia, stop being so naïve!' Candi shouted as she threw her plate in the sink.

" 'Well, if I fall, let me fall! I'm not a child and I'm certainly not a baby! Neither of you are my momma. Remember, she gave up on me for a man just like you two ganging up on me about a man!' So, I grabbed my shopping bags and purse, and stormed out the door.

"Candi shouted behind me, 'Fuchsia, if you leave like this, don't bother coming back, you Pig-headed immature brat!'

"Angrily, I jumped in a cab and went to the twenty-four-hour Walmart, thinking, *At least, there's a bathroom and food. It's just for one night, tomorrow I go on my mini vacation.* Careful to stay out of sight, knowing the layaway department was closed in the evening, I camped in that area. Early the next morning, I purchased a washcloth and a bar of soap to clean up for my mini vacation. I dressed in the new clothes purchased by Fred and prepared for my weekend date. I was to meet him at his Restaurant by ten in the morning, so, I hurried to catch a cab just barely making it on time.

Stopping for moment and remembering that day like it was yesterday, she sank into the chair she brought for Mitch's room. Her mind ran through the memory of that day as she began to share that experience with her brother.

"Good morning, darling. Thought you were going to stand me up," Fred said, caressing the side of her cheeks.

"Hello, no, I said I'd be here."

"Come, let's go. We have a flight to catch," motioning to his driver to bring the car around.

"Fly? You didn't tell me we were going to fly. I have never been on a plane before, I'm a little nervous for real now. Plus, I don't have the proper ID."

"Don' be afraid, and you don't need ID on my plane anyway."

"You own a plane?"

"Yes, I do, but I don't share that with everyone."

"No problem. I understand, remember I don't share my personal life either."

The rest of the ride to the airport was quiet. Fuchsia kept going over in her mind the argument she had with both Candi and Tommie. This was the first time anything ever happened like this. *Why would they both be so angry about nothing and an old man at that? Plus, he seems harmless, nothing that they expect, and they never met him. I can't believe Candi told me not to come back,* she thought. *She'll see when I get back that they made a mistake and they both too overprotective.*

"Well, Ms. cat-got-my-tongue, you ready to board the plane?" Fred said as the car pulled up to a small airport.

"I'm sorry. Just a little tired, had restless night, that's all, but I'm here now. Let's go."

Fuchsia was nervous stepping on the plane but when the door opened, she was stunned at the beauty before her eyes.

"I didn't know that a plane comes with all this! Wow! Big screen TV; it's like a living room for twelve people."

"I'm glad you are impressed. Take a seat anywhere, I'll be right back," he said and went to the rear of the plane.

"Thanks," she said to the stewardess who handed her a fruity drink.

Fred returned casually dressed, not his usual suit and tie attire. He changed into a pair of fitted jeans and a white collarless shirt unbuttoned to the top of his hairy chest with a gold chain hung around his neck.

"This is different," she said to him.

"Yes, when I leave town I like to be relaxed, you like?"

"Well, I love the way you dress normally."

"Thanks, you enjoying your drink? I requested it specially for you, a non-alcoholic fruit drink."

"Thanks, it's great. I taste the strawberries. How long is the flight?"

"Less than two hours."

"So, what time is your meeting today?"

"I won't know until we check in and see the itinerary. What would you like to do?"

"I really don't know."

"Here, choose something to watch," he handed her a brown wood box full of movies.

"Nice; you have all the latest movies, how awesome."

She chose the movie *Jumping the broom.* She curled up in the plush leather seats eating popcorn, thinking to herself, *This is the life. Why would Candi and Tommie disagree with this?*

The plane ride was relatively short and quiet as Fred nodded off a few times uninterested in the movie. Fuchsia smiled to herself as she looked in his aged face and chest. *He must be about seventy-five, at least*, she thought, as she stared at the white hairs making their shy appearance out of his ears and nose. "Yuck!" she snickered silently.

"Prepare for landing," the pilot announced over the intercom.

"Fred, they made an announcement."

"Who, what? Oh yeah, of course. Put your seat belt on, that's all."

Stepping off the plane, the heat met them both as they strolled to the waiting car.

"Hello, Mr. Frederick. How are you today?" said the driver.

"Hello, Carlos. How is the family?"

"Everyone is fine; my youngest daughter graduated last week. Soon, she will be off to college."

"Congratulations to you and your family."

"Thank you, Sir. May I ask which location this trip is?"

"My usual, Carlos. My usual."

"Got you, Sir."

The car pulled up to the villas sitting right on the ocean. Stunned with awe, for this was like nothing she ever seen before. While Fred went to the front desk to get the keys to their suite, Fuchsia strolled around the back deck overlooking the beach.

Man! This is the life, she thought. *If they could see me now, they would be proud of me*. When he had completed the check-in process, he met her on the deck. Fred walked up to her wrapping his arms around her waist with her back turned. Jumping at his touch, "Hey you all done?"

"Yes, all done. The bags are sent to the room already; you ready to change into your bathing suit and go on the beach for a swim?"

"I'm ready to put on my suit. It's so cute, but I don't know how to swim. I've never seen the ocean in person before."

"Really? Well, let's go change."

"I thought you had a meeting?"

"Well, yes I do but I wanted to have a little fun with you first."

"Okay, don't know how much fun I'm going to be."

As they entered the huge suite, the bellman was leaving the room.

"Did you put everything in?"

"Yes Sir."

"Thanks," Fred slipped him a tip.

"Fred, this is a beautiful hotel suite; you come here often?"

"On occasions, I come here. You can put your things in the room over here. The bathroom is in the room as well. Go on, change and freshen up, I have a call to make."

She gathered her things and walked to the double doors. As they swung open, the sweet smell of fresh cut flowers greeted her. Looking around, she was stunned to see one bed in such a large room; *where is Fred planning on sleeping*, she thought as she reached into her carrying bag for the swim suit he purchased.

"Nice bathroom," she said, smiling to herself while closing the bathroom door. "Hum I never been in one quite this nice before; this is different," she thought out loud. "A tub and a separate shower; this bathroom bigger than our kitchen at home." She slipped out of her cloths, debating whether or not to leave her panties on. She spotted a TV extended from the corner of the wall. "Oh snap! Who hangs out in a bathroom long enough to watch TV? Wait until I tell Candi this!"

Pulling up her swimsuit, looking in the mirror at her behind, "I should have tried this thing on!" she exclaimed. "All my cheeks making their private showings. Man! I just screwed up! I shouldn't have taken Fred advise on this one.

"My booty too big for this. Oh shoot! I thought my boobs were small but this thing make me look like I'm carrying balloons under this suit! Now, I know I can't keep on my panties; darn! Now, what am I going to do? I didn't even shave!" she said in fear.

"You okay? Who you talking to in there?" said Fred on the other side of the door as he was attempting to turn the nob.

"Boy! I'm glad I locked that door," she said to herself.

"Yeah, I'm okay; just talking to myself. I'll be out in a minute." Wiggling herself around in the bright red swimsuit, "It looked better on the hanger than on me.

"I can only imagine what Tommie would say if she saw me in this getup. This look like someone sown together two giant red letter Vs, you can't tell the front from the back," she squirmed at the thought of walking on the beach in this getup.

Reaching for a towel to wrap around her body, and mumbling, "Boy! I'm so glad this an old man and I certainly don't want to give him a heart attack." She opened the bathroom door.

"Well, it's about time sugar. Come, take that towel off so I can see how you look," Fred said, standing at the center of the room.

"Fred, were the rest of your clothes!" frantically shouting as she closed her eyes.

"What you mean? This is my trunks for the beach; you mean you don't like what you see?"

Fuchsia opened her eyes and was in shock to see what was before her very own eyes; he was dressed in the smallest – what looked like – black little boys' underwear. He looked like a big fuzzy bear in tights, and an old grey bear at that!

Fred was standing there actually posing like he was a pinup doll. Fuchsia looking at what was there before her, checked him out from his head to toe, trying so hard to hold back the laughter; then, she noticed something that made her cringe, *Oh, no, he's not standing there with a bulge!*

"You look shocked sweetie, didn't know a man like me was still packing huh?"

"I'm sorry, I don't understand. You need some help unpacking? Sure, I'll be glad to help you, what time is your meeting?" she said, ignoring his comments.

"I canceled my meetings. I decided I'd rather spend time with you over the weekend. Now, let me see that pretty suit I brought you. Come on, take down the towel. I promise I won't hurt you," he said reaching for her towel.

Teasing, she slid to the side just missing his hand. "I'll show you on the beach. It's a surprise; let's go."

"Boy! What have I done?" she said as they walked from the bedroom to the patio that led to the beach. "Now, I'm going to have to play cat and mouse the whole weekend. Who would have thought that old grey dude would try and turn into the incredible hulk!

"I should have listened to Candi and Tommie." Her heart, feeling doomed, started pounding like it did when Kevin came near her. "Okay, think now, Fuchsia. He is old, that bulge could just be a sock. He's just trying to impress someone, just not this someone. Yuck!"

"Sweetie, let's go on the side where there aren't many people so we can have some privacy."

Not on your life, Old man was her thought, but she said, "Oh Fred, I want to show off this wonderful suit. So, let's go around the crowd. I want everyone to see how nice you treat me."

"Do you? Okay, over here looks fine."

She could see all eyes staring at them both. Well, I'd rather have their eyes than his hands. So, I'll take the lesser of the two evils. Finding the perfect spot, she laid down the beach towel she grabbed on the patio before going down the stairs. He sat on the towel barely able to get down with ease. Fuchsia got the courage to take off the bathroom towel; it seemed as if all eyes were on her. The men stopped playing volleyball to stare, and the women looked in sheer disgust. Fred's beanie eyes were locked on her body like a bee in honey.

"Now, that's eye candy for sure," Fred muffled.

"Hey! Old man, you got a fine granddaughter," shouted one of the volleyball players.

Suddenly the volleyball sailed across the sand aiming right towards them.

"Look out, run away. Ball!" a burst of laughter rang across the air. "Heads up, old man"!

The ball barely missed Fred's head as he ducked, rolling into the beach lounge chair nearby. "Stupid, irresponsible kids!" he said as he regained his composure.

"Oh, are you okay Fred? Are you hurt? Need me to get a medic?" Fuchsia said as she jumped to her feet to aid him.

"I'm stronger than you think my dear. It's going to take more than a ball to slow me down this weekend," he jeered at her.

"Slow you down? Well, I thought you wanted to rest Fred."

"I can rest when I get home."

The sun glazing down on the ocean quickly caught her attention. She stared at the most beautiful site she's ever seen. Seemingly, she entered into a trance were the only voice she heard was the sun serenading the sea when, suddenly, she was interrupted my Fred's hand fondling her thigh. "Now, Fred, behave!" she snapped.

"I'm just searching for buried treasure. I love treasure hunts. I love playing pirates; it reminds me of my youthful days."

"Never played the game myself," she said as she rolled her hips away. "Hey, where shall we eat tonight?" she asked changing the subject.

"I was thinking in the room tonight. Having a private dinner, just the two of us; you know, under the moonlight."

"Oh, I thought you wanted me to escort you to that fancy restaurant you told me about, plus, I love to show off that beautiful dress you brought me."

"Oh yeah," he grunted as he pulled his stylish Marc Jacobs shades down on his eyes pretending to be resting.

Fuchsia with a sigh of relief pulled out her big flop hat from her bags, placing it on her head as she laid back in the beach chair.

"I can't believe I fell asleep on that beach. What a tan!" she said to herself while looking in the bathroom mirror as she exited the tub. Taking a long hot bath and rubbing herself down in the soft, fragrant oil she found in the basket alongside the sink, courtesy of the hotel, was what she needed. Pulling her long wavy hair up into a twist, she pinned it, staring in the mirror with awe; she looked so much like momma. She applied soft shadows of pink, gold, and white to her eyes, and finished with a soft frosty pink on her lips, remembering the words of momma and grandma Lydia, "A lady should always look her best, simply elegant." She stepped out the robe supplied by the hotel and glanced at her small figure in the full-length brass mirror. She then took the new red halter dress supplied by Fred and wore it. Fred stated red is his favorite color, so, he purchased everything red for this weekend. "It's a good thing red looks becoming on me," she muttered.

"Something must be wrong with this dress!" she grunted while trying to wiggle it over her buttocks. "This can't be the right size," pulling it off to check out the size. "A size four, that's right. Gosh, this must have the wrong ticket size in it." Usually, four would give her plenty of room. *Tommie always said, 'You need to buy a two, it would fit better.' Man! If this was a two, I would suffocate,* thinking to herself. Finally, holding her breath, she pulled it up and hooked the back loops around her neck. Then taking a step back to look in the mirror, she marveled at how beautiful she looked except it was too short. She doesn't wear dresses this short. The dress just made it past her back cheeks; it boasts of her shapely figure. She certainly did not want Fred to get any strange ideas or his hands to think it was open season. She pulled and tugged on the hem of the dress trying her best to make it a little longer.

"Hey sweetie, you ready? We going to be late. I made a reservation for seven. It's now five 'til..."

"Oh, I lost track of time. Just had a little dress trouble, that's all."

"You need my help?"

"No, I got it. Here I come now," she said while opening the door. "Boy! I am hungry; you hungry?"

"Simply stunning; the dress fits you perfectly, I must say," he said while adjusting his glasses. "Now turn around; let me see it from behind."

Normally, she would not be worried about an old dude looking but it was something different about Fred, it was almost creepy. *He didn't seem like he was like the other tired old men, even if they flirted, it was different. I can't seem to put my hand on it,* she thought. "Well, I guess a little turn won't hurt," she mumbled as she turned slowly.

With a big grin on his face, he reached to cup her buttocks. Fuchsia jumped as she was startled by the grope. His hand was so big and strong, and when he grabbed her behind, his fingers slipped in between her legs. The same feeling came over her like it did when Kevin tried to rape her. Suddenly, she cringed with fear and snatched away from his grip.

"Don't!"

"Don't what? I paid for this dress!"

"Yes, the dress, not the lady wearing the dress!" angrily grabbing her purse. "I thought you said we were late. Let's go, Fred."

166

"What if I tell you I'm not hungry anymore and my appetite has changed, then what?" he said as he snatched her by the wrist pulling her to him.

"Fred, we never talked about fringe benefits!" she exclaimed trying to break free from his strong grip.

"Well, the plans have changed! I've already taken my pill, and I'm ready now. We can eat later!" as he tightened his grip on her wrist with one hand and the other, he reached up her dress to her grab her panties.

"Wait! Oh no, Fred. This ain't in the plans. So, please, Fred. Let me go, and I will forget all about this ever happened! Now let me go before I scream!" she cried out as her small body began to tremble.

It was as though he didn't hear her; he pulled on her dress with such a force that the two buttons which held up the halter broke loose falling exposing her breast. She fought to get free until he slapped her across the face with such brute force. Falling to the bed almost unconscious, her eyes were waxed with tears and full of terror. Through her tears, she could see him taking off his pants with all his manhood in full readiness. With all the strength she had left, she leaped off the bed, holding the dress around her waist, trying to make it out the bedroom door to the sitting room.

"Somebody, please help me," she screamed.

Fred leaped across the room as a hot lion in heat and landed on her back. She could feel his breath on her neck as he grunted when they both fell to the floor. He again reached up her dress as she wiggled to get free. Suddenly, what seemed like a hammer hit her in the back of her head; then flipping her over, he swung again, this time landing across her right eye.

"Oh God, please," she cried out in a daze.

"God? You should have had him buy this dress and fly you here! You tease, and I'm going to get my due!" He snatched the rest of the dress off, exposing just her panties.

"Fred, I said No, and No means No!" she screamed at the top of her voice as she took the rest of the strength she had left and kneed him in his exposed private.

"Oh, God! He cried out as he rolled on to his side, holding himself. "Get out, Get out. Leave, you crazy broad!" sweat rolling down his head.

She crawled to the door, opened it and slid out into the hallway with just her panties on. She made it to a corner and balled up into tears. After catching her breath, she saw, ten feet away, the ladies' restroom. She crawled to it; just as she tried to push it open, it swung open.

"Oh my," cried the startled voice.

"I'm so sorry," Fuchsia said as she scrambled to get on her knees, covering her breast.

"Oh, dear God! What happened child?"

Fuchsia looked up from under the curls which had fallen out of place on top her head. Her eyes filled with tears of embarrassment and pain. She gazed at the older woman who had a look of radiance and dressed in a tailored navy pantsuit trimmed in white stitches. The woman's hair was a mixture of gray and black styled perfectly above her neckline with just enough tapered around her face. She had eyes of deep peace and the gentlest soft smile that Fuchsia has ever seen. The woman stooped down to her side and reached her hand towards Fuchsia's chin; she lifted her head and said, "Sweet child, why allow such pain in your life?"

Never has anyone asked her that question. Fuchsia, confused with no reply, dropped her head and cried. *Why have I allowed this pain? Could I have controlled this situation?* Thoughts were racing through her mind as the woman helped her into the bathroom sitting area. The woman was strong for such a tiny size; she helped her into the round leather chair. The woman walked over to the sink, got wet paper napkins and returned to wipe Fuchsia's face. Then again looking into Fuchsia's eyes, in a soft-spoken voice, she asked her, "Sweet girl, why are you here and what is your name?"

With her head hanging low, she replied, "My name is Fuchsia, and I thought I knew what I was doing," her voice cracked right as she was speaking.

The woman reached in her navy and white leather handbag with the initials MK hanging from the buckle and pulled out a bottle of cold water. "Well, I guess you are the reason I picked up this fresh bottle of water. Here, please, take a sip."

Barely able to hold the bottle of water to her lips, she took a sip of the cold water and mumbled, "Thanks," still covering her breasts.

"Here, wrap this around you. I always carrying a shawl because, sometimes, I catch a draft," she said as she pulled out a beautiful softly woven shawl and handed it to her.

In a sigh of relief, Fuchsia took the shawl and wrapped it around her. It was just long enough to wrap around her body. Fuchsia sat up in the chair quietly, adjusting her fallen hair all the while thinking, *Candi was right. Fred wasn't to be trusted. I've messed up big time. I don't even know where I am nor how I can get home. Oh, home; I forgot I have none any longer. The last thing Candi told me, 'if you leave, don't come back.'* The thoughts of the last conversation rang in her head like loud chimes of a church bell. The feelings of dread came over her like balls in a bowling alley rolling down the lane. She began to think; *I'm really doomed this time.*

She forgot all about the woman who now was sitting in the other chair staring at her with much concern. Fuchsia pulled the shawl tighter around her, rolled her legs up into the chair in a fetus position and began to weep.

"Now child, no need crying over spilled milk; you are not alone. Yes, you may have made a few mistakes but don't allow those mistakes make you. Are you from close by? I can offer you a ride home."

"No, I am not from nearby. So, you cannot offer me a ride because I have no place to ride to."

"Sweetie, life is a journey that can lead to nowhere if you don't know your destination. And, sometimes, the journey takes a sudden turn that is made to change the course of your life. The things that were meant to hurt you can actually be the very thing that leads you to the road of your true destination."

The woman's voice was so calm and soothing with wisdom. She continued, "Sometimes, a new road is created with you in mind. Life is full of decisions; wisdom knows which one to make. Every now and then, someone is sent along that journey to make life a little easier, and again, wisdom helps you discern whether that someone is to be trusted or not."

The older woman stood up and walked over to Fuchsia, held her hands and said, "We all have untapped wisdom waiting to aide in instructions, for wisdom is a principle thing. What you need to do right now is ask of wisdom what direction you should take. I'm going to my car; I will be parked right outside the front lobby entrance. I'll wait ten minutes; then I will pull off and go on my merry way. I won't be offended, and I will not ask you to trust me. I want you to ask wisdom what decision you should make because you have ignored wisdom so long. This might take you a minute, but you must get acquainted, and I promise you this, once you do, you will never again have regrets. Now, remember this is no pressure because I have nothing to gain or lose. I'm just available; that's all." She picked up her things and walked out of the restroom.

Fuchsia, stunned at what she just heard, suddenly heard the still small voice of grandma Lydia come to her, "There is a way called escape, take that road; it's the course of your journey, Fuchs." Peace overwhelmed her. She jumped up, dropping the bottled water, eyes wide open. She adjusted the shawl and walked out the bathroom straight to the lobby, and as the double doors slid open, there was a white car waiting at the door. Fuchsia began walking towards the car when, suddenly, a hand grabbed her by the hair.

"Where you think you're going? I paid for you and you going to pay up, you tramp!"

Fear gripped her heart as it began to race again. Her knees buckled as she swung around staring in the face of danger. "Please, let me go. I don't deserve to be treated this way."

"You don't deserve to be treated this way! Who you think you're fooling? It's sure not me, you little..."

"Sir, step away from the girl," said this voice with so much control.

Fred turned around to see the older woman who was in the restroom with Fuchsia. "Look, ma'am, you have nothing to do with this. So, please mind your business."

"I'm not going to say it again. Step away from the girl, and it became my business when I covered her nakedness when I wiped her bruised face. So, please sir, do not insult my intelligence with your simple games. One call and you would be arrested now, just try me," she shouted as she stepped out the car with her phone in one hand and mace in the other.

Fred's countenance changed as he released Fuchsia with a shove. "Here, you can have her. She's useless anyway."

"Something is only useless when we fail to realize it's value and purpose, and sir, at your age, it would seem as though you knew as much. Maybe through this situation, you have gained some knowledge, but again, you can't teach old dog new tricks. Have a good evening," she said as she unlocked the car door for Fuchsia to get in.

Fred was left standing at the curb speechless as they drove off.

"Oh, I left all my things behind in his room," Fuchsia said as she looked back through the side rear mirror.

"Your statement is true my dear; you left it all behind. Wisdom knows when to let go and leave it behind you. When any person finally makes up their mind to move forward, they also must make up their mind to leave the baggage behind. And, sometimes, we are not the ones to make the decision, life steps in and make a choice for us such as in your case my dear."

Looking in the rear mirror of her car, she continued, "From this point on, your life will certainly change; the only choice you have is to accept or reject it. Accepting is embracing what lies ahead, rejecting is holding on to what you left behind. From where I sit, by the way, it's not the seat of judgment or scorn; what I see is a life that was leading to destruction. What you have here this day is an open door you can either go through to see what lies ahead or close the door and remain where you are. I may be wrong and if I am, please, accept my apology and correct me, but it seems to me that you need a change."

"Who are you?" Fuchsia said as she stared at this woman who was so gentle yet so stern.

"Oh my, I apologize we never properly introduced ourselves with so much excitement going on. My name is Ms. Dorthea Lambert, but you can call me Ms. Dee. May I ask your name dear?" she said with such politeness while driving.

"Fuchsia. My name is Fuchsia," she said looking down at her hands.

"Well, that's an interesting name, and please lift up your head when you answer me. Again, I'm not here to judge but to help."

"Yes, ma'am. My grandma Lydia named me Fuchsia."

"Fuchsia, a plant that looks fantastic in almost any container. They are easy to grow and will reward you with extravagant blooms all summer if one respects her slightly fussy requirements. They attract birds, butterflies, and hummingbirds. They have to be fed regularly..."

"Stop!" Fuchsia interrupted her.

Ms. Dee matched on the brakes and looked at her with concern, "What is the matter?"

"I didn't mean to stop the car. I wanted to know how you know that? My grandma Lydia was the only person to say that to me. She told me about the flowering plant ever since I could remember, but I never understood why she would say that to me, especially if I was sassy. But how did you know this?"

"First, my dear Fuchsia," she said as she began to drive again; "I love plants, and I read a lot. That particular plant would always intrigue me even with its definition. Now, I know why because one day a Fuchsia would enter in my life or I, hers." She smiled at Fuchsia for the first time since their meeting.

"No one but grandma ever spoke of the flower."

"You are a very special girl, like the flower. You are beautiful in whatever you put on, or wherever you are placed, you stand out. You will grow in every change in your life because you are teachable. You can be a fussy one at times, but you mean no harm, it's just your way. You attract favor wherever you go; people are naturally drawn to you. The good and the bad, but especially the good. Wisdom is the one nutrient you lacked in your diet. You love knowledge, and you are a quick learner, but your inquisitiveness can, sometimes, land you in trouble, like the man you left behind."

"Ms. Dee, I like you I think, but you scare me at the same time."

"I scare you?" she laughed.

"Not in a bad way; it's just you remind me of grandma Lydia, but she died a long time ago. She would talk like you do. She knew everything; it was like she could see through me and tell me everything I was doing, couldn't get anything past her."

"Grandma Lydia was a woman of wisdom."

"Wow, yes she was. Just like you."

Ms. Dee made a turn into this huge driveway with the most beautiful home sitting at the top. Windows were all over this house; the front door was a white double door with brass knobs.

"We are here, Fuchsia. Welcome home. This is home for as long as you desire to stay. No worries, I live here alone with my dogs who will greet you at the door the moment I open it," she said as she parked her car in front of the door.

She picked her purse and opened the car door, "A housekeeper comes in a few mornings a week to tidy up, and at three times a week, my chef comes in to prepare me meals; other days, I eat out with my friends like tonight, we ate at the restaurant at the hotel."

There were only three short but wide steps that led to the white double front doors. Ms. Dee retrieved her house keys from her purse. "Been a while we were there, but now, I know why we had to dine there. My friends had left, but I had to use the ladies' room; I told them to go on for I was fine. There was no need in my rushing, I told them, but I sensed it wasn't time for me to leave there yet. I now understand why."

As she put the key in the door and opened it, waiting for her were the cute white dogs, and their names were Brice and Simba. "They are both nuts; mixtures of this and that, but they're the most loving animals not because they caught up in titles, they are just who they are." She winked at Fuchsia as she closed the front door.

Ms. Dee walked her to a room in the five-bedroom house. "This can be your room as long as you desire."

Each room had a private full bath with a vanity table and chair. Huge walk-in closets complete with hangers and full-length mirrors in each room. The room had a king-sized bed and a sitting area with a private balcony. It was like a mini hotel suite.

Ms. Dee then walked her through the enormous house. It was gorgeous; many rooms looked like a small version of a museum with incredible artwork. When they arrived at the gourmet kitchen, "Fuchsia, this kitchen is equipped with anything you could need. If there were any special needs or desires, please write it on the pad on the secretariat," pointing to the small area in the right corner of the kitchen, which had a desk and chair. "I would make certain it's in the house. I want you to be comfortable while you are here."

They walked to a small hallway that led to a closed door. Upon opening the door, "This is our laundry room, everything to wash and dry your clothes are also in here," Ms. Dee said.

Opening a cabinet door over the counter, she pointed to the different types of laundry detergents, fabric softeners, and cleaning products. "I only ask that you tidy up after her since the cleaning lady comes every other day to clean all bathrooms, bedrooms, and kitchen. The linen will be changed every two days, and fresh linen would be put on the beds of occupied rooms, which now includes yours," she smiled as they left the laundry room.

Ms. Dee was detailed down to her favorite smells for linen, and the types of fresh flowers added every few days. Nothing was allowed to die in the house; every flower was exchanged before their expiration. Ms. Dee loved orchids and lilies of all colors, so, the entire house was filled with them in elegant vases. The dogs both shared a tiny room upstairs, each with its own bed. Paying attention to details was a very strong point to Ms. Dee who was meticulous about everything.

Lost for words, Fuchsia stared at every detail of every room. Finally, she spoke up, "You have the most beautiful home I ever saw!"

"Well, thank you Fuchsia. I love beautiful things around me. My parents reared me to pay attention to the details; they were very strict about leaning towards perfection, and being I was an only child, that's all I heard."

"Well, now that I have toured you around the home, I must retire to my room. I advise you to do the same. In the morning, we shall get acquainted. This day has been full; you need to rest and allow your body to begin its recovery process. Would you want a cup of chamomile tea to aid in relaxing?"

"Chamomile? I have never had one, but I sure could use one," nodding her head.

"It's a very soft smooth tea. Come, let's both get a cup to take to our room. Oh, please forgive my manners, I didn't ask, 'are you hungry?' If you are, I can make you a sandwich."

"No, the tea is fine. I have no appetite."

"That's to be expected with the evening you had. Tomorrow, if you like, I can take you for a visit with my doctor to have your face examined, looks pretty bruised up," she said, picking, from the cabinets, two small teacups.

"Oh no, I don't want to be a problem. Besides, I'm just a little sore, that's all. I'm a little tougher than I look," touching the side of her face.

"Okay, the offer will remain if you decide you need to see a doctor. Do you like sugar or honey in your tea?"

"Which do you prefer since I never taste this kind before."

"My preference is honey," opening the cabinet to pick the honey.

"Honey it is for me too. Ms. Dee, I want to thank you again for looking out for me. I had no one to turn to or any place to go; I don't even know where I am let alone get out of here to return to where I came from even if I could."

"No need to fret and you are more than welcome. Okay, let's retire for the night; we can talk in the morning when you're awake."

Handing Fuchsia her cup of tea, she turned off the main light switches as they exited the kitchen, leaving on shadows of lights pervading the ground floor. They both climbed the staircase; Ms.

Dee went off in the direction of her room and Fuchsia, the opposite, to her room.

Fuchsia sat on the small dual sofa in the sitting area of her room; she rested the teacup on the table that was beside it. She took a deep breath; for the first time all day, she finally felt at ease. Having finished her cup of tea, she walked over to the bed ready to climb in and sleep the day off, but she looked down at her feet and realized she should bath first. The one thing she didn't want to do that night was to face herself in the mirror. She entered her private bath in the room, tried to avoid looking in the mirror, but it was impossible because the wall around the sink was one enormous mirror. She turned on the shower, unwrapped the shawl and slid out of the only piece of clothing she now owned, her panties. Stepping into the shower as the warm water ran down her body, tears ran down her face. Silently, she sobbed, bathing as though she could wash away the pain and loss. *I'm twenty-one and, again, I'm starting over alone,* she thought to herself. *What have I done so bad to deserve this life? So many other girls have their moms, dads, brothers and sisters, but I keep ending up alone or with strangers. Why me, why must I suffer these things?*

Hot tears seemed to stream down her eyes as if they were purging all the hidden pain of her young life. When it finally appeared that no more tears were left, she turned off the water and stepped out of the shower. Staring in the mirror as though she was twelve again, she bowed her head and wore the nightgown that Ms. Dee handed her earlier that evening. She climbed her small body up into the bed she now called hers, rolled into a fetal position and fell asleep.

"Fuchsia, Fuchsia," Ms. Dee was whispering as she tapped on the door and opened it. "Fuchsia dear, I'm so sorry to wake you."

"What, huh? Who?" Fuchsia jumped up in fear and shouted as she pulled up the covers to her face.

"I didn't mean to startle you, dear; please accept my apologizes. However, I didn't want you to wake up and not find me here. It's ten thirty, and I have to leave to attend church; I'll return around one-ish. Here is my cell phone number if you need me for anything, please don't hesitate to call. Have a good morning," she said and closed the door.

Still stuck at the moment, Fuchsia just stared around the room as the sun brightened every corner with its warm presence. The silence astonished her, never had she experienced an atmosphere of such peace. She got up, and her toes curled into what felt like fluffy soft cotton as they touched the floor. She looked at her feet, then noticed a beautiful pair of white slippers beside the bed. She slid her foot into one, checking to see if it fits, it was as though it was made just for her. The inner curves of the slippers welcomed her foot with a gentle snuggle. She then quickly put the other slipper on and hurried to the bathroom because her bladder was full. While she washed her hands, she noticed things she hadn't last night.

A pink and white robe was hanging on the brass hook behind the bathroom door, the large window overlooking the tub draped with exotic flowers. The flowers wrapped themselves around the window as they would a picture frame. Each flower had the appearance of being the center of attention; no one was left out without making its own statement. The view from the window was only the tops of palm trees with the sky as its backdrop. The sun pierced its way through the window between the trees, greeting each flower with a shine. The tub was oversized with knobs of the same brass as the hook with the robe. The drapery in front of the tub was sheer with hints of tiny flowers, same as those surrounding the window. Her panties and the shawl were gone from the side of the tub where she left them last night, in their stead was a tiny stool with perfectly folded underwear with tags still attached. She quickly visually scanned the rest of the bathroom, amazed at every beautiful detail that was attended to, nothing was left out. On the vanity table were beautiful bottles full of sweet scents as Fuchsia opened all their lids to smell their fragrance. She was cautious about making sure she placed them all as she found them. She smiled because each was unique in its own way. Suddenly, she was surprised when the bedroom door opened; she quickly grabbed the robe behind the bathroom door.

"Oh ma'am, I didn't mean to frighten you," said the accented middle-aged woman dressed in a simple buttoned-down white dress with pockets on both sides. "I'm Katina, the house attendant. Can I get you anything before I straighten your room?"

"Hi, I'm Fuchsia but they call me Fuchs. I didn't know someone else was here too, thought I was here alone," she replied with a soft voice as she kicked off the slippers in a hurry. "I'm sorry but they were so soft and comfortable."

"Ms. Fuchs, Ms. Dee sent me early this morning on an errand while you were asleep to purchase those, the undergarments and robe in the bathroom for you. I was there when the store opened and rushed back to place them for you, so you would have them when you awakened. I hope they fit well, do they?"

"She had you to do that for me, why?"

"Ms. Dee is a fine woman with a big heart, and if she warmed up to you, she would do anything for you. So, I guess she's warmed to you. I didn't know what type of young lady you were, so I was only comfortable in getting you those, a pair of jeans and top for the day. I hope they fit. I placed them in the closet over here," she said as she walked over to the closet door and opened it to show her the clothes she purchased.

"What do you mean the type of young lady I am!" she snapped.

"Oh no, not in that manner ma'am. I would never disrespect any guest of Ms. Dee," she responded quickly in a warm apologetic tone. "I meant, I didn't know if you like dresses or pants or if you were the fancy type like Ms. Dee. So, I glanced in on you while you were asleep and you looked to be like my daughter Mia, and Mia loves jeans, so, I chose jeans. If I offended you, please forgive me. In Ms. Dee's house, we never hurt one another. Ms. Dee says everyone matters and everyone must be respected. She teaches us all, meaning those on staff even matter; she's the best person we ever worked for."

"I apologize for jumping to the wrong conclusion and becoming wrongly offended, please forgive me. And by the way, I love jeans!" she exclaimed with a smile on her face. "How many people work for Ms. Dee?"

"You know we really don't call it work because she's so good to us all, it's a joy to come here and serve Ms. Dee but don't tell her I said the word serve, she says we keep her company and help her out around here. But any of us would do anything for her because she would do anything for us. Anyhow, it's three of us who come in during the week; me, Kimberly, and Archie.

"Kimberly, she does all the cooking, even feeds us when we here. Archie takes care of the grounds. He's the one who places the flowers in the house as well. Tell Kimberly all your favorite foods, she will make them and boy, she can cook too! Now Archie, if you tell him your favorite flowers or plants, you will spot them throughout the house. He's a master at that, even flowers Kimberly and I like are throughout the place. They may be in between Ms. Dee's but we all see them," smiling as she spoke of the others.

"Wow, Ms. Dee seems to be a remarkable woman," Fuchsia said as she sat on the chair while Katina made up her bed.

"She is. She really is. Well, if you are hungry, Kimberly is in the kitchen waiting for you to come down and make your request. The kitchen is fully stocked; there is nothing that's not available if you desire it."

"Well, alright," Fuchsia said as she pulled her robe tightly around her waist.

Katina led the way to a separate staircase that led straight into the kitchen. She introduced her to Kimberly. Kimberly was a middle-aged woman with a stout built. she was dressed in the same type of dress as Katina, only she had an apron on, and had her short haircut covered with a hairnet.

"Good morning, Ms. Fuchsia, nice to meet you," her voice was a deep southern tone. She smiled as she shook Fuchsia's hand.

"Good morning. Nice to meet you as well."

"What would you desire today for breakfast, well, brunch?"

"Brunch?"

"You know, breakfast is nearly past, and lunch is nearly here. So, you can have a part of breakfast and a part of lunch combined. It's your choice."

"Well, could you surprise me," Fuchsia's face lightened up as she responded.

"Yes ma'am, I can. Is there anything you don't like or allergic to?"

"I don't particularly care for mushrooms; don't think I have any allergies."

"OK, you can go and sit in the Florida room and relax if you want to. I'll bring it to you when I'm done," she said as she opened the large stainless-steel refrigerator.

"The Florida room?"

"Yes, it's just over here," Katina pointed, leading Fuchsia to the room.

"I never heard of a Florida room before."

"Really? Where you from, if I may ask?"

"Atlanta."

"It's nice there, I heard."

"Yes, it is."

"Well, here is the Florida room, make yourself comfortable. Here is the remote if you want music or to watch TV, the choice is yours. If you want, I can open the windows for fresh air, I'll just slide the door closed to shut out the air conditioner in the house. It's a pleasantly nice day, there is always a breeze blowing across the lake, and if you listen closely, you will hear the birds singing too."

"This is really beautiful; it's a different world in here. I didn't notice this last night."

"That's because we pull down the shades in the evening and raise them in the morning."

"Yes, let's open the windows."

"No problem. Do you want them all so you can get the cross breezes when it blows?"

"If it's no trouble."

"No ma'am, no trouble at all. I'm here to make you comfortable," smiling as she left Fuchsia alone.

The entire room was surrounded by windows that extended from the ceiling to halfway down the wall. The ceiling was like an open sky; it was like looking into heaven. When Katina lifted the window, it was if it disappeared in the ceiling and the breeze rushed in to greet them. The floor looked like marbled glass with tiny veins of gold running through it and was even cold to the touch. Flowers poised every corner in a charming way. In the side corner, right under the window, was a perfectly sized marbled stand with a TV, DVD player, and speakers. There were two double reclining chairs with a small round table next to each one, and in the middle of the floor was a four-chair natural stoned table spotted with what looked like gold shimmers throughout.

"What a beautiful room. What type of table is this? It's so smooth and yet heavy, are we allowed to sit at it?" she asked curiously as Katina returned to the Florida room with a tray of food.

"This is called granite, and of course you can sit at it! Ms. Dee only has the best in this house, you see. She says it's made with us in mind to enjoy, and if we can't sit, lay or eat there, then it's not worth the money paid for it."

"Nice," she said as she sat at the table in one of the high black leather chairs.

"Yes, it's nice. We sit out here at times and talk when we are done around the house, it's peaceful and a good place to meditate. You can turn on the CD player. Usually, the XM radio is set to the same station. If you change it, it's ok as long as you return it to the initial station, so, when Ms. Dee turns it on, it's already set. She loves music too. She listens to only two stations. The TV doesn't matter as long as it's not filled with sex and profanity, she's fine with it," Katina said and left Fuchsia alone in the room.

"Wow," Fuchsia whispered to herself as she looked at the tray full of food. "Who she think she was feeding!" She picked up a slice of cinnamon raisin toast, bit into it and began examining everything on the tray. "Oh, this is good, so soft. Bacon, eggs, grits, sausage and cooked apples, man, this is the kind of breakfast grandma Lydia would have made." Smiling, she continued muttering, "Grandma Lydia, you at it again! Making sure I'm taken care of as always!"

Eating more than she thought she could, she finished up most of the food on the tray. She then got up to pick up the remote that controls the entire system. Pushing the button marked CD, she relaxed in one of the recliners; she noticed two blue birds sitting in the tree playing with one another. Gazing a little further towards the lake, she saw what appeared to be a large duck standing on one leg, still as though asleep. The lake was still with gentle waves dancing onto it, as though not to disturb the large duck; the sun too was blazing onto the water.

Fuchsia sat quietly in the chair remembering the last conversation with Candi and how she really messed up. Candi was so good to her she thought, *she took me in, provided for me as though she was my momma. I really let her down, I let everyone around me down. What could she be thinking and what about Tommie? No one deserved to be hurt by me, I hurt momma and Sasha and maybe even Mitch.*

Her mind began racing with thoughts of all that happened; *I've messed up so bad, how can anyone trust or love me? All I do is cause pain everywhere I go. Ms. Dee don't deserve a person like me around, I will eventually bring her pain as well. Grandma Lydia, I wish you were here. I really need you. I miss you so much. You were the only person I didn't get a chance to hurt. Here I am at twenty-one years old with nothing, not one thing to offer. Never had a job, can't use my social security number because I'm too afraid someone will track me down. I was born in Maryland, escaped to Georgia and now thrown in Florida. I am miles away from my beginning and I have no idea about my future. Grandma Lydia, why did you have to leave me so young? Since you died, all I have been is a fallen branch. Anyone knows if a branch falls from a tree, it's only a matter of time before it dies. I feel like one of those branches I would see lying on the ground after a storm; no one picks it up to try and replant it. It lays there until it withers and is no more.*

Fuchsia took a deep breath as the words formed on her lips, "Grandma Lydia, I have fallen like that branch, and I can't seem to get up. Oh, how I wish you were here to help make things better." She began to cry as she rolled up in the recliner. Suddenly, something caught the attention of her ears. The lyrics of the song caught her heart as she sat up and reached for the remote to turn up the volume.

We fall down, but we get up

We fall down, but we get up

For a saint is a sinner who fell down and got up

This melody kept ringing over and over again. It was as though Grandma Lydia ordered the song just for her. "Get back up again. Get back up again," the melody continued to grab her heart. She stood up and looking into the clouds, she screamed on the top of her lungs, "I'm going to get back up again! Grandma, I'm getting back up!" Her voice echoed through the trees over the water; it startled the blue birds, the sleeping duck and even herself! Katina and Kimberly, running, burst through the Florida room's sliding door to check on the new house guest.

"What's wrong? What happened? Are you in pain?" They both sharply enquired.

Fuchsia stood there looking bewildered; she didn't understand what had happened. It was as though the heaviness that overwhelmed her for the last eight years was broken. She couldn't explain it. If she tried, she felt as though something was constantly holding her down, so, she never told Candi or Tommie about it. Sometimes, she would sit and cry. Yes, at times, she missed momma and Mitch but that wasn't it. It felt like the night that Kevin touched her, he left his invisible mark forever upon her. There were days she couldn't eat but had to force herself to eat so Candi wouldn't notice. There were nights where she could not sleep and, sometimes, felt as though something held her down in a death grip. She would fill her days trying to keep busy so as not to notice or bring attention to herself. The only reason she did the private escort was to avoid being alone when Candi wasn't home.

She made herself believe that the feeling was normal but now to feel the pressure finally released, oh, what a feeling! She wasn't completely honest when she told Sasha she was free in her letter because something kept hold of her. But this time, it was different. She spun around looking at the two of them and said, "I feel truly free! There was a song playing on the player, and it was as though the man was singing to me! I need that song; help me find it, please!"

Looking at the anxious look in Fuchsia's eyes, Kimberly said, "I understand how you feel at this moment. I see in your eyes something different than when you first came to the kitchen. Can you remember the words, maybe I can help since this station is all I listen to myself?"

"Really?" Now trembling with tears streaming down her face.

"Yes. What was the lyrics, do you remember any?"

"It... It kept saying 'we fall down, but we get up.' "

"Oh! Yes! I heard that one recently. I will look for it for you. I know it well. It's Pastor Donnie McClurkin; the song is a few years old, and the title is *We Fall Down*. I'll get you the CD if you like."

"Oh, would you!" she said jumping in her arms.

Katina and Kimberly both burst into laughter at the same time.

"What's so funny?" Fuchsia said smiling at them as she wiped her face with a napkin from the tray.

Katina said, "Young lady, we thought a lizard done got in the Florida Room somehow and scared you to death!" laughing out loud again.

"Well, let me bring out brunch since she's fine," said Kimberly.

The three sat, talked and ate together as though they were old friends.

It was as if time stood still since Ms. Dee left for church. The three of them had chatted for a while and eaten. Katina and Kimberly continued their chores while Fuchsia sat in the Florida room watching TV. She was so entranced at the movie she didn't hear Ms. Dee come in.

"Well, hello my dear. How are you feeling?" said Ms. Dee as she entered the Florida room dressed in a black tailored suit with matching hat.

"Oh, I'm sorry I didn't hear you come in. I'm better, thank you. How are you?

"You look better," she said as she sat in the other reclining chair. "Did you eat? Have you met Katina and Kimberly?"

"Yes, I ate the best food today! Kimberly can sure cook!"

"She sure can. I see your slippers fit, and the robe. What about the jeans, did they not fit?"

"I'm sure they will; I never made it back upstairs after brunch."

"You must be comfortable then; I'm glad."

"Ms. Dee, thank you again for taking such good care of me," she reached out to hold Ms. Dee's hand.

"Darling, everyone deserves a chance. Here, turn around, let me see your eyes. How is that bruise today?"

"It's better than last night. It's just a little sore, it will heal soon."

"Sweetie, you talk as if this type of thing has happened frequently, has it?" she said with a troubled voice.

"Enough to know it will heal in a couple of days," she replied in embarrassment.

"Not even an animal deserves to be whipped like this. When you learn your worth, you will know that you deserve better than what you have allowed yourself to endure. Anyone ever taught you your value when you were younger?" Ms. Dee said with a concerned tone, as she sat next to her.

"Sometimes, my momma but mostly grandma Lydia used to talk to me like this when I was little; she died on my eleventh birthday leaving a hole so deep in my soul. Before it could be filled back up, my momma came home with Mr. Kevin, and he filled the hole with terror every day for just about two years until I couldn't take any more. I didn't have momma or Mitch, my brother, to protect me and Grandma Lydia was gone, so, I ran. I ended up in Georgia where I met Candi; she was older but still too young to raise me. However, she did. She never let anything happened to me, then, I met Tommie, and they both looked out for me. I really love them, and they loved me, but I let them down. They both told me not to work with Fred, but I insisted. I thought he was harmless like the other old dudes I would escort but I was wrong, they were right. On the way out to meet Fred, Candi told me that if I left, I can't return. The look on her face when she said it was a look she never gave me before. That was a look she gave if someone pissed her off and she was about to cut them. I guess I got cut in the worst way, huh?" she said, dropping her head in shame.

"Fuchsia, sometimes, a branch has to be trimmed in order to grow and trimming means to cut away something. A Gardner can look at a beautiful tree and yet say the tree needs to be pruned to look even more beautiful. And if that tree is to bear fruit, the cutting may be intensified to make room for even more fruit.

"Fuchsia, it's not that you were bad, the Gardner saw a tree that was worth saving. A tree with more potential than it knew it had. I love plants and I, or most times, Archie goes into the garden and have to prune plants, even my flowering plants. The pruning is not to kill the plant but to make room for new growth. However, the one thing we don't do is throw away the flowers because some people use them dried for crafts; what we do is place them in water to encourage growth. You, my dear, are a flower who has been pruned and transferred into water to enable growth. So, as you can see, cutting is not all bad." She patted Fuchsia on the leg gently.

"Never heard that before. No, I guess cutting is not bad if there is another purpose for you. But can you tell me what my purpose is?"

"Time reveals to all who dare to reach beyond the limitations of life and tap into the greatness they possess. Most of us are one step away from knowing our purpose and then, there are some who are too close-minded to see what's there under the rubble. Unfortunately, some die not knowing because they failed to pursue, and others flourish like a running vine, nothing can stop them. The choice is yours."

"This time, I chose to get up from the rubble and live to fulfill my purpose," she smiled at Ms. Dee.

"Well, now, the journey begins. First, we must take you shopping for some clothes and shoes. Go get dressed, we have a few hours before the mall closes."

Fuchsia stood up and shook her head frantically. "Shopping? Oh Ms. Dee, you don't have to. I have no way to pay you back, and I don't want to worry about owing you something; the jeans and undergarments are enough. I can wash them nightly, hang them and wear the next day!"

"You can do what? How absurd, not when you live in a home that can provide for you. You see, this is why lessons have to be taught. Value your worth! I just offered to take you shopping. You did not ask me to take you, I volunteered, meaning the choice was all mine. I did not say if you do this, I will do that. Therefore, I am looking for nothing in return," she said sharply.

Her face wrenching, "Ms. Dee, with no disrespect to you, Fred, the guy from last night, took me shopping and purchased everything I flew into Florida with and when I could not produce, he took it all back, and beat me."

"No disrespect is felt. The only problem I perceive here is an inability to regain the sense of your worth. That Mr. Fred expected something in return, and you were fully aware of it..."

"Wait Ms. Dee; you promised not to judge me!"

"Now Fuchsia, how am I judging you? You didn't give me a chance to finish my lesson," she gently replied.

"Ms. Dee, you were stating that I knew what he wanted."

"No, I simply said you knew Fred expected something. I never mentioned what that something was now, did I?"

"No, you didn't," she responded as she lowered her tone and sat back down.

"Now, think my dear and listen to my question carefully. You were with him for a reason, am I correct?"

Nodding her head, "Yes. The reason he claimed was to escort him on a business trip to here?"

"So, he purchased your clothes to escort him on a trip correct?"

"Yes."

"Was he going to pay you, if I may ask?"

"Yes, I would not have traveled with that old geezer for nothing."

"Exactly. He wanted an escort, and you knew what he expected, correct?"

"Yes ma'am, I got it, but I didn't expect him to attack me," lowering her head in shame.

Ms. Dee reached over and put her arms around Fuchsia. "Now, now, no shame, we just talking, pointing out facts. I just want you to understand and know that I, on the other hand, have no expectations of you. The problem was trust and lack of discernment coupled with no self-worth. Not all was your fault, and it all can be corrected. Discernment means you see beyond your sense of sight and understand the motive of a thing. Now, do you believe that you are special?"

"I really don't know," Fuchsia responded in a soft voice.

"Do you believe you can be loved unconditionally?" Ms. Dee asked as she used her finger to lift Fuchsia's head.

"I don't know."

"That's some of the reasons why you could easily hook up with Fred because you don't know. It's what you don't know that can destroy you. Knowledge is power, and if you know who you are, then the ball will always be in your court. You can either serve it out or take control through possession of it. Now, it's getting late. Will you now prepare and allow me to take you to the mall?" Ms. Dee asked as she stood up.

"Yes ma'am, I'll hurry," she said as she ran upstairs to get dressed.

They spent the next few hours at the huge mall, in stores Fuchsia had never seen or heard of. Ms. Dee took her from the shoe stores to the underwear stores, she didn't miss anything. Fuchsia was so overloaded that Ms. Dee asked the store clerks to have the packages delivered. Ms. Dee looked not at the price, she just asked Fuchsia if she liked it and if she would wear it. The whole time, they chatted about simple things such as fabrics, stitching, styles and colors; they shopped until the mall finally closed. On the way back to the house, they branched by a quaint Italian restaurant to have dinner.

While at dinner, Ms. Dee suggested that Fuchsia should call Candi and Tommie, and assure them that she was safe and secure. "You owe them that much," she said. "And you will see them again, trust me, that relationship is not dead."

"Okay, I will, I promise but where should I call from?"

"What do you mean dear? You can use any phone in the house, you are not held captive. It is a safe house for you, a house of transitioning and rest. If they choose to come and visit you, they are welcome. If you choose to leave, you may, and yes, you can take everything I purchased for you today. It is called grace. You didn't earn it because you didn't need to, it's called an unmerited favor. Grace is given to whomever the giver chooses; this time, it happens to be you."

Fuchsia smiled at Ms. Dee as she enjoyed the fresh baked lasagna and garlic rolls. After dinner, they drove home, and they both went to their separate rooms to rest after the long shopping day.

The next morning, Fuchsia waited until half past one to call Candi from the house phone. She was trembling as she dialed the numbers unsure of how Candi would respond.

"Hello," Candi answered. Fuchsia heard in her voice great sadness

Fuchsia was trembling, fear had gripped her, but she managed to respond. "Candi, it's me, Fuchs."

"Fuchs! Where are you, where are you calling from? Are you okay?" Candi screamed into the phone.

The sound of screaming and running of Tommie as she got closer to Candi could be heard through the phone. "Oh God, tell me she's okay. Please, say she's fine! Tell her I will come wherever she is and pick her up. If necessary, I will take care of that old man!"

Trying to calm them down, "Tell Tommie I'm okay. Don't worry, Fred ain't worth it."

"What did he do to you, baby girl, what?" Candi began to cry.

Tommie snatched the phone from her hands with a high pitch voice and shouted, "Fuchs, I will kill him! Where is he? What did he do to you?"

"I'm so sorry. You both was right. Please, forgive me. I thought I knew better but I didn't, please, don't be angry with me," she cried.

"Fuchs, can you tell me where you are? Describe to me what it looks like; I promise you I will find you and cut his heart out!" Tommie still shouting while Candi sat on the bed, numb.

"Can you put us on speaker? I need to hear Candi too, I need her to hear me," Fuchsia said, wiping her tears.

"Sure, Fuchs," she said as she tapped the speaker on the phone. "Candi, snap out! Fuchsia wants to hear your voice."

"Baby girl, I'm here. Where are you? Let me and Tommie come get you."

Ms. Dee walked up to Fuchsia, seated in the Florida, and patted her shoulder, "Do you want me to talk to them?"

Nodding her head, she handed her the phone. "Hello, is this Candi or Tommie?"

"Both of us. Who are you, if may we ask, and why is our Fuchs with you?" This time Candi stood up in defense as she put on her jeans and tennis. "If you or that old man put one hand on my little sister, I promise you, I will hunt you down!"

"You got this all wrong," said Ms. Dee in her peaceful voice. "I rescued your sister, I didn't harm her. I kept harm from her."

"Wait, Candi, hush!" Tommie screamed. "Ma'am, is she okay? That's all we need to hear right now, is she okay, did he hurt her?" Tommie stood at the center of the room, hands over her forehead as she listened to Ms. Dee.

"She's okay now. Yes, he did hurt her," Ms. Dee began to explain.

"Oh God, Fuchs, oh no. Please, how bad? She's so frail, how bad?" Candi screamed in fear. "I should have demanded that she not go. I felt something wasn't right with him, please Miss, How bad?" Candi's heart beat faster as the words rolled off her tongue.

Fuchsia could hear the fear in her voice, a sound she never heard from Candi nor Tommie before. The sounds of their voices caused her stomach to turn, she felt nauseous and weak. Fuchsia began to cry uncontrollably, she could feel the pain she caused vibrating through the phone. The trio have been so close all these years and they have never hurt one another in this way before. Ignorant of what to do or how to fix it, she fell to the floor and wept harder than she'd ever cried.

Ms. June, hearing all the commotion upstairs and knowing that Fuchs was missing, came running upstairs through the unlocked doors straight into Candi's bedroom. She could hear Fuchsia crying over the speaker. She yelled out seeing Candi and Tommie in an unusual uproar, "What happened to her? What's going on!"

Candi turned to Ms. June with a tear-filled face said, "He hurt her, he hurt her."

Ms. June grabbed the phone from her, "Hello, this is Ms. June. I'm the girl's downstairs neighbor, whom am I speaking to?" she said in a demanding tone

"Ms. June, I'm Ms. Dee. I live in Naples, Florida. I found Fuchsia after she had a terrible ordeal with a man." Ms. Dee replied, holding Fuchsia in her arms as she narrated the entire ordeal. Looking at Fuchsia face, "She was pretty bruised up, but she looks better today."

"Oh, thank goodness!" Ms. June cried out, throwing her hands in the air. "Ms. Dee, thank you. Fuchsia is a wonderful young lady, she doesn't mean anyone any harm. I promise you, she's not a bad girl."

"Ms. June, right?" Ms. Dee said as she was rubbing Fuchsia's forehead. "Yes, I found out she's a wonderful young lady. She's just a broken vine, a little damaged but not destroyed."

Candi and Tommie, hearing the conversation, pulled themselves together with a solemn look on their faces as though they knew a change was coming. They could hear the compassion in Ms. Dee's voice towards Fuchsia.

"Ms. Dee, this is Candi. I apologize for going off on you, I thought you were some wacked old woman who was working with that sick man. Can I please speak to my sister? Ms. Dee, thanks for saving Fuchs. What do we owe you for her stay?" she said.

"Oh! You owe me not one cent! I did this because I wanted to! I saw she was in trouble, I decided to step in and help. There is no need to apologize, you were defending your sister, that's what love does - protect. Here's Fuchsia," she said and handed Fuchsia the phone, leaving her alone to talk with them.

"Candi, I'm sorry for not listening. You always knew what was best," sniffling as she spoke.

"Not always, lil bits, not always; because if I did, you wouldn't have been working the streets, escorting old men. I am so sorry, baby girl. Please, forgive me."

"You did nothing wrong, I made the decision. I was the one who did not use wisdom. Candi, is Tommie still there?"

"Yeah, I'm here, little bits. I'm here." Tommie's voice was soft and calm.

"Oh, I just wanted to make sure you didn't go looking for Fred."

"Trust me, I have, but the word is he's still out of town. So, I sent him a message and told one of his goonies to deliver it ASAP! I knew he did something, I felt it in my bones," Tommie said.

"Tommie, what did you do? I don't want you locked up for me!"

"Nothing yet, but I took a dozen of black withered flowers with a note, *You will not rest in peace*. Told his flunky driver to give him my message, and if my little sister does not come home safely, I'm coming after all who knew.

"Them old punks looked at me yesterday like mice stuck on a trap; all except one, he must be a new kid on the block. He walked up to me and stood in my face asking me who I think I am.

I pulled out my freshly sharpened blade from my backside, before he could blink, I had it at his throat about to slice him. Then some of my hood boys who knew I was on the prowl walked up, stood beside me, telling me 'Not like this, Tommie you in the open. it's broad daylight.' I let the blade down and my home boys back him in the alley, threaten that they would kill him first if he ever thought about coming near me again, and if Fuchs don't show up soon, it will be a massacre in the neighborhood. So, you can believe old man Fred got the message!" She said in her normal snappy voice.

"Tommie!" Shouted Fuchsia.

"Baby girl, did you not think we would turn this city upside down if we couldn't find you?" Candi said.

"Oh darn! I thought you didn't want to see me again. I was too embarrassed to call the last two days."

"Well, if you ask me, the old man deserved to be scared after hurting you," Ms. June said in the background with her hands on her hips.

"Candi, I didn't let him touch me. I fought with all I had, that old geezer was strong too. He hit me so hard that it knocked me down in a daze, but I was determined he wasn't getting me! I mustered up enough strength, kneed him something awful! You should have heard that old fart with his old grayed self; he even had to nerve to say he took his pill and wasn't going to waste it!" Fuchsia said as she sat up on the chair.

"He did what! I knew that old man was different, trying to be so slick. Well, I guess he going to sell his restaurant now because the word on the street is if he shows up, he's dead! So, we won't see him any longer unless he's stupid!" Tommie finally laughed.

Candi blurted in laughter too, "On the real note, baby girl, I'm glad you fought for your stuff! One of us got to remain pure!" Candi said, still laughing. "Did you shatter his crown jewels?"

The four of them laughed so hard Fuchsia felt peace come over her again as they laughed like always.

After a few minutes of laughter, Fuchsia stopped and said, "Hey, on a real note, I think I need to stay here for a while. Ms. Dee is sweet and kind, and I need to rethink my life and see what the purpose of my life is."

Silence filled the phone, no one said a word.

After fifteen seconds of stillness, Candi spoke up. "I kind of figured this was happening. I'm not mad, right now, it's for the best because I can't fathom something happening to you. And I ain't built to run up and down no prison, visiting Tommie either! Take your time, plus, I'm ready to hang up my panties; this makes me more determined to do so. I almost have enough saved to start my home for runaway girls like us," Candi replied softly as her voice choked.

"Wait one moment, hold up! Are you saying you not coming home yet?" Then turning to Candi, "And are you saying you about to stop the game?" She threw her hands up in dismay "Well, I be a fish in an empty bowl! What am I supposed to do now?" Tommie shouted. "With both of you off the streets, who am I going to protect!"

"Girl, you sick! You need to rest your old self too! Look at us, almost thirty; well, one of us is. This situation all happened for a reason. I started because I could do nothing else, then, when baby girl came, she gave me a reason and a purpose. I knew the first night when she laid crying in that bed, we aren't the only ones who had to be in this place. She had me, I had no one when I was her age like most young girls. So, I decided that I would be one to make a difference. That's why I kept telling you, Fuchs, it's only for a while and I would be done. Well, I guess I'm done," Candi stated firmly.

"I'm proud of you Candi," said Ms. June as she hugged Candi.

"Me too, Candi. Me too," answered Fuchsia proudly

With her hands on her hips and her lips poked out, "Well, I still need to think about this, all this is too sudden!" Tommie said in her sassy voice.

"Hey, we still sisters, right?" asked Fuchsia.

"Sisters to the end, thicker than blood!" replied Candi. "Thicker than blood."

Tommie interrupted, "You know us, the three sisters! One for all and all for one! We ride together, we live together, and we die together. And I ain't checking out no time soon!" shaking her booty as she twirled around the bedroom.

"Tommie, you so crazy!"

Pausing for a moment, Fuchsia spoke up again. "Hey, in all seriousness, you promise you will call me and please come see me soon. Ms. Dee said you can come whenever you want! She's so peaceful. I need to be here right now, thanks for understanding. I love you two and I love you too, Ms. June!"

Tommie, Candi and Ms. June stopped moving and in unison, responded, "We love you too."

Candi then spoke up. "I will call you in a few days, okay, baby girl. You will always be baby girl, and I promise to call you every other day, but if you need me, you call me right away!"

"Me too!" Tommie shouted into the phone. "But I will call opposite days of Candi, so, you will hear from us every day!" she said in a serious manner. "Also, I mean this: you need anything, you call us right away, and we will be there ASAP! And Fuchs, we ain't playing!"

"I promise, this time, I will call if I think I could be in trouble! I promise never to have you worry again!" Fuchsia answered.

After they ended the call, Fuchsia stared at the receiver as reality set in. Palpitations peaked, resulting in hot surges through her body; she wiped the sweat that began to form beads around her brow. The word, 'Bye' rang like an echo in her mind.

A sudden cool wet feeling tingled the tips of her fingers, only to see and smile at Brice who was wagging his tail happily. "Okay, okay. I get it, life moves on."

Fuchsia climbed the stairs to retire to bed. "Good night, Ms. Dee," as she passed by Ms. Dee's bedroom.

CHAPTER ELEVEN

(Wedding day)

Someone was sure looking out for you, Fuchs! I'm so glad Ms. Dee came into your life when she did!" Eyes wide-open, scratching his head, "Baby girl, you could have been killed and I would have been devastated even more." Mitch said having heard his baby sister.

Surprised at Mitch's response, "I know it must be hard on you hearing how your baby sister survived after you were gone. And yes, I know I had some type of guardian angel on my side." She reached over his head to pull the string to the ceiling fan. "It's kind of hot in here, you hot?"

"No! it's you. You just nervous because the hour is drawing nearer! Or you having early hot flashes! Now, tell me, when am I going to meet this wonderful saint of a woman, before the wedding or must I wait until after festivities?" He said, jumping to his feet, and rumbling through his suitcase to complete his unpacking.

"You're not," her voice dropped a few decibels.

"Why not?"

"She passed away a year ago yesterday."

"What? You should have said something." This time, there was a sudden sense of surprise in his voice as he dropped his shirt back into his suitcase.

"Would it have made a difference?" she questioned.

With a look of concern on his face, he responded, "Well, I guess you are right, what happened?"

"She was old, ninety-five"

"Really?"

"But she didn't look like or act like it either," she smiled.

"Man, Fuchs. So, you've been living here alone since?"

"I guess you can say that; me and Lady here," with a smile on her face, she caught Lady up in her arms.

"What happened to Ms. Dee's two other dogs?"

"They were both older dogs too. Strangely, not long after her death, the two of them both passed, a week apart. That's when I adopted Lady, she needed to be loved and I needed someone to love. Funny how things work out, ain't it?"

"What do you mean?"

"Time, that's all. Time."

Glancing over Mitch's shoulder to take peek at the alarm clock on the night stand, "Speaking of time, it's getting late. It's one-thirty, and those girls aren't here yet! The florist was supposed to deliver my flowers by one o'clock, no later than one fifteen, they promised me!" This time, the crack in her voice became sharp as her pulse hiked.

"Calm down, Baby girl. Do you have their number? I can give them a call," he said, reaching for his phone.

Lady jumped off the chair and ran downstairs as the sound of the door-knocks rang throughout the house.

"This better be them or I'm going to blow my top! I hate lateness!" Storming out the bedroom through the runway, she stumbled down the stairs as she ran to get the door.

"Slow down, Fuchsia, for you fall and break your neck!" Mitch said, trying to catch his sister before she fell.

Slinging open the door in a combination of anxiety and frustration, "You are late!" she chastened the man.

"Ma'am, I apologize. I made the wrong turn off the highway. It's my first day of delivery, please, accept my apologizes. The delivery to the church was on time. I just got a little confused coming here from the church," the young delivery man responded with trembled voice.

Such a small voice from a big man, Fuchsia thought as she escorted the young man through the foyer. Taking a deep breath to slow down her rapid heartbeat, she became lost in emotions as she laid her eyes on the most beautiful bouquet of flowers.

"Is this my bridal bouquet?" her voice mellowed down to a whisper.

"Yes ma'am, it is," he said as he handed her the open box, exposing the four types of Fuchsias - all perfectly sized, married together into one large bouquet with tiny calla lily tucked so neatly in their midst. Little sparkles of gold dust, as if they were rain drops, nestled on top the bouquet.

"I... I don't understand, there must be a mix up. Don't get me wrong, this is the most beautiful bouquet I ever laid eyes on, but this is not what I ordered. I ordered just a plain white arrangement of orchids."

"Ma'am, I don't know. I'm just the delivery guy, let me look at my delivery slip. Is your name Fuchsia?

"Yes, my name is Fuchsia. Is there a packing slip or a note?"

"Yes ma'am, there is a card attached, somewhere," as he opened his work pad. "Here it is," he handed Fuchsia the order form. "Where can I lay the other bouquets?"

"Here man, you can lay them over here on this table. Let me help you," Mitch took charge as his sister sat in the oversized chair.

"Thanks, you guys have a great day. Oh, and tell the lady I said congratulations," he said as he laid the last bouquet down and was about to close the door behind him.

"Hey man, let me give you a tip," Mitch said as he reached into his pant pocket.

"No man, I was late. Don't worry about it, just have a good day."

"Thanks man, we will. You have one as well," shaking the delivery guys hand, and closing the front door behind him.

"Fuchs! What's the matter? What is it? Why the tears?" kneeling to his sister. "Hey baby girl, what is it?" staring at the pages of a letter in her hand.

"It's…" she hesitated for a moment. "It's from momma," bursting into tears.

"Oh, baby girl, don't. Come on here." He wrapped his arms around her and held her as she trembled in his arms. "Ssh, come on, don't fall apart, not today. Put it away, read it later."

Mitch tried to calm her as her hands trembled with the slightly crumbled letter in the center. She pulled herself together and read the note:

My dearest Fuchsia,

This is the day I dreamed about since the day you were born, yet it is the saddest day of my life because I can't be there with you. I want you to know that I love you and always have. Yes, I messed up as a mother, I should have listened to you and not close my eyes to the signs that were right in front of me. I pray you can forgive me. I can never make up to you the years that was lost but I hope one day you will find it in your heart to welcome me back in.

Baby, Fuchs, you still momma's baby. I left Kevin about five years ago after many years of abuse. I finally got tired; it wasn't as hard to do as I thought. I gave him more power than he deserved or even had. Fuchsia, the day you left was the worst day of my life and this is the second worst day, knowing I should be with you to help you dress. I miss running the brush down your beautiful long hair. Baby, momma's so sorry.

The day I received your letter was the day my life began to change. From that day, it started me on my journey of soul searching. I still carry your letter with me in my purse everywhere I go. I always believed I would find you and would be able to tell you one more time how much I love and miss you. Losing both my children at young tender ages was as if I had died on the inside. Mitch told me you found him on social media, and I was so overjoyed and I hoped you would look for me as well. When Mitch told me you were not ready yet to see me or talk, I died again. He kept his word and would not give me your information. But a mother who has lost her child is a desperate mother who would do anything to hold her child in her arms again. I searched every society paper, all the social networks until I found you. There you were just as beautiful as the day I last saw your face without the tears. I tried desperately to grant your wish, but I couldn't let this day happen and not tell you how much you still mean to me. I drove all night just to get a glance of my baby, even if it's from a distant, I had to see you one last time before you became a wife.

Fuchsia, I should have known that Kevin was up to no good. All the signs were there, I was blinded like my momma was when I was a young girl. You see, baby girl, I too was a victim when I was a child. My aunt's husband molested me and no one listened to me; they told me that good girls keep their legs closed. I was treated like it was my fault. Then later in my adulthood, after grandma Lydia passed, I found out when she was a little girl, she too was molested by someone in the family.

She was shipped away, that's how she ended up in Maryland. She lived on a farm with relatives until she was eighteen, then she moved closer to the city. She was married for a short while and after my brother John was born, daddy left us all. Momma then became very strong in church and she thought she kept me safe until the summer. She sent us to the farm because she didn't want us to get into trouble over the summer. That was the worst summer of my life. I was thirteen years old and when I told my aunt, I was chastised; so, I never told anyone else because after she told me 'Good girls keep their legs closed,' and if momma ever found out, they would ship me off never to be seen again, I never opened my mouth. Until now, I want you to know I believe you and I believed you then, but I was in fear. I was afraid of being alone. I had already lost momma and I thought Kevin was my blessing, but it turned out he was my nightmare. I'm so sorry, please forgive me. I have learned to forgive myself and my momma because it was neither of our faults. It was the fault of the sick men that did that to us. Because of that happening in my life, it caused me to make mistakes when it came to you and Mitch. I asked Mitch to forgive me a long time ago and he did. I now ask you to please forgive me, my heart is broken and I long for the day to hold you in my arms again. If I could do it all over, I would but we both know I can't.

Please, accept this bouquet as my gift to you. When I found out your wedding day, I contacted all the florist in your town pleading my case until I finally found the florist you chose. I had to bribe and pay extra but you are worth it! I couldn't be there with you but this is my gift of love to you. All the different Fuchsia's wrapped into one, they represent the many facets of you, the ones I know and the ones I lost. I pray that you will carry this down the aisle, knowing that this day your momma deeply and has always loved you. And know I will be somewhere standing in the shadows, wishing you well.

Love, Always.

Momma.

A sense of relief and despair came over her all at once as streams of tears bubbled out of her. The overwhelming feeling of the urgency to run to momma coupled with the desire to run away sent a sense of fear flowing through her body. She dropped the letter, brushed her hands through her hair, and looked up at her big brother hoping for a solution in his eyes. Her mouth began to tremble as she mustered up enough strength.

"I'm lost for words, Mitch. I'm confused and scared at the same time. I don't know what to do or how to react. It's like one side of me always wanted this but the other side is so afraid. Why now, why on this day? Why could it not have happened before now? How am I supposed to handle this? I know she's sorry and I forgave her a long time ago in the letter I sent to her. Why couldn't she just leave it alone? Why come here and why now?" she cried out in frustration.

"Maybe you're not supposed to carry the burden any longer. Maybe, just maybe, Baby girl, God don't want you to carry the old baggage into your new life." He said, trying to console his frantic sister.

"What baggage, Mitch?" She said, frustrated.

"The baggage of your past and the pain it caused to rest in your heart. Baby girl, you still have some areas that need healing.

You've been through a lot for such a young woman. Yes, you are twenty-five, but the pain of being eleven still grips you.

"Acceptance is a part of healing, forgiveness is the key to your release. If it still hurts and makes you cry like now, it's still very much part of you. How can you truly give your heart to Marvin if it's clouded with the pains of your past? One day, you will have children of your own and you want to love with no hinderances, no fears. You want your children to have a grandma Lydia in their lives too, just like we had. Yes, momma made poor judgments, but who haven't a time or two? Is she deserving of true forgiveness? Yes, she is. Why, because we all had to be forgiven of something we done or didn't do. Does that make us bad people? No, we are just forgiven people."

Fuchsia tried to squirm away from Mitch, but he held her tight in his arms.

"Fuchs, baby girl, please hear me. I was angry at momma too as a boy. I always thought it was her fault that our father was not around. But I realized while locked up: we are the ones in control of our lives. If he wanted, he could have stayed around; if he chose to, he could have visited us. Nobody has the power over us to make us do what is not already in our hearts to do!"

Looking in her eyes, "Fuchs, I chose to go get locked up and I also chose to change my life; they were all my choices. You know as a people, we always look for someone to blame for the choices we make, when in fact the choice was ours from the start. I made the mistake of choosing to be angry with momma and I lost valuable time with her. Now, look at me, I'm a husband and a father. I don't want my kids to hold me captive for my mistakes; I want them to really understand that forgiveness is a choice and if they chose to remain angry or to hate me for my mistakes, their lives would be hindered because of that choice. But if they forgive me quickly and release me from my mistakes, their lives will be one of peace and no regrets.

"Fuchs, when I got out of the Juvenile home, I had my mind fixed on joining the Marines, but I also had a mission which was to look momma in the eyes and tell her 'I'm sorry. I'm sorry for the pain I caused her, for blaming her, for leaving her when she needed me most.' I wanted to look you in the face and tell you the same, but when I returned to the neighborhood, none of you were to be found. I asked the neighbors where my family was; some threw their noses up in the air and turned their backs on me. I was hurt but I understood because I caused a lot of pain and trouble in the neighborhood. I was changed and they didn't know it. Then, the little old dude who used to walk his dog everyday past our house saw me sitting with my duffle bag on the stoop, he walked over and said, 'You that little bad ass fellow, ain't you?' I said, 'No sir, I was him but I'm not him any longer.' That old man sat down beside me and talked to me for the first time, telling me about his struggles as a kid. He was once like me and he decided to change too. Then he said he was proud of me because many of my friends are locked up now serving big time; he said it was a blessing I got shipped off when I did because two of them are now dead. Then he told me the worst news ever, he told me that momma and you had moved about six months ago, and no one has seen or heard from you guys since. I broke on that stoop and cried like a baby because all I wanted to do was to have momma hold me like she used to and send me off to the Marines with love. I wanted to show her how much I changed, how much I grew up; I wanted her to see that her big man was now truly a big man.

"Fuchs, you both were gone. I had to meet my recruiter so that I could catch the bus to leave to camp Lajuene. I had to leave without seeing the two girls that meant more to me than the air I breathed. The old dude gave me a ride to meet my recruiter and he said a prayer for me and wished me well. He told me, 'One day, you will see her again and when you do, tell her how much you love her and never let a day go by without telling her that.' He said to me, 'I don't know what happened but whatever it was, it don't matter because you only get one momma and no one will ever replace that momma.'

"Fuchs, I thought the days of Juvie was rough without seeing you guys but uninformed of your whereabouts was killing me. I did basic training on the strength that one day, I would see momma's face again and she would be proud of her big man. It wasn't until I was first stationed that I ran into the girl named Sister, from the neighborhood, who too was in the service. Her mother kept contact with momma, and she gave me the information. Baby girl, I didn't call her. I got special leave and went to find momma; all I ever wanted was to see her again, face to face. When I got to the door and rang the bell, the woman I saw was not the woman I left. She was older, tired and worn. When she opened the door, at first, she looked at me with a look of confusion. Then, when I smiled, she lit up and said, 'Big man? Is that my big man?' I reached out and grabbed her by the waist, lifted her up and spun her around. We hugged and cried for what seemed to be hours, standing on that porch. I finally put her down and we went in the house.

" 'Where's baby girl?' I asked, and momma looked at me like an old woman and said, 'She's gone.' Fuchs, I made amends with momma because it was death without her. I told her about Patrice, and I wanted them to meet because we were getting ready to be married. I wanted her blessings and needed her there. Before I could embark on a new life and take a woman as my wife, I had to make certain that I left no open doors of pain and resentment in my heart. I wanted to be able to love, with a pure clean heart, the woman I was about to call my wife. Baby girl, this is your time before you say I do. Make room in your heart to receive the love that Marvin is about to give you. Hurt people will always hurt other people; holding grudges will shorten your life and who wants to shorten an already short life?"

Stunned at her big brother talking, she calmed down and really listened to him.

"Wow, again here you come and drop so much wisdom on me. You almost sound like grandma Lydia, you sure you Mitch? Anyway, I hear you, but I got to do this in my time, my way.

"Mitch, I'm not the same baby girl momma once held. I'm not her angel any longer. Time and life has run a course on me, and justice has not been my friend either." she explained.

"What do you mean justice has not been your friend? Fuchs, you almost sound bitter! Bitterness is a major root of destruction. Listen to me now, Fuchs!"

His voice got louder and strong. "How you marrying a man you told me is gentle and loving and you still warp with this bitterness! That thing will cause you to have an unhealthy marriage! Does that man deserve to suffer because someone else robbed you of a part, not all, of your life? Are you serious?

"All this time, I've been sitting around here talking with you. I was almost convinced that you are this strong powerful young woman living in this beautiful miniature mansion, but I was wrong! Right, you are not the same baby girl. None of us are the same people we started out to be, but does that make either of us better than the other?"

Trying to break away again, "Let me go."

"No Fuchs! That makes us equal! In a little less than five hours, you will be taking the hand of a man whom you said loves you and you love but do you really know love? Do you? Love is kind and patient and keeps no records of wrong! It endures, protects. It's to be cherished; even the love of your mother is to be cherished! Fuchs, you need to think about this and think right before you hurt Marvin! Forgive Momma before you say I do and ruin a good man!"

"Stop it! Stop it now! Just shut up! I don't need you or anyone to tell me about loving Marvin! I know I can love him, and I promised him that I would! Since when did you become so perfect and full of all this kind of talk? Who do you think you are, bullying me around about what I should do about my own mother?" she said and threw the pillow from the oversized chair across the floor.

"You mean our mother, Fuchs? She's our mother and she deserves a second shot at life with you! Fuchs! Man, Fuchs! Don't make me!" as he reached to pick up the pillow she threw.

"Make you what?" she jumped in the face of her six-foot brother with her hands on her hips.

Walking away from her, shaking his head, he sat on the living room sofa. "Nothing, baby girl. Time is supposed to heal all wounds, come on Fuchs! Listen to me, I love you and I love her, and I want the best for you both.

"Change is needed here. It's time to release yourself to love totally again. I know you; inside, you are struggling as I was too, but I had to find my inner peace. Things that come are not to destroy us; sometimes, they come to make us strong. Baby girl, I saw a lot, been through more than I can say but one thing I realized while I was in Juvie was I had to have inner peace, and that peace gave me strength to become the best I could be! Now I serve my country, but I served myself first! I had to come to grips with being locked up and realize that though I'm locked up, I'm not locked out, and if change was going to come, it had to start with me," he shouted at her, his eyes fixed and red.

Standing in front of the bay window, staring at the sky, anger had filled her mind. "But Mitch, I'm not you! I have forgiven in my heart, and I had peace until this very moment! I'm entitled to my feelings too!" she snapped back in defense.

Fuchsia stared out the window in silence; she watched as her neighbor down the road was walking with her kids. One was in a stroller and the other was a toddler holding her mother's hand. Peace and love overwhelmed her because she remembered when the baby was still in her mother's womb. She remembered how the neighbors got together to take up an offering to bless this family after the husband lost his job. She remembered that the toddler, two years ago, may never walk because of an illness as pronounced by the doctor, but they were wrong. One day, that little girl got up and walked in spite of what her parents were told. She remembered how Ms. Dee said, 'Anything can happen in twenty-four hours. Everything could change, nothing is certain to remain. Then Fuchsia saw the most beautiful butterfly land on the front bush, it was as if Ms. Dee and Grandma Lydia was speaking at the same time.

Turning around to look her brother in the eyes, "Mitch, you've changed so much. I'm tripping as I listen to you. I'm so selfish, please forgive me."

She walked over and knelt down before her brother, "Was Juvie that bad? How did you become this man? I've been sharing so much about me that I never thought to ask you how you became this wonderful man I now see?"

He rubbed his hands across her brow, "Fuchs, I learned that the man I am now was locked up inside of me waiting to come forth; all I needed was someone to help bring it forth. When I first got locked up and sent to Juvie, I tried to be hard, but it was just a charade, I missed my momma. I would just sit around all day, dragging my face until one day I found my inner self."

He turned from her and stared across the floor, out of the window into the clouds. "No, it wasn't easy, but it was about the lessons I needed to learn. Sometimes, we need serious hard lessons to bring out the best in us," he said, remembering the days his life began to change.

Looking at his sister, "It's not about what I been through, it's about how I made it through."

"Tell me Mitch, what changed you into this man? The last time I saw you, you was cold and hard, not warm and compassionate," she sat there wanting to know about the years she was estranged from her brother.

"It's not important, Fuchs; it really isn't. Just know this: Juvie made me realize the man I wasn't. Military made me into the man I desired, and marrying Patrice helped me become the man. Remember this: we are not defined by the past or mistakes; we are defined by our ability to change, and it's also a plus to have great mentors in your life.

CHAPTER TWELVE

Fuchsia could see the gleam in her brother's eyes, something she never saw when they were growing up. She could feel his passion in his words. For the first time in years, she felt a real connection to her brother.

"Hey Mitch, I'm so proud of the man you have become."

"Thanks, Fuchs. I'm proud of myself as well, but if it hadn't been for a great mentor in my life, I believe I would have stayed in that cycle of destruction, never seeing my total worth or purpose."

"Nice!" smiling at him. "Do you still keep in touch with him?"

"All the time. He's like the father I didn't have and the father I choose to be, he's my hero. He doesn't have a big house, drive fancy cars, wears designer suits or own a large corporation but what he does have is compassion, loyalty, and a genuine love for humanity. This man will share wisdom with anyone; will give you his last to make sure that you have, and, most of all, he shares time. He invested time in me, and I will never forget that. I cherish every conversation we have 'til today."

"You know Mitch, I really never gave to much thought to the fact that we had no daddy. I was so used to me, you and momma, and momma took care of us, so I never paid any attention. It wasn't until she married Kevin that a man sat at our table or lived in our home. So, when Kevin tried to rape me, it confused me so much because 'Was this what having a father meant?' I would often ask myself because if it was, I didn't want or need one."

Shifting her position on the chair, "You know that messed me up as a girl, not knowing the love of a father; the provision, the protection, all those things that a little girl needs in order to grow into womanhood. So, because my perception was jacked-up, it made it hard for me to recognize what true love was. I grew to not trust a man, or respect one either. Kevin was a misrepresentation of fatherhood and husband-hood; that poor excuse of a man messed me up!"

Mitch stood up and walked over to the fireplace and rested his elbows on it, holding his head between the palms of his hands. For few minutes, there was complete silence. After about three minutes, he turned around to Fuchsia who was seated crossed-legs on the chair, staring at the gold etching on the wall: In True Love, there's Unity; No divisions.

"Hey baby girl, it's conversations like this that reminds me of my purpose in mentorship of young men, so another daughter won't have to cry or suffer from lack of a father. Mothers are necessary but so are the fathers! Young men need to know their worth as well. To know they are needed, and also chosen to do great things so that they don't grow into worthless men like Kevin. If they can be taught as boys to value and know their worth, to pursue their dreams, to have a healthy vision for their own life first and, most of all, to love themselves, then, we would have real fathers raising daughters in love, sons in strength, and wisdom to become great men. I believe if our father would have stuck around and been a dad, both our lives would have been different; that's my opinion."

"Yeah, I believe so too, but if he didn't have what it took to be that, maybe we was better off without him. And you know that ole saying that is so true, 'It takes a village to raise a child.' I'm grateful for my village people. My village taught me this: In true love, there's unity; no division. That's why I had it etched in my wall," she said pointing to the wall.

"Yes, you are right. I was wondering why you had that written in the wall, it's beautiful."

"It's my daily reminder. I understand that love has no gender, color, religion, or class. It's the one factor that brings us all together. There's no division in love, only unity. My girls and I come from different places, different experiences, but there's one factor in our lives, we love each other and that's the bond that keeps us together. If people would just let down their guards and fears, they would see we all want the same, and that is to be loved and give love; that's what unifies us all."

"Wow! And you talk about me! Who is this love guru here? You didn't do badly yourself, Ms. Soon-to-be Bride!"

He gave his sister a high five as they walked towards the kitchen arm in arm.

Suddenly, Lady jumped off her dainty little dog-chair, ran out of the Florida room and dashed towards the front door, wagging her tail and jumping.

"Well, I guess the girls finally made it an hour later," Fuchsia said, laughing and running towards the door to greet them.

"How do you know? No one knocked on the door."

"Because Lady knows they are here." She swung the door open to greet her friends.

Laughter, giggles, hugs and kisses filled the foyer as Candi, Tommie, and Sasha all walked in.

"Sasha! How did you meet up with these two?"

"We just happened to be coming off route I75 at the same time. You know these two heifers tried to run me off the road! You know I was tripping, saying to myself, 'I thought this was a nice area with rich nice folk! Who let this feline team out!' " Sasha laughed out loud, dropping her purse on the floor to hug Fuchsia.

"Feline! Hunty, you know you looking at a well stacked cougar over here!" Tommie said as she shook her behind and jokingly shoved Sasha.

Laughter filled the house as the three girls continued laughing and joking on their way to the kitchen, and Lady running alongside Candi, jumping and panting.

"I know, Lady, I got you. Look here," giving Lady one of her favorite treats.

"You spoiling my dog, and she better not be sick when I return from my honeymoon."

"You thangs! Took long enough; you know I like to have my food well digested before I take my bath and get dressed," Fuchsia said as she opened up the bag containing her Sushi.

"Oh, we know, miss prim and prime," Candi said as she tugged Fuchsia's hair.

"I know Ms. Dee spoiled her rotten; she so rotten that her poop got to be timed just right!" sneered Tommie as she opened the drawer to get her a fork.

"You a mess," Sasha laughed.

"No, Fuchsia is the one with the mess problems. Now, hand me some of that shrimp salad," Candi belted in and got herself a plate.

Sasha stood there in the middle of the kitchen space with an expression that made it seem as though she was waiting on something.

"Oh, oh, girl, I forgot. Here is another boogie valley girl. Alright, please, can you hand me some of that gourmet shrimp salad, madam?" Candi *dissed* Sasha.

"That's better," Sasha said in her high-pitched tone as she handed the container to Candi.

"What I tell you ladies about all that snapping at one another?" Fuchsia shouted.

"I told you, a bunch of felines acting like they all in heat," Sasha said, smiling at Candi.

"Honey, ain't no kitty-cats running up around here! At least not over here!" Tommie shouted. "Now, pass some of that shrimp salad, for the real cat come a-scratching!"

Mitch, who had gone to bathe, walked into the kitchen doorway. He stood there a few minutes before anyone noticed him. He cleared his throat, "Excuse me, is that salad any good? Is it alright if I join you ladies?"

Spinning around to see who the man behind the voice was, "Oh my lucky day! Who, may I ask, do I have the pleasure of meeting this day?" Tommie blurted out with a surprised look. "Fuchs, you didn't tell us we were not alone, and who is the good-looking eye-candy here?"

"You must be Tommie. Hello, I'm Mitch."

"Mitch! Oh, my goodness, it's been such a long time since I saw you!" Sasha jumped up from the kitchen table in a sprint and leaped into his arms.

"Sasha? Wow, look how you have grown up. You look incredible," he said as he embraced her. "Look at you! You still got the looks!" Quick flashbacks ran across his mind as he remembered how he had such a crush on her as a child.

"Alright, alright, that's enough of that. Leave some for the rest of us here, Sasha." Tommie chimed in as she stood on her feet, walking towards them. "I saw him first, and he called my name, not yours. How did you know who I was, Mr. tall, fine and sexy?"

He let go of Sasha, smiling at Tommie who was standing in front of him with her long black wavy hair just exposing enough of her slanted hazel eyes and almond complexion. "You're not what I pictured. I'm sorry. I meant to say you are more beautiful than baby girl described you."

"Oh really, you not half bad yourself, soldier."

"He's happily married, right Mitch?" Fuchsia interrupted.

"Yes of course, I am," snapping out of his trance. "Yes, I am. Baby girl has told me a lot about you ladies. I kind of pictured you a little different, that's all; my bad."

"Well, now that the felines have all tried to mark the ground, I would like to introduce myself. I'm Candi, it is finally a pleasure to meet you. We heard so much about you over the years, and like yourself, Fuchs did not tell us how fine her brother was."

"Candi, it's my pleasure and honor to meet you and you certainly ain't bad yourself. I guess I jumped to the wrong conclusions on what you ladies would look like. First, I want to thank you for taking care of my baby sister and raising her in the earlier years of her life. Words cannot express my gratitude to you. If there is anything I can do for you please, don't hesitate to ask me. The same goes for you too, Tommie. She has been talking all morning about you two; so, I feel as though I know you both."

"Shoot! Not the way, I would like to know you better. You bring your wife with you or do we get to have you to ourselves all day? How long you staying so I can make sure I get my fill? Here, you can take my seat and I will just stand over here watch you eat!"

"Tommie!" the trio shouted together as they shook their heads laughing.

"Some things never change," Candi said, "and he's married as well!"

"What! The man said he was married, he didn't say buried. Come on, give this cat a break; ain't nothing wrong with a little cat chase every now and then," grinning as she winked at Mitch.

"Don't worry, Baby girl. I know she's all talk. Besides, I ain't ready to die yet, and that's what Patrice would do, she would kill me. Above all, she never has to worry about me stepping out on her. Now, don't get me wrong, sugar; you fine but you family to me."

"Hahaha, I guess he told you. Now, sit down and eat your food, you house cat!" Candi said as she put a fork full of shrimp salad in her mouth.

"Shut up, you just jealous, and I'd rather be the house cat than the alley cat!" Tommie shouted back.

Laughter filled the atmosphere as the four of them reminisced while eating.

Fuchsia's mind went back to the letter she received from momma. *Mitch was right; I never thought I was still carrying so much pain about momma. I thought I was strong, only to find my weakness tucked deep inside my heart.* The thoughts ran across her mind while she sat amongst her bridal party. *Maybe I should call Marvin and ask for his opinion about this. No, he would say the same things Mitch said, and I don't want to raise an alarm because he will drop whatever he is doing and run right over here. I don't want that.*

"What's up, little bits?" Candi said with concern. "Come on, you want to go talk?"

"No, I'm alright. It's just that I got a letter today from momma."

"Really, what she say? Where is she?"

The four of them stopped eating and talking, focused on Fuchsia who brought the bridal bouquet into the kitchen to show the girls.

"Wow! That's beautiful and so big; it's a bouquet fit for a princess!" Sasha squealed with excitement as she looked in the box, then, reached for the second large box on the dining table.

"One... Two... Three... Four; hey Fuchs, they gave you one too many bouquets, it's only three of us in the bridal party."

"No, it's no mistake. It is four of you."

The three of them stopped in mid-tracks as though they saw a ghost and yelled at the same time, "Who?"

"Come on, y'all. Calm down, I got enough on me right now with momma in town somewhere and I don't know what to do. The last thing on my mind is you not wanting someone else in the wedding, and if you must know, her name is Melondy. She has been a friend to me since Ms. Dee passed; she's a friend from church."

"What? Wait a minute, how come we just finding out about this now? And you expect us to just accept this new chick? Fuchs, you know us better than that. You know how long it took for me to get used to Ms. thang over here. No offense, Sasha but you know you kinda stuck up; however, you my girl now.

"Well, where is this Ms. Melondy at? She's late!" Tommie snapped.

"Why you tripping, Tommie? I didn't ask you to take her home with you; she's my friend, Tommie, that's all and that settles it! Plus, it makes Marvin happy that I asked her, she's known him for years. She's like a sister to him, so if you don't mind, can you please put the gangster away for today?"

The tone in her voice echoed the blood she felt boiling in her veins. "You heard me say I got other troubles I need to sort through, or didn't you hear me?" Fuchsia screamed at Tommie

"I know she's not shooting me wolf tickets."

"Tommie, shut up! It's Fuchs's day; we all promised her to support her and be here for her. Now, stop being jealous about another cat in the pen," Candi said, standing between them.

"Fuchs, you okay?" Candi turned to her.

"Yeah, I'll be alright."

"I never saw you like that before, especially not with Tommie. Where's that letter cause this is not our Fuchsia?"

"Here," handing Candi the letter from her pocket.

Mitch walked over and pulled her close to his chest, squeezing tightly.

"Baby girl, it's your day. Whatever you want, it's all up to you; don't let nothing take your joy or peace this day. If you don't want to see her, then don't. If you do, I will make it happen for you, but it's all up to you."

Candi sat in the chair to read the letter, then, passed it to Tommie and Sasha. For a couple of minutes, they stared t Fuchsia.

"Look, honey, I nor anyone in here can tell you how to feel or what to do. However, that was a long time ago, and you have to move on now. What if this is the door that needs to be closed in order for you to more on. I'm just saying, baby girl; things have a special way of showing up in order for us to move on.

"Fuchs, you know I lost both my parents when I was young, and I never got the chance to say good-bye to them. They never had the chance to see me grow up. I'm just saying you got a chance that neither Tommie nor I ever had."

Turning to get Tommie's attention, she continued, "You don't have to be concerned about how I or anyone feels. I know I got a place in your heart, but I also know that you have a heart big enough to hold all of us."

Sasha walked over to her, took her by the hand and looked her in the eyes. "Fuchs, your momma loves you. She never stopped. Yes, she hurt you but you not seeing her is going to hurt you worst."

She smiled, nodding her head and turned towards Candi. "You the best. For the last twelve years, not only were you my big sister, you were a mother figure to me. From the day I met you, you have always been there as my teacher and rock. Nothing or no one can replace that."

Turning to Tommie, "I'm sorry for yelling at you. I'm so overwhelmed right now. From the first day we met, you became my sister and protector. I trust you so much, and nobody can separate us. You don't have to be concerned about Melondy; when you see her, you will see she's so gentle and loving. I didn't need another Candi or Tommie or even Sasha because you all are originals in your own rights. Melondy is a part of the woman I'm becoming or trying to get to know. She brings something different into the atmosphere.

"When Ms. Dee passed, I didn't know what to do or where to begin. I know I could have called you three, but I didn't and I'm sorry it happened fast and unexpected. I had to grow up fast and take on a whole different level of responsibility. Melondy was the only one at the funeral to come up and sat on that empty pew with me. I actually was Ms Dee's only family; I didn't it was true until she died. The church was full except for the family row. I was all alone on the family rows until Melondy came off the choir stand, sat next to me and held my hand. She rode with me to the burial in the limousine and afterwards came to the house to make sure I ate.

Ms. Dee had given the workers two weeks off and sent them and their families on an all-expense paid cruise two days before she died. That's the kind of woman she was. So, there was no one but me here in the house. Melondy came every day to check on me and to pray with me. That's why she's special because she helped me to see the gain despite the loss.

"I thought I was over the pain of momma not being in my life. Now, on this day, I find myself having to deal with a bandaged wound. Can you please embrace Melondy, she's no threat. Believe you me; she's such a wonderful person. And can you promise me that if I get the heart to call my momma, you would help me not to run again."

Tommie and Candi both, from each direction almost knocking Mitch over, embraced her with so much assurance.

"Hey, we are the three sis-keteers, one for all and all for one. You hurt, we hurt. If it's best for you, like it was for you to stay with Ms. Dee, then, it's best for us as well. We got you through thick and thin, we in this thing together." Tommie said and kissed her forehead.

"You know we got you," Candi chimed in.

"Well, what about me? Don't I count for anything?" Sasha said trying to get in on the group hug.

"Yeah, you here just in case someone gets sick!" Tommie blurted out.

"Tommie! Behave!" Fuchsia broke into laughter.

The sounds of chimes rang throughout the house as the doorbell rang out. Lady ran towards the door excited to greet the incoming guest.

"Boy, this little doggie loves people, don't she?" laughed Mitch as he opened the door.

"Hello, I'm Melondy. I'm here for Fuchsia," she said in a soft-spoken voice.

"Hi Melondy, I'm her brother, Mitch. Come right on in, she's expecting you."

"Mitch, I heard great things about you," she said as she entered the foyer and began walking towards the voices. "Hello everyone, sorry I'm late."

"Hey sweets, come on in and meet the rest of the maids!" Fuchsia said as she walked over and hugged Melondy. "This is Sasha, Tommie, and Candi. Everyone, this is Melondy."

Sasha got up, walked towards Melondy with her arms extended to hug her. "Hi Melondy, I'm so glad to finally meet you. Do you want something to eat? I can make you a shrimp salad sandwich if you like."

"Oh thanks, I guess I am a little hungry; have been running errands all morning, that's why I'm so late."

Staring at Melondy for a few seconds, looking her up and down, she let out a loud awful belch. "Excuse me, I'm Tomika. Nice contacts, a little much though."

"I'm sorry, contacts?"

"Tommieee! You promised. I'm sorry, Melondy, her medication wearing off. Tommie, they are not contacts. That is her God-given green eyes!" interrupted Fuchsia.

"Don't pay her any mind, she's just joking. Hi, I'm Candi and, like Sasha, I'm glad to meet you too. Tommie is too, she's just messing. You really do have beautiful green eyes, they are so deeply piercing. I know you get a lot of comments on your eyes."

"Thanks, yes but I'm used to it now," she said as she took her garment bag and hung it in the closet in the foyer.

"Oh snap! We left our gowns in the car!" Candi jumped up after seeing Melondy hang up her things. She ran out to the car to get their clothes as well.

"Well, I guess you are good for something, aren't you Miss Green eyes?" Tommie said as she met Candi at the door to gather their things.

"Hey Tommie, come on, lay off the lady. Fuchsia just asked us to accept her friend," Candi whispered to Tommie as they hung up their clothes.

"I'm just teasing, but I'll lay off," she sneered.

Meanwhile, in the kitchen, Mitch, Melondy, Sasha and Fuchsia were talking and laughing. They were all happily talking as though nothing had taken place.

"What's so funny?" Tommie said as she entered into the kitchen.

"Melondy was just telling us how she picked up the wrong dress at the tailor yesterday and didn't notice until this morning when she began getting her things together."

"Wow, what a bummer. It's a good thing you found out before you got here with this nervous bride," Tommie chimed in.

"Yes, I'm so happy too. Don't want to upset the bride," smiling Melondy responded. "Plus, I really don't want to upset the groom either; I will never be live with it."

"Speaking of the groom, did you see him this morning?" Fuchsia asked Melondy.

"Yes, I made sure he was taken care of, and he had everything in order, so he could rest. He's just as nervous as his bride!" she said with excitement in her voice.

"Thanks, I appreciate you looking out for him today. He would say he doesn't need any help, but I know better."

"Hmm, seems like you know Mr. Wonderful real well," Sasha stated as she began tiding up the kitchen.

"Yes, I have known him for a few years now," Melondy responded.

Fuchsia opened the pantry to get clean trash bags, then, spun around to face Tommie. "She's his personnel assistant and have worked with him for many years. She's trustworthy and faithful, your honor."

"Why you looking at me? She asked, not me!" Tommie shouted.

"Because I know you and what you were about to say, so, I stated my case first."

"Well, I was just thinking, plus, who told you to be all up in my mind like that?"

"What! As crazy as you are Tommie, we'd be surprised if there's any room in there to think anything else!" Candi burst into the conversation.

"Hahaha, funny! Anyway, how much time do we have before we need to leave? I'm tired, you know how it is when I eat a little something," Tommie said, stretching as she walked towards the staircase, picked up her white Coach bag and tossed it over her shoulders. "I need to take me a hot shower and a quick nap, then,

I'll be good. Can I take my normal room or is it Ms. Green eye assistant's room?" She said sarcastically.

"Take the room and shut up please." Candi chimed in as she began gathering her things too; they left and headed up the staircase. "Any particular room you had in mind for us and what time to be ready?"

"The time now is two forty-five exactly! So, please be ready to leave at six forty-five precisely!" Fuchsia shouted.

"You ladies go ahead, I'll take whichever room is vacant," Melondy said as she looked at Fuchsia and smiled, nodding her head, indicating that she was fine in any room.

Whenever she would stay over with Fuchsia, she would sleep in the room she called sunshine. The room was painted the color alabaster, and everything was either trimmed or accented with the warmest yellow she has ever seen. She loved how Fuchsia had the house remodeled; every room had a meaning and purpose. No matter what room a person stayed in, the colors and atmosphere of that particular room greeted its guest with a warm embrace.

"Hey Ms. Green eyes, we left the yellow room for you; it seems to suite you better, being that you all sunshine and all!" Tommie shouted as you could hear her close the bedroom door, walked into the next room and close it shut behind her.

"I apologize Melondy, but I gave you a heads-up last week!" smiling at her as they climbed the staircase. "See you in a few. Mitch, get some rest like the others."

Fuchsia opened her bedroom suite and a sudden sense of nervousness came upon her. Light dampness filled her armpits, and tiny beads of sweat formed on her forehead. *Am I ready for this, can I do this? These are my last moments of singleness; it will never be just me and Lady any longer. Do I really want kids? I, a mother, a wife? I never thought this day would come; no, I never thought I would give in and allow someone else into my heart or space.* Burying her head in her pillow with her feet straddling across her bed, fear leaped upon her mind.

Maybe I won't be a good enough wife for him. What if he wakes up one morning and says he's not happy or fulfilled, then what? Could he change his mind like that, would he? Maybe I should just save myself and him the future heartache and call if off. Man, all the money that he spent on this wedding and the honeymoon, not allowing me to add one dime except for my dress and shoes. He would lose a lot of nonrefundable money; he probably would kill me for that one. Better dead than hurt again.

She reached for her cell phone to call Marvin. Suddenly, the sound of light tapping on the bedroom door caused her to lay the phone down beside the pillow.

"Yes, who is it?"

"Melondy, may I come in?"

"Sure, what's up?"

"I was told to bring you this note," opening the door with a note in hand, she handed it to Fuchsia and walked out, closing the door behind her.

"It's from Marvin. Oh, what if he called it off? Coward! I should have expected this," she mumbled to herself as she tore open the note.

Dear Fuchsia,

Today is the day that I choose to marry my friend. Today is the day I choose to make you my wife. As the sun was making its grand entrance for this day, my heart leaped knowing that today is the day we join as husband and wife.

Fuchsia, the day that you showed up in my life was the day I began to see new life. I thought I understood the verse, 'He who finds a wife finds a good thing and obtain favor from the Lord,' but that day, finding you, it all became so clear. I know you falling in love with me was not on your agenda, but boy, am I glad that you allowed me in and allowed me to love you. Today, you may be nervous, questioning if this is real or not but let me assure you that our love is as real and pure as they come. I promise to love you, to protect you, to cherish you, to never put anyone before you, to never neglect you, to always be a dependable husband and a nurturing lover, to never be selfish, and never too demanding, to always look for the best in you and to always give you the best of me. You will never be second place or an afterthought; I will keep you as the apple of my eye. I will never judge you, always giving you room to make mistakes as we will but never holding you captive because of them. I will always give you room to grow and explore the greatness in you that you may fulfill your purpose and never become stagnant.

Fuchsia, my promise to you this day is more than standing before the altar and Bishop; it's standing in a holy realm of matrimony before God and His angels to say to you, "I do." I want you to hold this part of my heart in your heart, that as you walk down the aisle, not only will I take your hand as my wife, but we will join heart to heart, soul to soul, as one husband to one wife till death do us part. This is my covenant to you this day, my bride, my wife.

See you soon,

Your husband-to-be.

Tears flowed down her cheeks as she gently folded the letter and kissed it. She let out a sigh of relief, picked her phone and dialed.

Before she could say 'Hello,' the voice chimed, "Hey Sunshine, you okay?"

"Yes," she sniffled. "I just wanted to hear your voice and tell you I love you with all my heart, and thank you for loving me, even the broken me."

"Babe, Sunshine, we've all been broken a time or two. The good thing about being broken is that we are amendable. You may have been broken but you were not destroyed. I count it an honor to love all your brokenness 'til they all become whole. You give me joy because when I thought I couldn't love, you proved me wrong. I never knew love 'til the sun shined on this beautiful flower and presented her to me. You brought back the sunshine, Fuchsia. Were you resting? You know it's a big evening ahead and a bigger night a-waiting"

They both started giggling like young kids on their first date.

"Tonight, I will celebrate my love with you," he sang.

"Hey Marvin, you know I'm really nervous about tonight. I almost called you and cancelled."

"Really? Hey Fuchsia, you think I didn't know? That's why I gave Melondy the letter; I told her the minute you go off alone to make sure she gives it to you. You know, I'm supposed to know my wife, and knowing her means cognizant of her needs, her emotions and her desire, especially if I want to live in a peaceful house."

"You are a mess, but a thoughtful thinking mess, and my mess. Can I say I'm so glad you chose me to be your Mrs. Mess! I wouldn't have it any other way! Thanks for the letter, you know it broke me down, took my running shoes and threw them away! I'm ready to be your wife, and I mean I'm ready! Inside and out,

I'm ready. For real, after that note, we can slip out of the church into the Pastors study and get it on!

"Hahaha! Oh, babe, I feel you on that!"

"Whew! Man, oh man, I wish."

"No, I really feel you on that. You know I'm still a man, just not a married man at this moment. So, on that note babe, it's time for the shower."

"Aw, ok, I love you, my husband-to-be. See you in a few."

"I'm waiting your arrival, love you more."

Giggling, she rolled around *on the ultimate luxury bed linens* in her one hundred percent Egyptian cotton, the *Clemys Border collection* bed set from Frette; *this was one investment that totally was worth the five, seven thousand plus dollars spent*, she thought every time she snuggled into her bed.

"Man, I'm so madly in love with him, Lady," as Lady was rolling around the bottom of the bed panting as if she was giggling with her. "In a few hours, it won't just be you and me, it will be three! Oh wow, I'm really going to tie the knot," she said, looking down at the three-karat heart shape diamond engagement ring on her hand, remembering the day she first laid eyes on this ring not knowing that one day she would be wearing it.

CHAPTER THIRTEEN

(Eighteen months ago)

G azing out the window of the small office she shared with her co-worker Susan, the wind blowing a slightly cool breeze that afternoon; *such a beautiful afternoon,* Fuchsia thought.

"Hey, I think I might be a little longer on my lunch break, it's a good day for an afternoon walk, and plus, I want to grab a smoothie from that new juice bar. You want me to bring you one back? My treat if you cover my calls 'til I get back, deal?" Fuchsia said as she swung her chair around with a cunning grin.

"You a trip, Fuchsia! Ok, and make it a large smoothie!" Susan replied.

The sun peeked through between the trees as the wind danced around Fuchsia, blowing her hair across her face. She strolled along the pavement, window shopping. There, as she sipped her tropical freshly made smoothie, the most stunning ring caught her eyes in the jeweler's shop.

"Come on in, get a better look. It's a remarkable piece, isn't it?" a voice sang as her eyes were locked on the most beautiful ring she ever saw.

"Oh no, I'm just window gazing, plus, I was just strolling by."

"Well honey, this piece here only attracts a certain type of girl, and you my dear must be her! No harm in seeing up close, come on in," she said as she motioned Fuchsia into the store with her finger glistening with diamonds.

"Oh ok, I'll just take a moment."

Fuchsia stepped in.

"Here, try it on, so you can get the full effect of its brilliance."

"Wow! I never had the pleasure of being introduced to such an amazing ring!"

"It's three karats platinum," the jeweler paused as a gentleman entered the store. "Oh sir, I will be right with you in one minute."

A deep voice responded, "No problem, Ma'am; just here to pick up my watch from repair. I'll browse while I wait."

This voice grabbed her attention like none other, Fuchsia turned to see who was behind such a unique tone.

"Hello there, that's a beautiful ring you have there. Someone is a lucky guy," he said as he smiled with a warm glean in his eye.

"Oh, no! I'm just admiring! Plus, why does it have to be a lucky guy? Can't a lady be shopping for herself? she sarcastically responded with a slight grin. *Man, he fine*, she thought to herself as she handed the ring back to the sales lady. "I will put this on my dream list as I wait for my dream guy," she turned to walk out the door.

"Hey, please don't leave on my account."

"Really, you think you got that much power? Hahaha," she laughed as she took a sip of her smoothie and closed the door behind her.

Strolling along, enjoying the beautiful day, she smiled to herself about the encounter she just had when, suddenly running up behind her, the deep voice startled her. "Hey, what's the hurry? I want to apologize, I didn't mean to offend you."

Stopping in her tracks, "Offend me? Do I look like I'm offended or a weak damsel that needs saving?" she replied with a snappy tone.

"Whoa, I apologize. I didn't mean any harm, let me start over. Hello, my name is Marvin, how are you today?" he said in the most gentlemanly tone she ever heard.

"Hello Marvin, I'm Fuchsia, and forgive me. I'm always in defensive, protective mode, I deeply apologize. My God-mom says it's a bad habit I have," she said as she bowed her head in shameful smile.

"No need to apologize, I was too forward. Tell your God-mom it wasn't you this time, it was my fault."

"Hahaha, yeah right, like she would believe me," she said as she lifted her head and smiled at him.

"Wow," he stared with a look of amazement at her, thought she's beautiful! "You out for lunch on lunch break?"

"Yeah, you can say that. I'm supposed to bring my co-worker a smoothie, but I got caught up in how beautiful the day is. I should return but I just wanted to hang out a little longer, today is so beautiful."

"It sure feels like it, and unusual. Can I walk you back, if that's not to forward?"

"How do I know I can trust you? How can I be sure you won't try to snatch me up off this street? She grinned.

"Well, we can stop back by the jewelers on the way up the street, and you can tell them I'm walking you back to work. They have my information because I just had a watch repaired there, would that work?" he said with all sincerity.

"Oh no, I was joking!" laughingly, she said. "For some reason, I feel comfortable with you, and I'm usually a good judge of character. I only made one mistake in my life about a person, and that was because I got side tracked, but you can bet that won't happen again!"

"Don't you have to get back to work somewhere also?"

"No, I'm good. I don't have any afternoon meetings today, so, I'm all yours."

"Mine? I don't even know you!"

"Not yet, you don't but I feel like I've known you a long time," he said as they strolled along heading to her office building.

"Well, this is where I leave you. I need to get in here and act like I have a J O B!"

"Shoot! Shoot! Shoot! You distracted me, and I forgot Susan's smoothie! She's going to kill me! Darn!"

"Oh man, I apologize. Let me run to get it for her, that's the least I can do since I distracted you. I hope it was a good distraction! What flavor would she want?"

"Really, sir? You a trip. If I didn't know better, I would say it's a setup! Thanks for covering me! I owe you! Any fruity flavor, just make sure it's large," she said as she reached in her purse to take out cash.

"I don't want your cash. I got this, it's the least I can do."

"Thanks. When you come back, ring the top bell and I will buzz you in. Take the elevator upstairs; I'm in the second office to the right. Thanks, I owe you a smoothie," she said as she disappeared into the building.

"Fuchsia, girl, where is the smoothie you promised me? I knew I couldn't rely on you!" Susan shouted as Fuchsia danced through the doorway. "And you have the nerve to come back here dancing, what's wrong with you?"

"Girl, I just met the most handsome incredible man! I think I could actually let my guard down for once and date this man!"

"What? Who? Wait a minute, hold up. Say this again, I think I'm hearing things!"

"You heard me!" she giggled as she sat at her desk.

"How did you meet him? Do tell!"

She began explaining her afternoon encounter with such excitement leaving no details out.

"Girl, is he married, have kids, own a house?" Susan questioned.

"I don't know! I didn't ask the man for a resume!"

Looking cross-eyed at Fuchsia, "Why? Nowadays, I want to know everything! And know it before our first date! That way, I know if I even want to go out with you!"

"See, that's our difference! I'm not even trying to date! I don't need no man hovering over me!" Fuchsia snapped.

"You right cause I don't care if he hover, roll, or sit as long as it's on me!" bursting out in laughter, she swung her chair back around, facing her desk.

(Wedding day)

She looked at her ring, smiling. *Who would ever have thought that because of you*, (staring at her engagement ring) *I would find the man of my dreams or that he would find me?* She reminisced on how she, because of her fears and insecurities, almost lost him forever until she saw him at Ms. Dee's funeral. She sighed at the thought of Ms. Dee being gone and at the same time smiling because she believed Ms. Dee had it in her plan. However, sad that it didn't happen until after she passed.

"Sweet child, why you keep running from love? Why won't you answer this man's calls? When am I going to meet him? You've been running from that man for weeks now but one day, love is going to catch up with you and there will be no more running! I know just the man for you, and when you ready..." Ms. Dee would say, pointing her finger at Fuchsia, "When you ready, he will certainly find you."

Fuchsia rolled over and balled her pillow under her head, thinking out loud. "Did you have to leave me for him to find me? A funeral – what a way to begin a relationship. I guess it's a true saying: something has to die in order for something to come to life. I can't even believe it myself; I'm marrying a Pastor! Me! Fuchsia, a first lady," sighing again. "Lord, what did I get myself into? Nonetheless, I love Marvin so much and I love the way he loves me even more."

She turned over to pick up, by her night stand, the small glass vase containing a single Fuchsia flower that appears to be floating in a clear jellied liquid. She remembered what Marvin said the day he gave it to her – the day she knew she was in love.

CHAPTER FOURTEEN

(9 months ago)

Feelings of empty pain filled every part of Fuchsia's being as she felt all alone on that church pew, thinking to herself, *I forgot to call Candi and Tommie; they would have been here with me. I can't believe Ms. Dee really had no family. What am I going to do without her in my life?* She sat and stared at the beautiful white casket decorated with beautiful flowers, and Ms. Dee laying there as if she was only asleep with such an astounding peace on her face. The choir was singing, Fuchsia could hear people's sniffles all around. Trying not to show irksomeness as the people lined up to shake her hand, and give their "I'm sorry for your loss," she closed her eyes. *Please, please, stop. Just leave me alone. Please, no more hugs, no more I'm sorry. Don't you see I just want to sit here and say goodbye to my God-mom in peace? Just let me cry alone, and grieve on my own. You have nothing to be sorry for, she lived a good long life. She's in a better place as she would often say of others who passed on before her. Hey grandma Lydia, please take care of Ms. Dee because she took great care of me. I love you both so much, and I'm going to miss you both. I can't even begin to think about me; who's going to love me now that you are both gone?* The thoughts of being alone again began to sink deep in her soul. She felt the warmth of her tears streaming down her face which caused her to tighten her closed eyes even more, as if she never wanted them to open again. She could feel hands touching her on her head, then her back, and on her knees. She almost screamed "Please, please, stop touching me" when, suddenly, a familiar voice broke through her thoughts.

"Sister, Sister," the voice said.

"Ma'am, I'm Pastor Marvin. I want to know if it's okay to close the casket? I would like to begin the home going memorial now." This time the voice came closer as if he was kneeling in front of her.

A familiar peace came upon her as she tried to open her tear-filled eyes. Having blinked a couple of times, trying to get a focus, and as her eyes cleared a path to see, she lifted her head in the direction of the voice.

"What? What are you doing here? How did you find me? Are you following me?" she said, whispering to him.

"No, I assure you I haven't followed you. This is my church; I've pastored here for years and Ms. Dee was a faithful member. I didn't know you knew her. So, you are the young lady she often spoke of, her god-daughter, right?" He responded in a compassionate tone.

"Yes, yes I am, and yes, you can begin," she said softly.

As pastor Marvin went back to the pulpit, he motioned one of the ladies on the choir to go sit with Fuchsia. The young lady sat beside her and held her hand as they covered Ms. Dee and closed the casket.

"I love you and will miss you, Ms. Dee," Fuchsia said softly as the undertaker fastened the casket.

The young lady didn't leave her side during the rest of the service. When the service was complete, and were about to roll Ms. Dee out of the church, the young lady whispered to Fuchsia, "Can I ride with you to the burial?"

"Yes, I would like that, thank you."

As she was about to board the limousine, a hand reached out to help her. She looked up to him, "Thank you, thank you. That was a beautiful service; Ms. Dee often spoke of you, how she loved her pastor."

"Thank you. We all here loved Ms. Dee. Will you be ok?"

Melondy walked up towards them, "Pastor Marvin, I'm going to ride along with her to the burial."

"Great, thanks Melondy."

Just as he was about to close the limousine door, he pulled out his business card from his suit coat pocket, and handed it to Fuchsia. "Please, give me a call. I'm here for you," he said, holding her hand a second longer, his eyes locked in on hers. "Call me, please." He closed the door.

"Pastor Marvin; he is a wonderful man, a very sincere man."

Fuchsia never said a word the entire ride to the burial nor on her way home.

The evening sun was beginning to set, the breeze was warmly blowing as the palm trees swayed gently. Sitting on the fancy white iron bench Ms. Dee would often sit on, Fuchsia watched as the birds were flying in and out of the bird feed houses that nestled at the end of the garden. Ms. Dee used to say it was the most peaceful place to sit, right there in that beautiful garden. Sitting there, sipping her warm cup of tea in her favorite mug that grandma Lydia gave her, it was almost as though she could feel Ms. Dee's presence right there with her. Wiped out from the funeral, all she wanted to do is sit in peace.

Fuchsia could hear the doorbell chiming throughout the house, but knowing she wasn't expecting company, she didn't move except to place her tea cup on the white iron table beside the bench. The door chimes rang again. None of the dogs budged; they rested beside her in the garden as though they weren't expecting anyone too. Closing her eyes as the warm sun was setting directly on her face, she was startled by the sudden sound of footsteps. She stood up abruptly and turned towards the sound.

"I apologize, I didn't mean to startle you."

"Marvin? Is that you? What are you doing here?" She questioned in a peaceful manner.

"I came to check on you. I was concerned if you were going to be okay," he said as he walked towards the garden where she was sitting. "This has always been her favorite place to mediate, she often said."

"May I sit with you?" he asked

"You don't give up, do you?"

"Should I?"

"Why do you keep calling me even though I won't answer?" She asked him as she shifted for him to take his seat.

"The question is why won't you answer when you know I'm calling you?"

Her focus was on his face as though it was the first time seeing him. The sun appeared as though it was resting right on his shoulders, his features were so bold, and his hair so dark. Everything about him seemed too good to be true. Without saying a word, she just stared at his face.

Slowly, he lifted his hand to her face and gently stroked down her right hairline, down to her cheek.

"Why are you afraid of me, have I given you a reason to fear me?"

His touch was soothing; it was like something she longed for. She wanted to melt in his hand but quickly pushed his hand away.

"What are you doing? I never gave you permission to touch me! By the way, I'm not afraid of you or no man! So, let's get that straight first!"

"Okay, let's calm down, I meant no harm. I just was moving the hair that was about to get in your eye, that's all. Why so defensive? I am not the man who hurt you. Whoever he was, please don't take his anger out on me." Standing up to leave, "Look, I'm not that guy. I don't hurt women, and you being afraid of me makes me uncomfortable. So, I think it's better that I leave," he said.

"Wait, wait. No, don't go. I apologize. You are right, you have been a perfect gentleman every time I see you. Please, sit. Let's start over, and no, I'm not ok. I really don't want to be alone in this house tonight."

Finally, she felt relieved to tell him her truth. "Listen," she touched his hand, "The truth is I have never been on a real date, never had a boyfriend, never had a real kiss, or an invited touch. I don't know how to date but the crazy thing is I have been exposed to a whole lot. I don't know my father, I haven't seen my mother or brother in years, I don't smoke or drink, I'm learning not to cuss. Yes, I'm angry but not at you. You wanted to know about me, so, Mr. Pastor Sir, this is me."

"Okay, okay. I didn't mean to get your history in one paragraph, that's what time is for but I'm glad you finally opened up," he humbly responded.

Her face became so tensed that her eyebrows began to wrinkle. "Okay, now that you know that I am a messed-up soul, do you still want to continue chasing me?

With a serious look, "Fuchsia, I'm not chasing. I'm pursing my wife." His response was direct with a certainty, however, said in a calm manner.

"What! Wait a minute! Your what?" For the first time she burst into laughter. "Okay, now I know you kinda crazy!"

Marvin's eyes gleamed with a thin smile. He reached out to touch her fingers, "Fuchsia, from the first moment my eyes caught your eyes, I knew you were special. That afternoon walk, though short, was the most amazing day I had in a very long time. I knew you were the lady for me that day. As for being messed-up, that's your opinion, and seeing you've never dated, never had kissed or anything like that, it would be my honor to take you on your first date and to court you in a proper manner. I would love to hear your dreams and aspirations, to share new discoveries with you. I promise to not push you and allow you to get to know me, learn to trust me, give you space when you need it. I'm willing to share my love with you, and most importantly to wait for you.

"Fuchsia, I already know you are one day going to be my wife. I have waited months to see and talk to you again, and I'm not going to lose you again. If I have to come sit in this garden every day, I'm willing to do so." He gently squeezed her fingers, then released them as he stared directly into her eyes.

Nervous to open her mouth not knowing what to say to him, she finally nodded and spoke up. "I hear you, I really do, but what makes you certain I'm the one? What makes you think I want to be married let alone married to you?"

"Fuchsia, Ms. Dee was like a mother to me when I first relocated here. She would come to the church every afternoon and bring me lunch. We would talk for hours if I had no appointments; that woman was so full of wisdom. She asked me one day if I was married, then asked why I wasn't. I told her I don't know, I ever thought about marriage, more so, I'm a loner. Besides, I didn't feel as if I was a good candidate for a husband, my past and all.

"She looked in my eyes and said to me, 'Pastor Marvin, you are forgiven, now forgive yourself of whatever you have done.' She began telling me that I, too, was worthy to be loved and one day I would have to open my heart and allow myself to be loved. That sounded crazy to me because I thought that I was open for love, but when she finished breaking it down to me, I realized that she was right, and I had given myself only to the ministry and I totally blocked my very own needs. She told me that I had so much love to give and one day the door will open, and I will come out and experience the life and love that has been ordained for me. She also told me, one day, I will find my wife and I will know it when I see her. 'When you find her, hold on to her and don't waste time, marry her.' So, that day when I saw you, I finally understood what she meant," he smiled, "Even though I didn't know you were going to be a runner, and I was going to need patience and keep pursuing until I caught you!" He chuckled.

She burst in laughter. "We will see. We will see."

Silence pervaded the atmosphere as they stared at the bright orange sun that was setting behind the trees only with a glimpse of its outer edges. Fuchsia sat back on the bench, holding on to every word. A sense of peace came over her like she never experienced before. She thought to herself, *Ms. Dee was right, maybe he is the one for me.*

As they sat there quietly enjoying the sunset, she slowly rested her head on his shoulders and he, in turn, held her hand.

Dusk began to fill the garden and the lanterns began to glow softly. Marvin positioned his chin on her forehead, "Hey it's getting late, and a little cold. I don't want you sitting out here too long, and I'm not trying to overstay my welcome. Let's get you inside. I will make sure you are fine, then, I will leave and return tomorrow, okay?"

Lifting her head off his shoulder, "Yes I guess you are right." She stood up, adjusting her sundress.

He took her by the hand and led her through the garden to the patio door of the Florida room. As they entered, Marvin closed the door and made sure it was locked; he also adjusted the curtains and checked the windows.

"What you doing?" she asked in curiosity.

"Making sure everything is locked and secure."

"Oh, okay," she said as she stood there watching him go around checking everything.

"You think something's going to happen to me or something?"

"No, I'm making sure nothing can."

Standing in amazement as she watched him check and closed the windows. Never in her life has she experienced a man making sure she was safe before.

Turning to look at her, "Okay, everything is secure. Is there anything you need before I leave?"

"No, thanks. I'm fine," she said softly as they walked towards the front door.

She unlocked the front door, paused for a moment and looked him in the eye. "This is new for me, so, please be patient with me. I have never allowed a man to get close, and if I can be real with you, I don't even know how to begin. I am nervous but at the same time, I'm willing to try."

Gently, Marvin touched her cheek, then he slowly moved close to her and kissed her forehead. "I'm a patient man, you don't have to be nervous. I promise never to bring you harm; we going to allow the natural nature of love to take its course."

A warm feeling came over her, one she never experienced before. She smiled at him as he stepped over the threshold.

Before closing the door, he looked back at her, "See you tomorrow, rest well tonight. Oh, and if you need me, just call, I will be here."

After closing the door, Fuchsia locked the door, then leaned on the closed door. "Ms. Dee, you a mess! I know you set this up," she giggled as she ran up the flight of stairs. She ran into her room and jumped on her bed, grabbing her pillow and squeezing it tight.

"Wow! Wow! OMG! His lips were so soft!" she screamed into her pillow. She laid there, reminiscing what just happened the rest of the night until she fell off to sleep.

Waking up to the sound of the trash men tossing cans around and shouting, she jumped up looking at the alarm clock that sat on her night stand, "Eight o' clock! Man! I must have been tired!"

She noticed she was still in the clothes she had on yesterday. "Oh now, Fuchs, you broke your cardinal rule. Never Ever get in the bed in your outside clothes." She grunted to herself as she slid out the bed and began removing the bed linens. Having placed them in the hamper, she undressed and tossed the clothes into the hamper as well.

Naked, she walked to her in-suite bathroom. Just as she was about to use the toilet, she heard her phone chimed, letting her know she just received a text.

Mumbling to herself as she sat on the toilet, "Who in the world is texting me this early?"

She washed her hands, then reached for her toothbrush when her phone chimed again. "Okay, okay, give me a second!" she shouted as if the messenger could hear her.

She took a clean face cloth as she continued her daily ritual. Afterwards, she jumped into the hot shower. Her favorite shower gel scent lit up the bathroom with the awakening scents of citrus with hints of vanilla and ambers. As she stepped out of the shower with her body wrapped in an oversized plush towel, a strange feeling turned in her stomach. She opened her eyes wide and blurted out. "Wait a minute, was I dreaming last night?"

With the towel still wrapped around her, she hurried out of her bedroom suite down the hall to Ms. Dee's bedroom suite. Knocking on her door as she opened it, "Ms. Dee, are you awake? I need to tell you about this dream I had last night!"

A sudden feeling of loneliness came over her like a flood. Ms. Dee's bed was just as she left it; her satin white robe laying at the foot of her bed. She could smell Ms. Dee's favorite perfume that filled the room. Standing there in the middle of the room, fear and pain overwhelmed her at the same time. She began to tremble; her legs became weak. Immediately, she turned, closing the bedroom door. Stumbling down the hall, she held her stomach as she made it back to her bedroom suite. She fell on her bed and curled up into a fetal position, holding her pillow under her head, she cried uncontrollably until she drifted off to sleep.

The smell of bacon with the sweet aroma of cinnamon filled the kitchen, reaching Fuchsia's bedroom. A soft tapping began to arouse her from her sleep, she could hear soft footsteps coming towards her as she tried to pry her puffy eyes open.

"Ms. Fuchsia, Ms. Fuchsia," Katrina said as she stretched her hand to touch Fuchsia's forehead.

Startled, "Katrina!" she said as she leaped into Katrina's arms, her bath towel fell off her body.

Tears again filling her puffy eyes, she mumbled, "I'm so sorry. I didn't know how to reach you guys, but..." it was as if the words were stuck somewhere inside her chest.

"Shush now, it's ok, dear. Kimberly and I came home last evening, we left vacation a few days early. It was as if something or someone was calling us home. We both felt it. When we arrived here this morning, we knew as soon as we opened the door, then we saw the beautiful obituary laying on the glass table in the foyer."

Katrina bent to pick up the bath towel to cover Fuchsia's naked body; she wrapped the towel around her as she helped her to sit on the bed.

She, sniffling, trying to not let Fuchsia see her cry, "Kimberly and I rushed up the stairs looking for you, and we saw you curled up on top the bed in your towel and Brice laying on the floor beside you. So, we took Brice down to feed him and Kimberly started breakfast for you. Come honey, we know you haven't eaten much, and you need to eat. Let's get some clothes on you," Katrina said as she went to the dresser drawers to pick out some underwear.

"Thank you, Katrina, I'm so glad you home. I didn't know what to do. I woke up this morning, took a shower and went running to Ms. Dee's room. I thought it was all a dream but when I opened the door, it hit me hard, so hard," shaking her head in disbelief.

"I know honey, I know. Don't worry, Kimberly and I will take care of everything. We are here now," she said as she handed Fuchsia her undergarments and her two-piece loungewear.

As she helped Fuchsia down the stairs, she could see how frail she had become. "Honey, when was the last time you had a meal?"

"Oh, I don't even remember. Maybe a couple days ago," she responded.

As they entered the kitchen, Kimberly was at the oven removing the homemade cinnamon rolls. She looked up as they came in, placing the hot pan on top the stove, she walked to Fuchsia with her arms extended. "Oh sweetheart, I'm so sorry we weren't here for you," she said as she hugged her tightly.

"No, I believe Ms. Dee sent you on vacation cause she knew she was leaving and she wanted to make certain you would have a great vacation."

Adjusting her apron, "I made your favorites this morning; hot cinnamon rolls, bacon, eggs, and fried apples!" Kimberly said, trying to smile through her pain.

"Thank you, I love you guys so much!"

"Do you want to eat in the Florida room, or do you want me to set a table in the garden for you?" Katrina said.

Looking at the wall clock in the kitchen, "Wow, it's noon already?"

"Yes, you needed to rest," said Katrina.

"Okay, let's eat in the garden," Fuchsia replied as she headed out through the French doors.

Katrina began setting the small round marbled table that was just off the patio at the beginning of the garden. Then dusting off the white patio chairs, she could hear a car pulling up into the front driveway.

"Are you expecting company this afternoon?

Sitting in the chair that Katrina just dusted, "No, I'm not."

The chimes of the doorbell rang throughout the house, the sounds could be heard from the patio. Kimberly placed the pot holders down and walked to the foyer to answer the door while Katrina was busy on the patio with Fuchsia.

Kimberly opened the heavy oak and beveled glass door. "Hello, how may I help you?" She asked the gentleman whose back was turned as he stood on the front porch.

Turning around to respond, "Good morning, I'm..."

Interrupting him before he could finish his sentence, Katrina blurted with excitement, "Pastor Marvin, what are you doing here?" She extended the door to allow him to enter.

"Good afternoon, how are you today?"

"I'm fine, thank you."

"I'm here to check on Fuchsia, is she available?"

"Yes, Pastor. She just went to sit on the patio for brunch, would you like me to take you to her?" Katrina said without thinking or asking Fuchsia if she was up for company.

While Kimberly went back to the kitchen to continue preparing brunch for Fuchsia, Katrina lead Marvin through the great room towards the Patio. Shaking her head, as she walked over to the stove, Kimberly muttered, "Hope Fuchsia don't chew her head off bringing a man to her."

Opening the French doors and stepping onto the Patio, Katrina announced who was coming her way. "Ms. Fuchsia, it's Pastor Marvin from Ms. Dee's church coming to check on you."

Then she turned to Marvin, "Would you be joining her for brunch?"

Fuchsia surprised at Katrina's announcement quickly turned around with a surprised look on her face. Just as she was about to open her mouth to yell "No," her eyes met Marvin's, and she just nodded.

"Hey there," she said softly as she remembered last evening and how pleasant it was to have him there with her.

"Katrina, just please have Kimberly prepare for Pastor Marvin as well. Oh, and thank you," she said in a whisper.

Marvin walked over to the patio table, pulled the chair out and sat down in front of Fuchsia. "Hey, how are you today? I started to call you, but I didn't have a direct number for you, so, I took a chance on coming by hoping you would let me in." He adjusted his chair, "But I was prepared to sit and wait until you did," he chuckled.

"You a mess," she said as she shook her head sideways.

"I told you last evening I would check on you today."

"Yeah, you did, but I thought maybe later in the evening, not early noon," she said as she tried to adjust her loosely flowing ponytail.

"Hey, you fine. No need in trying to fix perfection. Besides, I was up early for my morning workout, and I tried to wait as long as I could, but I wanted to see you as soon as possible," he said as he reached his hand across the marbled table to touch hers.

Nervously she wiggled her fingers under his hands, gazed into his eyes for a moment, then she turned to watch a bird that landed in the bird feed. Looking back at him, she softly spoke up. "Really, why me? What is it about me that makes you keep on trying?"

"My question back at you is why not you? But my answer is: from the moment I laid eyes on you at the jewelers, there was something magical I felt about you that I have never felt before. Believe me when I say every time you rejected me, to myself I would say no more but then my spirit would not let me give up. So, I vowed to myself that when the day comes and I'm able to see you again, I would not let you go. So, here I am, and I'm not letting go."

Silence filled everywhere as she sat there, staring into his eyes; her heart started beating fast, one side of her wanted to run but the other side encouraged her to stay and listen to him.

The silence was interrupted by the sound of the patio door opening up, Kimberly and Katrina both with trays in their hands stepped onto the patio. Each holding the tray in one hand, they began placing the food in the center of the table. The warm aroma of the hot cinnamon rolls made its way to both Marvin and Fuchsia's nose; simultaneously, they both gave a warm sigh, "Hmm."

As Katrina was arranging the food nicely on the table in front of Fuchsia and Marvin, Kimberly went into the house and brought back a tray of white with gold trim dinnerware, and a small teapot of green tea with hints of apples and mangoes.

Katrina placed a set of dinnerware in front of both Fuchsia and Marvin, along with beautiful floral white and gold tea cups and saucers. Kimberly poured tea into both cups and placed the teapot on the table. The only prominent sound was that of the hummingbird flying around the garden as they waited patiently for either Kimberly or her to finish. Placing the last dish of cooked apples in the center of the table, Kimberly looked over the table and said to Fuchsia, "Is there anything else I can get you?"

"No, I think we are good. Thank you both," Fuchsia replied.

Katrina and Kimberly both returned inside, closing the patio door behind them.

Marvin, with amazement in his voice, spoke up, breaking the silence, "Wow! This is breakfast fit for a queen!" He stretched his hand to bless the food.

"Amen," Fuchsia echoed as Marvin completed the blessing.

"Do they always cook breakfast like this?"

"Yeah, pretty much. They do change up on a variety of things, but Ms. Dee was a breakfast and dinner kind of woman. Lunch, she liked simple but enjoyed a variety of choices. I think she also did this so that the ladies could eat well too and take home whatever was left for their families. Her heart was so gracious towards people," she responded while breaking apart the hot cinnamon rolls.

She bit into the cinnamon roll; its sweet butter taste smeared her taste bud. Taking her napkin, she covered her lips, "These are my favorite! Please try one, you will see why I go for these first!"

He reached for one and took a bite, his eyes lit up and he also covered his mouth, "OMG! These are incredible! Man, I would be a fat boy with these in the house every day!" He burst into laughter as he took a second bite.

Laughing along with him, "I know, I know! However, she knows only to make them once a week because I would eat the whole pan myself!"

"This breakfast is amazing; the cook knows her way around the kitchen! Hey, will they stay on with you now that Ms. Dee has transitioned?"

"Oh, I don't know. I haven't even given it a thought. Today is the first time I saw or talked to them; Ms. Dee sent them and their family on a paid vacation. So, they were not here when she passed; they only found out today when they arrived at work.

"Katrina found me in a bad way this morning when she woke me up. I had a really rough early morning. I thought it was all a dream; I went rushing into Ms. Dee's room, thinking I was going to tell her about a dream of you but reality hit me hard, and the pain overwhelmed me so bad that I crashed on my bed and cried myself back to sleep still wrapped in my bath towel. I don't know how long I was out before she awakened me."

Placing his fork down unto his plate, he reached out and touched the side of her face, "Hey, why didn't you call me? I told you I'm here for you; it doesn't matter how late or how early, I will be here."

"I know, I heard you, but I've never ever had to depend on a man before to comfort me. So, I really didn't know how to reach out and I really didn't know if you really meant it," she said as she used her free hand to wipe her mouth and hand with the napkin.

"Listen, I meant what I said. I'm here and I'm not going anywhere. If I have to sleep in a guest room so that you are not alone at night, I will. Whatever it will take to make you comfortable and ease your mind, I will do it."

Marvin then lifted her hand and gently kissed it; a warm feeling came over her as she felt his soft lips rest on her hand.

They continued eating, listening and watching the two hummingbirds fly around the garden playing tag. The silence was peaceful as they concluded their meal. The opening sound of the patio door broke the silence.

Katrina walked over to the table with an empty tray in her hands, "May I clear the table Ms. Fuchsia?"

"Yes, thank you Katrina."

"Can I get you anything else, Pastor Marvin?"

"No, thank you. Everything was wonderful," he replied. "Oh, please tell the cook that was the best cinnamon rolls I have ever tasted. I'm a fan forever too!"

Smiling, "I will certainly tell her that," she said as she cleared away the dishes and leftovers.

Marvin stood and began walking towards the center of the garden. "You know this is the first time being in Ms. Dee's garden."

"Really! It's amazing and so peaceful," she said as she stood up and joined him.

The sweet fragrant smell of the Honeysuckle drew them in as they walked along the garden path.

"Ms. Dee had the gardener plant this particular plant along the entire garden," she said. "Because it's vibrant – apricot orange and yellow with the most beautiful creamy white color – and the sweet fragrance that fills the garden, I just love the sweet smells as I walk through my garden," Ms. Dee explained to Fuchsia when she came to live there.

As the two of them strolled through the garden, sounds of playing birds in the bird bath, sounds of birds feeding, the sight of butterflies flying along the Honeysuckles, the sun shining brightly as the wind gently kissed their skin, Marvin took Fuchsia by the hand, and ever so gently pulled her arm under his as they walked along.

A feeling of peace came upon her again as her arm was nestled under his. Taking a deep sigh, she slowly moved closer and rested her head on his shoulder. They walked the entire garden which was a circle path on grey and white French Pattern Pavers. When they reached the end of the right-side circle garden, there was a beautiful cushioned white swing bench for two. The custom-made swing was made in the form of an arbor with a ceiling fan; the swing was nestled on its small patio surrounded by rocks with soft lights and speakers. Fuchsia tapped her foot on the switch that was on the patio floor beside the swing, it began to sway slowly. Marvin helped her unto the swing, and he sat down beside her holding her hand.

"You like swinging?" she asked him.

"Yeah, actually I do."

"Me too, ever since I was a kid. The playground was my favorite place my grandma Lydia used to take me."

"Growing up in my neighborhood, we had swings on the school playground if the kids didn't tear them down," he replied.

"Did you grow up here?" She questioned.

"No actually, I grew up north."

"Up north? So did I!" She responded in surprise.

"Really? Where up north? I'm from Maryland."

"No way! You're kidding me, right?" She burst into laughter.

"Nah, please don't tell me that's where you are from as well!" His face lit up.

"Well, Yeah, that's where I'm from. I grew up in the city."

"Wait, wait, I grew up in the city as well on the west side," he chuckled. "This is too funny."

Placing her hands over her face, "Are you for real! I have never met anyone from my home state let alone my city, and the same side of the city! This is crazy!"

He removed her hands from her face. "Well, I guess this means this was meant to be. We were destined to be together, our paths were meant to cross paths," he said and kissed her hands.

They sat on that swing and talked for two hours reminiscing the old days and finding out if they knew the same people and played on the same streets. Fuchsia interrupted Marvin when he wanted to tell her about the street life he once lived, and how he gained the nickname he once was known by.

"Hey, that's not important. That was your past, we all have a past," she said softly in hopes of not having to tell him hers just yet.

Marvin immediately noticed the look on her face. He stretched to place his arm around her shoulders and pulled her close to him. "You are right, we all have a past. I just want you to know that I will never hold your past against you, and I ask that you will never hold mine as well but I also want you to feel safe and secure. One day, I will tell you all about who I was. I don't believe in secrets, especially in relationships. Secrets can come back to haunt people and, in turn, can destroy relationships. Now that I found you, I don't want anything or anyone to come between us, including you and I."

Her heart began to melt in his arms, thinking to herself, *who's this guy?* and if he was real. She closed her eyes trying to fight back the tears that was filling up underneath her lids. Slowly, she felt one tear escape as she tried so hard to keep it locked inside her closed eyes. The warm tear rolled down her nose and dropped onto his other arm under which she tucked her arm. Her warm tear rolled down his arm to rest between their arms, followed by a second tear. Fuchsia's body began to tense up as she couldn't control the tears and she didn't want him to see her cry. She pushed her head closer to his shoulder as the feeling of insecurity began to fill her soul. In her mind, she was shouting, "Stop. Fuchs, stop," but her body was becoming unraveled with fear that now caused trembling.

Feeling her trembling in his arms and the sudden drops of water hitting his arm, he gently lifted his tear-filled arm from its resting spot and raised her chin so he could look into her face.

"Fuchsia, did I say something wrong?" His voice was so patient and calm.

Trying to avoid looking into his eyes, her body trembled even more as both eyes were now flowing with warm tears. She shook her head side to side as she tried to mutter the words "No," her lips formed but no sound exited her mouth.

Worried that he said something to upset her, he spoke up again, "Hey, I apologize if I said anything to cause you pain."

She wiped her eyes with her fingers and dried them using the top of her loungewear, then, she spoke. "No, no. You didn't upset me, you actually surprised me. Never in all my life have I met a guy like you. You are so kind and compassionate, the warmth of your touch and your gentle heart is something I have dreamed of but never thought it was real, until this moment."

Marvin leaned over and kissed her forehead, then both cheeks, then her nose and, lastly, kissed her lips. She, resting his lips on hers, could feel the warmth of his breath as he whispered, "I'm here to be whatever you need. Whether it's a shoulder to lean on, an ear to listen, arms to hold you or to wipe your tears, I promise to do it all with the same love and compassion you feel this moment."

As he was about to lift his lips from hers, she leaned in closer and opened her mouth to his. He opened his mouth to receive her open lips as she slowly let her tongue meet his. The kiss lasted what seemed like a lifetime to her; feelings she never experienced before began to overwhelm her: the fluttering felt like butterflies in her tummy, her heart was beating faster, her trembling stopped. Her body was reacting in ways she never felt before, a warm sensation had totally taken over her. Their lips finally parted, and with her eyes still closed, she laid her head again on his shoulder.

What in the world had just happened? Why am I feeling like this? Feelings of damp moisture invaded her entire body. *Oh snap, this is what Candi was talking about! OMG, this feeling, I don't want it to end.*

"Hey, you alright?" Marvin whispered in her ear.

"Yes, I am. Why did you ask me that?" feeling embarrassed, wondering if he could tell what she was feeling.

"No reason; making sure you okay with me kissing you."

"I was a little surprised and nervous at the same time, but it's all good," she responded, blushing.

"Yeah, it was good," he chuckled.

"Really, you think so?"

"What, do I think so? I know so! Oh, you do think it was?"

"I... I..." she said, stammering.

"Aww man, I didn't impress you, huh? Oh, I'm embarrassed," he burst out into laughter.

"No! No! It's not that! It's... Oh wow, how do I say this... aww... please don't laugh at me," giggling and shaking her head.

"No, never. What is it? Go on, say it, I'm a big boy."

"Yes, I know you a big boy," raising her eyebrows as her voice pitched higher. "Okay, okay. It was my first real kiss," she said, covering her face in embarrassment.

"Nah, you kidding me, right? That didn't feel like a first-time kisser," he laughed as he tried to remove her hands from her face.

Releasing her hands from her face, "Yup, it is. It really is. I have never let a man kiss me before or any part of his body enter mine." This time her voice was strong, as this is the one thing she has been sure of all her life.

"Ain't nothing wrong with that, I'm actually pleasingly impressed. Of course, this is not my first kiss but it is the first in quite a long time. I have been practicing celibacy for some years, so, I truly understand and I'm just as passionate about it as well."

With a sense of relief, she said, "Really, a man like you? I know women falling at your feet, how do you handle it, and then why you kiss me?"

"Well, I don't allow myself to be put in position for anything to happen. I haven't dated in a long time because I made up my mind that until I found that one woman I wanted to spend my life with, I won't do random dating. And as for why you, because I found the one woman I want to spend my life with."

"You keep saying this; like how you know I'm the one?"

"I knew the moment we met. When you responded to me, your aura was bright with positive energy. I felt your strength and determination, yet, I felt your soft compassion. I also felt your pain and pureness like a genuine lady with a lot of love, a lady who don't trust much but can be trusted. I felt that you were my soulmate. Today, I know you are the one I truly been waiting for, I know that you are my soulmate."

"Wow, OMG. That's a lot to take in."

"I'm willing to wait until you trust me and fall in love with me."

"Wait, who said anything about falling in love, plus what makes you think you can love me? Also, how do I know this ain't some trick to get in my panties?" She became defensive.

"Well, you can forget about all you just said because I'm already falling for you. Secondly, I made a commitment to myself and I live a life of covenant. When I take you as my wife, that will be the first time I make love to you. So, until then, it will be getting to know each other and cold showers!"

"Falling for me, wife, make love to me? Wait, what?" Shaking her head in disbelief, "This is some kind of a joke or are you just cray-cray?" she snapped.

"Cray-cray? Oh man... Well, I think it's time for me to go." He stood up, grabbed her hand, kissed it and began to walk off the patio.

Fuchsia sat there in disbelief, and then suddenly jumped up.

"Hey, hey, are you serious? You just going to leave like that?"

He, turning back, took three steps towards her. He put both hands on her shoulders, looking her in the eyes.

"Listen, I know what I want but I can't or won't force you to love or believe me. Why do I have to be crazy? Plus, it's getting late, the sun will be going down soon. I have been here all day, not that I would want to be anywhere else with anyone else, but I want you to want me around as well."

"I apologize for calling you cray-cray; this is all new to me. I enjoy you being here with me all day. I have never experienced anything like this before. I'm green to this but I'm willing, for the first time in my life, to let my guards down with you. I just ask that you please be patient with me because I have trust issues and fear will cause me to try to run. The truth is I'm feeling you as well, but I don't know what to do with what I'm feeling."

She took his right hand off her shoulder, placed it on the side of her face and gently rolled her cheek in his hand.

Marvin pulled her close into his chest. "Thank you, all I'm asking for is a chance to let me love you."

"Now, for real, it's better that I leave so that neither of us would do something we may enjoy and regret at the same time; I'm really falling and if I don't go now, there will be no turning back!"

"Oh yeah. I think you are right," she smiled as she walked him to the front of the house.

"See you tomorrow?" He asked as he boarded his car.

"Well, of course, you better!" She blew him a kiss as she went back through garden gate.

Feeling like she was floating through the air as she entered the patio door, it was if time had stood still. She glanced at the clock on the microwave and realized that they had been out in the garden all day. A handwritten note was laying on the island countertop addressed to her:

"Miss Fuchsia, I prepared dinner for you. I placed your plate in the microwave and extras are in the refrigerator; didn't want to disturb you two. We will see you tomorrow, enjoy your day." It was signed with two smiley faces.

Smiling, she tossed the note in the trash and opened the microwave. She opened the plate to see what was prepared; as always, Kimberly made her favorite dishes: Fresh salmon with lemon butter herb sauce on top of sautéed spinach with onions and garlic. Placing the plate back inside the microwave and setting the timer, she walked over to the refrigerator, grabbed a bottle of water, danced around in a half circle and reached for silverware just as the microwave beeps. She took her plate of food upstairs to her room, still smiling as she was remembering the kiss, her first kiss.

Having placed her leftover on the nightstand, being unable to finish her dinner with thoughts of Marvin on her mind, she fell back on her bed, staring at the ceiling, whispering. "Ms. Dee, I finally think I know what you meant about knowing when it happens. I think it's happening, I think I'm falling for him!"

"OMG," she shouted out loud. "OMG! How in the world? Ms. Dee, you a mess! It's just like you orchestrated this! OMG! This can't be happening!" She laughed as she rolled around on her bed. "OMG! This can't be real! Pinch me somebody and wake me up!"

While she rolled around on her bed, and kicking her feet up and down like a kid full of joy, the sudden ringing of her phone caused her to sit up and look at the clock. "Who in the world is calling me?"

"Hello," she answered.

"Hey, beautiful. Just checking on you before I turn in for the night, you good?" said the voice on the other end of the line.

"Oh, hey. Yes, I'm good. Just laying here quietly on my bed," she responded softly, trying to masquerade her excitement.

"Great, do you need anything? Did you make sure everything was locked up before you went upstairs?" His voice was so caring.

"Aww, no..." feeling embarrassed that she didn't check the doors, assuming everything was good.

"No, you don't need anything or no you didn't check?"

"Aww, no to both." She realized that she was so used to Ms. Dee doing the nightly rounds that she completely forgot.

"Hey, while you are on the phone, I'm going to check right now, okay?"

"Okay. But from now on, before I leave, I will do the checking. Need to make sure my sweet gift is safe when I'm not around."

With her phone, she ran down the stairs, checking the front and patio doors, making certain no window was left open.

"Locked, locked, and everything is closed, sir. Is that better?" she said as she turned off the kitchen light, leaving only the night lights shining throughout the downstairs. Then walking back upstairs, "Are you always this protective?" she asked.

"Well, as a matter of fact, I am. It's a part of me, you remember the streets we grew up in. *Never give a thief an open invitation* is the motto I lived by. And now that I found you, oh, I got to protect my gift!" he chuckled.

She walked into her bedroom, closed the door and began removing her clothes to prepare for bed.

"Why you always referring to me as your gift?" She curiously asked as she walked into the bathroom.

"Because you are my gift. God favored me when He allowed me to find you. You are precious to me, and when someone presents you with a gift such as you, you cherish it with every fiber of your being. The way that I show God that I'm grateful for such a gift is to love, honor and cherish that gift. Not to misuse it, toss it around, belittle it or cause the gift any harm. So, look for me to always cherish you, watch over you and, most importantly, love you." He spoke his words in a soothing tone.

She stood there, at the center of the bathroom, staring at herself in the mirror over the sink.

"I don't know what to say. Love me?" She questioned.

"Yes, love you, Fuchsia Greene. You are easy to love, and I promise you this day that the love I'm willing to share with you will not judge, drag you down, suffocate you, but will always seek the best for you and in you; will allow you to breathe and encourage you to soar. That's my promise to you," he responded gently.

"Wow, Ms. Dee always told me that one day, the right someone will enter my life and love me the way I'm supposed to be loved. And... and..." she hesitated.

"And what?" he asked.

"And she told me to open my heart and let him in," she said as she sat on the stool beside the tub.

"Well, Ms. Dee was a wise woman. The question I ask today: Fuchsia Greene, will you please open your heart and let me in?"

"Well... I think I already did," covering her face as if he could see her, she blushed.

"Thank you."

There was a moment of quiet between them. Marvin broke the silence first, "Hey, you okay?"

"Yes, I'm fine actually, never felt better."

"Okay, it's getting late. So, I'm going to turn in but if you need me, no matter the time, please promise you will call me?"

"Okay, I promise. Good night," she whispered.

"Good night, talk to you tomorrow."

For a month, Marvin, like clockwork, arrived at the house every day, except Sundays, for brunch. They sat in the garden, then walked and talked for hours. On Sundays, Marvin would come after church with a bouquet of fresh flowers; she would put them in the vase on her night stand in her bedroom.

This particular Sunday when he arrived, instead of the regular fresh flowers he would bring, he handed her a large pink box.

"What's this?" She asked as she began opening the box.

"Hey, it's no fun if I tell you first," he replied as he sat on their usual swing.

A sweet aroma entered her nostrils. "Hmm, smells divine," she said as she lifted the pink tissue paper from the box.

Her eyes lit up as she gently pulled out the beautifully etched clear vase, allowing the box to fall to the ground as she raised the vase to eye level. Flopping onto the swing next to Marvin, she took a deep breath as she said, "Wow! This is stunning."

She turned the vase around in her hands to see every detail. The single most beautiful Fuchsia flower looked like it was floating in water, but the water was solid as it drowned the entire flower. The vase had a glass lid that was etched in pink and gold. She stared at the vase, then noticed the gold lettering etched on the front that read, 'Forever, Fuchsia.'

With tears in her eyes, she spoke softly, staring into his eyes. "This is the most beautiful flower I ever saw, and the most precious gift I ever received. Thank you." She let out a deep sigh. "Is this the name of the flower, forever Fuchsia?"

"No, that's not the name of the flower. That's how long I want to love you - Forever," he responded as he kissed her hand that was cupped around the vase.

Lost for words, she held the vase closed to her chest as a single tear feel from her eye.

"I had this specially made for you, it's an original. I had to go online to order this deep color Fuchsia flower, then I had someone to make this for me to present to you."

"Really?" smiling as she stared at the vase.

"Yes, I started on this gift after our first garden walk. It represents everything that you are: your captivating beauty, your resilience to withstand all you endured. You are mine forever, Fuchsia, and I want you to place this somewhere you can see it daily as a reminder that I promise to love you forever."

Holding the vase still close to her heart, she laid her head on his shoulder and thought to herself, *he's a keeper my game changer.*

A cool breeze danced across Fuchsia's face as she sat on the Patio waiting for Marvin to arrive. This Sunday felt different to her, it was as if she could feel his presence near. For the first time in her life, she felt safe with a man. She was like an excited kid waiting with expectation for him to arrive. The sound of his car as it pulled up into the driveway caused her stomach to flutter with excitement. She could hear the car door as he exited the car and began walking towards the garden.

Standing up to embrace Marvin as he stepped closer to her, he suddenly stopped. He then pulled out, from his pocket, a navy-blue satin box with a navy ribbon wrapped around it and slowly dropped to his knees. With the box in his left hand, he took Fuchsia by the hand with his right.

Fuchsia stood there with a shocking, confused look on her face.

"What are you doing? Why are you down there?"

"Fuchsia Greene, from the very moment I saw you, I knew you were the chosen one for me. You are the gift I chose to spend the rest of my life with. I promise, if you would have me as your husband, that I would spend the rest of my days learning how to love you better. I promise to be the husband that you need, to be your listening ear, to be your encourager, to be your protector, to be your provider, to shelter you, comfort you, laugh with you, dance with you, sing with you, and to father children with you. I promise not to smoother you, to give you space when you need it, and learn the things you love and the things you dislike. I promise to never judge you or demean you, to never focus on your flaws but to embrace every inch of you. I promise to never go to bed angry with you but always seek peace in every situation. Fuchsia Greene, will you be my wife?"

Smiling with tears flowing down her cheeks, "Marvin, you had me the moment you kneeled down. Yes, Yes! I will be your wife!" She said in excitement.

Marvin stood up and swooped Fuchsia in his arms, lifted her high off the ground above him, spinning with her in his arms as they both cried with excitement. With her arms wrapped around his neck as he was spinning, she threw her legs around his waist. He stopped and lowered her down to his face; they stared into each other's eyes, and as he slowly pulled her close to his face, he whispered, "I love you, Fuchsia." He then locked his lips to hers.

(Wedding day)

The continuous knocking that came from her bedroom door interrupted her thoughts.

"Yes, who is it?" she sang as she sat up in bed, waiting for a response at her bedroom door.

"You decent?"

"Haha, it depends on what you consider decent," jokingly, she responded. "Yes, come on in."

Opening the door, she peeped, "I just wanted to check on you. Chat a minute if it's fine with you."

"Of course, Melondy. Come on in. Sit, let's chat. What's on your mind?" She hopped off her bed and motioned Melondy to join her in the sitting parlor. Fuchsia held on to grandma's Lydia's words, "Fuchsia," she would say. "When you become a woman and you purchase your own bed, never let any and everybody flopping on your bed. That's the one place you keep all to yourself; that bed is your place of rest and restoration, your place of refuge and one day a place for you and your husband. So, you don't want to be chasing off other peoples' crazy! You hear me Fuchs?"

"What you mean everybody crazies, grandma Lydia? So, everybody crazy?" She would burst into laughter every time Grandma Lydia came into Fuchsia's bedroom saying those words. Nonetheless, she never forgot and did as Grandma Lydia said.

"Fuchsia," Melondy said as she sat down. "At Ms. Dee's funeral, when I came to sit with you, I could feel you had a warm spirit and I later found you are a great person. You have such a magnetic personality, always full of life, never judgmental, always welcoming. I really understand why and how Ms. Dee took you in and loved you like her own. I don't know if I ever expressed my admiration and thanks to you, so, today I want to thank you, and thank you for allowing me to be a part of your wedding."

"Aww Melondy. Neither Marvin nor I would have it any other way! Plus, even though I didn't attend church with Ms. Dee, she would come home and tell me all about the service. She often talked about you; how she really liked you and said you had such a wonderful spirit. She told me that when you first came to the church, she wondered what brought you to a church full of people of color, but she soon found out you were just like the rest of them - just wanted to be in a safe place with no judgements and full of love. 'She just fit right in with the rest of us misfits,' she would say."

Fuchsia held Melondy's hand, smiling and said, "I'm the one who needs to thank you; you were there for me through the whole ordeal of me losing Ms. Dee so suddenly. If it was not for you, I would still be in that daze, crying, shaking with fear as Ms. Dee's lifeless body laid on her bed. I was stuck standing there, I couldn't move when you rang that door bell. Those chimes broke through my crying. It was as if Ms. Dee shook me and said 'Go to the door, sweet Fuchsia. Go to the door.' When I finally opened the door, all I could see was those piercing green eyes looking at me with such a welcoming warmth, and I knew who you were instantly because of how Ms. Dee described you."

"I know that was such a strange day because Ms. Dee never invited anyone to her home. She was so private but so loving at the same time. I was so nervous when Marvin called me and told me he received a call from Ms. Dee early that morning and asked if he could send me to her home this afternoon because she needed my help with something personal. I thought, *why would she asked for me*? But when you opened the door that day, I understood. She needed me to look after you because you were going to need some help," Melondy said.

"Melondy, Ms. Dee was such a woman of grace, beauty, elegance and order. She already had everything prepared for me, all written down tucked in her dresser drawer. She told me a year earlier that if anything happened to her, there is a letter addressed to me in her top drawer with all important names and numbers. Little did I know it was more than that! Imagine little ole me inheriting everything she owned, from this house in which she instructed me to remodel asap to the car, jewelry; she put my name on bank accounts and left me bonds, but the most important of them all was the Transitional home for women she developed in my honor. It was just completed and furnished, with a scheduled opening date of my birthday which she never got to see. Can you believe such a woman lived and had no family to share such love with?"

"Did she ever talk of her family?" Melondy asked as she sat with her legs folded under her.

"No. She only said she was an only child. Her mom died a little after her birth and her father was a business owner who taught her the principles of smart work. He sent her to boarding schools all her life; she had the finest of everything but never the pleasure of love. When she was around fifty-ish, I believe, is when her father died, and she started going to church. As she put it, she started realizing love was the missing link in her life. She then started focusing on helping people, even though she was very private.

"Ms. Dee confessed to me one evening as we sat in great room watching a tv show that I was the first person to stay in this big house ever! Can you believe that! She said there was something about me that made her want to bring me home with her to protect me. She said it was like she heard the angels say, 'Save her if she will let you, and teach her and give her all the love you can.' She needed me and I certainly needed her!" Fuchsia said as she leaned back in the reclining chair.

"She changed my life, it was as though she was prepping for this moment..."

"Actually, that's why I came to talk to you," Melondy interrupt Fuchsia softly. "You are right, Ms. Dee planned everything down to the day you'd get married."

Fuchsia sat up in the recliner, "What do you mean, Melondy?"

"Well, I believe it was like six months before she passed that I was in my office at the church, and Ms. Dee surprised me by stopping by. She asked me if I would be an angel, keep something safe for her and be her messenger when the time was right because she may not be around. Of course, I was like 'Sure, Ms. Dee but you scaring me talking like that.' She smiled and said, 'No need to be concerned. I'm not going anywhere just yet, but at the rate my sweet Fuchsia is going, I may not be here,' she said as she gently laughed. Ms. Dee handed me this box and this card; told me to make sure to give it to you on your wedding day, no matter how long it takes." Melondy pulled out a beautiful, blue box with a small card addressed, My Sweet Fuchsia, from the deep pocket of her fluffy white bathrobe and handed it to Fuchsia. She walked over to Fuchsia and gently kissed her forehead as she was instructed by Ms. Dee before leaving the room and closing the door behind her.

Sitting in awe, Fuchsia felt the warmth of tears running down her face. She opened the envelope, it was a beautiful embossed blue and silver card with white clouds on the front of the card. She took a deep breath and opened the card.

My dear sweet Fuchsia, you finally stopped all that running and allowed love to find you. I didn't want you to spend your precious years all alone not experiencing love, wasting the gift given for all mankind. Love is powerful and should be experienced by all. You taught me how to receive love in its purest nonjudgmental way, and I want you to love like that the rest of your life. Enjoy the love of a husband and, one day, children. I wish I could be there with you today, but God had other plans and plus, I have gone all the miles with you that was needed. Now, I pass the baton to the luckiest blessed man alive, whoever he is. Now, wipe those tears and look in the box, here is a symbol of our love we shared. I may not have been your biological mother, but you were always my sweet daughter Fuchsia. The two hearts are mine and yours, and the blue diamond is for that something blue for your wedding day. Please wear this on your right today, knowing I'm with you holding your hand as you walk down the isle.

Love Always,

Ms. Dee.

As she opened the beautiful blue and silver box, her eyes gazed upon the most beautiful diamond bracelet she ever laid eyes on. Two - one large and one small - hearts joined in the center at the opening, each with princess-cut diamonds coming from its side till they both were joined at the center with a single blue diamond.

Gasping for air between her tears, she held the bracelet to her breast and said, "Ms. Dee, I will always love you. You were the mother I needed at that time in my life." She placed the bracelet back in the box and walked to her dressing closet to place the box among her bridal attire. She walked into her bathroom, to the face basin, to run water on her face. Looking in her vanity bathroom mirror, she, now with puffy eyes, stared at her small round face. "You know, Fuchs, you've been blessed by the wonderful women placed in your life." Sighing, she looked at the small gold clock in the bathroom. It was three thirty. "Let me try and rest a moment." She stepped on the oak stepstool for her raised bed and laid across the top of the bed as Lady moved from the foot of the bed and laid next to her.

Fuchsia, much like the women in her life from momma, grandma Lydia and Ms. Dee, never had much company in her home. So today, it is huge having so many people, much more, at the same time. At first, the thought was overwhelming, but she soon gave into the notion and came at ease. It reminded her of how she felt the next morning after meeting Marvin for the first time. "But this time after all, they are just my only brother and the only girls who mean the world to me. If it had not been for any of them, I wouldn't be the woman I am."

She has been living with Ms. Dee for about two years, working her first real job as an office clerk - a work that Ms. Dee helped her to get. "Sweet Fuchsia," Ms. Dee would say. "If you can read, you can file, and you certainly know how to use a phone and take a message, all you need to do is show up for the interview and be your normal self and the job is yours." She was right as always but she failed to inform me that the owner of the staffing company was a woman who was a member of her fancy organization, so, she hired me with no skills.

She had been working there three months, sharing an office with Susan who was a little quirky most of the time but much fun to work with. When Marvin brought that smoothie back to the office for Susan, her eyes lit up and she had the biggest grin on her face. Smiling Susan asked him, "Do we know each other, seems like I know you from somewhere?"

He responded in his gentleman tone, "I don't believe we've ever met."

"Oh, you must have one of those familiar type faces," she replied as she collected the smoothie he brought for her. "Thanks, I apologize for my co-worker having you to run get my smoothie," she said as she stood up with that big grin on her face.

Before Susan could finish her comment, Fuchsia interrupted. "Yes, thank you so much. We don't want to keep you any longer again, thank you." She stood to walk him to the door.

He stopped, turned, and handed her a neatly folded paper and said, "I took the liberty of writing my name and number. If you like to take another walk or would agree to have lunch, please call, or if you want to just talk, I'm available."

Fuchsia took the note out of his hands and nodded her head, then closed the office door.

"Girl, what's wrong with you? Mr. Tall, dark, and Fine is obviously interested in you and all you can do is nod! My word, Fuchsia Greene, My word!" Susan blurted out as she ran to the office window to get another look at Marvin.

"Oh, shut your mouth! Plus, I never told you I needed an assistant with my love life! So, mind your little business, little Miss Susie!" she said laughing as she sat at her desk.

That evening after work, she went straight home and all she could think about was that handsome man she met at lunch today. She briefly mentioned her lunchtime experience to Ms. Dee at dinner.

"Really!" she said excited at the thought.

"Don't get all excited, Ms. Dee, plus, who said I'm going to call him anyway? That's why I'm not going to tell you his name," Fuchsia snickered as she flopped on the chair at the kitchen table.

"My sweet Fuchsia, honey, you can't keep running every time a nice guy comes your way."

"Oh Ms. Dee, I knew I shouldn't have told you," she said with a smirking laughter as she picked up the dishes from the table to put in the sink.

Afterwards, she went off to her room. *Boy, he was good looking. Nah, he probably has a girlfriend or wife and bunch of kids somewhere. Plus, he was too nice, that got to be a con. Fine dudes always got a trick up their sleeves.*

"Ain't nobody got no time for no drama," she mumbled to herself that night as she tore up the note and climbed into bed, shaking her head. "But he sure was fine!"

The next day at work, Fuchsia couldn't get in the door and the first thing out of Susan's lips was, "Did you call him?"

"Girl, no. Bye!" She walked to the file cabinet, "And do me a favor, don't ask again please," Fuchsia snapped back at her with rolling eyes.

"Well! I guess your period musta came on this morning cause you sure snappy."

"No, it didn't if you must know, but I just don't feel like talking about my personal life, if that's ok with you?" She slammed the file cabinet closed and walked out the office they shared to the rest room down the hall.

Feelings of guilt and fear began to overwhelm her. She sat in employees lounge for thirty minutes, sipping on a bottle of water she got out the machine. Finally, she walked back down the hall to her office. When she opened the door, Susan spoke up. "I'm sorry, you are right. I had no right to impose, please accept my apology."

"I accept, and I'm sorry as well. I know you meant no harm," she responded calmly as she sat at her desk.

Three days had passed since she and Marvin met. She was on a call with a future client who was inquiring about needing staff for big project. The other phone line started ringing, Susan answered the call, "Can you hold, please?"

Turning to Fuchsia, "You have a call on line two."

Motioning with her lips, "Can you ask who it is, please?"

"Sir, may I ask who's calling? She's on another line with a client."

The look on Susan's face made Fuchsia uncomfortable. "Well, who is it?" she again motioned with her mouth.

Trying not to show any excitement, "He said his name is Marvin, the smoothie man," she answered.

"Can you hold, please," Fuchsia said as she put the call on hold.

"Look, tell him I'm busy and will be all day," Fuchsia said in a low stern tone, then returned to the call she had on hold.

Susan not wanting to interfere again, returned to the gentleman on hold. "Sir, can I take a message? She's on an important call and will be in meeting all day."

"Yes please. Tell her I called, thanks," Marvin said as he hung up the phone.

Neither Fuchsia nor Susan mentioned his call after she got off the other call. She just continued to work as if the call never came. All day, while sitting at her desk, she felt her stomach knotting up every time she thought about the call, but she was determined to never return his call.

It was as if Fuchsia's life was all mapped out, and when she detoured from the plan intended, something or someone helped her to get back on track. Like grandma Lydia used to say, "*We all come into this world with a hidden road map and invisible secret agents to help be our guide. Every now and then, when we stray from the path, we get signs to turn right, turn left, even stop and make a U turn. Fuchs, we all will make mistakes but if we all pay attention to the little voice inside, we will find our way again.*"

As a child, she could never understand some of the things grandma would say. She would say them over and over again like she was drilling them in Fuchsia's head. Now as an adult, those words have so much meaning. Thinking through her life, she sees how there was always someone, placed strategically, to help her back on track every turn she made in the wrong direction. If it had not been for Ms. Dee, there would not have been a Marvin.

(Wedding Day)

Laying there on her bed, she tossed from side to side. Attempting to rest before getting dressed seemed to be one of the most unlikely thing that was going to happen. Everything was racing through her mind: did she pack enough clothes? Should she pack her hair curlers or not? "Hmmm," thinking out loud, "I don't think going to bed with hair curlers on my honey moon will be cute or sexy! Uhh snoot! What am I suppose to do with my hair? If I don't, that means I will have to get up every day and curl it if I want flowing curls! Man, the things women have to go through to be cute! Damn! Well I can always just wash it after the honey moon night and let it air dry with my natural wavy curls. Hmm, let me see if I have a bottle of that curl activator left?" she said as she jumped off the bed.

"I promised myself I would not be running around with no last-minute stuff! Come on, Fuchs, where you put it?" She asked herself as she went through her vanity cabinet. "Great, found it!" She made her way to her walk-in closet again to pull out her luggage. She picked up her king-size toiletry bag and having put in the small bottle of barely used curl activator, she zipped it closed. "Man, one would think I'm going away for a month, not 10 days."

She double checked to make sure she had everything in order. Glancing over her Louis Vuitton luggage, "Okay, I have my Carryall for everything I need in case my luggage don't arrive with me. A girl always need fresh panties and a toothbrush. Check! Toiletry Pouch, Check! Keepall for my sandals and slides along with Shoe Pouch, Check! Jewelry case, Check! Deauville for my beauty products, Check! And lastly, my P'egase L'egere 55 for everything else. Oh snap, where is my..." Worried, she began searching everywhere in her closet. "My overnight honeymoon piece, Whew!" She picked up her Keepall Bandoulie're 50. "Okay now, everything is in place; ready to roll out the door!" Sighing, she exited the closet.

"Who can rest on a day like today?" She, smiling at herself, passing by her long length hand-crafted maple oak mirror, "Certainly, not me." Running her fingers along the ivory tapestry drapes that dressed the oversized windows in her bedroom suite, she stood gazing out the French doors that opened to the small intimate patio that overlooked the flower garden. Ms. Dee had the gardener to plant a beautiful Asiatic Lilies garden organized in groups of types and colors.

"The Dimension Lily," she would say, "Is her mysterious one because of its rich dark color. The Black Out Lily signify strength because of its rich bold red which gets darker in the center, and my favorite, The Starlette Lily." She said it was her joy because it reminded her of Fuchsia with its center and tips; a beautiful glow of yellowish golden orange that embodied the dimensions of the color. "Fuchsia, what a beauty to behold."

The grass was perfectly manicured, the sun was shining so warm and bright over the garden, glistening over the small lake that flowed behind the houses in the community. "A perfect day to get married," she said as she left the window, blushing at the thought of what it would be like waking up with her husband in this very room. She was all prepared for her new husband to share the room which has only been occupied by her since the day Ms. Dee had the house built twenty-two years ago. As a part of Ms. Dee's wishes, she had the entire house updated and some rooms completely redone. "Make it your dream house, the way you desire it to be, spare no expense for I left enough money for you. Do to it as you please. I just ask that you design some breathtaking rooms in the process," Ms. Dee wrote in the letter addressed to Fuchsia.

As she requested, Fuchsia obeyed but the garden she left as Ms. Dee designed. Fuchsia made sure her bedroom suite was everything a lady could ever dream of and could make her husband feel welcomed. Warm colors of Ivory, gold, with hints of soft pink and royal blue filled the entire luxurious suite, flowing even to the master bath. The wood framed archway so eloquently separated the bedroom and the sitting room with its sleek curves running along both sides, draping together in the center of the archway as if it was custom drapes in a theatre house. Tapping her fingers on the archway that was duplicated in both rooms, "I hope this not too fancy for you Marvin," she whispered to herself, walking through to her bedroom.

"Momma used to say, 'Fuchs, if you gonna dream, you might as well dream big. Boy, who would have thought my dreams would become reality, you know what I mean, Lady?" She held Lady as the sound of her voice woke the pet from a short nap.

"Lady, I know you used to just me and you but after my honeymoon, we going to have a third person. I can't even begin to imagine a male in my room let alone my bed! Oh my, I didn't think about where you will sleep now. I never asked Marvin if you being on the bed would bother him. Oh well, I guess we will find out soon because I refuse to give up either one of you. So, you two will have to work it out, okay, Lady?"

Lady wagged her tail and licked Fuchsia's arm as if she understood and was willing to comply. "Lady, I love you so much. You always going to be my girl, I know you've grown accustomed to this beautiful bed and this soft fluffy spread, but I just might have to find you a little fancy dog sofa. We can put it right over there by the fireplace, okay, girl?" she said in a cheerful, assuring tone.

Her king-sized upholstered sleigh bed with its grand scale classic design of Ivory Jacquard with elegantly flowing shapes of diamonds; each peak filled with crystals that married itself to a rich dark mahogany wood with side rails that connected to the sleek 's' figures curving its way from top to bottom of both the head and footboards. *Still the most beautiful stunning bedroom set she laid eyes on,* she thought. Barefoot, she walked towards the night stand she cleared out for Marvin, twiddling her toes in the cream California Cozy Plush Shag Rug at the center of the room, which was bordered by a dark and rich bamboo floor that flowed throughout the master suite until it reaches the bathroom. Opening the top drawer of the night stand which matches the mahogany wood on her bed, she reached in to pull out the small black velvet box that contained Marvin's wedding band. Marvin insisted that she shouldn't spend a lot on his ring; he is such a humble man who does not like a big deal to be made of him but would spoil her to no end. Lifting the box lid, she thought, smiling, *I didn't do bad if I must say.* The 18 karate Rose Gold and Platinum band that matched the Rose Gold, Platinum and diamond wedding band he picked out for her. Having closed the box, she tucked it in her satin champagne with rhinestone trim clutch Bridal Bag along with an extra lipstick, mints, Kleenex, bobby pins, and the dreadful tampon, if needed.

Startled by the banging on her bedroom door, almost dropping her bridal bag on the floor, she shouted, "What in the world! What's wrong?" She swung her French door opened as Lady, also startled, came barking.

"Girl, nothing's wrong. Why you so jumpy! I'm checking on you, you been so quiet and all. So, I wanted to make sure you didn't run out and leave us here to cover for you!" Tommie burst into laughter.

"Tommie, you know you sick, right? You almost scared me to death! I'm not used to having folk around, you know. Then you going to be in here banging like you the PoPo. Plus, you don't have to worry if I'm running; the only running I'm doing is straight into his arms!"

"I know, that's right," they both burst into laughter as she let Tommie into her room. "What the!" Tommie exclaimed as entered her room. "Fuchs, what? Oh my God, your bedroom is stunning, I knew you was remodeling but damn! This look like a magazine layout! Did Candi see this?"

"See what?" as she burst through the door. "What you two Siamese cats up too?" Candi froze with mouth wide opened. "Good God! Wow! Who are you? What you do with my girl? Dang, aliens done took Fuchs and brought us some bougie princess bride!" laughing as she grabbed Fuchsia and jokingly began to shake her. "Where is she? Come on, where is she?"

The three of them laughed so hard until tears came running out. Then, they broke free of their embrace. "Oh shoot, I got to pee! I can't hold my bladder like I used too, guess I'm getting old," Candi said as she crossed her legs trying to get to the bathroom.

"Nah, it ain't that, miss kitty-kat. It's because you used your kitten like it was a tunnel! Every vehicle that was able to gain entrance got in no matter the style, size, color, all aboard!" Tommie burst into hysteric laughter.

"Aww man, Tommie, that was low!" Fuchsia said as she laughed even more. "Boy, how I miss days like this when the three of us were together?"

"Yea, Right! You got all this now and the man of your dreams plus an old cute dog. What more ya want, Ms. Bougie?" Tommie said as she walked into the sitting room. "I ain't forgot. Don't go sitting on your bed! It's not me you need to keep off your bed, it's Kitty-Kat Candi in there with the open kitty-kat that can't keep her bladder," they screamed in laughter.

"Look, you unknown bred in a dress, I ain't thinking about you. All I want to know is if I can please take this whole bedroom suite home with me; that bathroom is to die for. My Randy, (her latest, steady guy friend) would have to peel me out of this room, I would be up here trying to cook and all!" Candi said laughing as she came out of the bathroom. "Man, Lil Bits, you did this thing. You done well like Ms. Dee asked."

"Yeah, you done real good," Tommie concurred.

"I miss them so much at times, especially times like this," Fuchsia said as she sat on the loveseat reclining chair.

"Them, which them?" Candi said as she scooted in the Loveseat next to her.

"Aww nah, you going to have to move over a little more," Tommie said as she squeezed in from Fuchsia's other side. "You know how we do when it's girl talk time, like little Oreos. Fuchs in the middle cause she's the sweetest one and we on both sides of her. I know you bought this chair with us in mind, didn't you?" she said, shoving Fuchsia comfortably.

Before Fuchsia could answer, Candi chimed in with a gleaming smile on her face, "Nope, she remembered what I taught her!"

"What's that? How to loosen your kitty! Oh, my bad; how to use your kitty to tame a man," Tommie reeled in laughter.

The three of them began laughing again.

"No crazy! I told her to make every room a love room, have something she can always lay on or over for her and her hubby to get busy on!" she said, twerking her body in the chair.

They laughed again.

"But real talk, lil bits. I almost feel like a mom to you, not a big sister. When you came into my life, it changed me. You gave me purpose, and you were my reason to leave the streets life. You even inspired me to actually settle down and allow myself to be loved. Oh, I almost forgot, Randy sends his love. He just couldn't take off after starting the new job just two weeks ago, I told him you'd understand.

"Fuchsia, I'm... Well, we..." looking over at Tommie, "We are very proud of you, of the woman you have become; how you have kept yourself for this day. Your beginnings, like us all, was rough but you made it through with determination. We watched you unfold like a blossoming flower, eager to know each layer of your existence. When you fell, you got back up stronger than before; you weathered every storm you encountered, and your wisdom is beyond your years.

"You made us better women; it's because of you Tommie and I are the women that we are. You came into our lives when we needed you. It may have appeared that you needed us, but little momma, we needed you, and we, the lonely ones, became the happy three. If it wasn't for you coming into our lives, Tommie would have been in jail, and me, well, you know I would still be selling my precious body because we didn't know our worth. However, you helped us define them.

"Fuchsia, the day you left with that old man, trying to be grown, I never..." her eyes began to burn with tears, "I couldn't sleep nor eat until you called. My body shut down. I didn't even work. I couldn't work. I sat by the window, hoping to see you jump out of a car or get off the bus, and when the sun began to set, so did my heart." She swallowed back the tears. "I never knew I could be so protective and so loving at the same time. All kinds of thoughts raced across my mind: *if he raped you, or worst, did he kill you?* I was so angry at myself for letting my pride not stop you that day. I never prayed before that day; I never felt like I needed to, or I could, but I tell you I prayed, I prayed all that day and the next. I prayed every time I thought about you. I was like, 'Look God, I know you might not know me, but I often heard Fuchsia talking to you. I think she might be in trouble and we need your help. If you would please look out for her, please bring her home safely and I promise you from then on out, I will stop this life.' " Dead silence filled the room.

Fuchsia, bowing her head, broke the silence. "I'm so sorry for causing you two pain," she wept.

"Hey, no. I didn't tell you this to make you cry or feel bad. I shared with you so you can know the impact you had on my life," Candi said as she wiped Fuchsia cheeks. "Lil Bits, you the hero in this story, Marvin is so lucky to have met you."

Tommie interrupted, "He sure is and you pure and all that, not like me and Candi was. That's why we fought so hard for you to remain a virgin. All jokes aside, I know I'm the hard ass and all, I act like nothing bothers me or I'm not afraid of anything, but the truth is I do have fears, and there is a little Tomekia inside who cries too."

For the first time since meeting them, Tommie broke down in tears. She tried to fight back the burning in her eyes; her lips began to quiver, and her right leg rocked as her left leg which was draped over the other's began to shake uncontrollably. Fuchsia and Candi both placed their hands on her leg as to reassure her that it's okay to be vulnerable but she's in a safe place with them.

Trying her best to pull herself together, words choked out of her mouth as her voice cracked. Her slanted hazel eyes now filled with tears, her once soft almond complexion was now as red as her cute pug nose. Moving her long straight dark hair off her tear-filled face, "I never told you everything about my life. Yes, my dad owned a boxing gym; he was a trainer, but what you don't know is my dad began beating me at the age of five. He would beat me with his closed fist, said he was making me tough. My dad was a big man, tall and handsome. My mom used to say he was once a good-looking man.

"His mom was Cuban, and European descent. He said he didn't know his dad but was told he was African American. My dad had a hot temper and I always tried to make sure I did everything right so he wouldn't be angry with me. All five of my brothers, when they reached seventeen or eighteen, left home and didn't return. So, it was my mom and I left home with my dad. My dad was so hard on my brothers, forced them to be rough and tough, they hated him. I was the last of the liter, my mom would say, because there was twelve years difference between my immediate brother and myself. I wanted my dad to love me and I tried to be so good so my mom would come back to get me or just see me again."

Taking a deep breath, trying not to let her voice crack, Tommie swallowed hard.

Candi stroked the top of Tommie's head, running her hand down her hair. "Hey, Hey, it's okay. We are here, you don't have to talk about it."

"No, I need to talk about it, I've kept so much inside; kept you, my sisters, from knowing my true pain." Tommie leaned back her head and continued.

"I would clean and mop the entire apartment every Saturday, thinking this Sunday would be the Sunday that mommy would return because she left on a Sunday. She said she was going to Sunday Mass. So, I believed in my heart that she would return on a Sunday after Mass. Every Sunday, I would rise early, brush my teeth, brush my hair, put ribbons on it and put on my favorite jeans, the same jeans that mommy dressed me on the day she left. I wanted her to know that I waited for her just like she left me. This went on for one whole year, I was eight when she left me with him." Sniffling, she reached for the Kleenex on the table and wiped her nose. "That was the only year that my dad didn't hit me.

"One Sunday, I did my same Sunday ritual except this time, dad interrupted with rage in his voice. He burst into the room, 'Why you still sitting here, waiting for your momma. She don't want you! She never did! She wanted another boy like I did but she couldn't, had to make a girl this time, no boy! She was weak when she had you! You made her weak, that's why she left. She left because of you; why do think we named you Tomeika and call you Tommie? The day your mommy left, you was in those same jeans cause you was supposed to be a boy! My boy!'

" 'I ain't no boy! Mommy loved me and told me she loved her girl! And I was her girl!' I shouted back at him with tears streaming down my cheeks! in a rage I never experienced from him, he leaped across the floor like a bear and with his fist balled up so tightly, he punched me in my face so hard I fell back over the chair. I screamed out in pain. 'Shut up, you spineless girl! Don't nobody like a crying ole girl because your type turn into weak crying women like your mommy. You the reason she's gone!'

"I screamed back, choking on my tears, 'That's not true! You are the reason cause you hit her every day!' My dad drew back his fist with those flames tattooed on them and hit me once again in the face; I felt the pain so hard I thought my cheeks was busted open. Then, he hit me again in my stomach; I buckled over, throwing up and gasping for air. Then, he picked me up and threw me in the bathroom, told me to clean myself and clean that floor. I cried so hard silently, 'I want my mommy.' I cleaned up myself and the living room floor. That night, I didn't eat dinner. I wasn't hungry and my mouth was swollen shut, nor did my dad come in to offer me dinner. He ate at the kitchen table with his usual vodka bottle. I cried myself to sleep.

"The next morning, my dad came in my room to wake me. He looked at my face and said go back to bed, you look a mess. I stayed in my room all day with the shades down, my dad left me alone for work. I remained home the rest of the week. When Sunday came, I didn't put on jeans, I put on a skirt instead. I never let my dad know I was still longing for my mommy. I dreaded every Saturday night because I knew Sunday was coming and my dad would have a long night with the vodka bottle well into Sunday morning, and if I made the least sound, I became his punching bag. After a while, I became numb to the punches and would just lay there and try to block the punches to my face which made him swing the more. I knew to stay home from school if the punches landed too much hard to the face. Eventually, I began to put on makeup I found in mommy's makeup bag to cover up the bruises.

"One day, at the age of twelve, it all came to a head and my life took another hard turn. Dad gave me his usual beating but this time he caught me off guard. It was a Monday morning, I was getting dressed for school. He slept all that Sunday, it was mommy's birthday. I got up early for school because it was my first day at middle school, I was excited I had a good Sunday, no daddy drama. As I was getting dressed, I put on a cute jean skirt one of the neighbors in the building had given me because her daughter had outgrown her clothes. I was so happy as my dad didn't take me school shopping this year.

"I got used to the idea that my mother was no longer coming, so, any help from any of the mothers in the building was a plus. The clothes fit my small framed body perfectly. I was so happy until my dad woke up. I was in the mirror, brushing my hair and checking out how good the skirt looked on me, I began to see curves in my body that I didn't see the school year before. Suddenly, I felt my dad's hand snatch my left shoulder and spun me around and shouted, 'Tramp like your mother! Take off the whore skirt.' At the same time, he hauled and slapped me so hard in my face; the sting was unlike what I felt before, it felt like fire on my face. I stood and held my face and stared fearlessly at his hungover face, not batting an eye. He reached back and struck me again this time on the other cheek and his nail scratched the corner of my lips. I looked at him again with that fearless look and said, 'That's your last hit. Next time, I will kill you!' My dad looked at me as though he saw a ghost and walked away.

"I left the house immediately and went to school, not thinking that my face was bruised. I walked to school that day. I felt too many emotions to be sitting on no bus, so I walked. When I arrived at school, everyone was looking at me with a look of concern. It still didn't dawn on me that my face was messed up. No one dared to say anything to me because I was known to fight if need be. So, my homeroom teacher called me into the hallway to ask me.

'What happened, dear?'

'What do you mean?' She looked at me so strangely and said to walk to the teachers' lounge. I walked with her but instead, she walked me to the nurses' office. When the nurse looked at me, my heart sank because that day I stood my ground but forgot to cover my bases and my secret was out.

"That day, my life changed from bad to worse. I had no one that could take me in, no mother or grandmother. I was sent to my first foster home. The couple's seventeen-year-old son raped me the second week I was there in the middle of the night. So, the next morning in front of his parents, I pulled a knife out of the drawer and went up behind him and said I will slit your throat if you ever come in my room and touch me again. The mother begged me to put down the knife and the father called 911, police came and took me away. I got placed again in another foster home.

"This time, a family with two small daughters whose dad thought I was sent there to please him due to his wife being pregnant again. At first, he would try to feel me up and I would block his hands. Then, one day, he jumped on top of me while I was in bed. I tried to scream, he covered my mouth with his big hands, but I bit him. He struck me in the face, that did it because I promised myself that not another man would never get the pleasure of hitting me in the face again.

"That was the first time I cut a man. I reached for the small paring knife I snuck to my bed and placed under my pillow the first day he tried to feel me. I pulled it from under my pillow and closed my eyes, screaming and swinging. The wife rose from her afternoon nap and came running into the room filled with screams. Seeing her husband in his underwear and bloody tee shirt with me standing in the corner, crying and holding a bloody knife. She screamed at him, 'What did you do?' Then turned to me and shouted, 'Get out of my house!' I lived on the streets for about a week. Then, one day, someone called the police because I was caught trying to steal a bagel and orange juice. When police arrived, they ran my name and birthdate, and found out I was wanted for assault. That wife had me arrested for cutting her husband, so, I was sent to Juvie.

"I spent the next six and half years there. I fought daily, the first five years. I was such an angry kid. The last year and a half, I just stayed to myself and no one bothered me because I had a reputation and a bad temper. When I got out, I was sent to a halfway house for six to twelve months. Then, I left the Bronx and hitchhiked to Georgia, I needed a fresh start. That's when I met you, little momma, I had only been out six months. The street was my home. I stayed wherever I could, that's why I never brought you to my house in the beginning. Cleaning the boxing gym was my first job ever but I knew I needed a place of my own, plus, I could train there whenever I choose. Also, if you wanted to follow me home, I had no home to take you to. My fears are being alone with no one to love me, not being a good mother to Travone, or good wife to Arthur, or losing one of you. I talk a good talk but deep down inside, I'm so soft.

"I cried too when you disappeared with that old fart, but I turned my fear into someone's pain. I busted up a few low-lifes when I went looking for you. I felt as though it was my fault, I should have scooped out the old geezer, but I didn't. I went against my better judgment and we could have lost you for good. I might not show many feelings, but I love you two to pieces, you are my family. I used to not believe that I was worthy of anyone loving me, that I was some type of mistake my parents had. I went years with no hugs or kisses, no one to run to with happy moments, no one to laugh with or share my feelings until I met you that day." She looks at Fuchsia, "That day, you changed my life forever. Seeing you that young on the street and knowing those guys and what was about to happen, I saw a young me except I wasn't green and as young when I hit those streets. I normally wouldn't interfere with other's business but this time it was something different about you. It was as though a voice spoke to me and said, 'help her,' so I did. That was the beginning of my life.

"Candi is so right, it wasn't just you who needed saving and protecting, it was us as well. It was like the stars in our lives all lined up at the same time and caused an alignment that forever changed our lives. You taught me how to love and trust with your innocence. I felt like it was my job to keep you safe and I wouldn't change one moment of our journey together. You helped me to let go and let love in, but I'm still working on that forgiveness part! Watching you grow up and making sure you was good everyday was a responsibility I took seriously. No jokes, for real, it was like Candi and I were your parents. Before you, the only responsibility I had was me, never had a dog, cat or fish but I was handed a Fuchsia." Smiling at Fuchsia, "So, it tripped me out when I got pregnant by Arthur. Man, was I scared inside. I kept thinking this was not supposed to happen to Me! I'm the tough one, the fighter, the dragon slayer. I'm the girl who don't get attached, just handle my business and out the door!"

Fuchsia, sitting up, blurted out, "I was so confused when you got pregnant! Was like, who? Tommie? How?"

Candi jumped up from the chair they were sitting in and ran around in a circle, screaming, "Me too! I just didn't want to say anything!"

The three of them laughed and laughed.

"Tommie, tell us, how the heck did you know Arthur was the one? Oh, wait and when you told us his name was Arthur, we screamed inside. What the heck was an Arthur?" Candi and Fuchsia slapped each other a high five and Candi fell over on the carpeted floor and laughed so hard.

"Oh, you hussies are a mess!" Laughing with them both, "Wait, wait let me finish!"

"That Arthur kept catching me in that gym. I think he would stay late boxing and sparing so he could see me and catch my attention. He used to wait good until he knew I was coming through that door, then, take off his shirt and step in the ring. At first, I would ignore him, and then he would shout from the ring, 'Hey there legs, can you hand me a towel?' He did that every night for a week! Then, one day, I shouted back, 'Why the hell you keep calling me legs? Why don't you ask me my damn name!' He stopped right in the center of the ring where he was shadow-boxing and said, 'Well, it took you long enough to ask me why!' So, I said, 'Well, I'm asking you now.' He walked over to the corner rope and motioned me to come to him. I walked over to him, he looked at my short black denim skirt. His eyes landed on my muscular thighs, he touched my right calf and said, 'These legs here are no normal legs, they stallions.' He ran his hand up my leg and stopped at the edge of my skirt. For the first time ever, I almost melted at a man's touch! Then he went on back and continued his shadow-boxing, and I was made as hell! So then, I kept coming in at the end of his workouts, making sure my skirts hit all the right places exposing my freshly oil legs fully 'til the day he said, 'Hey, I heard you can box. Come spar with me.' I hopped up in that ring, we did a couple rounds. He was tripping, was like, 'Legs, you got a punch like a man. Where you learn to box like this?' I answered, 'Never mind that,' and got in a quick right hook. He dropped his gloves, grabbed me and we knocked boots right in the ring! For the next two weeks, I met him at that ring! He took my fight right out of me!

"When I started feeling sick and Candi told me to take a pregnancy test, I was blown away, but never once was an abortion a thought but my fear was real!" The tears began to swell up in her eyes again. "You girls was my rock during the whole pregnancy. You never knew I cried myself to sleep every night out of fear because I couldn't shake the feelings of abandonment from my mother. My daily visits to your place was because I felt safe with you guys, no judgements but real love.

When I finally got the nerve to tell Arthur after ducking him for a month, it blew my mind when he said, 'I couldn't find a better lady to have a family with. I'm here with you all the way, and know this: one day, you will be my wife if you would have me.'

"You know half of any battle in life can be won with the right support around you. You two are my support system. I know I never shared my story or my pain, it's because I didn't know how to express myself any different. After all, I'm Tommie, the tough one who's not afraid of anyone or anything but the truth of the matter is, inside, I have fears too." Grabbing Fuchsia by the hand, "Hey, tonight is a big night, your life is about to take on another journey. I want you to be happy, enjoy the ride of all that life brings you. There will be up days and down moments, sometimes you will have to cry but it's okay. Sometimes, you might want to throw in the towel but don't unless it's absolutely the last option. Never let your family or friends dictate the climate of your married life and that includes me and Candi because you know we will be bias in the situation, we going to always be on your side. Only let us in if you are in danger because you know we will fight for you 'til the death.

"I want you to learn to love your husband even when he's un-loveable. Find new ways of learning and exploring love with him. Allow him to be the man, the husband, the leader and the father; doing this does not mean you are weak, it shows you understand his role in your life and the life you are building together. Sometimes, you going to want to have that last word, but think first, lil bits, think. *Is it worth it at this moment to have the last word? Would it make or change the outcome or make it worst?* Timing is everything in a relationship. Sometimes, it's a time to speak and sometimes it's a time to listen, but all the time is to love. Fuchsia, let love fill your marriage, your home and your family. Me and Candi will always be in your corner, just a call away, but we promise never to be in your marriage because once we release you to Marvin, it's all about you two." Tommie reached out and hugged Fuchsia, "I love you lil bits."

"Wow! Wow! Wow! Is this our Tommie? All that up in there! That's the most I ever heard you say in one whole day! That was incredible, so beautiful, I mean, what you said to Fuchsia," Candi said as she joined in the hug. "Man, I knew you was rough and tough but sentimental too!" she said, wiping her eyes.

"So, tell me, what's the reason behind the skirts every day? I understand the jeans, I mean you stacked and all, and look incredible in your skirts, but I always wanted to ask you that."

"I wear my short skirts every day as my reminder: no, I'm not the boy my dad wanted, I'm the strong powerful beautiful girl my mom had!" Tommie explained.

Fuchsia still holding on to both Candi and Tommie's hand, "You know what? I knew I loved you girls but today is confirmation of my love and our unbreakable bond. I could not imagine this day without you two, I used to dream about my wedding day and the talk that my mom or grandma Lydia would have with me on this day or even Ms. Dee, and none of them are any longer with me, but my incredible sisters have made my day so touching and special. You give me peace when I'm confused; you have been my rock, my shelter, my protectors, my teachers, and now my inspirations. My day would not have been complete without you. Thank you for loving me!"

Candi squeezed her hand tighter, "Lil bits, we can't even begin to imagine what you are feeling right now, knowing your mom is around somewhere and is aware that today is your wedding day but no connection between you two. I know what it's like to lose a mother but only through death. However, to lose her and she is alive is a whole different level to me. If I had brought a daughter into this world, there would be nothing that would keep me away from that child. The both of you having to grow up and face this world alone without your moms was both your moms' choices, not yours. Please understand I'm not judging either of your moms but a person like me who desires a child can't fathom how a woman who is blessed to give birth would turn her back on the baby she carried in her womb, gave birth to, watch grow for a few years, then walk away or not love enough to believe them, and instead take the word of someone else over that child!"

Candi's emotions started rising because of her own pain of wanting a child coupled with the doctor's report that she may never conceive. "Man, I'm just saying, if either of your moms could just see you two now, the women that you blossomed into, the joy you bring to the lives of the people around you." Turning to look at Fuchsia, "I can't tell you how to feel and nobody has a right to tell you that. All I'm going to say is: it may not be today and I totally understand that but in the near future, try to find a way to meet your mom, listen to what she may have to say. She may have changed. We all know life can throw us curves and who we were yesterday is not who we are today. We all make mistakes on this journey and no one deserves to be held in the captivity of judgement because of our mistakes, especially if we have matured from that place and now trying to rectify our mistakes.

"So, lil bits, you may find that that's the state she's in, wanting to right her wrongs; give her that chance to do so. Now, if she still blaming you, keep on moving because you don't have to be tortured by the negativity. This time, it will be your mature choice. Listen, I'm not saying not to forgive her if she's still in that place of negative vibes, I'm saying forgive her, love her but it's okay to love her from a distance. That's all I'm going to say on that subject, and we won't bring your mom up any more today.

"Fuchsia, you are about to enter a new realm, and this one is one of love and experiences you have never had before, and possibly through this union, give birth to children. To give birth, you must have sex!" Candi now smiling as she looks into Fuchsia's eyes, "That's right, I'm finally saying the sex word to you!"

Fuchsia started to blush and giggle, "You finally going to have this talk, huh?"

Candi, interrupting her, snapped back, "Girl, you better shut it, listen and give me my mother-daughter wisdom moment! Now, this serious talk here. Lil bits, you being a virgin and all. For your first time, you may not see fireworks and volcanic eruptions. It may be painful, but I promise you it gets so much better after that! Tonight will all depend on how your new husband prepares you; how he marinates your body with his tender love and fills your every being with passion 'til your secret garden longs for him to enter in and welcomes him to join her in the magical world of ecstasy. I want you to enjoy every moment of exploring his body, every muscle of his being. Don't be afraid to touch him, caress his manhood, stroke him tenderly in ways that assures him that tonight, you'll give him the awesome pleasure of entering your secret garden that you saved just for him. Lil bits, don't be shy; tonight is the night that ushers you into a whole new realm of womanhood. Enjoy your debut, let the tigress in you loose and show him what is now his."

"In other words, put it on him! Make him scream your name! 'Whose your momma!' " shouted Tommie as she jumped off the recliner, they all were sitting on and started gyrating her hips across the floor.

The three of them burst into laughter like little girls just exploring boys for the first time.

Tommie, dancing in a circle, shaking her hips, "Say my name Marvin, oh say it louder. Oh, Pastor Marvin, what big hands you have. Oh Pastor, what big feet you have. Oh, Oh, Oh Pastor, I didn't know you was built like this!"

Tommie, still laughing and spinning around, "Oh, I would love to be a fly on that hotel wall tonight!"

"Girl, shut up! You so crazy and nasty!" Fuchsia said laughingly with a baby voice and covered her face in embarrassment. "You two are a mess!"

Suddenly, there was a knock on the bedroom door, then it opened slightly. "Hey, what's going on in here with all that laughter and commotion?" said Sasha as she entered the room, walking towards the sitting parlor. You three waking everyone up from their naps with all this loud laughter, what's so funny? Then again, I don't think I want or need to know because I can only imagine!" she said looking at the three of them, shaking her head in amusement. "Hey, look, it's four forty-five. I think the bride needs to begin getting prepared, don't you?" she said as she smiled at Fuchsia who was now standing up from the recliner.

"Yeah, you right! I can't be late! I told Marvin I would be at the church on time tonight," Fuchsia said as she rushed to her master bath to run the water in her claw foot tub which sat in the middle of her oversized bathroom. Then, she poured her bottle of luxurious milk and honey bubble bath into the running water. Walking back towards her girls, "Okay, you three better be ready on time too! And someone tap on Melondy's bedroom door, please, to make sure she's up as well."

"First girl, what is that you poured into your bath? it smells so good! That some type of aphrodisiac? You about to put a spell on him!" Candi said as she walked to the gold bottle resting on the small glass table beside the tub. "Wow, this stuff ain't no joke! Who' this by?" She opened the lid to take a deep whiff.

"I purchased it at an exclusive boutique in town. I loved the scent and feel so much that I bought the layering set; it came with the luxurious bath, the silky body mousse and perfume. I bought two, packed one for my honeymoon," she said as she walked over to her bathroom vanity table, picked up both the gold jar and gold perfume spray bottle, and motioned them to come smell. "When I smelled this, I knew this was the scent for my wedding."

"Girl, you gonna make that man horny. I know he'll want to snatch that wedding dress off right there in the church! Me-Tarzan-you-Jane type of action!" Tommie laughed as she started gyrating around again.

The four of them began laughing uncontrollably till their stomachs were in knots.

"Get out! It's time for you ladies to go!" Fuchsia said laughing so hard tears were streaming down her cheeks. She motioned them in a fanning way, walking them to the door. "Go, go, get, scat," she closed the bedroom door behind them. "They so crazy," she said, wiping tears from her face.

Undressed, she walked towards her bathroom, tossing her clothes into the hamper bin masquerading as a drawer in the wall. Grabbing her head towel, she wrapped it around her head. She opened the linen closet beside the toilet room, pulled out a fresh gold towel and two fresh new bath cloths, one white for her face and another gold for her body. She tossed the gold bath cloth into the warm bubble that filled the tub and slid her small framed body into the inviting, warm, bubble water containing glistening scents of exotic Milk and Honey with a hint of soft musk and almond. Laying there, she allowed her body to soak in every sensual moment. A gentle tap came from her bedroom door followed by Melondy's soft voice calling out to her, "Fuchsia, it's me, Melondy. I have something for you from your husband-to-be, may I come in?"

"Sure," she said as she slid deeper under the bubbles. "What do you have? What has that sweet man done this time?" A curious grin on her face, Melondy made her way to the bathroom with a beautiful crystal champagne flute, trimmed in gold sitting on a gold tray and a bottle of Non-Alcoholic Sweet Sparkling Pink champagne. She sat the tray on the glass stand beside the tub. On the tray was a handwritten note addressed to:

The future Mrs. Marvin Drake, cheers until we meet at the alter.

Loving you Always.

Without a word, Melondy walked to her room to get dressed.

"Who could run from all this love?" she smiled as she sipped the poured glass of champagne. "Cheers, my sweet lover 'til we join as husband and wife."

Stepping out of her tub unto the plush rug towel, she dried her body off as she stared into her full-sized bathroom vanity mirror. Her eyes captured every inch of her small framed body. She turned slightly to see her side and back view. She couldn't help but wonder if her soon-to-be husband would love her even more or any less when sees her nakedness for the first time. She reached for her new-found love Milk and Honey Body Mousse. Opening the jar released the sensuous aroma which filled the air around her. Scooping out a generous amount with her finger tips, she began applying the Mousse from her tiny feet up her freshly waxed legs and thighs, carefully making sure not to miss one spot.

The intoxicating aroma was engaging her body with the silkiness and sensuousness of the Mousse. Gently, she further applied it to her lower back and buttocks, working her way to her womanhood. She stopped for a moment and looked carefully at her vagina, hoping Marvin would be pleased as she had all the hair removed except a tiny patch manicured into a well-groomed heart with its peak resting so perfectly at the top of her Labia. She applied a small amount of the Mousse on the top and sides of her smooth vaginal area, endeavoring to get none inside. Blushing at the thought of her soon-to-be husband being the first man to ever see or touch that intimate part of her being, she glided her hand with the Mousse around her small waist upwards to her small firm breast, applying it upon every inch of them, leaving behind the sensuous aroma and its silkiness. Reaching her neck, shoulders and arm, the warm, inviting and intoxicating scent raised her emotions to a feeling of readiness.

She picked up her silk nude with Ivory lace panties and gently slid it up her body, making the needed adjustment as she put on her matching strapless bra. She took another quick glance at her body in the full-length mirror before making her way to her walk-in closet, unzipping the large bridal bag hanging on the valet. She unzipped the bag and allowed it to slide to the carpeted floor. Her eyes began filling with tears, "Grandma Lydia, this is it: the big day. Oh, how I wish you were here to share it with me. I chose the hand stitched pearls on the breast of the dress as a reminder that you're in my heart" she said as she patted herself on the chest. She stared at the intricate details of her wedding dress, ensuring everything was perfect. She smiled at herself, knowing Grandma Lydia would approve. From the drawer of her vanity closet, she pulled out her nude silk with Ivory Satin, trimmed garter with a tiny gold key resting in its center. She slid it up her smooth bare left leg resting up high on her thigh. Excited by the thoughts of Marvin removing this garter and truly being the first man to ever enter her special garden, she thought out loud, "Funny how I used to think it was just a funny or sexy gesture for the reception until finding out that the garter was symbolic of purity or a bride's virginity which made me want to have a key attached to mine. Boy, I'm all yours and I can hardly wait! You won't be tossing this garter, No sir! That's why I'm placing it way up here!" she said as she pushed it up further. "No worries Babe, I got one for the other leg for you to toss but this one means business!" she said as she did a slow motion gyrate in her closet vanity mirror.

Now blushing at her thoughts, "Wow girl, I guess this is really it." Nervousness began to come upon her, and with trembling in her hands, she reached for her wedding dress.

Tommie, Candi and Sasha burst into Fuchsia's bedroom all at once, startling her. "Miss thing, where are you? We, your maids, are here to assist you into that dress!" They all shouted in one voice.

"You know you shouldn't scare a bride on her wedding day, right?" she shouted back as she stepped out of her walk-in closet. "Really, you three? And where do you think I would be?"

"Well, damn!" screamed Tommie as she glanced at Fuchsia's well-formed small half naked body. "Don't kill the man on his wedding night! That's some sexy secrets you have on there, except it ain't no secret! I see all your goods through those panties and that ain't no bra either. It's just some lace holding onto your boobs! Lil bits, Wow! I ain't no dude or nothing but boy, you looking good. Marvin may not be able to handle all that sexy, you know, he a preacher and all!" she said with screaming laughter.

"Wait, wait. Is that a heart I see through those see-through panties!" My word, you are going to kill your husband on his wedding night! Shoot, I might have to go get mine done like that!" Candi said as she spun Fuchsia around to get a better look. "I can't take it! You are all grown up and everything."

"What! Oh, you two, please shut up! I'm a ole virgin! I ain't got time to play! I figured I'm going in all the way. Plus, between you two, I learned from the best! Did you really expect anything less?" Fuchsia said as she did a slow dance move.

"Now me, I'm stuck on that garter! A key? Oh Lawdy, what you got up your sleeves for the Pastor?" Sasha said screaming in laughter.

They all stood there, laughing like young school girls.

"Wait, where is Melondy?" Fuchsia said between laughs.

"Probably somewhere picking daisies," Tommie laughed harder.

"Don't say that! You promised me, Tommie. Don't start," Fuchsia said, wiping away laughter tears. "Look, all this laughter gonna have to stop when I put on my makeup!"

"Makeup? Oh yeah, you mean the little eyeliner and lipstick you wear? You can reapply that in one minute because I can't promise you I won't be laughing anymore today cause you know how that crazy Tommie is," Candi said as she tried to pull herself together. "Shoot, I'm the one who has to touch up her face now!" she says as she takes a glance of her fully done face in the mirror.

"See me, I'm just natural. I like it simple," Sasha chimed in.

"Ain't nobody ask you, Miss wonder woman. Sasha girl, please you can use a little som'n too, you know?" Candi snapped back.

"Oh no, not you two!" Fuchsia laughing at them both. "We need to get moving, the limo will be here soon."

As she walked into the closet, Candi stopped and turned saying, "What about the photographers, what time are they coming?"

"Oh, they are meeting us at the church," Melondy responded.

With a quick look and snap of the head, Tommie turned to Melondy, "Is there anything you don't know? But on the real tip, girlie, I was talking to Fuchsia."

"What's the problem? I was just responding to the question on the floor," Melondy responded in her soft voice.

"O-okay... the photographers are going to the church. Now, that that's clear, let's do what we are all here to do, assist this beautiful bride on this day. Are we good?" Sasha said as she stood between them.

"You right Sasha, I apologize Lil bits. I apologize to you too Melissa," Tommie said.

"Melondy. My name is Melondy."

"Hey Fuchs, where are your bridal shoes?" Candi said, changing the subject

"Over there in the closet beside the vanity table," she responded as she stood in the full-length mirror, watching herself as Tommie brought her wedding gown.

"This is amazing, Lil bits, so gorgeous," Tommie exclaimed as she lifted it out of the unzipped garment bag.

"Thanks, Tommie. Oh, I think I should step into it. Sasha, please help Tommie hold the other side? Candi, can you help lift the train and Melondy, please help keep me balanced so I can step into this dress?" Fuchsia gave directions to her all four of them.

"Sure," they said in one voice.

They all took their positions as Fuchsia assigned them. Candi lifted and flounced the train while Sasha and Tommie held the dress from both sides up as Melondy helped her step into the dress. Slowly guiding the dress up over her small frame hips and waist, they slid it up until she was able to slide her right arm into the one sleeve. She wiggled her body into the perfect position as the dress seemly melted on her body like a well-tailored glove. Tommie began buttoning up the small round crystal buttons with the Ivory loops, beginning at her butt then up her waistline, ending at her back. She counted as she fastens each button, "One, two, three... Fifteen, sixteen, seventeen... Well, damn lil bits, how many of these damn buttons are on this dress? Twenty - two, twenty-three, twenty-four, twenty-five, Finally! Who would ever think you needed twenty-five freaking buttons on your little body! Marvin gonna snatch them off as one goddamn button!"

Standing there in awe of Fuchsia in her wedding dress, the four of them were speechless; their eyes fixed upon every tiny detail of the dress.

It was important to Fuchsia that the designer captured her vision down to every detail, even the Ivory pearls in the center in memory of Grandma Lydia. She chose Ivory because of her favorite picture with her mom and Mitch; that was the color of the dress she remembered her mom wore that day. She had her wedding dress designed all nude sheer fabric from the top throughout the train, but double layered the breast area along with her butt and vagina areas to conceal her intimate parts. The nude right sleeve ran down her arm, ending at her wrist in Ivory laced ribbon, leaving her left arm bare as the nude silky fabric came around and wrapped around her breast and tiny waist. Large Ivory pearls were hand sewn into the front center of the bodices of the dress, giving the illusion that she had pearls resting on her entire breast and upper stomach area which tuxedoed at her waist with Ivory Satin ribbons that dropped into a deep V cut just resting on the hips of both her front and back. The silky nude stretch fabric formed a flattering A-lined Silhouette that hugged every curve of her hips and thighs, then slowly opening up around her knee area getting wider as it climbed down her legs which flowed into a six-foot Ivory ribbon laced train. Every three inches of the dress from her hips throughout the train was embellished with a 3D Flower Appliques with Ivory ribbons.

Marveling at the sensuousness of Fuchsia's dress, they all stopped and looked at the picture - perfect Bride and her court, for they stood next to her, looking in the large full-length mirror at their reflection, smiling as they saw it all coming together as one complete piece.

Candi, Sasha and Melondy, her Bride's Maids, all wore a Blush colored strapless soft Tulle A-Lined gown with a sweetheart Neckline trimmed in Ivory satin ribbon. Tommie, her Matron of honor, wore a Blush Colored off the shoulder sheer left arm sleeved Soft Tulle A-lined with a V neck line gown. Standing in bridal line formation: Bride, Matron of honor, then Bride's Maids was the most incredible sight. Fuchsia's and Tommie's sheer sleeved arms side by side with Fuchsia's bare arm and Melondy's bare arms forming perfect bookends of a picture just as she envisioned.

"Can someone just say stunning! This is going to be some kinda beautiful bridal court! I hope Marvin's groomsmen ready for all this action right here!" Candi said, striking a vogue pose.

"You so right, girl. I hope they ready for all this feline glamor cause we hot and sexy up in here! Oh, you too, Melondy, you clean up pretty good yourself," Tommie snickered.

"Well, Tommie, I may just have to agree with you on this one. I have never felt so pretty, and I don't know if this is right or not, but I feel kinda sexy too," Melondy blushing as she stared at herself in the mirror.

"Hey, I was kinda uneasy that you wanted us all to have our hair in a down sweep flowing to the right pony tail with this Ivory pearl holder on it, but I get it now because this bridal court is on point!

Now that I see your slightly curled bouncing pony to the left, it makes so much sense!"

"I visualized the look I was aiming for, and you girls made it come to pass cause for real, you ladies have snapped the radar of beauty!" Fuchsia chimed in. "Now, for the finishing touches, so we can be out here; I got a man to marry today!"

Motioning with her hands, "Alright. Candi you get my tiara. Melondy, you get my Diamond stud earrings. Sasha, you get my shoes and Bridal bag, and I'm all set and ready to roll. They are all over on my closet vanity table."

The four of them hurried, following directions. Melondy began putting the diamond studs in Fuchsia's ear lobes. Sasha carefully kneeled down in front of Fuchsia, placing her Ivory transparent peep toe slide on 4" Silk heel Stiletto in front of each foot. She stopped, looked up at Fuchsia, and held her by the hand.

"Fuchs, I count it an honor to serve as one of your Bride's Maid today. You and I have been friends since elementary school. We have so many memories together from laughter to tears. Who knew our friendship would have lasted this long? I have watched you through your struggles of youth into a blossomed woman.

"When you ran away, I thought I would never see you again. I will never forget the day you left: my mother opened the door as she heard the banging, I watched your mom's frail body fall into my mother's arm, crying and shaking her head in disbelief, saying she don't believe you left like that, telling my mother to ask me where you were.

I told her, 'Ms. Angie, I really don't know where Fuchsia is. All I know is she said she had to get out of that house because she couldn't take it any longer.' When I said that, she looked at me and said, 'What you trying to say? My lovely home isn't a good home?' My mother had to interrupt her, 'Angie, she's only telling you what your daughter told her, that's all.' Your mom stormed out of my house, crying, saying, 'It's all lies.' My mother closed the door and held me so tight. She told me I did right in telling her the truth, 'We are just going to pray that that poor child is safe and found.'

"Days went by, no word. The detectives questioned everyone in the school and neighborhoods for weeks. They stopped questioning when your letter came and my mother called a detective to show it to him, and we gave the one you sent to your mom. Fuchsia, those were the darkest days of my young life. We missed so much growing up together, but I'm so glad you found me again.

"Now, that was the best day of my life for sure! I don't know why you waited all those years to reach out to me again but I'm glad you did. The day my mother called and told me you called, it was actually my first date with Sonny. We went out for coffee at some new coffee spot everyone raved about, but the coffee was okay, nothing special. I remembered thinking why my mother was calling cause I spoke with her before I left my apartment. So, I answered a little annoyed; all I heard her say was Fuchsia, and my heart stopped. When she told me you called and left your number, a tear ran down from my eye. Poor Sonny thought something terrible had happened. When I hung up, I told him about you. He said he remembered about the missing girl, but he didn't know that the girl was my best friend. That's the afternoon we bonded, because of you.

"See, as the years passed, I never talked about you to anyone because it was too painful. I wasn't sure if you were even alive. I didn't want to answer anymore questions, I didn't want people to keep asking if I was okay because I wasn't. Every time I heard on the news about a young girl missing or found dead, I cried my eyes out. I couldn't sleep at night; my mother finally took me to therapy, and I had to finally move on with my life.

However, secretly, I never stopped looking for you. As the years went on and I began to mature into a young lady, I often wondered what you looked like at this age, that age. So, when you left that message, Sonny was the first person I spoke your name out loud to and he listened and held my hand as we walked and talked. That evening when I phoned you and heard your voice, one side of me was excited but the other side was kinda angry at you for being gone so long without calls or letters. However, I quickly got over it when you said you wanted to see me and would purchase a plane ticket for me if I would come. I could hardly wait to see your face, and when I did, I thought to myself, *she's even more beautiful than I imagined*, but I could tell life wasn't as simple for you as it was for me.

"My little friend, Fuchsia, was no longer here, she had been replaced by this stunning woman who knew life in ways that I couldn't imagine. You were once a delicate wild bud but now, you were this stunning kinda reserved woman whose eyes held her secrets. I knew not to ask you questions but embrace the woman you have grown to become. So, on this your wedding day, I salute you. You have endured and experienced much, more than you may ever tell but one thing I know is that you are truly an overcomer; you are my Hero-rella, that is, my Cinderella Hero!"

Picking up one shoe at a time, she continued, "As I have this honor of placing your glass slippers on your feet today, I pray your dark midnights hours never come again. That you will never have to feel pain like you experienced again; that your days be full of sunshine even when it's raining. That love will always encamp around you."

Lifting up the front of Fuchsia's wedding dress, she slid on her right shoe, then left. She stood up and kissed her friend on both sides of her cheeks. "Friends for life," she whispered in her ear.

"For life," Fuchsia whispered back as she fought to hold back tears.

"Oh, here we go again! Can we just leave before we cry ourselves out of a wedding!" Tommie said, handing Fuchsia a kleenex.

Again, laughter filled the room as Candi placed the final touch. She placed the sparkling crystal tiara on Fuchsia's head, setting it properly in place and kissing her forehead as a mother. "Love you, lil bits."

"Love you more, Candi, and thanks again for being my guardian angel," Fuchsia whispered.

"Hey, wait. Look, we forgot to put this garter on; you know those dudes don't want to skip this part!" Tommie said as she picked the second garter out of the shoe box.

"Whew! Thanks, I almost forgot this one. We would have just had to skip that part at the reception because this other one is strictly for Marvin's eyes only!" Sighing with laughter, she chuckled as Tommie slid it up her right thigh.

Mitch interrupted their laughter by knocking on the door. "Alright ladies, your chariot has arrived. Let's get moving, we got a bride to get hitched in forty minutes," he said as he opened the door.

Frozen in place, with his eyes seeming to lose focus, he blinked. A sense of numbness came to his legs, he felt as if he couldn't move. Not knowing what to say to his once baby sister, he took a deep breath.

"Well, I got to say baby girl, I have mixed emotions right here: one part of me want to say, 'Oh no, you're not leaving this house like that,' then, the other part is saying 'Fuchs, you make the most beautiful bride I ever have seen.' I don't know if I should be a father or brother of the bride; should I let you go today, handing you over to a man I have never met, or should I prepare to fight to keep you as my baby girl forever? I... I just don't know what or how to feel... I just got you back and now I'm giving you away. Either way, Fuchs, you look so beautiful. I'm getting too emotional, so I think you better take my hand and let's get going before I change my mind."

Taking her gently by the hand, he escorted her out the bedroom. Lady was prancing in front as if she was escorting the bride who was walking carefully downstairs with her bridesmaids following close behind, and Candi holding up her train.

"Lady, I love you. Please, be a good girl for Melondy while I'm away," she reached down carefully and rubbed Lady's little head. Lady wagged her tail as if she understood, she ran to stand beside the door as Fuchsia preceded out.

Melondy, picking up their bridal bouquets, "She will be fine. We will have a great time while you are away."

The chauffeur's assistant met them at the door. Mitch handed Fuchsia over to him and watched him walk her to the waiting Ivory Limo as the driver opened the door, welcoming them and helping each one board the vehicle.

Mitch, motioning to the assistant, "Sir, when you get a moment, I need your help with the bride's luggage please," he said as he turned to go up the staircase to Fuchsia's bedroom. Having gathered her luggage and done a final check to make sure she has everything, he called for the assistant. "Sir, you can come on up, she has a few pieces here. I'm going to need your help bringing them down."

After taking down the last of his sister's luggage, he ran upstairs to grab his overnight bag, as well as the others'. He patted Lady on her little head and then turned on the foyer light and the porch light by the front door. He locked the door and, with the help of the assistant, put the last things in the trunk.

"Hey big brother, you know I love you so much," she smiled as he boarded the limo.

CHAPTER FIFTEEN

The ride to the church seemed to be a long journey. Mitch could barely look at his babe sister who is now a full-grown woman; how time had passed. Sasha could see the worried look on Mitch's face. She softly spoke up, "Hey there, what you thinking about?"

"Ha, ha, ha, why? You trying to read me?

"Just thinking to myself, wondering what life would have been if I hadn't made the wrong choices I made. I would already know this Marvin, not getting to meet him for the first time. What if he is not the one? What kind of past did this guy have? Everyone has a history, even the pastor.

He paused to look over his shoulders, making sure his sister could not hear their conversation; then he continued.

"If only I had stayed close by, I could have protected her from Kevin, and she would have still lived home with Momma. If that one night I had gone home early instead of getting caught up with turf wars, trying to prove who had a right, who was better and the tough ones in the neighborhood; If only I didn't take on that challenge to go and kill Stink, I would not have been caught off guard and got stabbed myself. Man, that guy didn't know how close he was to his life being snuffed out. I wonder what ever happened to that smart mouth joker. He is probably dead by now cause he made a mess wherever he went, just trouble that Stink was. So, if it wasn't going to be me who did kill him? Somebody else sure was going to do it. Well, at least that's what I tried to convince myself of. Boy, I will never forget that dude's face with that crazy looking gold grill in his mouth, and that stupid "S" tattooed on his hand."

Shaking his head, "Boy, we all was kinda stupid back then. That "S" shoulda stood for stupid not Stink."

"Hey, that conversation looks kinda deep up there, what's up? I see you shaking your head," Fuchsia said, smiling, as she glanced at her brother.

"Nothing, we just thinking about us as kids; what our life would have been like if I made better choices, that's all."

"Hey, we all have different paths to our destination. We all here today; we all came by one form or another, but the only thing that matters is that we are all here together. Besides, the past is behind us. Let's look forward to our future."

"Baby girl, what if Marvin and I don't vibe together, then what?"

"Well, I'm going to say it like this: you both are a part of my life and always will be. So, no matter what the issue could be, you better work it out and show up like men. You two are the only two men in my life. So, if you love me, you will find a way to make it work."

Tommie chimed in, "Well, I guess we going to be one big happy family even if it kills us!"

"No worries, we all will get along just fine. Besides, it's not about either of us; it's all about Fuchsia and Marvin," said Sasha.

"You right, Sasha. You are right," Mitch responded, looking out of the limo's window. He remained quiet for the rest of the drive to the church.

As the Limo pulled into the parking lot of the red brick church, Fuchsia's stomach began to flutter as though butterflies had taken over her body. On each side of the stairs that led into the double glass doors of the church, there were the beautiful large bouquet on the white pedestals. Two men dressed in black suits with white shirts and black ties came out of the church doors and walked to the door of the limo to speak with the driver's assistant.

"Good evening, I'm Brian, and this is Calvin. We are the ushers for the wedding. We are here to assist in any way we can. First off, we would ask if the bride or bridal party needs anything? Also, if the Father of the Bride here with you?"

Candi responded before the driver's assistant could answer. "Good evening, we are fine, and the brother of the bride will be escorting the bride down the aisle."

Mitch cleared his throat. "Hey man, I'm Mitch. I'm standing in as father of the bride."

"Great. Hey Mitch, glad to meet you. Can you please come with us? We will take you to where the groomsmen are," said one of the ushers as the driver opened the door for Mitch.

Mitch followed the two ushers up the stairs of the church, then, down the hallway until they stopped at the door labeled, 'Pastor suite.' One of the ushers knocked on the door of the suite. The door was opened by another gentleman dressed in the same attire.

Calvin, the usher with Mitch, spoke up first. "Hey man, the bride and her ladies are here, waiting in the limo, and here is her brother who will escort her down the aisle, Mitch, right?" He confirmed as he escorted Mitch into the study. "This is Donald; he got you from here."

Mitch entered the suite with the three groomsmen and best man. The four men were all dressed in navy blue tuxedo's with Navy Cummerbunds and bow ties, Ivory shirts and Navy shoes; each had a corsage pinned on his lapel. There was a round cocktail table prepared with fresh fruit, water, and mints. The men were all standing around it talking as Mitch, and the usher approached.

"Everyone this is Mitch, the Brides brother. He will be escorting her down the aisle," said the usher.

"Hey, Mitch, nice to meet you," they all said at once. Each one of the men introduced themselves as they shook his hand. Mitch joined in with the men standing around the four-foot round cocktail table. His eyes scanned the large Pastor's suite; one side of the room was a large oak desk, and burgundy leather chair with two chairs sat in front of the desk. A bookshelf, filled with books, covered one side of the wall across from the desk and a large gold eagle with spread wings was hung. *Nice,* he thought to himself.

The side of the room where he and the other men stood was situated the four-foot round cocktail table, a large burgundy leather sofa and two burgundy leather arm chairs across from the sofa. Picking up bottled water, Mitch was curious as to where the groom was. He opened the bottle, took a sip and openly ask the other men, "Has the groom arrived yet?"

"Oh, yes he's here. He just stepped out the office for a few, he will be back soon," responded one of the groomsmen.

"Thanks, I just need to introduce myself before the ceremony begins," replied Mitch.

"You haven't met Pastor Marvin yet?" responded another groomsman.

"Nah, I live out of town. Just flew in this morning. I surprised my babe sis; she didn't know I would be able to attend."

"Sweet! We know she was ecstatic to see you," the shortest groomsmen said. "Such a beautiful sweet lady, your sister."

Mitch replied with a grin on his face, "Yeah, she is. It's been a minute since we had time to sit and chat; we had a great morning catching up."

Suddenly, the office door opened and in walked a tall, well-built man, hair neatly groomed, fading around the sides and back. His features were very distinct as his eyebrows perfectly framed his eyes with remarkable precision as if they were placed there to match his piercing brown eyes. His nose was keen with a groomed mustache resting between it and his small lips. His skin looked as smooth as a rich creamed olive butter...

A tap on his shoulder interrupted his evaluation. "Hey Mitch, right?" one of the ushers said as he motioned for Mitch to follow him. "That's the groom, Pastor Marvin. Let me introduce you to him." They walked across the floor towards Marvin who was leaning over his desk into the file drawer.

"Hey, Marv. I want to introduce to you to your future brother-in-law, Mitch."

Marvin, immediately lifting with a smile to greet Mitch, stretched out his hand to shake Mitch's hand. As his hand approached Mitch's, Mitch froze and dropped his hand to his side.

With surprise and anger, Mitch looked at Marvin closely, "Wait, you're Marvin? This some kind of joke, right?" he said as he reached for Marvin's right hand and firmly held it.

CHAPTER SIXTEEN

thought you said this is going to be a small wedding? Tommie said, watching the guest walk up the walkway of the church. "I see a whole lot of people going in."

"It is small. I only have a small guest list; I don't have many people in my life who I wanted to invite. Everyone who matters is in the wedding, just a few from the office and the Jewelry clerk who sold us this ring. Everyone else is the church family and a few of Marvin's friends. He, like myself, don't have many people in his inner circle. His mother is passed now, and his father is old in a wheelchair. Marvin helps take care of him. He used to live in Ohio, but after Marvin's mother died, there was no one to take care of him, so, Marvin sent for him. They are very close now, but when he was a kid, they wasn't because his dad was locked up most of his youth."

"Wait, so, you telling us that ole preacher boy didn't grow up with a silver spoon attached to his hand?" Tommie interrupted.

Fuchsia, looking at Tommie and Candi, realizing she never shared Marvin's background with the closest people in her life. "Oh, it never dawned on me that I never told you about where he grew up, I just assumed you knew. I apologize."

"Wait, is there something we should be worried about Fuchs?" Candi said with a questioning look.

"Really, baby girl, really?" Tommie snapped back.

Sasha jumped into the conversation. "Come on, ya'll. Whatever or whoever he was, he is not that person any longer. People have a right to change. Look at everyone in this limo; none are who we started to be, plus, I don't believe now is the time to bring up the past."

"Hold up! Sounds like you know something we don't know, Sasha," waving her finger between her and Tommie, Candi shouted.

"No! Stop it! We are not going to go here with no blame game! It ain't that deep, you two. Sasha only knows because he came from our old neighborhood, that's all! When I found out who he was, I called Sasha to ask her if she remembered him, that's the only reason she knows, and you don't! Sasha don't remember him from the neighborhood either because we are a few years younger than him and Sasha, like me, wasn't allowed to hang in the streets. The only encounter I had with him was on the bus when some guys were picking on me, and he shouted from the back of the bus for them to leave me alone. I only glanced at the guy with the voice that helped me, so, I didn't know who he was until we were talking one night, and I told him where I grew up. We were both shocked that we grew up in the same neighborhood. I told him who my brother was, and he was stunned. He said to me that he knew it was something about my eyes that reminded him of someone but couldn't put his finger on it. However, when I told him that Mitch was my brother, he shouted 'That's it!'

"He reminded me of the bus ride; that he was the guy on the back of the bus who told the other guys to leave me alone. He also confessed that I was actually his first crush as a kid! He's three years older. He said he used to watch me walk through the neighborhood with my mom; thought I was the prettiest girl he ever saw but one, I was too young, and two, Mitch was my brother."

"So, you telling us that he and Mitch are friends? Does Mitch know this? Questioned Candi.

"No, not exactly. They were not friends, nor does Mitch know who Marvin is. I haven't seen my brother in years neither did I expect him to be here for my wedding. Besides, I'm not worried. Marvin is not the same boy from those streets, and neither is Mitch, and I prayed about it after I found out; that when they meet, all will be well. I didn't expect them to meet on my wedding day!

"They are both now two matured men who made it out of those streets, overcame obstacles and are successful, loving guys whom I just happen to love. So, they must work it out, especially if they both plan to be a part of my life because I'm not going to choose one for the other!

"Can you imagine the guy who saved me on the bus all those years ago is the same guy who stole my heart? When I found out who he was, I fell more in love; it's like we were destined to be together. Who would have even thought all those years and miles ago that we would connect and become husband and wife?" smiling at Candi and Tommie. "I love Marvin and Mitch, and I know they both love me. It may be rocky at first, but it will work out for the good of us all."

Tommie, shaking her head in disbelief, "I hope so lil bits. I hope so."

Melondy, who was listening quietly spoke up. "Listen, I know I may be the outsider of the group, but I'm a good judge of character. I believe like Fuchsia said, that it will work out. Pastor Marvin has always been open with the congregation about how he grew up and what he used to do, but he always told us how his life changed. And just like Sasha already said, we are not the people of our past. We all have overcome obstacles, and we all have our hidden scars of battles; they stand as reminders of how much and how far we have come. I know you see me now and possibly think I came from some prestigious family and had it all. Yes, I did, but being born in a prestigious family didn't stop me from becoming an addict, it didn't help save my life.

"You see, most people look at my outer woman and get stuck there, they don't see the hidden scars of my painful fifteen years as a junkie. Yes, I was addicted to heroin. Yes, I shot drugs in my veins. I stole and sold my body for fifteen years to support my addiction. Yes, I know I don't look like who I used to be. You looking at this quiet white little church girl now, but this little white woman bears scars of her past as well. I'm thankful I'm no longer her and no longer going in and out of some rehab, lying to myself.

"My family, the struggle was real. My inner demons were real, and it wasn't until I faced my truth and dealt with them that I could successfully be set free from my addiction. I have been through so many programs I can't even count. My parents tried everything money could buy, but it wasn't until I hit my bottom that I could also look up to get out. My story may not be your story, but I have a story. I didn't lose a parent; I had both my parents. I didn't grow up in the inner city. I grew up on a beachfront estate with a nanny and housekeeper. I had the privilege of going to the best schools, but I was lonely and left alone most of the time as my parents were focused on building their wealth and giving me everything but themselves. So, I filled my little lonely days exploring and experiencing; one day turned into many days and then, I was on the course of destruction.

"It took my parents two years before they even noticed that I was different. I was not their little girl by the time they opened their eyes to see, I was already too far gone, and eventually, I took to the streets. I'm sharing this with you to allow you to see we all have history, some bad and some worst but our past does not define our future. I, like you, am not who I once was and don't desire to be reminded of who I once was or judged for what I once did. We all are positive proofs that there is life after death; that there is resurrection after the burial; that there is sunshine after the storm; there is laughter after the tears. We are overcomers. We have been through the fire, but we overcame. So has Pastor

Marvin and Mitch. Neither of them is the same people they started as; they too have overcome and changed."

"Holy crap! I'm shocked! Miss purity white is just like us!" Tommie screamed, bursting into laughter. She hugged Melondy, and said, "Girl, you alright with me," as laughter filled the limo.

CHAPTER SEVENTEEN

Tension began to fill the pastor's suite as Mitch stood still, holding firmly unto Marvin's right hand, staring at the tattoo that stretched from the bottom of his thumb and disappearing under the sleeve of his tailored Ivory shirt.

Mitch, studying Marvin's tattoo as he had done many years ago in Shorty's old garage, remembered it like it was yesterday. He remembered the day he first ran into Stink. Stink was a trouble maker and leader of his pack. All the guys he ran with looked up to him like he was some god.

Listening to the rain hitting the roof of that old garage, Mitch remembered momma told him to get the leaves up from around the house before the rain.

"Mitch, come on! It's your turn, go on, roll the dice! Stop staring out into space, you holding up the game!" Shorty shouted at Mitch as he shoved him in the shoulder.

"Man, shut your mouth and don't push me no more!" Mitch said as he rolled the dice.

"Six! Move over and let the pro in!" Curtis shouted as the dice Mitch rolled landed four on one and two on the other.

"Man, I'm going to have to run home for a little while. I forgot to clean those leaves around the basement steps before it rained or else it will cause the drain to be backed up. I don't feel like hearing momma's mouth!" Mitch said as he stood up from his kneeling position.

"Sit your punk ass back down, mommas boy!" shouted a voice coming into the garage.

All four of the boys in the garage stopped the game and turned towards the voice. They stood to their feet all at once as they saw the face behind the voice. The medium olive colored skin, dark wavy hair, eyebrows that looked like dark caterpillars with a freshly tattooed "S" on his right thumb that stretched from the base of his thumb to top of his wrist. In the bend of the "S," at the bottom, was a broken red heart.

Shorty, standing up from his squatting position, responded first. "Look, don't be stepping up, dissing nobody in here."

"First of all, I ain't no damn punk! What, you mad cause I can find my momma and you can't?" Mitch belted out.

"Ooh! You got served! Coming on up in here with that shit. Ain't nobody up in here scared of you! Take that somewhere else, son, you got the wrong house!" Little man said as he walked toward the guy standing at the entrance of the garage.

"Ain't nobody get served shit! And you," pointing at Mitch, "You say another thing about my momma and I'm going to burst you in the mouth!"

"I wish you would try it. You may have those flunkies over there jumping but not over here! Ain't nobody thinking about you in here!" Mitch responded.

"Oh, you not scared. Well, you better ask somebody, and you better sleep with one eye open cause I'm gonna come to visit you and your momma, then, we will see who is scared of who."

Mitch aroused in anger as he moved towards the guy with the 'S.' "Man, I will kill you if you come near my house or my momma," he said as he picked up the baseball bat.

One of the guys who came into the garage lifted his shirt to expose the handle of his gun. "You sure you want to do that?"

Shorty grabbed Mitch. "Come on, Mitch. Not here, not now. These punks just looking for trouble!"

Then turning to the guy with the tattooed 'S,' "Look, ain't nobody beefing with you in here. So, why you come up in our spot, bringing trouble? Let's just squash this here!"

The wavy hair guy and Mitch stared at each other for five minutes, then, the wavy hair guy and his friends turned to walk out the garage. "You better watch your back," mumbled the wavy-haired one.

"What he say?" Mitch shouted back as shorty was holding him back. "Shorty, let me go. Ain't nobody going to threaten my momma!"

"Mitch, calm down. Come on, not now! That dude is trouble. That's the guy that Leon was telling me about; he's trouble and dangerous. Did you see that tattoo on his hand? His name is Stink. The 'S' stands for Stink. He came down from New York; he lives in lower Park Heights, and I heard he don't have a mother. Take his threat seriously, but you going to have to sneak him first cause he means what he says. I know where he hangs out, so just tell me when and we will meet so you can handle him."

"Stink, what kind of name is that? Well, tonight, Stink, we gonna pay you a visit cause don't nobody threaten my momma!" Mitch shouted as he threw the bat across the garage in anger. "Stink, you mine!"

CHAPTER EIGHTEEN

Hey Mitch, you ok, buddy?" Marvin said as he pulled back his hand from Mitch's grip,

"I don't know, you tell me," Mitch replied with a stern tone as he backed up from Marvin.

"Mitch, let's talk."

"About what? How you trapped my sister in marrying you? Or how you planned on killing your future wife's mother? I'd like to hear it Stink. That's your name, right? That's what they call you!"

"Mitch, I know you upset, and you have every right to be but please, as men, let's talk about it calmly and let's do it out on the patio where we can have some privacy. No need in upsetting or bringing undue attention, can we please do that? I promise you I will explain everything," Marvin pleaded calmly to Mitch as he motioned him towards the patio door right outside his office.

"Do you really think I care about attention right now? Do you? Man, that's my sister out there in that limo waiting to marry a man she believes is the man of her dreams!"

"Mitch, I'm asking you, kindly please hear me out?"

Suddenly, an usher walked up to them. "Pastor, is everything ok?"

Before the usher could finish his words, Mitch interrupted. "Yeah, everything okay!" Turning to Marvin, "You better make this good because I swear, I will tell my baby sister everything!" he mumbled as he followed Marvin out to the patio.

"Please, have a seat," Marvin said as he pulled out one chair from the round table.

Mitch took his seat, even as his heart raced, staring at Marvin. Marvin also sat at the table, cleared his throat, rested his chin on both hands which was crossed together and held up by his elbows resting on the table.

"Mitch, I promise you that when we first met, neither of us knew who the other was. It wasn't until months later that we connected the dots of our past. We met here in Florida a long way from our old neighborhood. I guess Fuchsia shared how we met; it was all innocent.

"Mitch, we were kids then, we men now. I made a lot of mistakes in my young life, and I'm not that guy any longer, I promise you that. One day, when she and I was talking about my dad, I mentioned where I was born and we both at the same time realized that we were from the same place. I remembered her as a little girl, and as the young girl, I had to tell some boys on the bus to leave her alone, but I didn't put the pieces together until she told me about her brother, Mitch, who was sent to Juvie. Then, it hit me who you were. I told her I had a beef with you a long time ago. She replied, 'Who didn't have a beef with Mitch?' So, I never proceeded any further.

"Mitch, I would like to apologize for that day in the garage and I was an angry child whose mother walked out on as a boy. I couldn't see the value of a mother, and I equated them all the same. Mitch, I realized that hurt people always hurt other people. I was so hurt and angry with my mother that when you stated you had to do some chores for her, I just snapped in my anger. I could never tell anyone how hurt I really was; how I looked for her daily and as the days went on, my pain turned to anger and built into a rage that I took out on any and everyone. It wasn't until my dad heard the word on the streets that there was a hit on my life that he decided that we should relocate, and he sent me to Jersey with his sister and family. I was sixteen years old and was being shipped out. My dad moved to Ohio and sent me to Jersey; he said it was for my best.

"It was there that I began changing my life; started going to church, reading the Bible. It began to make sense to me, and as the years rolled by, I changed more and more until I became this man sitting before you now. I became ordained minister at twenty-five and served at my home church for three years. Then, I took the plunge of faith and moved here and began bible studies in my condo which grew into a church. I have been pastoring here now, eight years.

"Mitch, I'm no longer the same. The only thing that remains from that hurting, angry boy is this tattoo, and the only reason I haven't had it removed is because it keeps me grounded and humble. Every time I look at my hand, I am reminded of the grace of God; how he spared me as a teenager. I shouldn't be here today, but God! When my dad got the word that someone was coming after me, he packed us up, and we left dodge like in three days. Boy, I was so angry with him for shipping me with my aunt, but as I grew in God, I understood it was for my good unto God's glory. I never found out who had a hit on me because I had so many enemies then. I pray for that guy daily that his life would forever change as well."

Mitch, stunned with Marvin's story, looked him in the eye, "Well, since we being open and all that, they used to call me Big Man. I, like many, was one of those who had a beef with you. I had it out for you. I wanted you dead after you threaten my mom's life; the night I was planning to take you out was the night my life changed."

"Wait, what? You Big Man, it was you? I threatened your mom? How come I don't remember that?"

"Yeah, you did. My first encounter with you when you walked into my buddy's garage; you came straight for me about my mom and threatened to take her out."

"Man, I do apologize for everything I said or done to you or your family. I was a messed-up child. Nothing can ever excuse my behavior."

"Well, does my sister know who you are?"

"Fuchsia knows of my past, yes. Does she know about my wrongdoings? Yes. Does she know the names of all those persons I wronged? No, because I don't know myself. Mitch, I was a troubled young man whose life was destined to end young or in prison, but God had another plan, one I didn't know myself. I was introduced to the power of real love, self-love; love that conquers all fears; the love that reaches beyond my imagination; love that keeps no records of wrong or being wronged; love that does not judge, extends itself with hope.

"Mitch, I'm no longer that child with destructive behavior searching for love, and when he didn't feel like he found it, demolished everything in his site. When I felt like no one cared, I went after those who seemed to have it all together. I was jealous of people's relationships, so I went after the ones that appeared to have what I was missing. So, yes, I could see me wanting to attack you or your mom. I wanted people to feel like I felt, hurt like I hurt, become damaged goods like I believed I was. Again, I sincerely ask for your forgiveness. I, with all the love in me for your sister, ask you today for her hand in marriage, and If you say no, I would understand but I will go against your wishes and marry her and pray that you, one day, could forgive me.

"I desire this day that you give us your blessings. Fuchsia would love to know that the only two men who matter in her life are standing together in spite of our past, in spite of our differences, but we put aside all of that because we both love her and always will. She needs us both but will settle for just me if she is pushed to make a choice. How do I know this? Because we talk about everything. She always talked about you; how she missed you and loved you more than life. And when we realized that we came from those same streets, she said she felt in her inner being that our paths have crossed, but it may not have been positively. She stated that if that were the case, she hoped we could work it out because it was so long ago and she needs us both, but if we cannot come to some agreement, she would be hurt but would still marry me because she was used to you not being in her life. However, she couldn't live her life without me. So, again, I ask of you; Mitch, I deeply love and adore your sister. She's the light of my life, everything I prayed for and more. Will you give us the honor of blessing our union?"

Mitch tried to speak, but the words got choked in his throat. He took a deep breath and exhaled.

"Marvin, when I first noticed it was you, Stink or the once Stink, everything in me that I left behind years ago began to rise in my soul. All I could think about was my lil bits, my sister. I wanted to protect her all over again. The blood began to rise in my veins, all I could see was blood; your blood to be exact but the moment you started to say how much you loved her, my blood began to rescind back to normal. My heart was no longer vexed with anger.

"You are right; love conquers it all. I was stabbed the night I came looking for you. I went from the hospital to Juvie; that changed my life. Looking back at the pain in my mom's eyes and the tears that streamed down my sister's little face, it was then that I vowed I would never hurt them again. I spent the rest of my teenage years in Juvie, but it was the best thing that happened to me. It made me the man that I am today. So, you are correct; love is everything I have for Fuchsia, and if I lost her again, I would never be able to look myself in the eyes. Her happiness is level one in my life, and if that means letting go of the past, I let go of this very moment.

"Marvin, it's with honor that I release my only sister to your hands. I trust you will love her, honor her, cherish and protect her." He wiped the tears from his eyes and opened up to embrace Marvin. "Our past will not dictate our future."

Marvin responded to Mitch's embrace when suddenly the patio door slide open. "Pastor, is everything ok? It's five of six. We have five minutes until your bride steps out of the limo. So, we need to get in place now," said the head usher.

"No, we good. Thanks for the timely reminder. Well, let's go get in position, my brother-in-law," Mitch said as they walked back into the Pastor's study room and joined the rest of the groomsmen. With one last look in the mirror, Marvin, Mitch along with the other groomsmen walked towards the sanctuary. The Male ushers stood in the opening of the sanctuary door. The three groomsmen and his best man lined up behind Marvin and Mitch as the music began to play.

Marvin turned to shake Mitch's hand. "Well, I guess this is it. Thank you for being here for us both."

"It will be my pleasure to release my sister into your hands. Go on, get in place while I wait for her to enter. By the way, she's stunning!" Mitch said as he took a step back from the doorway.

Marvin and his best man walked down the center aisle of the sanctuary as the musicians played softly. They took their places at the front of the church alongside the minister.

Mitch stood at the opening of the church door and nodded to the limo driver assistant who was waiting in the middle of the walkway of the church. The assistant turned to face the limo driver who was now standing beside the limo door.

"Well, this is it, Fuchs. You sure you don't want to back out cause we can right now! Say the word, and I will jump in the driver's seat of this limo, and we will ride on off into the sunset!" Tommie sneered with excitement as the driver opened the limo door.

"Shush, Tommie! Plus, you don't know nothing about driving this big ole vehicle!" Sasha shouted as she was helping Fuchsia adjust her dress to exit the limo.

"What? You know my saying: if you can handle one big boy, you can handle all the big boys. You know it's not the size of the car; it's the power behind the wheel!" Tommie geared back.

Laughing, she stepped out of the limo and reached for the hand of the driver. "Oh boy, here we go again! Tommie, can you please stop! You going to make me pee on myself!"

"Oops, I apologize. She can't help herself," Fuchsia said, looking at the driver.

"No worries ma'am, no worries. Laughter is good," the driver assured Fuchsia as he helped her up the walkway, and Candi, holding up her train, the other three followed closely behind.

The glare of the sun was bright as if it was making a grand entrance along with Fuchsia. There were a few passing people who stopped on the sidewalk, catching a glimpse of the bride. Fuchsia could hear the "wows" and "beautiful" as she slowly stepped onto the church steps. As the church door swung open, she looked up and caught Mitch's eyes. They stared into each other's eyes as she stepped on each step. Trying her best to discern if he was upset or happy, her stomach began to flutter as if butterflies had invaded her body. As she took the last step into the church building, Mitch reached for her left hand. He nodded to the driver, "Thank you, I got her from here."

The driver released her hand into Mitch's. "Congratulations, ma'am."

Nervously, in a soft voice, "Thank you," Fuchsia said.

Holding her small hand in his, he whispered, "I got you, and I will always have your back. I just ask, next time trust me." He leaned over to kiss her cheek.

The warmth of Mitch's kiss seemed to calm the invading butterflies. Instantly, it reminded her of the days of their youth when Mitch would hold her hand as he walked her to school; they were the times she felt most safe. A feeling of peace came over her as Mitch's cheek touched hers.

"I do trust you with everything in me. I trust you." She squeezed his left hand with her left hand, and with her right hand, hugged her big brother so tightly. They embraced for what seemed like forever. "Yesterday is gone and today opens the curtain for our tomorrow. Time was suspended until this second, now we all can live beyond our yesterdays."

Mitch kissed his sister on the forehead as the music began to play in the sanctuary. "I will always love you."

"Always and forever will I love you, Mitch."

"Hey, that's our cue. It's time to get married," Sasha said as she did one last dress adjustment.

Melondy, Sasha and Tommie walked down the aisle of the church, each taking her place on the opposite side of the minister. As each one stepped to the top of the aisle, in front of Marvin, he smiled and nodded.

As the musician began playing the bridal song, Mitch whispered to her, "Well, I guess it's time I give you a new name. From now on, you are my blossom."

Looking at him strangely and thinking to herself, *He has lost his mind. Really, Mitch? Right now, you gonna do this?*

"I know you think I'm nuts, but I'm not. Why blossom? Because Fuchsia you are like a budding flower who has been through all the dirt and pain, yet you blossomed into this beautiful flower which stood the test of time. My blossom, I'm so proud to escort you this day to your future."

A tear bubbled in her left eye even though she tried to blink it away. "Mitch, you the best, and yes, I love Blossom."

The music began to change its cord which was the cue to begin her walk down the aisle. As she and Mitch stood at the doorway of the sanctuary, the minister motioned the awaiting congregation to stand for the entrance of the bride. It was as if she was floating down the aisle to her awaiting groom. Smiling the entire way, and staring only into Marvin's eyes, she and Mitch finally reached the front of the church.

The minister motioned, "Who gives this woman to be this man's wife?"

Mitch responded, "It's with great honor; I place my sister into your hands."

Marvin took three steps forward, embraced Mitch and received Fuchsia's hand. Then he walked her into place, in front of the minister.

The minister motioned the guest to sit and continued with the ceremony. "The couple have written their vows that they wish to recite to each other this day."

Marvin held Fuchsia's left hand, reached for her right hand. At the same time, Fuchsia handed Candi her bouquet.

As Marvin placed the wedding band on Fuchsia left hand, he began his vows. "Fuchsia, from the beautiful sunny day that I first laid eyes on you, I knew you were special and divinely sent to me. You are my gift; a gift that I promise I will always cherish. I promise to love you in all seasons of our lives, to always put you first, hold you when you need to be held, to let up when you need space but still reach to draw you back to my arms. I promise to pray for you, cover you, lead our household with wisdom and tender love, to be your strength when you are weak, to listen to your dreams, and to dream with you, to be the last voice you hear before bed and the first kiss you receive when you rise. I promise to honor and respect and love you 'til the last breath I draw. This is my covenant to you, my bride.

Fuchsia, placing Marvin's wedding band on Marvin's left ring finger, "Marvin, thank you for loving me; for showing me that love really does exist. I promise to cherish that love and never take it for granted. I promise when I get afraid, rather than run from you, I will run to you. I promise to respect and honor you, to hear and listen to your wisdom and advice, to never judge you, to be your partner for life, to laugh with you and share my dreams, to be your lover and your friend in all seasons of our lives. I promise to be the last smile you see at bedtime and the first lips to receive you at rising. This is my covenant to you, my groom."

Having led the congregation in prayer, the minister concluded with, "Amen. Marvin, you may kiss your wife."

Lifting Fuchsia's chin, Marvin leaned his tall body over and placed his lips on Fuchsia's lips and gently shared a very passionate kiss with her. He held her tightly in his arms, lifted her small framed body off the floor. Fuchsia, in turn, held on to him tightly as she felt her inner woman suddenly came alive. They both could feel the other's body tremble as he slowly lowered his new bride to her feet.

"I love you, my wife."

"I love you more, my husband."

Candi and Tommie, snickering at the same time, "Whew!"

The congregation stood in joy, applauding. Candi handed Fuchsia her bouquet as she and Marvin turned to walk down the aisle. The wedding party followed suit as the newlyweds exited the church. As they walked down the church steps and made their way to the Limo, the guests were tossing bird seeds.

The sun was again piercing through the clouds. Beyond the limo, a figure appeared. Fuchsia stood still as sweet fragrance blew past her nostrils. She caught a glimpse of a familiar long flowing white dress; her heart started beating faster as they walked and got closer to the limo. To her eyes, it seemed as though the flowing dress was moving closer. She stared the dress upwards; towards the waist, breast, neck and then, her eyes eventually rested on the face.

"Momma," she gasped as she squeezed Marvin's hand. Oh, she fought back her tears. Small, fragile hands reached out past the driver standing beside the opened limo door; slowly, Fuchsia reached out her hands until they locked arms, still holding her bouquet of Fuchsia flowers.

"Momma," she choked in her tears.

"My Beautiful Fuchs," her mother said gently.

Lady Carolyn Byrd

Some say that purpose can be found in the challenges that we faced and overcame, which causes a grip in our heart when we see others go through the same or similar challenges in life. Lady Carolyn has a firsthand knowledge on what it means to fight for and realize your personal destiny. She's on a mission to help other young women love themselves- to not live according to the standards the society has set for them, rise above life's obstacles and realize their peculiar destiny.

This passion drove Lady Carolyn to mentorship where she guides young women in navigating through uncharted paths of their life. For over thirty years, she has consistently served and inspired women to reach beyond the pain of the process and move into the full potential of their life.

Lady Carolyn is a native Baltimorean, has two incredible married sons and a grandmother to seven grandchildren.

Her impetuous towards seeing others live a fulfilled life has drove her to co-author three books (Yes! You Can Have a Happy Marriage, The Memorial Stones of Marriage Journal, and Birthing from Obscurity to Promise) with her husband.

She is constantly in search of ways to reach out to as many people as she can, and this book is a way of her further emphasis on the ever-growing drive to bring out the best in everyone she has a contact with.